SEDUCED BY GRACE

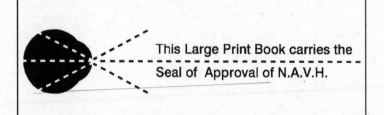

This Large Print Book carries the
Seal of Approval of N.A.V.H.

SEDUCED BY GRACE

JENNIFER BLAKE

THORNDIKE PRESS

A part of Gale, Cengage Learning

GALE
CENGAGE Learning·

Detroit • New York • San Francisco • New Haven, Conn • Waterville, Maine • London

GALE
CENGAGE Learning®

LIBRARY OF CONGRESS CATALOGING-IN-PUBLICATION DATA

Blake, Jennifer, 1942–
   Seduced by grace / by Jennifer Blake. — Large print ed.
     p. cm. — (Thorndike Press large print romance)
   "The Three Graces of Graydon Series; #3."
   ISBN-13: 978-1-4104-4428-8 (hardcover)
   ISBN-10: 1-4104-4428-7 (hardcover)
   1. Kidnapping—Fiction. 2. Man-woman relationships—Fiction. 3. Large
type books. I. Title.
PS3563.A923S43 2012
813'.54—dc23   2011041059

Published in 2012 by arrangement with Harlequin Books S.A.

Printed in the United States of America
1 2 3 4 5 6 7 16 15 14 13 12

To the NOLA Stars,
North Louisiana Chapter
of Romance Writers of America.
For all the grand accomplishments —
and all those to come.

1

June 1497
England

He rode toward them out of the sunset, a knight upon a milk-white destrier with his armor burnished to eye-stinging splendor by rays of orange and gold. The white plumes that topped his helm danced and swayed. The gilt embroidery on the white tabard worn over his armor shimmered with his every movement. The nimbus of brilliant light surrounding him made him appear incredibly tall and broad, a figure of legend.

The knight slowed his mount, turned broadside so he blocked the road. Sitting at his ease upon his monstrous warhorse caparisoned and armored as if for war, he raised a gauntleted hand in a gesture of command.

The mounted column with which Lady Marguerite Milton was traveling to her wedding came to a jangling halt. Just ahead of her, the captain of the men-at-arms exchanged an inquiring glance with Sir John Dennison, the emissary for her future husband. That gentleman's broad face creased in a self-important frown and his mouth tightened as he stared at the apparition before them.

The noises of early evening faded to breathless silence. Not a bird, frog or cricket was heard from the copse of oaks and alders that crowded the roadway. For a moment, a soft breeze fluttered the pennon of pale blue marked by a green-leaved crown that rose above the opposing horsemen. It sighed into stillness so complete it was almost possible to hear the dust trail of the column settle into the ditches.

"The Golden Knight . . ."

The whisper came from somewhere behind Marguerite. A shiver moved over her as she heard that strangled sound with its edge of awe. Her heart stuttered in her chest before rising to lodge in her throat.

Everyone knew the name, one awarded by the king of France after a grand tournament, along with a priceless suit of armor chased with silver and gold. Champion of champions, bravest of the brave, boldest of the bold, the man who held it was celebrated in song and story, known across the reaches of Europe and up down the length of Britain. Invincible, they called him, unconquered and unconquerable, though never arrogant withal. He fought like the devil himself, so it was said, using intelligence and honed instinct instead of brawn, though he had the last, as well. Known to be of a learned turn, he could debate any issue. As handsome as one of heaven's militant archangels, he was a favorite with the French queen, and a gallant of tender prowess and renown among her court ladies and their nubile daughters. The very soul of honor, not an ill word could be said against him.

Such a paragon was he painted, so full of strengths and virtues, that many doubted his existence. Marguerite had been among them. Until now.

He appeared all too real, a solid presence blocking their passage, as immovable as the mountains of the northern marches from whence she had ridden on this, her nuptial journey. A shiver of dread ran down her spine with a prickling like the scrabble of mouse feet. Marguerite jerked with it, so the mare she rode danced a few steps to the side, arching her neck before Marguerite could bring the palfrey under control again. Through the brief struggle, she kept her gaze upon the knight, her mind churning with doubt and a healthy measure of distrust.

"Good day to you, sir!" Sir John called in testy greeting as he eased his considerable weight in the saddle with a great creaking of leather. "Know you that we are upon the king's business. Stand aside at once."

"That I cannot do. No, nor would I if you rode under Henry's own dragon banner, which you do not." The answer was courteous yet layered with steel.

Sir John swelled with indignation. "By what right do you stay our progress?"

"By right of arms."

The reply was followed at once by the slithering rasp of metal on metal. A great sword flashed silver fire as it appeared in the knight's hand, its blade chased with gold near the hilt in the same pattern as his armor.

Jostling chaos ensued for long seconds. Marguerite's guard shouted as they reached for their own weapons. Her serving woman screamed. Horses whinnied in alarm.

"Hold or die!"

Such grim authority rang in the Golden Knight's hard command that the men-at-arms around Marguerite stilled with their swords half-out of the sheaths. In that moment, a flurry of movement appeared at the edges of the tree-lined road. Eyes wide, faces flushing dark red with choler and sudden horror, the soldiery stared around them.

They were surrounded. From shadowed and leafy ambush, a band of knights rode forward at a slow walk. Some fifty in number, compared to barely twenty in Marguerite's guard, their lances were in their hands, leveled and ready. Heavy armor, polished yet showing the hard use of battle, marked them as a fighting force it would be unwise to meet while protected only by chain mail topped by woolen tunics.

"Hold!" Marguerite cried in echo of the knight's command.

Her voice was high-pitched, sharp with fear that the men with her would go to their deaths trying to protect her. Against a more equal, less well-armed foe, they might have afforded her some chance of escape, but not here, not now. She'd not have them fall for nothing. Though a half dozen had been sent by her betrothed, the rest were from her brother-in-law's keep of Braesford Hall, detailed by him to guard her on her journey. She had known them since coming to Braesford a decade ago.

"Hold! For the love of God, hold!"

That cry came from Sir John Dennison as

he stared around him with bulging eyes in the frog-belly pallor of his face. His major concern seemed to be for the sharp and glittering tip of the Golden Knight's blade that was now centered on his barrel chest, requiring only an instant of cold effort to drive it through him.

The curses, the snap of reseated swords, rattle of bits and bridles and stamping of hooves died away. Sir John, his breathing hoarse, turned to the knight again, speaking in guttural outrage. "What is your purpose here? If it be thievery —"

"Nay." The reply was deep and scathing, resounding in hollow dissonance from behind the Golden Knight's helm. "I seek the mounted escort taking Lady Marguerite Milton to the lord who would claim her as his bride."

Beside Marguerite, her aging serving woman, Gwynne, muttered a dire warning of rapine under her breath. A cynic to the core, she had supported Marguerite's two older sisters through their weddings, had seen the disasters they were forced to endure before their vows could be spoken. She had predicted a similar disaster for Marguerite. This was based on the curse of the Three Graces of Graydon, as she and her two sisters had been known when they first appeared at Henry's court. The dread prophecy foretold death for any man who attempted to marry them without love.

"Nonsense," Marguerite answered the woman in reproof, though the sinking feeling in the pit of her stomach belied it. The hard gaze behind the nosepiece of the Golden Knight's helm had turned in her direction. It seemed to scorch through her dark blue cloak that hung open in the heat to reveal her riding gown of rust-red summer wool, to strip away the veil of red-edged cream linen that covered her hair. He centered his gaze upon the shape of her female form, the lift of her breasts, the turn of her waist and span of her hips crossed by her jeweled girdle. Only then did it lift to her face.

His eyes were metal-bright blue glimmers behind the face guard of his gold chased helm. Pitiless in their assessment, they weighed her, plumbed her and sought her essence. Nothing of what and who she was escaped him, or so it seemed. He knew her sorrows and her joys, her fears and bad habits, understood the fey, retiring side of her nature as well as the bravado she held up like a shield for it. He knew her past and present, and appeared certain he could change her future at will.

13

Marguerite's heart leaped in her chest, pounding into a frantic beat. Her gloved hands clenched upon her reins while vulnerability pooled in the center of her being. She had prayed to be delivered from the marriage decreed for her as a ward of the king, prayed until her voice was hoarse and her knees callused from the chapel's stone floor. But not like this, never like this.

The arrival of the order to wed had been an unpleasant surprise. So many years had passed since Henry VII had arranged marriages for her elder sister, Isabel, and middle sister, Cate, that Marguerite thought herself blessedly forgotten at Braesford Hall. Why the king had suddenly remembered her, none could say. It was also a mystery why he had chosen Alfred, Lord Halliwell, a pompous and spindle-shanked braggart with a son older than she was, as her future husband. Gwynne swore Marguerite had naught to fear from the match, that the curse of the Graces would protect her. If this confrontation on the road was its work, she did not think highly of it.

Could this be it? Had it come, here and now?

Oh, but what if this was no rescue at all, but something infinitely more dangerous? The messages she had sent flying across

England and Scotland, to France, the four corners of Europe and beyond, had not been to any man so terrible in his magnificence as the Golden Knight. No, not at all. They were meant for David, her brother-in-law's onetime squire, sweet, humble David who had pledged his heart to her when she was only a lass. Dear David, who had been knighted after saving the king's life at the Battle of Stoke, and neither seen nor heard of since.

"Aye, and you've found the wench's escort, so you have," Sir John said to the leader of the mounted company that held them at bay. "What would you now?"

"Why, what else?" the knight answered behind his mask of a helm, "I would have the lady."

He sheathed his sword with whistling slide and snick, and then set his destrier in motion. Marguerite gathered her reins as she watched him push through her escort to where she sat beside Gwynne. A tremor shuddered over her. The closer his approach, the larger he seemed until he took on mythic stature, as if a knight of ancient Camelot, stronger, braver and more daring than any mortal man had the right to be.

She flung a swift look around her for the chance of escape. There was none. She was hemmed in, unable to move her palfrey more than a few steps, much less flee.

"Milady —" Gwynne began in nervous warning.

The knight reached a gauntleted fist for her bridle with its blue leather trappings. Marguerite hauled on her reins, forcing her mount backward into the men-at-arms behind her. Her retreat shoved them into each other, forcing them closer to the lances that hemmed them in on all sides. Hearing their curses, she regretted the necessity, but would not be taken easily.

"What is your purpose, sir?" she demanded in breathless haste. "How came you here? Who sent you?"

"No one sent me. 'Twas my own desire, held through a journey of a thousand leagues and more. As for my purpose, have I not said it was to take you?"

"Nay, it cannot be!"

"Yet I hold to it."

Hard on the words, he reached for her, circling her waist with a mail-clad arm. Such power was in it that she was snatched from her palfrey as quickly as a hawk takes a sparrow. She seemed to fly through the air in a sweep of skirts while the sky and trees wheeled around her.

Air left her lungs in a hard gasp as she

landed with her back against the unyielding surface of an armored chest. She could not draw breath for the constriction of tempered steel across her rib cage, could not see for her veil that flew around to cover her face. The great stallion beneath the knight reared so she was flung back upon the large and rigid form of the man behind her. A shudder ran over her from the top of her head to her toes. Her skin tingled, burning as if she had landed in a flaming pyre. As the horse's front feet struck ground again, the knight held her tight, supporting her with what felt oddly like protection.

The steel mesh-covered thighs beneath her bunched with the flexing of strong muscles. The destrier immediately plunged away. That first leap snapped her teeth together so hard she bit the inside of her cheek. Thrown off balance, she clutched desperately at the mailed arm that threatened to break her in half.

A shouted order roared out above her head. The white stallion beneath her galloped off at ferocious speed while somewhere behind them Gwynne screamed and Sir John shouted curses. In mere seconds, the hooves of mounted men thundered after them. The horsemen pounded closer, ever closer, but became nothing more than the knight's men pressing in on either side. They closed ranks about their leader, a defensive cordon bristling with lances and grim purpose.

Disbelief gripped Marguerite as surely as the powerful hold that clamped her against her captor. This could not be happening. Her life was staid, even boring. Nothing occurred beyond the childish ailments of her nieces and nephews or an occasional noble visitor to her brother-in-law's keep. To transfer to her bridegroom's possession had promised little in the way of change beyond the necessity of submitting to a lust-ridden graybeard. She might have dreamed of being rescued from that act, but such fantasies had not involved being carried off by the renowned Golden Knight.

Dread rose inside her, along with disturbing, febrile excitement. What he wanted with her, she dared not think. Yet she feared she would discover it soon enough.

She greatly feared it.

He had her. It was done.

The fierce satisfaction of it thrummed in his blood, heating the top of his head under his helm. The woman he held would belong to no other man, not now, not ever.

The ambuscade had gone as planned; the

surprise of it had been complete. He'd expected more resistance, in all truth, but was pleased by the lack. There were advantages to the fierce reputation that preceded him wherever he went.

To shed blood was never his intention. He had, nevertheless, been more than prepared for it. Some things were worth the risk.

The men-at-arms from Braesford Hall would not attempt to overtake him and his men. Their number was too small, though greater than the paltry handful sent by the bridegroom for this important journey; the noble lord the lady was to marry obviously did not value his betrothed as she deserved. If the men of Braesford had been inclined to fight, the battle would have been joined at the outset — though the order of Lady Marguerite had helped prevent it, an unexpected boon. The most obvious course for them now would be turn back and report the loss of the lady.

What else could they do, after all? To continue southward to face the wrath of the disappointed husband-to-be would be foolish. It was enough that they must report back to the bride's relatives, Baron and Baroness Braesford, with their news.

No one was likely to follow after them then. There would be ample time to make himself known to the lady. Yes, and to discover what she made of it.

God, but she was fair to look upon, even with her hair covered by veiling. A few golden-brown tendrils escaped to curl in the damp air, accenting her delicately colored, fine-skinned face, while the dark pools of her eyes, as richly brown as the finest ale, carried every secret of womanhood. In her fine fabrics, vivid as the sunset that stained the western sky, she was like something from another world, one he could never know. Yet she was a luscious armful, her slender curves a perfect fit against him. He had almost forgotten how soft a female form could be, how sweetly scented, how pliant . . .

Or mayhap not the last. She was clawing at his arm, twisting and turning in his hold while wheezing like a winded mule. She could not hurt him, nor could she escape him, as she must know, but that didn't prevent her from —

An oath scorched his lips. He lowered his grasp to her waist, then tightened it again as she reeled in his hold, sobbing as she gasped for air. Allowing her just enough room to draw a whistling breath, he castigated himself for a fool unable to judge his own strength. Well, or one carried away by the triumph of having this woman in his power at last.

"What are you . . . doing, you great oaf?" she gasped. "Trying to murder me?"

"Never," he answered at his most laconic.

She struggled upright, though without relaxing against him. "It seemed . . . otherwise to me!"

To that, he made no answer.

She swallowed, a movement he felt as much as heard above the thundering of hooves around him. "Where are you taking me?"

"Away." He pulled her back against him and held her firm. After a moment, she realized how unbreakable was both his hold and his resolve and ceased her struggles, though she remained stiffly upright.

"Away from what? Away . . . away where?"

She sounded enraged. Now there was gratitude for you. "Away from the strutting fool chosen as your bridegroom. As to where, how should it matter?"

"It matters because I don't know you!" She tried to turn her head to see his face, but her flapping veil and his helm made that impossible.

"You will," he said, enjoying the way her bottom fit into the apex of his thighs, jouncing against him, the feel of her flat abdomen where his arm enfolded her, and yes, even the shiver that rippled through her at his touch, there at her abdomen where it was doubtful any other had trespassed.

She had taken his words as a threat. It was possible he had meant them that way.

"Besides," he said, his voice a bass rumble in his chest, "how well did you know the man you were journeying to marry?"

"What has that to say to anything? Lord Halliwell had the favor of the king at the very least."

"So Henry decided it was time you were wed."

" 'Twas certainly not my choice."

"You meant to be a spinster the rest of your days?"

She tried to sit forward again. "What do you know of me, sir, that you can ask such a thing?"

She was quick, he thought, even as he exerted pressure to bring her back against him. "I know what I see."

"Meaning I look the part, I suppose. In that case, I cannot imagine why you went to the trouble of taking me."

"You mistake me. I meant nothing of the kind."

"What did you —"

He went on without pause, his voice

dulcet against her ear. "And 'twas no trouble at all to take you, Lady Marguerite. As to why, mayhap you should think on it, think long and hard."

If she answered, he did not hear. Nor did she speak again as the miles flowed beneath his destrier's hooves. He did not make the mistake of thinking her resigned, however. He could almost hear the scurry of her thoughts, the half-formed plans to escape him when they were forced to stop or, at the very least, make him suffer for his daring. That she would try, given half a chance, he had no doubt. That she should succeed was something he could not permit. No, no matter how much he understood the instinct.

With him, she was marginally safe. Freed from his grasp, she would be a tender young hare dropped among slavering hounds.

She was, just possibly, too tender. She had commanded the men-at-arms with her to hold rather than fight him, preventing their efforts to save her. Any other lady he could name would have cowered behind their swords, though the blood of every one of them flowed to stain her skirts. Most telling of all, however, was that those hardened men-at-arms had obeyed her. He did not make the mistake of thinking it was from fear, whether of her or of Baron Braesford who paid their wage. No, it was a mark of their respect gained from watching her deal with fairness, kindness and generosity toward all who came within her reach inside her brother-in-law's keep. He'd seen it before, long years ago.

The thud of hooves drawing close brought his head around on the instant. It was Oliver of Sienna, a companion of the tournaments who had become his squire some six years back. His Italian friend did not speak or look at the lady, but only tilted his dark head to indicate a dim track that left the main road just ahead. It gave access, without doubt, to the position the squire had been sent to scout out for their retreat. As one, he and Oliver and the men behind them plunged into it, entering a dim green tunnel created by the interlaced branches of the trees that grew close upon the rutted way.

The sun had dropped below the horizon. Though twilight lingered, it scarcely penetrated this wood that had never felt axe or wedge, never heard the grunts and shouts of those who took timber for His Majesty's ships or manor houses for nobles. Coolness crept from under the great limbs along with the dank smells of lichen, decaying leaves and bleached bones of animal kills. They swept deeper along it, the noise of their passage echoing both before and behind them until it seemed certain they were being pursued. No horsemen showed themselves, however.

In due time, the smell of wood smoke came to them on the cooling air. Small fires appeared. They multiplied, flickering in the gloom. A woodsman's cottage, little more than a hut, stood silhouetted by their glow. Lantern light glimmered behind its rough shutters and smoke drifted from the opening in the thatched roof. Beyond it lay what had been a horse barn, with a low shed leaning against it meant to house pigs.

He pulled up before the cottage, while Oliver and the other men-at-arms cantered past to where the whiff of roasting pork drifted from the fires. The lady riding upon his thighs still said nothing, though her body turned as stiff as a nun's starched wimple as she sat staring at the primitive accommodation before her.

Irritation touched him. The cottage was no manse, no moat-encircled castle or nobleman's ancient keep, yet it was clean, dry and safe. He had suffered far worse and no doubt would again. Lady Marguerite could bear it for one night.

"Why are we stopping here?" she asked

finally, the words stifled in her throat.

What did she expect? A fast and lusty tupping followed by being shared among his men? Or was it only a straw mattress and shared blanket, with him to keep her warm in exchange for the right to discover what was under her skirts? He could find out soon enough, if he pleased.

The ache in his groin warned against the idea. It was entirely possible he would not be able to stop short of plundering the tender treasure he found.

Regardless, and against all reason, he was affronted that she could imagine it was possible.

"It is our lodging for the night, milady," he said, his voice rigorously even.

"Ours." The word held flat disdain.

"What would you? We must lie somewhere." He could feel her quick, uneven breathing now that they were still.

"I prefer private quarters."

"Without protection, and while sleeping among men-at-arms? Unwise, milady."

"And you are to be my protection from them? Forgive me if that seems . . . less than satisfactory."

There was defiance in that reply as well as in the set of her shoulders, the lift of her head. He allowed himself a private smile.

He did not want her cowed and afraid. "It's how it will be."

She gathered her veil to the side, turning her head to stare up at him in the gathering twilight. The dark slashes of her brows drawn together over her nose turned her frown into a scowl. The familiarity of that look smote him like a blow to the heart, and he was suddenly glad of the face and nose guard of his helm, which shielded his face from her view.

"Who are you?" she demanded. "Why are you doing this?"

He could put an end to her apprehension, might have except for some deep-felt need to gain acceptance in spite of it. It was unfair, mayhap, but there it was. "You know how I am called, I believe."

"Oh, yes, the Golden Knight. The tales say many things, but I never heard that you make a habit of abducting females."

"Nay. I am selective in those I snatch away to my encampment," he drawled while enjoying the way her breasts rose and fell under her cloak with every breath she took, brushing his arms that enwrapped her.

"If it's ransom you require, you should know that I am a ward of the king. He will pay if I am returned unharmed."

It was a valiant effort, that suggestion. Too

bad it was for naught. "You are certain?" he inquired with a thoughtful tilt of his head. "I'd heard Henry VII was a close man with his coin."

"He has affection for my sisters, also a certain obligation to our family from deeds useful to him in the past. He could be generous because of it."

"Or not, as he has already been put to the expense of a dowry for you. Or did Lord Halliwell pay him for the great advantage of getting his hands on both you and your portion of your father's estate?"

She was still for a long moment. "You know an uncommon lot about my affairs for one last heard of in France."

"It is a subject of some interest." The irony of that observation invaded his voice in spite of his guard against it.

"And why would that be? Have you gained all you desire except . . . except for a wife of wealth and good family?" A tremor shook her though she stilled it at once. "Is your purpose to force a marriage between us?"

"An interesting idea," he conceded as he allowed his hand that pressed her abdomen to slip to her lower belly, just above the apex of her thighs. "How would you feel about it?"

She slapped a hand against his wrist,

preventing him from pressing into the soft, warm depression he had discovered. "How do you imagine I would feel?"

"Gratified?"

"I despised the thought of marriage to a peer seen only once or twice in my life. Think you being tied to some strange knight would be more to my taste?"

"You might find it so," he murmured close to her ear. Heat mounted to his head, burning under the metal of his helm, while the drawing sensation in his groin brought a stabbing pain worse than a battle wound. The fluttering of her belly muscles under his hand was so intriguing he cursed his gauntlet that prevented fuller appreciation.

"Never!"

"Ah, well. 'Tis a prospect you need not face as marriage is not my aim."

She swallowed, for he heard it plainly above the dull thunder of his heartbeat in his ears. "Then . . ."

It was time to end this, for the torment was not restricted to the lady in his arms. He made no answer, but shifted her forward to gain room. Swinging from the saddle, he eased her down and set her on her feet. He did not release her, but drew her with him toward the cottage door.

It opened as they neared it, spilling light

out upon the leaf-strewn path they trod. A short figure stepped beneath the lintel, one that came nowhere near filling the low doorway. The lantern light behind her showed a miniature veil over fair hair that trailed near to the ground behind her, a tiny gown with a skirt scarce longer than a child's, short, well-formed arms and hands, yet the face and torso of a woman full grown.

"Lady Marguerite, at last!" the dwarfed lady exclaimed as she tottered toward them. "What joy to see you safely brought here! Aye, and that no harm has come to the gallant knight who rode to your rescue!"

"Astrid . . ."

The name was a whisper as the lady at his side stumbled to a halt, dragging against his hold. The color in her face drained away then surged up again with flame-kissed redness. Slowly, she turned to face him, spoke in stunned accents. "You have Astrid. She is here, here with you."

"As you see." Her amazement should have pleased him. Instead, it was near unbearable.

"Who are you, sir? Who are you in truth?"

He closed his eyes an instant, oddly reluctant to satisfy that question. Still, it could be delayed no longer. Releasing Lady

Marguerite, he reached up and unfastened his helm and steel mesh coif, drawing them off slowly over his head. He tucked both under his arm, squared his shoulders and faced her.

2

Marguerite stared at the sun-bleached gold of the knight's hair that was darkened in streaks by sweat, the rich blue of his eyes, the regular features that followed exact Greek proportions for male beauty. He had a scar in one eyebrow which gave it a slight ironic lift, and his nose had been broken at some time in the past so it had a slight hump in the middle. These small imperfections merely added a rugged, almost dangerous allure. He was taller than the doorway beyond them and had the muscled shoulders earned by a master of the broadsword, while about him, like a comfortable cloak, hung an air of natural command. Facing her, he waited, features grave, his well-formed mouth unsmiling.

Marguerite's heart tripped in her chest, accelerating to a suffocating beat. She couldn't move, couldn't speak, could barely think.

"Milady," Astrid said in scolding incomprehension, placing her tiny hands on her hips. "Do you not know him?"

Marguerite stirred, shaking herself from her odd reverie. Yes, of course she knew him. How could she not?

"David," she whispered.

"My Lady Marguerite." His gaze held hers as he made that solemn acknowledgment.

How different he was from the boy she had once known. It was not just that he was older, taller, broader, stronger, but as if the very essence of him had changed. It seemed an alchemist had burned away all warmth and tenderness, forging him into something harder and brighter than he had been before.

The Golden Knight.

He was a stranger.

And yet. And yet, not quite.

For long moments, he stood unmoving. Then he went to one knee before her, his armor creaking in its metal joints and his cloak settling in deep folds around him. With one gauntleted fist clanging against his cuirass over his heart, he bent his head, exposing the strong column of his neck where the curling gold of his hair grew thick at his nape.

"Ah, David." It was insupportable, that

gesture of homage. She sank down in front of him, reaching to touch the chain mail that covered his bent knee. "You received my summons after all."

"Astrid found me something over a month ago and a far journey away, almost to the Aegean Sea."

"I had given up hope, thought you dead or else that you had forgotten . . ."

His head came up, though something guarded remained in his expression. "Forget you? Never, my lady."

He had remembered. The astonishment of it, and the pleasure, swelled her chest until she could hardly speak. "It has been a long time, so very long."

"An endless age," he said in simple agreement, "each year the span of a life."

Consciousness of his size and his strength struck her again as she ran her gaze over his shoulders, his chest under his tunic embroidered with an odd device almost like a crown of thorns. She moistened her lips. "You . . . it seems you have done well. We heard you were following the tournaments, had taken a nom de guerre, but never dreamed you had gained such fame."

"No. Why should you," he said, cutting across all mention of his renown.

"You might have sent word to Braesford

that you had become this Golden Knight."

He lifted a shoulder with the quiet rattle of its steel mesh covering. "It was nothing much to boast of as a title, being based on the French king's whim and a pretty suit of armor. I only kept it as I had none of my own."

"Oh, but . . ."

"I was a bastard called David at the will of the good sisters who reared me, milady," he said, his features like iron. "Though I styled myself David of Braesford when I became squire to Sir Rand, I had no surname then and have none now."

The facts of his birth might be true enough, but he had proven himself over and over during the time he'd lived at Braesford Hall. Though some few years older than Marguerite, he had served as friend, companion and self-appointed protector on her rambles over the vast estate. He had been Sir Randall of Braesford's good right hand, had won a knighthood for defending Henry VII and protecting the king's standard in battle. His lack of a known father mattered so little to Marguerite that she seldom thought of it.

It had mattered to him. It seemed that it did still.

Astrid, standing in the doorway, took two

steps toward them. "Milady? Sir?"

Marguerite paid no attention to the little serving woman as she studied the face of the man before her.

"You used your fame to overawe my escort," she said on a note of discovery. "That was well done. Yet you might simply have come to Braesford when you reached England. Sir Rand and my sister Isabel, also Cate and her Scotsman husband, would have been glad to welcome you, to show you the fine broods of children they are rearing."

"Come to Braesford?" A shadow passed over his face. "What is there for me? Sir Rand, Baron Braesford, has no use for my sword while peace reigns."

"You are more to him, more to all of us, than a sword," she protested.

"Beyond that," he continued without pause, "descending on Braesford for your rescue would surely have involved Sir Rand. To cause bad blood between him and the king would be unworthy."

"Yes," she said with a thoughtful frown, "I suppose that would not have done."

"Besides, you might have decided I was too laggard, after my delay in arriving, might even have changed your mind about being wed."

"Hardly that!"

He watched her, his eyes darkly blue, giving nothing away. "Why not? Many a woman has married where commanded in hope of children as her reward."

She shook that away with a small movement of her head. "I was content to remain in my sister's household, to be fond aunt to her little ones. I would be there still but for Henry's decree. But you must indeed have duties elsewhere, have lands, castles, people and men-at-arms dependent upon you. It was wrong of me to take you from them."

His smile was grim. "You had every right, Lady Marguerite. There was a vow between us."

"You remember that, too."

"Aye," he answered, his voice deep and sure. "I vowed to defend you with the last drop of my life's blood, to serve you in all things as a knight should serve his lady, to protect you, holding you in chaste reverence, keeping you forever pure in my heart. 'Twas the day I rode away to battle. How could I forget?"

"So do I recall," she answered, her voice not quite even. It had taken her breath away, that solemn oath given as he knelt before her. She had relived it in a thousand dreams, thrilled to the touch of his hands upon hers, the blaze of exultation in his eyes, the nobility of his sentiments. She had revisited it in daydreams, touched somewhere deep inside that she did not care to examine, though uncertain she was worthy of the honor. Yes, and while half suspecting the sentiments were too exalted by half.

"Ah," he whispered.

Her smile trembled at the edges. "We . . . we were young, and you have traveled far from that time, far from Braesford's great hall where the pledge was given."

"Still I am bound by it, and will ever be so."

Was that all? Had he answered her summons from no more than the obligation of honor? She had no right to think anything else or to expect it. Yet she had, she had.

"Milady?" Astrid said again.

Marguerite glanced at her small henchwoman, then back to David. "In spite of it, you never came back," she said, shielding her eyes with her lashes, aware of a trace of accusation in her voice that she had not intended.

"To be squire to Sir Rand was no longer possible or necessary after I was knighted, and I had my way to make in the world." He tilted his head. "And you? You were never tempted to take any other man as husband?"

"The offers that came my way did not suit."

"Did they not?"

She wished she could be nonchalant about it, but that was impossible. "Not that there were so many, given the reputation of the curse of the Graces. Henry let me be, mayhap out of gratitude for past aid from my family or, more likely, because I slipped his mind, being so seldom in his sight except for the occasional court visit. That was until this past winter. His decree ordering me to marry came without rhyme or reason."

"You first sent for me at that time."

"Soon enough, as it began to look as if Lord Halliwell, my erstwhile groom, would remain hale and hardy despite the curse." She shook back her veil. "I sent far and wide, a dozen messages, two dozen and more, though all for naught. It was Astrid who suggested she should go after you, to seek the road you traveled."

" 'Twas a tavern where I found him," Astrid said, crossing her arms over her chest.

"You should have seen her when she approached me, a miniature gentleman with her hair wound up inside a hat big enough for her to sleep under, strutting about in doublet and hose as if ten feet tall. I thought her mad when she flung herself upon my lap and would not get down."

Astrid gave a screech. "You thought what?"

"You will admit it looked odd in your male garb." David threw her a crooked smile. "I did listen when you began to whisper in my ear."

"And set forth to come to me," Marguerite said, refusing to be deflected. "You are here, even if you did terrify me." Her gaze darkened as she recalled other things he had done, other liberties he had taken while she was in his arms.

"Your pardon, milady, but it was necessary. I preferred you not know me while in earshot of your escort, not identify me too soon."

She took his meaning, though in her opinion it did not explain all. "No, I would not have you become an outlaw over this business."

He shifted a shoulder in a deliberate movement that sent golden glimmers over the engraving at the neck of his cuirass. "That part matters not."

"It might, should Henry learn what you have been about. Yes, and discover this encampment. But what's to do now?"

To return her to Braesford would be useless, she saw easily enough, as Henry would likely send after her again with a larger company of men-at-arms as her wedding escort. Such a troop could not be barred from entry, for Henry might then lay siege to the manse and its pele tower as an example. That would endanger Rand, Isabel and their children, as well as their people and holdings. Rand might feel it worth the risk, but David seemed determined to avoid it.

What else had she expected, however, when she sent Astrid after him as her messenger?

She hardly knew, in all truth. It had been an instinct based on the safety she had always felt in his company, aligned to unconscious faith in his pledge to serve her. Or mayhap she did know, but cared not admit it even to herself. She had hoped David might make a stealthy return, after which there could be a quiet wedding that would forever bar her marriage to Lord Halliwell. The friendship between them would have made any solution more bearable than the alternative.

She must have been dreaming, still.

"For now, we eat," Astrid said in interruption, a fierce scowl on her small face that dared them to disagree. "The soup is hot and I hate when it grows cold. Besides, the ground is damp, and the two of you look ridiculous kneeling there when you could be inside where it's warm."

She was privileged to say such things because she was one of the Little People, and had been with Marguerite for nine long years. Once assigned to Elizabeth of York as the Queen's Fool, she had been riding on a pleasure barge that capsized in a sudden storm during the entertainment for Henry's second royal year. Marguerite had been on the same barge and gone into the water with everyone else. She'd fought her way to a floating ale barrel, then, seeing the doll-like person sinking under the waves, reached out and snatched her to safety. Henry, applauding the rescue, said that Marguerite, having saved Astrid's life, must be responsible for her forthwith.

Astrid had been thankful to be quit of court life, of the need to perform every moment of her day, to watch her every word and be eternally watchful against cruel jests. A tempestuous creature too small to punish, she was used to having her way. She soon routed Gwynne from her tasks as Marguerite's serving woman, taking these upon herself. She served Marguerite at table, overseeing every bite she ate. She entertained her upon the lute while she sewed in the solar, and was her close confederate in her more daring larks and outings. So determined was she in her guardianship that it sometimes seemed she felt Marguerite belonged to her rather than the other way around.

She ladled soup into carved wooden bowls and put them in front of Marguerite and David, placed a round, dark loaf on the deal table that sat in one corner, added beakers of water and then joined them. They ate in silence for long moments. Marguerite was hungry as she'd taken only dry bread and a slice of cold beef early that morning. She could feel her strength and her spirits reviving as she enjoyed chunks of bread dipped into the rich soup. She looked up after a moment, making ready to question David further about her future.

He was not eating. Instead, he gazed at her with his bread hanging forgotten from his fingers and a suspended look on his face. He met her eyes an instant before his lashes came down, shuttering his expression. Muttering something about seeing his men were supplied with food, he picked up his wooden dish and vanished into the night.

Marguerite stared after him with a frown gathering between her eyes. She turned to

Astrid. "Has he been like this since you came upon him?"

"Worse," Astrid answered while using a bit of bread crust to chase a beef chunk around the bottom of her bowl. "He drove his men so hard I was astonished there was no rebellion. As it was, a quarter of them fell by the wayside before we reached Calais."

"It must have been a hard journey for you," Marguerite said with a sympathetic wince.

"Not so bad." She lifted a small shoulder. "Sir David found a pony for me that was much better for my short legs than my rouncey from Braesford. Then being in hose and doublet, I was able to avoid a side-saddle."

Marguerite looked down at her bowl, and then pushed it away. With the edge of her hand, she wiped bread crumbs from the table, watching them fall to the packed earth floor. Clearing her throat, she spoke in careful neutrality. "Did David chance to say what he meant to do with me once he had me in his keeping?"

"Not to me. I suppose it shall be whatever you will."

Marguerite was not so certain. This new David appeared to have ideas of his own, also a great liking for seeing them carried out strictly to his order. "I can't go back to Braesford as Henry will surely look for me there, and the same is true if I should take refuge with my sister Cate and her husband at their holdings. David might keep me with him when he returns whence he came yet to remain with him and his men-at-arms will soon have me named as a camp follower. What else is there?"

"You have the favor of Henry's queen. Will she not intercede for you?"

"Well she might, but what odds Henry will listen to her."

Astrid lifted her tiny hands in a fatalistic gesture. "Hi ho, we shall be camp followers then."

"We?"

"Wherever you go, there must I go also."

Marguerite gave her an astringent look. "Don't become Biblical, please. I'm not sure I can bear it." She went on after a moment. "In any case, I think David too aware of my station to allow such a pass."

"Your station."

"As Lady Marguerite, daughter of a lord. He has always been far more conscious of the difference in rank between us than I."

"He didn't seem particularly humble on the journey."

"Did he not?"

The serving woman lifted miniscule brows. "Have you taken note of the man, milady? I mean, really looked at him? He is no youth, but a hardened soldier. He has fought in dozens of campaigns and gained recognition and honors far beyond most. What need has he to feel beneath any man, or any woman?"

"None whatever," Marguerite said, heat rising in her face. Of course she had taken note of this changed David. How could she not when he was so fair to look upon. She had sensed the power he held in such rigorous control, too, and felt his hands upon her in a manner he would never have dared before. Yet he had knelt before her, seemed reluctant to sit at the same table with her whom he had served at meals while her brother-in-law's squire. "The difference seems to be there, all the same."

"You refine too much upon it."

Marguerite gazed at the opposite wall for long moments before dislodging the conundrum with a swift shake of her head. "I should still like to know what he intends."

"You will have to ask him. He said nothing to me."

It was to be expected. As far as Marguerite had been able to tell while living with

Braesford, men enjoyed keeping their plans secret. She had never been sure if the cause was lack of trust in female discretion or only that they preferred to make decisions in midstream, as it were, and without tedious explanation. "He can't remain in England," she said with a worried frown.

"Can he not?"

"He could be accused of all manner of crimes. I never meant for him to risk so much, never dreamed he might abduct me on the road."

"What did you think he would do? Come for you in the dead of night?"

"Something of the sort," she said, looking away. "I could have gone to meet him if he had sent word."

"And then what?"

Marguerite preferred not to say. The only sure prevention for an unwanted marriage was to take another groom in place of the one assigned her. "I don't know. That he might come was such a forlorn hope, I hardly thought beyond it."

Astrid continued to eat, unperturbed. "I feel sure Sir David will know what to do."

"He must ride for the coast, I think, and take ship as soon as it may be arranged."

"With or without you?"

Now there was a question, one that left

47

her oddly breathless. She would be safe if she went with him. Or safe from marriage to Lord Halliwell, at least.

From the turmoil inside her arose a shaft of anger. "How can you be so calm?" she demanded of Astrid. "Only think what it will be like if Henry sends a company of men after us that is twice or thrice the size of David's."

"First he has to find us. Fear not, milady. Sir David will see you are not wed against your will, even if he has to do the deed himself."

"It's all very well for you to say so, but you were not there when he said he had no thought of taking a wife."

"He said that?"

Marguerite's nod was brief. He had been speaking as the Golden Knight at the time, still she believed him.

Not that she wished to be wed to any man if it could be avoided. She much preferred being a maiden, even if it did make her dependent upon her sisters and their husbands. There was nothing greatly wrong with going back and forth between their two houses, playing the loving aunt to her nieces and nephews, helping out when they were ill or when one of her sisters gave birth again. Yet watching Isabel and Cate with the men they had married, she often knew an aching need for similar closeness, for something more of loving affection than had been hers thus far.

David did not return.

Marguerite sat staring into the flames for an hour or more after Astrid had curled up, fully dressed, in the middle of the thin straw pallet that lay against one wall and fallen into her usual deathlike slumber. She had thought to question his plans, to discover if he had a better idea than she of where they must go and what was to be done. Finally, the peat on the hearth smoldered down to flame-edge chunks of ash. She sighed and wrapped herself in her cloak, then lay down beside Astrid and pulled a woven wool coverlet over them both.

Sleep would not come. She lay staring at the dark shadows that wavered on the ceiling in what was left of the fire glow. She could not rid herself of the fear that David might yet hang for his bold daylight abduction. Far better if he had come and taken her away by night. She would have met him at the postern gate at Braesford if he had only sent to tell her when. She would have gone with him without question. There was no man she trusted more.

No boy she had once trusted more, at any rate.

What had she done with her fervent request for aid? She could not bear it if he was forced to pay with his life for answering it; the mere chance was a knife twisting in her heart. Why had she not thought the matter through to its end? She had been desperate to avoid becoming Lady Halliwell, yes, but she would never have sent Astrid to find David if she had known it would come to this.

How strange it was to see him, however, and to discover the man he had become. His face and large form stunned the mind now with their masculine perfection. He was so self-contained, so rigid in his dedication to honor and valor. Somewhere deep inside, she was a little frightened of him, though she would die before admitting it. What hardship and labor, danger and horror he must have endured to turn him into such a fearsome knight. Thinking of it was more than she could bear.

Regardless, he had paid homage to her just as he had so many years ago, before he marched away to fight for Henry at the battle of Stoke-on-Trent. His vow given that day seemed as meaningful to him now as it had then, as valued as his vows of knighthood. The Golden Knight was, just possibly, as strong and brave, as true and pure of heart as the ballads claimed. Mayhap the troubadours who told of such things had not lied. She liked to think they had not, at any rate.

The David of years ago had been a handsome lad, strong and stalwart, courteous yet with a vein of endearing humor. How proud he had been to be Sir Rand's squire after her brother-in-law saved him from a beating by street thugs. This was after he had run away from the tannery where he'd been apprenticed by the nuns who had reared him from an orphan babe. Truth to tell, Marguerite mourned the gentle, painfully self-effacing boy who had wanted nothing from life except to serve Sir Rand and be her friend and guardian.

Why had he gone away after the carnage and heroism of Stoke? She had never known.

Oh, but how they had laughed before war came upon the land, running with the wind, eating food stolen from the kitchen while lying beside a cool, clear stream, talking, talking as they sat in the grass making crowns of spring clover. He had kissed her hand once, his mouth soft, smooth and warm against her skin. Another time, she had leaned over him as he slept with his head in her lap, and, greatly daring, touched her lips to his forehead. Such sweet memories, they almost made her cry. She had kept them close, so close they were almost like a dream. . . .

She woke of a sudden to the quiet creak of the door hinge. Lying rigid under the coverlet, she watched the shadow that stepped inside, stretching, moving over the wall beside her. The shape, the height and width of shoulder could be none except David. She sighed in soundless relief and closed her eyes for a moment of thankfulness.

He came closer, stepping with a tread so silent she would not have known if she had not wakened. He stopped beside the narrow pallet. Long moments slipped past as he stood staring down upon her where she lay. Goose bumps prickled over her under her clothing. Her heartbeat quickened, pounding in her chest until she thought surely he could hear it. Her eyelids fluttered a little before she could still them. She wondered what he saw that he did not turn away at once.

Clothing rustled, a whisper of sound, as he knelt beside her. She thought in scattered irrelevance that he must have removed his armor for the night. She waited, wondering what he was about, wondering if he meant to slide in beside her, wondering in shivering anticipation if he would take more liberties of the kind he'd ventured while she rode with him.

He put out a hand, almost touching her face, for she could feel its warmth hovering above her cheek. Yet he did not touch, did nothing except reach to pull the edge of the coverlet higher over her shoulder. A whisper, too soft to understand, shifted in the air above her head. Then he withdrew, his movements amazingly soundless for so large a man. Cool air swirled inside as he pulled open the door. It closed behind him with the softest of thuds.

In time, the fire died away into darkness. Only then did Marguerite sleep again.

"You are in danger if you stay. You must go!"

"In good time," David said in calm reply to that urgent command from Lady Marguerite. He might have known dawn would bring more argument. She was accustomed to thinking herself able to command him, at least in small things. It had been his privilege and pleasure to obey in the past, but that was long ago and in much smaller matters.

"First, I must see you to safety."

They walked the track that stretched past the cottage, he and the lady, away from prying eyes and ears. Morning mist hung like white bed curtains in the treetops, shot through with the silver, slanting rays of the rising sun. Birds called in melodious trills above the droning voices and occasional laughter of his men. The air was fresh and sweet, layered with the fragrance of some blooming vine along with the smells of smoke and horses and bread toasting on sticks held above campfires. It was a good day to be alive.

"I was wrong to send for you," she said, twining her fingers together at her waist. "I should have realized how it would be. Now you must return whence you came. If you ride hard, you and your men can be at the coast well before Lord Halliwell or . . . or Henry comes up with you."

Her concern for his safety touched a place inside him that had grown so callused from blow after blow upon it that he'd thought it beyond feeling. He watched her with raw concentration while regulating his breathing to an even cadence that might control the stirring of his body. Reaching out, he removed a piece of bed straw that had become entangled in the veil covering her hair, then allowed his fingers to trail along her jawline to her chin before closing them in a fist that he lowered to his side.

"Am I to leave you here, unguarded?" he asked in quiet reason. "That would be foolish after taking you from the safeguard of your escort."

"You cannot sleep outside my door for the rest of your life!"

Heat bloomed across the back of his neck. "I did not intend to offend. It seemed a way to make certain none entered and that . . ."

"And that all knew you had not lain with me during the night, yes, I know," she said with asperity. "I am grateful for the thought, as was Astrid when she stumbled over you as she started out for water this morning, but it only adds to the problem with this abduction. To remain in your company is as much a threat to my future as the marriage arranged for me."

"To remain here without protection would be a threat indeed," he said in hard disagreement. "I can't go, can't leave you unguarded."

"If you will be so kind as to send a messenger to Braesford, Sir Rand will come for me. Astrid and I may stay inside, out of sight, until he arrives."

"You would return to Braesford's keep,

knowing Henry will only find you there again?" He would not mention the mind-searing possibilities involved in two females left alone, at the mercy of any stray game-keeper, forest outlaw or band of mercenary soldiers from either of the armies gathering in the land. The mere idea turned him cold and sick inside.

"If you would speak of foolishness, then my hope of avoiding the marriage arranged for me was surely that." A corner of her mouth curled for an instant. "It is woman's part to accept these things in all modesty."

"I cannot accept it," he answered with tempered steel in his voice. "Not now."

"What would you have me do instead? You have no idea of marrying me."

"No. That I can't do."

She swung toward him, a frown in the rich brown depths of her eyes. "Why is that? Have you a wife in France?"

"Nay, no wife. As to the why of it, you know well."

Color like the bloom on a peach spread across her cheekbones. "This sacred vow, sworn upon the cross, to serve me in chaste and knightly fashion, without desire, without stint, without regard for life?"

"Sworn upon the hilt of my sword, rather, though it's the same thing."

"It was long ago. We were children."

"Not entirely." His smile was brief and a little twisted.

She clenched her fingers upon each other until they appeared as pale as candle wax. "There is of course the curse of the Graces, but I thought, I know you once said . . ."

"Oh, aye, I am beyond its effects, for I cared for you from the moment I saw you, will always care for you," he answered, the words a renewal of a different vow made long ago. To say them satisfied something inside him, in spite of everything.

Her eyes widened, dominating her whole face. "But if you have no fear of the curse . . ." she began, only to trail into silence.

"Milady?"

"To marry me would be . . . a service you may perform for my good."

That she could suggest such a thing set his heart aflame, burning like a hot coal in his chest. He was touched by the trust of it, also that she understood him so well. Still, some things had obvious answers. "Ah, Lady Marguerite, it would be an honor beyond any I've yet gained, but it can't be."

She searched his features for a fleeting instant before looking away. "There need not be anything of a physical nature between us."

"Even so." His voice was like a sledge being pulled through a rock pit, and he put a hand on his sword hilt in a much-needed reminder of all he had sworn and foresworn, clenching it until his fingers ached. The simple fact was that he could never take her to wife, not and keep to his vow of chastity. To tell her so was impossible, of course. A man did not hand a weapon to one sure to use it against him.

The color in her face deepened, as did the frustrated anger in her eyes. "You have no wish to be my husband. Very well. But do you never intend to marry?"

He hid a wry smile for her feminine curiosity, even as he wondered if a weapon might not be forged from it. "I never said that."

She stared at him, her gaze clouded. "What do you mean?"

"My vow was made to you alone, my lady. It extends to no other."

"So you are free to love elsewhere."

"And have been free these ten years," he answered with determined hardihood.

A short laugh left her. "So the verses sung to your prodigious, near insatiable appetite for love do not exaggerate."

"I wouldn't say that."

"But neither do you deny the stories told of your prowess among amorous French ladies and their daughters."

He lifted a moody shoulder, for he could not tell her nay. He had not been bound to resist the lures of such women. He had been far from Braesford, and thought never to see its walls or to lay eyes upon Marguerite again in this life. The physical release he had found had nothing to do with the tenderness and idealism of what he had felt for her when they were young and carefree. She had always been above such driven animal lust in his mind, as she had been above him.

If his carnal appetites turned her against him, then might that not be for the best?

She walked on, and he moved at her side, watching as she took one corner of her veil and began to nibble it in a well-remembered habit when she was upset or thoughtful.

"What would you have me do, then, if you don't mean to keep me with you?" she asked in exasperation. "Where am I to be settled? If I shelter with any lord of standing, he will give me up to Henry as soon as his men appear. Well, or else call for a priest and make himself my husband for the sake of my marriage portion."

"Not for that alone," he murmured, allowing his gaze to flicker quickly from her face to the tender curve of her neck and downward to the sweet mounds of her breasts under her gown. It might have been better for his peace of mind if carnal matters had not been mentioned.

"And not if he should happen to follow the white rose of York, I suppose. Such a one might keep me hidden to thumb his nose at a Lancastrian king."

"Or he might decide raping one of Henry's wards would be a fine revenge," he returned in hard warning.

"What then? Shall I follow in the train of your men like the merest camp drab?"

"No." The denial was sharp, primarily because the idea had violent attraction as long as she was his drab alone. Though that was as impossible as becoming her husband.

"What is left? I would not — Oh." She came to a halt as comprehension rose in her eyes.

"Indeed," he said in iron agreement.

"A convent. You intend that I become a nun." The words were as dull as the expression in her eyes.

"Will it not serve?"

It was not an uncommon solution. There was sanctuary within a convent for a lady of

Marguerite's station who wanted to escape marriage. It would be a life of peace and prayer, one well removed from the avarice of men, removed from their lust. If the last appealed to him more than it should, then so be it. In spite of the iron bonds of his vow, he was no saint.

She lowered her lashes and released her veil, clasping her hands at her waist. "I fear I lack a vocation."

"As do half the women who enter nunnery walls."

She pressed her lips together an instant then gave a small sigh. "But you will ride for the coast when I am with the good sisters in some such place?"

"When you are settled," he agreed with a nod. "Not before."

"Well, sir," she began with unhappiness threading her voice.

It was then that the clarion call of a trumpet blasted the morning air. It startled the birds to flight and echoed back from the distant sky. Hard upon it came the trampling of hooves and the jingling of saddlery. The noise grew louder, came closer, until it seemed to shake the ground and rattle the leaves on the trees.

Mounted men burst into view then, riding two abreast down the narrow woodland track, yet winding back as far as the eye could see. Above them waved a mighty pennon showing a snarling red dragon on a yellow ground, mark of the man who rode beneath it.

David cursed with soft and raging invective in three languages. Beside him, Marguerite drew breath with a sharp gasp, then stood perfectly still.

The yellow pennon carried the device of Henry Tudor.

Henry, seventh of the name, king of England.

3

Grunts, yells and the clatter of arms rang through the trees. In the blink of an eye, or so it seemed to Marguerite, David's men-at-arms formed a phalanx that bristled with pikes and halberds, bows and swords. They lined the rutted track, presenting a solid bulwark between him and the king's men. A command rang out, full-throated, rife with authority. Every man froze in position, offering no attack yet giving not an inch of ground.

The king lifted a gloved hand. The cavalcade behind him clattered to a halt. Alone, he walked his horse forward, an unmistakably royal figure in clothing suitable for the hunt yet of the finest cloth dyed in the richest of colors. He drew up, eased his seat as if stiff from his ride. His expression judicious, he stared down at David and Marguerite where they stood.

Marguerite's heart thundered against her

rib cage and tremors ran over her from her chest to her knees. She made her curtsy, aware at the same time of David's respectful obeisance on one knee. At a brief, stern word from the king, David rose and took her hand, drawing her up beside him, placing her hand on his arm and his other over it for support. They waited for Henry VII to make known his displeasure and what he meant to exact of them for it.

The king had aged since coming to the throne, Marguerite realized as she gazed up at him in the bright, unforgiving light of morning. His shoulders were more stooped and lines of care grooved his long, patrician face on either side of his thin blade of a nose. Strands of silver glinted in the sandy-blond of his hair that hung below his hat with its upturned brim cut in jagged points like a crown drawn by a child. Ten years past, when she first appeared at court, he had seemed a man in his prime. Now, at not much above forty, he looked much older and tired beyond reckoning. It seemed the weight of England rested upon his shoulders. Who could say it did not?

"Here we are together again, David of Braesford," Henry said. "At last."

"Your Majesty," he returned in grave acknowledgment, and not the smallest trace of subservience.

Marguerite, watching the two men, was aware of an odd undercurrent between them. One or two of the king's courtiers seemed to feel it as well, for they glanced at each other with raised brows. Did it relate to that day during the bloodletting at Stoke, when David had saved the king's life and raised the fallen Lancaster standard in victory? She could not imagine what it might be otherwise.

"You are no doubt surprised to see us," Henry went on, employing the royal plural with easy familiarity.

David inclined his head. "As you say, sire."

"We will go inside where we may be private." Henry indicated the cottage a small distance away with a brief wave of his hand. "We will then discuss how we arrived at this happenstance."

There was little mystery to it in Marguerite's mind. Someone must have ridden in haste to the king with the news of her abduction. Another man had no doubt followed after David, that he might lead Henry to this hidden encampment. The only way either could have brought the king here in such short order, however, was if Henry had been hunting or else upon royal progress nearby. And what evil chance had allowed that?

Marguerite, uncertain she was included in the command to attend the king in the cottage, hung back as they neared the low doorway. David did not release her, however, but drew her with him as he stepped inside.

Astrid was caught at the window where she had been standing on a stool to watch Henry's arrival. She curtsied from atop it with aplomb not unmixed with bravado. Henry gestured for her to jump down and bring her perch forward. Taking the stool, he made a gesture of dismissal. Astrid's face creased in a worried frown, but she backed from the cottage and closed the door behind her.

Marguerite and David were left alone with Henry VII.

The king made a brusque signal which indicated that Marguerite must take the stool. It was not a mannerly gesture, she thought, but rather that he wished to avoid the low seat which would have put his knees on a level with his shoulders, not to mention requiring that she and David sit on the earthen floor so their heads would not be above his.

Or mayhap Henry merely preferred to

remain on his feet. His manner was un-settled, and tension robbed his movements of their usual deliberation. The same sense of strain wavered in the air, crackling like the low flames on the hearth.

"You will have guessed that we have been kept informed of your movements since you left France," he threw at David, speaking over his shoulder as he strode toward the single window, then turned back again. "Lady Marguerite's as well, from the time she passed out of the gates of Braesford."

"Aye, sire, it seemed likely," David allowed, his thick, gold-tipped lashes shielding his expression.

"What may not be so obvious is that the betrothal from which you saved her with so little difficulty was no more than a ruse."

"A ruse," Marguerite repeated in stunned disbelief.

Not a shadow of remorse lay in the king's face. "Regrettable, but necessary."

"I feel certain there was a purpose." Though the words were polite enough, David's voice sliced like honed steel.

"She was a lure, nothing more or less." Henry gave him a jaundiced look.

"One meant to draw me back to England."

"If you had answered our many letters, our many messages that invited you to appear before us, if you had met with the representative sent to request your presence, then the fright for Lady Marguerite — this entire charade, in fact — need never have taken place."

"The fright for her? You are saying she knew nothing of this ruse of yours?"

Though David spoke to the king, his gaze, as hard as blue glass, was bent upon her face, Marguerite saw. She ceased to breathe as she awaited Henry's answer.

"Lady Marguerite is intelligent beyond most, but we do not make a habit of confiding matters of state to females."

Marguerite lifted her chin as she absorbed the backhanded compliment. That her escape from an unwanted marriage could be construed to be a matter of state was as difficult to accept as that no union had been intended in the first place.

"To Halliwell's men then? Or Braesford's?"

"It was considered, in order to prevent bloodshed, but we decided that might be best left to you. To encourage Halliwell seemed unwise. He has recently shown signs of being overeager for this marriage."

"Has he?" David asked, his voice soft. "Enough to prevent the rescue?"

Henry's features congealed into hauteur.

"What mean you?"

"I noted a man at Calais with uncommon interest in my route of travel."

"Ours, no doubt." The king shrugged. "If he attracted your attention, we are employing inferior servitors and must look about us for replacements."

" 'Spies,' you mean to say, sire," David said in clarification.

"What would you? If every crowned head in Europe has its network of agents, then we must have the same or be left naked in our lack of information."

"Keeping watch on your own subjects as well, sire?" Marguerite asked, entering the conversation with determination.

The king acknowledged her sally with a grim smile. "There is where the lèse-majesté lies, Lady Marguerite, and the threat of sedition that goes with it."

David watched them, his gaze considering. "Halliwell was never a party to this ruse of yours."

"As you say."

"He did not seek her hand."

That explained, for Marguerite, the peer's continued health. If he had not attempted to defy the curse of the Graces, then he had never been in danger from it. "The betrothal was a mere ploy then," she said in her need

69

to clarify where she stood. "There was no possibility of a marriage."

"Lord Halliwell did not disagree when it was proposed to him, and he will naturally be compensated for any mortification he may now feel at the loss of his bride. Of course, if the Golden Knight had not appeared . . ."

Her lips tightened as she saw Henry's point. She would have been married off with scarcely a qualm, thrown away upon Lord Halliwell as easily as disposing of a lure refused by a hunting falcon. "I fail to see why you thought he might trouble himself."

"The ability of the Three Graces to draw men to them has been proven in the past. We depended upon it."

"Yet how could you know there was any reason he should, anything between us then or now."

The king merely looked at her. Anger roiled inside her as she realized she was a subject who must have been watched along with the rest.

David stirred, his gaze upon the king. "So you had your spies in all camps, and used them to come upon us once the lady was rescued. Why go to such lengths? What can you want of me?"

"Well, you may ask." Henry tugged at his

70

bottom lip, as if deciding how much to say, or else how to say it.

The strained feeling in the cottage tightened, gathering close. Marguerite, sensing it, was suddenly afraid. She jerked a little as the king dropped his hand, facing David as if in sudden decision.

"You have heard of one Perkin Warbeck during your travels over the continent?"

"The Yorkist pretender? I saw him once or twice in Burgundy."

"How did he strike you? What think you of him?"

Henry's reign to date had not been particularly peaceful, Marguerite knew. Hardly had he settled into his role as king when the first pretender appeared. Young Lambert Simnel, barely twelve years of age, had been presented as the younger son of Edward IV, miraculously escaped from death in the Tower. His followers had been defeated at Stoke, after which the boy was proved to have been sired by an Irish carpenter. In the years since, there had been trouble with Charles VIII of France and other skirmishes on the continent. Now there was this specter of the man called Perkin Warbeck.

Warbeck had been agitating for at least six years, going slowly from one court to another to gain support and add to his war chest. He was a more formidable foe than Simnel, being older and more self-assured. More than that, he had the Plantagenet coloring of fair hair and blue eyes, also their supreme confidence that amounted to arrogance. It was said as well that he had more knowledge of the family descended from that grand old tyrant, Geoffrey of Anjou, than any should know who was not born to the purple.

Whether from sincere belief in his lineage or mere political expediency, James IV of Scotland had taken up Warbeck's cause to the point of giving him a kinswoman in marriage. The duchess of Burgundy, supposedly Warbeck's aunt as she was a sister to Edward IV, had extended her blessing and promised an army of mercenaries. Charles VIII of France had entertained Warbeck in royal state as well, since anything which might shake the English throne was seen as a benefit for his regime.

"I liked what I saw of him," David answered with studied calm.

Henry grimaced. "That he is likable does not make him a Plantagenet prince. Did you speak to him? Had you a sense that he might actually be who he claims?"

It was telling that Henry thought it possible. Some liked to claim he had ordered the deaths of the princes in the Tower, Edward IV's sons, before he invaded England to fight for the crown. That was unreasonable on the face of it. If he'd had certain proof Simnel and Warbeck were false pretenders, surely he would have produced it before now?

"Anything is possible, sire. He spoke well and had the royal air, yet there are those who could have made certain he knew enough to be convincing."

"It can be done, yes," Henry said, rubbing his chin with his knuckle. "We were not brought up for royal office, but soon gained the knack of it. As for his looks . . ."

David gave him a smile with a sardonic edge. " 'Tis well-known Edward was blessed with a number of sons born of unions without a priest's blessing."

"Before and after his clandestine marriage to Elizabeth Woodville," Henry said in agreement. "His dealings with women, particularly the poor lady to whom he was promised before he took the throne, were less than admirable. Some by-blows he acknowledged . . ."

"And some he did not," David finished for him, his eyes cool. "It's been suggested my own mother may have known him too well for her own good."

"So we've heard," Henry replied with no surprise whatever.

Marguerite listened to that charge with an odd pang under her breastbone. Her older sister, Isabel, had once mentioned that David had a familiar look about him. She had gone on to speculate about his parentage and how he had come to be brought up by nuns. Marguerite had paid scant attention. David was David, his own person, and she had no interest in anything more. It was odd to hear him speak of it now, for he had never indicated in those younger years that he cared who might have fathered him.

"Forgive me, Your Majesty," she said in controlled patience, "but I don't understand the purpose of this hoax."

"We are coming to that, Lady Marguerite. In fact, it is this accident of birth which is of most interest to us."

"My resemblance to Warbeck," David said, his eyes narrowing with thoughtfulness. "Is that it?"

A wintery smile moved over Henry's lips that had once been sensuously full but were now pinched and thin. "Or rather to the man who may have been his father."

"To Edward IV."

"There you have it. These are treacherous times, so require treacherous measures. To

74

the ruse we planned involving Lady Marguerite, we would add another."

"Sire . . ." Sick dread spiraled up from deep inside her as she caught the vague outline of Henry's intention.

"And that would be?" David asked, his voice quiet, almost contemplative.

"We would create another Yorkist pretender."

Silence fell with the swiftness of a headsman's axe. The peat fire whispered on the hearth. Wind soughed through the trees that waved over the cottage. Beyond the log-built walls, the low murmur of the men-at-arms and stamping and blowing of horses could be heard.

David stirred, squaring his shoulders. His voice was deep and without inflection as he spoke.

"Another pretender, sire? In addition to Warbeck?"

"Warbeck is a serious threat, more dangerous by far than young Simnel a decade ago," Henry answered with a brief gesture of acceptance. "Old enough to command from the throne in his own right, he has gathered an impressive array of supporters, both here and in Europe. The numbers of his followers increase day by day, and include the highest in the land. What is required is a way to dilute his effect, to divide his supporters, draw a portion away to another banner while preventing others from joining the insurrection he is fomenting."

"You believe he will actually invade?"

"Oh, yes. The Scots made a foray in his support last year, hoping to catch us off guard. Those behind him will not miss the opportunity to try again this summer."

"You think to confuse the issue with a second pretender to the throne, another man claiming to be one of the princes who disappeared from the Tower."

"Just so." Henry VII's smile was chilling.

"And I am chosen."

"No," Marguerite whispered, though she could not be surprised when neither man spared her a glance.

"You have the correct appearance and bearing. News of your exploits in tournament and battle has been carried far and wide. Few will be surprised if told you have royal blood in your veins. They will see your fame as proof of it."

David gave a short laugh. "So I am to be made legitimate."

"Warbeck claims to be Richard, Edward's second son. Would you do the same? Or would you prefer to take the name of the eldest as your own?"

"No!" Marguerite sprang to her feet. "David, sire . . . this is madness!"

"Edward would suit me very well," David said, "that is, if I agree to the scheme."

"You must not agree," Marguerite said in an urgent undertone as she turned to him. "Only think what it will mean!"

"I am aware," he said, though he met her eyes for the briefest of instants.

"Are you? Are you, really? The Yorkists who follow Warbeck will not sit idly by while you destroy their plans. They will remove you from the field if they can, will kill you without a qualm to achieve it. The Lancastrians loyal to Henry will see you as a threat as well, for it can hardly be made public that you play a part at royal behest. Every hand will be against you! If you are caught, you will be condemned as a traitor. You will be drawn and quartered, and your head put up to feed the ravens."

"She is right, of course," Henry said without expression.

"The question then," David answered, "is why I should undertake such risk."

"You would be rewarded?" The king's eyes narrowed to gray slits. "What is it you want? Lady Marguerite and her dowered lands as your prize?"

"Sire!" The suggestion came so near to

taking her breath that the protest had the sound of a moan.

David's lips curved in a wry smile. "What, with so little likelihood of being able to enjoy either? Nay. I require greater favor than that."

Henry's features turned chill, though he did not withdraw. "What would you then?"

"I require your pledge that Lady Marguerite will never again be given in betrothal to any man. I'll have your written word that she may be allowed to live in peace wherever she so desires, to retain the properties that are hers by right of inheritance from her father and stepfather and to enjoy all proceeds from them without let or hindrance."

"David," she whispered, staring up at him, her eyes filling as the full meaning of his request came to her. He was bartering for her security and nothing more, nothing for himself in return for the dangers he would have to face. He meant to see that she was safe from marriage, safe forever.

"I require," David finished, turning his head to hold her gaze while his own shone darkly blue, "that you extend to her your protection, guarding against all who might seek to trespass, all who might violate her person for the sake of possessing her and her dower lands."

"And that is all?" Henry asked in blank amazement.

"It is enough."

"Done," the king said, and offered David his hand upon it.

"Done," David agreed as he accepted the king's pledge.

"Done," Marguerite echoed in a hollow whisper, and thought the repeated word had the sound of a death knell.

4

David gave orders for a hearty midmorning meal to be prepared for the king's men, and called Astrid back into the cottage to do the same for Henry. It had been a wearisome ride for the king's party to reach the encampment this day, and all would soon take horse, heading back to the castle currently providing shelter for the royal party. He and his cadre of half a hundred would go with them, as would Lady Marguerite and her small serving woman. Meanwhile, Henry had plans to unfold in this matter of a second pretender, or so it seemed. A deliberate man was Henry VII, and much given to detail. Doubtless, it was a large portion of his success.

David had ideas of his own, but was content to see what the king had in mind before he presented them for discussion. Unless an absolute necessity, it was foolish to butt heads with a man who wore a crown.

The main points were laid out while he and Henry strolled the wooded track, well out of earshot of the others. Marguerite watched them walk away, but made no effort to join them. Henry issued no invitation, it was true, but David suspected she would have refused. She was angry with both of them, he knew, foreseeing nothing but disaster in this venture.

She had always been perceptive, as he remembered. She had not changed in that.

In so much else, she was not the same. She smiled less. She was more forthright in her speech, less malleable in her thoughts and opinions. She had softer and more obvious curves, greater awareness in her eyes. True, she had been little more than a girl, her personality unformed, softer in feature and mien, smaller in stature when he had left her. Not that she was particularly tall now, of course. And she still had a fragile air that made him want to wrap her in his cloak, gathering her close for protection.

He desired a great many things when it came to Lady Marguerite, none of which he was likely to receive. He had given them up long ago, and could not expect them now, would not go back on his vow in order to achieve them. No, he could not do that, no matter the temptation.

Temptation there would be in plenty. Once ensconced at Henry's present keep, she was to help tutor him. She would guide him in the various graces that would be useful if he was to appear in the guise of Edward, prince of the house of York, once hailed as Edward V. Such closeness could become a sore test of his resolve, heaven help him.

He had almost laid hands upon her the night before. Her hair had been uncovered, as she had removed her veil for sleeping. Its thick braid had gleamed like interwoven strands of silk, the fine tendrils that escaped it shimmering as she breathed. He'd been carried back to a day in summer when they had run through the thick grass of the meadow below Braesford. She had tripped and fallen and he had plunged to the ground with her, both of them laughing like young fools. Her veil had loosened in the chase, her hair escaping from its confinement. She had sat up, leaning over him where he lay on his back among the clover, the daisies and wildflowers. Her glorious tresses had fallen around him, enclosing him within their silken curtain. The sunlight striking through them made tiny rainbows along the luminous strands, picking out a dozen blazing colors other than mere brown, shades of gold and russet and auburn and the soft coral-brown of beech leaves in autumn. He had been struck breathless by the magic of the moment while somewhere deep inside his very being stilled in awe. He wasn't sure he had ever quite recovered from that enchantment.

"Are you listening, Sir David?"

"Aye, sire." It was not exactly a lie.

"Well, then?"

David cleared his throat before answering. "I am to join your supposed hunting party, effectively going into seclusion at the castle that is your base for now. Over the next few weeks, I will be instructed in all the rules of behavior, the manners and forms of address that a future monarch should know from birth. I am to be outfitted for this part, also provided with the nucleus of an armed force."

"Together with your own men-at-arms, this force will become the vanguard of the army you will gather around you," Henry said in agreement. "Once trained to your orders, they will make a fine show of strength when you begin to be seen about the countryside, so it will appear men are flocking to your standard. Speaking of which, I believe a phoenix, symbolizing the rise from the ashes of old rumor about your death, would be appropriate."

"My apologies, sire, but I have a device."

"We are aware. A crown of thorns or some other vegetation, we believe. It is hardly suitable for this enterprise."

"A crown is a crown," David said at his most stubborn. "This one is of my own choosing and design. It has served me well. I would not depart from it."

"If you would be accepted as Prince Edward, son of Edward IV, you must display something more martial. Perhaps even the Plantagenet golden lions."

David stopped and turned to face Henry, placing his hands on his hips. "Why is that, when I have won what recognition I have on a foreign field, am come to this business full grown? Why would I not have chosen something of my own, even if I were Edward?"

Henry eyed him with disfavor for long moments. "It means this much to you?"

"It does," he said in deep-voiced precision.

The device came from a crown tendered to him on that same hot summer day while he lay with his head in Marguerite's lap. He had watched while she made that clover crown, her brow furrowed with concentration, her brown eyes holding all the softness in the world and his heart ached with hopeless longing that seemed to have no beginning and no end. She had placed it, more than a little askew, on his head, and he had felt a very king. He still had the crumbling remnants of that woven circle of clover in his baggage, folded into parchment and silk and tucked into a purse slipped into one of his spare boots for safekeeping.

How long ago it seemed, so very long ago.

The king inclined his head. "You may fight under your device if you must, but will be supplied with another showing the Plantagenet lions. You will display both when you ride out to rally men to your cause."

"As you command."

Henry was too wise a man to show his satisfaction. Walking on, he continued with the instructions he thought imperative for the success of their undertaking.

David stopped again. "I would point out, sire, that I have ample excuse for any lapse in manners or memory. If you will have it that Edward has been absent from England these many years for safety's sake, then clearly there will be much he's forgotten, including details of the Plantagenet family. Added to that, I've met a few princes. Most were less than pattern cards for royal conduct."

"Nor were they setting themselves up as would-be kings, I'll warrant," Henry answered. "You will be judged everywhere you go. It can be no other way. To discover in private the things that may trip you up when you go into the public view will be far better."

David thought to himself that he had more knowledge of court etiquette than Henry, or Lady Marguerite for that matter, seemed to realize. He had fought at a king's side and called him friend, had dined with kings and princes, spoken with them in audience, and stood about while they spoke with others.

He let it go. He'd no wish to be found lacking in any detail. Moreover, long days spent with Lady Marguerite while she aided him with the finer points of royal behavior were not to be scorned.

As for this business of impersonating a prince, he had his doubts. The line he would be treading was fine indeed. Its dangers were easily as apparent to him as they had been to Lady Marguerite. He must avoid being taken by either Yorkist or Lancastrian factions while building his base of support from which to challenge Perkin Warbeck. It would mean hard riding as he showed himself hither and yon, speaking to market crowds and gatherings of nobles, seldom remaining in one place for more than a few hours, staying always ahead of those who would destroy what he sought to build. Yes, and him with it.

He did not shrink from the danger, but neither did he underestimate it.

There was an additional peril that had gone unspoken by Lady Marguerite. Had that been from diplomacy or simple failure to recognize it? Either was possible, though it might also be that she rated his chance of success too low to trigger it.

In simple fact, attracting too great a following could become his greatest threat. What would Henry do if the support rallying to a new Plantagenet standard proved mighty enough to shake his throne?

He had sworn fealty to King Henry VII, but the king had sworn nothing to him.

"A question, sire," David said in contemplative tones.

"Aye?"

"What of afterward, when this rebellion has been put down and Warbeck captured or killed? Will you make public the stratagem we have agreed to pursue, or will you denounce my part in it and banish me across the channel?"

A thoughtful frown crossed the king's

face. "We've not looked that far ahead. An oversight, it must be admitted."

"Before it comes to that point, I could possibly discover proof that I'm not legitimate, after all, and fade from contention." Even as he made the suggestion, David could not forebear wondering if Henry had not failed to consider this eventuality because he had no expectation that his new false pretender would be alive when it arose.

"It's a possibility," Henry allowed.

"One that may smack of cowardice if left too late." David shook his head. "I would prefer the right to fight at your side, should that time come."

"And I would be honored to have you there once more." Henry clapped a hand on his shoulder. "An announcement it is, then, when events are in order and the pretended defeated, one telling all of the service you have rendered us."

David would have liked to ask His Royal Majesty to swear it. He might have, except where would he be if Henry refused?

Within an hour of the king's arrival, the combined cavalcade of David's men-at-arms and those of the king left the forest retreat. Whither they were bound, Marguerite had no sure idea. Her palfrey and the pony allotted to Astrid were brought to the cottage door by a dark-haired man who identified himself as David's squire, though he was of an age with David himself. He presented his commander's compliments and request that they mount up. Minutes later, they were a part of the galloping multitude.

Marguerite thought David might drop back to ride beside her in good time, mayhap to tell her what had passed between him and the king in private audience. She was troubled in mind about what had been proposed, had a thousand fears and questions that she would put to David about it. He had his responsibilities, of course, and she would not have him shirk them for her sake, yet surely he could spare a short while to let her know where they were going and what they would do when they got there?

He didn't appear. Instead, he seemed to have appointed his squire as his substitute.

The man introduced himself as Orlando of Sienna, though called Oliver by the English. He was an engaging rascal, with his black curls flying in wild disarray around his head, dark, shining eyes and the appreciative grin of a satyr. Though stocky of build and none too tall, he carried himself with aplomb. He had ridden with David for the past six years and more, so he said, after being captured in a tournament. Having no money for ransom and no relatives who might redeem him, he had thought to forfeit all he owned, horse and trappings, armor, shield and sword. When offered the post of David's squire instead, he had folded the banner of his ancient family, doffed his knight's plumes and accepted with gratitude. David being no stickler for form, the two of them had become companions of the tournament and battlefield. More than that, they were friends.

Astrid didn't care for the Italian. He was, she said under her breath, too charming by half and without proper respect. She cut her eyes at him and sniffed at the pleasantries he directed her way. She also did her best to keep her pony between his charger and the palfrey her mistress rode, though it was a little like a puppy trying to ward off a mastiff. That her disdain made the thin mustache favored by the squire tilt up at both ends only caused her to fume more.

Marguerite might have discounted her small maid's attitude but for the knowledge that Astrid had been with David and his men for some weeks now. It was possible she had reason for her dislike of the man.

"Have you any idea of our destination,

sir?" If she could not put the question to David, his squire seemed her most promising source of information. She made her voice light and airy, however, as if the answer mattered not a whit.

Oliver of Sienna gave a light shrug. "Talk among the king's men is all about the hunt. Your Henry is mad for it, so they say. Most see this outing as a search for deer and boar, and happening upon our cadre as an accident. Finding no great supply of game, they are now returning whence they came."

So that was Henry's story. Admittedly, it had an authentic ring to it. "Did they mention where that might be?"

"Some castle belonging to a petty noble who is exhausting his stores to feed his guests. It seems to be a chilly stone pile enclosed in a damnably thick forest that's a hard day's ride from a town of any size. The cook earns high praise, but the host's good wife is a strict chatelaine, and her serving women inclined to scream if cornered."

"I can imagine," she said, her voice dry.

"Can you now?" His eyes were bright, as if he would gauge her experience with such matters.

"It requires little effort, given the nature of men-at-arms." She kept her features bland as she turned her gaze to the column ahead, searching it for a glimpse of David's broad shoulders. That she had no experience whatever beyond drying the tears of maidservants who'd had indignities forced upon them was none of his affair.

"Pity the poor fools, who are as God made them," he answered. "Or as He made us, since I don't hold myself above the average man. No doubt it is His private jest."

The Italian's inclusion of himself in that rather disparaging assessment brought her head around. "Or mayhap His test for manly self-control?"

"Alas, so few are equal to the challenge. But then there is David."

Her eyes narrowed as she wondered how much he knew of the vow David had given her. "David?"

"It's helpful, of course, that he need not exercise restraint with the entire female population."

"Apparently," she answered in chill accents.

It seemed clear that Oliver knew all. What was she to make of that? Why, what else, except that David's promise of chaste servitude to her had become a different kind of jest, an oddity that affected her alone.

The idea pained her in some manner she could not describe, though it angered her, as well. She had thought, more fool she, that he was hers, would always be hers, regardless of the lack of intimacy between them. She'd assumed the closeness of mind they shared was all he required of any maiden.

She had been wrong, it seemed. It had never been enough for him. Other women might know his kisses, his touch, his powerful possession behind the bed curtains, but not her. Never her.

"Well, but what would you?" Oliver went on in cheerful reason. "The ladies do fling themselves at his feet, you know, as he is ever the champion, the celebrated Golden Knight. To step on them would be unkind. And if he steps over one, there is always another, and another. So tiring, such tribute."

Astrid entered the exchange with a snort. "So he puts himself to the trouble of picking up the most beauteous, I suppose. No doubt with your help."

Oliver chuckled and reached to chuck her under the chin. "What else are friends for?"

Marguerite was silent as she tried to adjust her thinking to this view of David's renown. It was not easy, when he had been so respectful, almost reverential in those long-ago days at Braesford. How far he had come since then, what prodigious feats he must have performed, to reach the pinnacle he now held. What greatness he had achieved that his deeds, appearance and gallant manners, gallant way with the ladies, were touted in the chansons de geste of a thousand minstrels and troubadours.

How changed he was. It was a loss.

Astrid slapped at the Italian's mailed fist, her face set in lines of suspicion. "You are uncommonly eager to have my mistress know of all these conquests. Why is that, I wonder? Do you seek to puff off your own part in them? Or would you make certain my mistress cannot overlook them?"

"What a devious mind you have, *cara,* and so busy, too." The squire's voice had a pained undertone that suggested the small woman's words had struck home.

"Better that than the latrine that is yours, oaf. You'll not put my mistress off Sir David, however, for she knows how to take what you say."

"A pity, as she's likely to get him killed."

"Sir!" Astrid began.

"Such was never my intention," Marguerite said at the same time. She would have liked to deny the charge, but there was too much truth in it. How could she convince Oliver it would not happen when she could

94

not convince herself?

"Intentions matter little when a man's neck is in the noose. What passed between David and Henry of England concerning you, I know not, milady. Still, it is a bad day when common men are pulled into the affairs of kings."

"Yes," she returned in laconic agreement.

"The hold you have upon him is uncommon strong. I've never before seen him so harried as on our journey to reach you. Still, it's plain as a wart on a pig's bum that this rescue was a trap. I fear it's one that will entangle us until there is no hope of escape."

"Your concern for him does you credit," Marguerite said, keeping her voice even with an effort.

"He is too good a man to die for no reason. Yet make no mistake, milady. As I am under his command, my concern is for my own neck."

She turned her head to search his face, studying the set of his mouth under its line of mustache, the tilt of his chin, the grim look in his black eyes. The cynicism was there, as expected. Beneath it, however, lay brooding edginess that suggested real anxiety for his friend. She liked him the better for it, in spite of herself.

"What would you have him do?" she asked

quietly. "Turn about at once and ride for the nearest port?"

"If I thought he would."

"You must know it's too late for that."

He turned his head to stare at her, his face set with anger. "I don't know it, no. Here I am, jaunting merrily down the road to what may be a slaughter at the end. As far as I can see, it's all for your sake, Lady Marguerite. What should I do, do you think? Shall I join your noble cause or knock our good David senseless and remove him from the king's clutches. And yours."

The idea was so beyond reason that Marguerite jerked on hearing it, causing her mare to dance away a step or two. Bringing the palfrey back around and under control, she spoke over her shoulder. "That is your decision, sir."

"So it is," he muttered as he swung his charger away from where he matched her pace in the line of march. "So it is."

Marguerite frowned as she watched the Italian gallop forward again. Was his lack of commitment a reflection of the attitude of David's men toward the undertaking that lay ahead? She did not like to think so, as it could mean trouble in the ranks. That was David's concern as their commander, of course, yet she felt responsible in some fashion. They would not be here but for her.

The business with Warbeck seemed headed for yet another confrontation between York and Lancaster. Some declared the eternal strife between the forces under the white rose of York and red of Lancaster, called by some the War of the Roses, had ended after the Battle of Bosworth Field, which brought Henry Tudor to the throne. Certainly he had held sway since then. Regardless, the jockeying for position and final supremacy had never really ceased. Nor would it, so it seemed, until the last drop of Plantagenet blood was shed, the last Plantagenet claimant to the throne banished or dead.

Here was David, now, set to proclaim himself a new contender for the crown at Henry's behest. To successfully divide the forces of the York contingent, he must attract a sizable following. Yes, and what then? She had not dared breathe the thought in the king's presence, yet her great fear was that David's campaign as a rival York leader might succeed too well. He could become such a danger to Henry's Lancaster regime that he must be eliminated. If that happened, she could not bear it.

David was far too good to die for no reason. She and Oliver could agree on this if on little else.

The muffled thud of hooves dragged her from her morbid preoccupation. David was riding toward her down the line, the sun glinting on his chain mail he wore without helm or armor here among friends, catching random gleams from the trappings of his destrier. As he drew closer, he smiled with a flash of white teeth in the sun-bronzed planes of his face. And her heart smote her with so violent a blow that she lost her breath.

"Why so glum, ladies? Oliver is a fine one with a compliment, but you can't be missing him already."

Astrid made a sound of disgust. "Yon cockatrice? Never!"

"No?" He slowed, turning his mount to come up beside them. "I was sure the journey would go more swiftly for his presence."

He spoke to Astrid, but Marguerite thought his gaze was upon her face. "He is well-spoken," she said with care.

"Is he not? He has held the men enthralled on many a night, reciting some song of Roland or Richard the Lionhearted."

"Did he, by chance, compose those about you?"

David looked away while a hint of color

flared in his face. "Mayhap one or two, though only in jest."

"Little comedy and much derring-do marked those I heard."

"All greatly exaggerated. But have you all you require?" he asked in a firm change of subject. "Your mount is carrying you all right? You've no need of another, no need to rest for a few minutes?"

"We go on quite well." To abandon the subject of his fame seemed best, as it discomfited him so.

He glanced at Astrid then back to Marguerite. "Oliver was not being a nuisance? I mean, he shines in female company, but can sometimes be forward."

"Not at all," Marguerite answered. The man was his friend. Nothing Oliver had said was reason to cause a problem between them.

"Preening ape," Astrid said at the same time, though under her breath.

"If he was too encroaching . . ."

Marguerite could not prevent a smile. "I would know what to do, I promise you."

David gave a hard nod. "You have nothing to fear from his blandishments. He means little by them, you know."

"Certainly." She felt sure what Oliver might mean if a female chanced to be a maidservant or tavern wench was something else again, but that was neither here nor there. What was interesting was the suspicion that she was being warned away from him. It was unnecessary, but David was not to know that.

He studied her for an instant longer, then began to speak of when and where they would make their next stop, and what they could look forward to as their midday fare. From there, the two of them moved on to the many changes that had taken place at Braesford since he went away, and continued with the health of Madeleine, the girl-child Rand and Isabel had adopted at the behest of the king, as well as their other offspring. They also spoke of the keep where Cate and Ross now lived with the four babes born of their marriage.

Marguerite answered questions, smiled and told of petty happenings within her family, but her attention wandered. Her gaze rested upon David again and again. He had been a handsome youth, fair of face and form. The years had added weight and height to his frame. The width of his shoulders, with their musculature perfectly defined by the steel mesh draping of his chain mail, made her long to smooth her hands over them. The sensual yet intensely masculine molding of his bottom lip caused a pool of heat in her lower body. His eyes gleamed richly blue, yet gave away nothing of his thoughts. Such a powerful figure he was upon his great destrier, armored in intelligence and tempered resolve, so self-contained it seemed nothing could touch him.

It was impossible that she had ever thought she knew him. Impossible, too, that he had answered her summons from past friendship alone.

Yet if that was not the reason he had come to her, what could it possibly be? What?

In this manner, the miles passed away behind them. And in late evening, as the sky turned violet-blue, rooks called and gloom surrounded them from the deep forest through which they passed, they came at last to the castle where Henry VII intended David should prepare to become a royal prince.

5

David cursed at length and in heartfelt virulence. He could do many things with ease. He was able to defeat most men at swordplay, to unseat an opponent on the jousting field nine times out of ten, send an arrow flying farther than any of his acquaintance and drink all but the most hardheaded under the table. He could keep his own counsel about his private affairs, and discern the motives behind those of his enemies. What he could not do was remember that he must accept the bows of other men while returning mere acknowledgment, take the head of every procession, and initiate all conversation between him and any other. He kept forgetting to eat slowly so none would go hungry because they must stop stuffing their guts the instant he pushed back his plate, and he must walk without haste because otherwise the bows and curtsies rendered to him looked like the jerky movements of badly constructed marionettes.

It was maddening.

Nonetheless, the instruction in kingly manners and protocol continued by day and by night. It was conducted by one or two courtiers close to the king, for the most part, and in secret. That was, until it came to the dancing. Every prince was apparently supposed to be able to caper with ease.

If he was to suffer through the indignity of such tutelage, it would not be under the guidance of some aging musician with spindly shanks and no teeth, no matter how discreet he might be. He demanded Lady Marguerite as his instructress.

"Where have you been?" he demanded, his fists on his hips as he watched her come down the long gallery toward him, a sylph-like figure in pale green silk embroidered in a tracery of green vines that made her look as provocative yet illusive as a wood nymph. "I've scarcely seen you except at table since we got here."

"As the castle has been taken over by the king's hunting party, our host's good lady and chatelaine, Lady Joan, considers it prudent to keep to her solar. Her daughters and I attend to her, given she is blunt-spoken and with a clout like the captain of your men-at-arms." Her brown eyes held a bright sparkle of humor. "You would not believe the prodigious amount we have embroidered on a wall hanging drawn to the lady's design, one destined for the great hall. It's to be a record of the king's visit, though the deer look as if they have tree roots growing out of their heads and the rabbits resemble mice."

He smiled, he couldn't help it. Her drollery had always amused him, even when it was a trifle sharp-tongued. More than that, she gladdened his heart. He did not remember her being quite so shapely before, or moving with such grace and unconscious allure, but could appreciate it now. And if his wayward body responded with a painful form of enthusiasm, at least his doublet was not of the ridiculously short mode that would make the results obvious.

"Poor Lady Marguerite, stitching was never a favorite pastime. I seem to recall helping pick out half the stitches you put in."

"And kind it was of you to lend me your aid," she answered as she came to a halt before him. "I'm somewhat more accomplished with a needle these days, but dare hope it's not a skill you require just now."

He told her what was needful, and waited

to hear what she would say to it.

"Teach you to dance?" she asked, the slashes of her brows drawing together in puzzlement. "This is at Henry's order?"

"None other."

"I can see that you might have to take an empty floor to lead some merriment, but surely —"

"You can do it?" he interrupted, in no mood to hear objections. "You know the steps and turns in the latest style?"

"Yes, but —"

"Excellent. We will begin at once."

She gave him a darkling look from under her lashes that made him wonder if he hadn't become more autocratic than he realized. She did not demur, however. Not a little relieved, he turned and gestured to a manservant standing beside a screen set at the far end of the otherwise empty gallery. Moments later, music began to issue from behind it, a spritely tune played with a will upon viele and lute, pipe and horn.

"Very convenient," she said as she took the hand he offered and walked with him to the center of the floor. "But are these music-makers hidden for a reason?"

"I am to remain incognito during this time of preparation."

Skepticism appeared in the rich brown of

her eyes. "Surely they will be curious?"

"They have been paid not to be, I believe."

"Ah."

For long moments, he stepped and turned and pointed his toe to her example, walking as if in the midst of a line of other dancers. Her hand in his was slender, with long fingers and well-shaped nails. Clasping it kicked his heart into a faster beat. The brush of her skirts against the calves of his legs was like the sting of a hundred bees. To allow his gaze to rest on the gentle bounce of her breasts under her bodice was a temptation difficult to resist, while the delicate scent of field flowers and warm female that wafted between them when she drew near made him as drunk as a robin feasting on fermented berries.

He had thought Marguerite a lady beyond the ordinary when he was callow and easily impressed. Nor had his opinion changed; she was beauty and elegance personified, and kindhearted withal. He'd also once considered, being an idealistic idiot, that leaving her untouched was his only honorable course. How was it that he'd never realized others might see her as he did, yet have fewer scruples?

When they came together to form a bridge of their hands, pretending to allow other dancers to pass beneath them, she made a wry grimace. "This would be easier with more dancers. Could the king not arrange it?"

"He could, mayhap, but displaying my clumsy attempts to copy my betters is not princely conduct."

She sent him a frown, possibly for his too modest comment. "But they won't know you are supposed to be Edward. You would be only the Golden Knight."

"True, but some may remember my lack of skill later."

She studied him, her attention so close that he felt the back of his neck begin to burn, as well as other regions of his body. He could see himself reflected in the cinnamon-brown surfaces of her eyes, see the shadows cast on her cheekbones by the sweep of her lashes. He wondered how she would appear in the height of passion, if she would share her joy or hide it away behind closed eyelids.

"Are you certain you want to do this, David? You need not, you know, not if it's for my sake alone."

His name on her lips was like a melody he could listen to for hours. So distracting was the sound that it was necessary to cast his mind back over what she had asked to find the sense of it. "I am certain," he said, his voice firm, "and would change nothing of the agreement."

She did not appear convinced. "You could leave the castle tonight. If no one knows why you are here, the men at the gate can have no reason, no orders, to stop you."

"I gave my word, my lady."

Her open gaze met his for endless moments before she sighed. "So you did."

"I am honored that you would have a care for my safety," he said, the words a low murmur near her veil as he walked beside her to the music, her right hand in his and his left arm resting lightly behind her back. He could feel the warmth of her skin through her clothing, sense silken smoothness that made his mind drift to the silkiness of other parts of her.

"I don't merely have a care," she said with a flash of her eyes as she flung back her drifting veil, "I'm terrified for you. This is wrong, I feel it. It cannot turn out well."

"You have a presentiment?" She had always been the most intuitive of the three sisters, more given to looking for signs and portents. He would like to ignore such things, but had seen them turn out right too often for true skepticism. Besides, he would not annoy her with any suggestion of unbelief.

"You might say so, as I see problems everywhere I turn. This Warbeck has spent years building his base, so is far ahead in drawing followers to his cause. How can you possibly compete? And how will you go forward, given those who will be ranged against you? Spies are everywhere, a traitor behind every curtain and informer under every bush. If you are not killed in the first week you ride out as a new pretender, it will be God's own miracle."

His heart thudded against the wall of his chest. The harder it pounded, the softer his voice became. "I have been hunted before, Lady Marguerite."

"Not like this, surely."

The muscles of his arm behind her back were like iron, his lower body strained against his hose until there was no give left. That she seemed unaware of her effect astonished him. That is, until it occurred to him that she might well be as innocent now as when he had left her years ago.

"There are many different kinds of enemies," he said with artful intent. "You must have discovered that much for yourself."

"What do you mean?" Her gaze was clouded before she separated from him in the dance, skipping around an imaginary corner couple and returning again.

"Surely you were pursued while at court? Men would have to be blind not to be drawn to you."

"Don't forget my portion of my father's estate," she said tartly. " 'Twas a more powerful attraction by far."

"Still you are unwed. Was there no man who appealed, none who could tempt you to abandon your sisters — or at least taste forbidden pleasure in some dark corner?"

Her gaze turned suspicious. "You are forgetting the curse of the Graces, not to mention the safeguard provided by the formidable gentlemen my sisters chanced to marry."

"No daring flirtations, then? No midnight trysts? Nothing to regret?"

She lifted a shoulder. "Those desperate enough to pay serious court were pox-ridden, spavined or graybeards willing to risk shorter lives for the sake of fatter purses. For the rest, I was of no mind to be pursued as a mere novelty."

"You do yourself an injustice," he answered at once. "There would have been much more to it."

"But not enough to tempt me," she returned with simple candor.

She was untouched, she must be. The

miracle of it took his breath. It also sent a shaft of fierce, protective joy through him. Stupid and ignoble it might be, also less than generous, but he could not prevent it. She was untouched and would remain that way for all time if he had any say in the matter. If he could not have her, then no other man would take the prize.

"You have done this before," she said with a glance from under her lashes. "Dancing, I mean. I think you are not so ill-prepared to lead out a set as you wish to appear."

"Do you, now?" He had forgotten the role of novice he was playing in his preoccupation with her lack of experience. He could pretend to trip over the train of her gown, but wasn't sure she would be fooled.

"It stands to reason, now that I think of it. You could hardly cut much of a figure at the French court otherwise."

"Supposing to cut a figure was my aim." He whirled her around at the end of the room and started back the other way.

"And why would it not be," she asked in light disdain, "considering the plenitude of French ladies available for your pleasure?"

He almost laughed, but swallowed the surge of mirth as he realized she could not mean that as it sounded. Jealousy had never been a failing of hers. His hold tightened, nonetheless, and his gaze caught and held on the curves of her mouth with their lovely fullness. He felt his own mouth water with the need to taste that sweetness, to probe for the source of it.

A tremor ran through her there in the circle of his arm, for he felt it, felt it drive into him like a stake. He glanced down to plumb the soft brown depths of her eyes. In them swirled such an enchanting mixture of doubt and awareness, candor and unconscious invitation that he dipped his head toward her. Stopped. Lowered it again.

She swallowed, and the edge of her tongue, moist and pink, flicked over to leave a moist sheen on her lower lip. The sudden heat and swelling ache in his loins was so vicious it made his eyes sting. She was innocent but not ignorant of the animal needs of men, he thought. She knew to beware the tightening of his muscles, the heat in his face. God's teeth, but what was he thinking to let her see?

He had grown used to responding to female charms, used to expecting glad welcome for his rampaging desire. That was not the case here, and he'd best remember it. His responses must be controlled with iron will.

Coming to a halt so she was forced to do

the same, he straightened, removed his arm from her waist and stepped in front of her. When he spoke, his tone was as light as he could make it. "Could be I learn quickly. Have you thought on that, Lady Marguerite?"

"Could be you're a master of deceit, or else you've been watching the dancing with particular care since we arrived here." She gazed up at him, scanning his face, searching his eyes as if only half-convinced he was blameless in what had just passed between them.

"Oh, aye, that would be it," he said at once. "I've been watching you, you see, and with the greatest care possible."

The color that sprang to her cheekbones was caused by something more than the exertion of the dance. "Is that why you asked Henry for me as a teacher?"

"Who else should I choose?" He smiled into her eyes while his heart ached at the truth in his answer. "You are the lady I know best, the mistress of my young heart and truest friend. There is none other I would trust so much."

"You are a scoundrel," she said with mock severity, "and also my truest friend. Now may we dance again?"

The warm joy of her return to trust so

filled his chest that he wanted to laugh out loud, to catch her to him and spin around until she was dizzy or they both fell down. He had done that once or twice, long years ago in the halcyon days at Braesford. He could recall with minute clarity the feel of her in his arms, the press of her firm, young breasts against his chest and the way she had fit so perfectly against him that it seemed she had been made to be in his arms.

Impossible.

Impossible then, impossible now, and he was a fool for letting it slip his mind for even an instant.

David was her friend. Yes, of course he was.

That was what he had meant earlier when he'd said he cared for her. She should have known.

Well, and so she had, Marguerite told herself later that afternoon as she stood at the castle window and watched the king and his male guests ride out for a twilight hunt. He had set her apart and meant to keep her there. His deference had always been apparent, even when he teased her as he might a sister, or when she drew him into the family her sister Isabel and Rand had created around them at Braesford. It was only for that brief moment a few days ago that she'd thought he might have felt differently.

She should have known better. She faced that now, in spite of feeling strangely bereft by the knowledge.

Why had he made such a point of their platonic affection? Could it be because she had shivered as he clasped his arm around her? She had not meant to; it had just happened as she saw the way he looked at her, a predatory gaze like a hungry wolf eyeing its next meal. Had he hastened to reassure her she was safe from him because he looked upon her as his lady-mistress still, someone above his touch?

Oh, but that suggested he thought she feared his male reactions. He was wrong. It had been a lightning strike of excitement that shook her, white-hot and impossible to deny.

She and David had always understood each other before, being both without parents — he from being left a foundling at a nunnery, she because her father died when she was young and her mother remarried but died in her turn, leaving her and her sisters to the mercy of a stepfather. The misery of that life was put behind her soon after she and David met, yet the effects remained. She had her sisters, but still felt set apart from the greater belonging of a true family circle. That David was even more alone had endeared him to her from the first.

She frowned now as she thought of it. She had felt many things for David in the past, but never anything quite like the near painful awareness of his size and strength as they danced, or his scent compounded of sun-dried linen, leather and strong, virile male. He had been servitor, guard and near foster brother when they were younger, detailed by Rand, Baron Braesford, to act as her protector when she left the keep. It should have been a task beneath him as a squire, yet he never complained, always acted as if it was his own inclination. They had grown inseparable, the two of them.

It had been an odd companionship, however, for the gulf between their stations had been wide — she an heiress with several castles and villages in her dowry, he a nameless bastard with only brains and brawn to secure his advancement. So good had he been at self-effacement that she'd seldom thought of him as being a man almost grown, never considered him in the light of a future husband. She had been brought up to expect that her male guardian or, later, the king would direct her choice of husband, marrying her off to a lord of power and position who would likely be much older. To contemplate anything else was useless.

It was strange to watch David riding away from the castle now, and see him in so different a light.

"Tell me something, Astrid," she said over her shoulder.

"Aye, milady?"

Marguerite turned to face her. "What is it a man truly wants from a woman?"

"Now, milady, you know that as well as I." Her small serving woman looked up from where she was smoothing fresh-washed body linen with her hands and putting it away in their traveling box. A question flickered in her pale eyes.

"No, I mean really."

"The good Lord made Adam master of the world and all that was in it, but he only sat and sighed," she quoted in her light, singsong voice. "He made a naked woman then, and Adam smiled."

"So men want a naked woman?"

"Most of them. Yon Oliver, the whoreson, would no doubt want two."

Marguerite gave her a wry grin. "You are not fond of him, are you?"

"He'd couple with his own self if he could, being that fond of his manly bits."

"Oh, Astrid."

"Well, maybe not, but you can be sure he'd rather dip his wick than eat."

"Dip his . . ."

"Have carnal knowledge of a woman."

"I know what it means!" Marguerite colored as her mind presented the image of a candle wick dipping in and out of warm wax or tallow. Or something doing it. Again, and yet again.

"Aye," Astrid said in dry accord.

"But he can't be so bad, not really, if he has David's approval."

The tiny serving woman shook her head, obviously disagreeing but unwilling to make a point of it.

"Anyway, I wasn't talking about anything so obvious. What else is it that men like in a woman?"

"A fine pair of . . ."

"Breasts?"

"I was going to say legs and what's at the top of them, but that, too."

"Surely they think of something else," Marguerite insisted.

"Not that you'd notice. Oh, some might, like our David. He's a man, still, for all that others scurry to do his bidding as if he's a cross between the greatest ogre ever born and a newly crowned king."

Marguerite sent her a straight look, wondering what she'd heard. Servants' gossip could be swift and uncannily accurate, and Astrid had a way of hearing whatever was said. However, her small face was calm as she went about her task. "I don't believe he's an ogre."

"No more do I. He's a leader, though, right enough."

"Yes," Marguerite said thoughtfully. Would that be sufficient to see him through the task Henry had set for him? Would the strength and hardihood gained as the Golden Knight keep him safe?

When David had first gone away, she had daydreamed about him returning in triumph. More than once, in the months before he rode away to war, he had spoken of earning his spurs as a knight, then competing in tournament to seek his fortune. It was one of the few ways open to a penniless and nameless squire. Others had done it in the past, so why not he? The knighthood had come at Stoke. The rest would follow, or so she had reasoned.

Now here he was, returned in greater triumph than anyone could ever have imagined. He had returned, and it was all wrong.

Fear for what he was doing, what he meant to do at Henry's behest, was with

119

her every waking moment. She could not bear that he had embarked upon it for her sake. The idea of him being captured, tortured or killed was horrifying, the dread of it a constant ache inside her.

"If a woman wanted to stop a man from doing something, Astrid, how would she go about it?"

"Depends on the woman. Well, and on what this something might be."

"Just speaking in general," she said with an airy wave of one hand. "Would he, do you think, listen to a woman who surpassed him in rank or was . . . close to him?"

Astrid paused in the act of folding monthly cloths. "How close?"

"A lover, mayhap?"

"Happens, betimes, though usually in small things."

"What if he got her with child?"

"With or without being wed to her?" The pint-size serving woman put a fist on her hip.

"Either." Marguerite paused. "Or both, if he could be persuaded to marriage."

"Some men might feel it made no difference at all, others that it meant the world. What are you thinking, milady? You would not do anything foolish?"

Would she? Marguerite sought blindly for

the corner of her linen veil and put it between her teeth as she considered. She had suggested marriage as a solution and David had refused her. Was it truly from knightly principle, the idea that she was above him still? Or did he have no wish to be her husband? Would he change his mind if convinced it was the only way to keep her safe?

Yes, and could she abandon pride and go to him again with such a proposal? Would it serve if she did? Or must there be something more?

Mayhap if she were compromised in the way she had suggested, it might make a difference. Still the idea called forth more doubts. He had such strength of will. What would it take to persuade him to put aside his principles and take her to his bed? Would he ever allow himself to be seduced?

Marguerite might be virtuous, but had seen enough of the backstairs affairs between men-at-arms and serving maids to understand the act of coupling. She had never been able to think of such activity with Lord Halliwell, had shuddered away from it in her mind.

This was different. Her breasts swelled under her bodice, tingling at the tips as she pictured David touching his lips to hers, undressing her, caressing her. She ached low in her belly at the thought of being in his arms, her breasts molded to the hard surface of his chest and his weight pressing her down into the mattress as he fitted his hard body and her soft one together, one into the other. Curiosity for what it would be like burned in her mind with the heat of Samhain fire.

She would have to think long and hard about so drastic a venture. But not now. No, not now.

"Is there no other way to make a man do something against his will?"

Astrid pursed her lips. "There's wine and ale, if you've enough of it. Failing that, you'd need a few strong men with cudgels."

"Really?"

"Nay, milady! A poor joke only. Leave off thinking of this pass. It won't help and may make matters worse."

"Yes, I'm sure you're right. I know you're right. But am I to stand back and do nothing when so much is at risk?"

"Happens yon knight is used to peril," the serving woman said in tones of acid reason.

"Even so." Marguerite turned back to the window, contemplating the dwindling figure on horseback.

She was aware of Astrid's frowning regard

upon her for endless moments. Then the little serving woman shook her head. Muttering under her breath, she went back to folding linen.

6

To an outsider, or one who had never commanded men, it doubtless appeared Henry VII had no thought in his head other than pastoral pleasures. David was not deceived. He knew the king worked far into the night, that he received couriers, read dispatches without number and penned answers in his precise hand; that he received visitors who came by the postern gate without being heralded and left the same way. David knew because he was often kept waiting in an antechamber until Henry was ready to hear his report on what he had learned of the statecraft during the day, what he knew of his presumed Yorkist relatives, their titles, habits, appearance and ancestors. He knew because he kept the same hours as the king.

It was not all labor. Every evening now, he was expected to dance with Lady Marguerite in the king's chamber, displaying his increasing skill at treading a fine measure.

As that part of his training proceeded apace, Henry dismissed his original tutors. At David's request, he wrested the lady from the castle chatelaine's control, entrusting her with honing his court manners to a fine edge. Accordingly, he was required to show his ability to raise a lady from a deep curtsy, to accept the bow of her noble father, brother or uncle and to make conversation while saying nothing of importance.

It was a game Marguerite played to perfection. David, on his mettle, did his best to match her at it. What Henry thought mattered little to him, but he did value the smiles from his teacher when she thought he had acquitted himself well.

If David had not known better, he might have suspected His Royal Majesty of throwing the two of them together. He did know, however, so assumed it to be a test of a different kind, one which sought to see how well he could keep his head when faced with temptation. A man who could resist the fascination of Lady Marguerite when she was flushed and breathless from the dance, or else encouraging him to address a pair of sheep as if they were a duke and his duchess, could surely refrain from snatching a crown.

"Pitiful," Oliver murmured as he came to

stand beside him near a pillar of the great hall that had been cleared of tables for the evening. "Do you know you have been watching the lady half the evening, and with the most revolting look upon your face."

"No, have I?" David did not remove his gaze from Lady Marguerite's spritely form where she played a game with a cup and a ball in company with Lady Joan and her daughters. It was such a blameless occupation that he was reminded of evenings at Braesford Hall, when he had sat in a corner watching Marguerite and her sisters tease and entertain each other.

"Don't think she doesn't know it, either. What a flirt she is, glancing this way to make certain you're still here. I wonder that she wasn't married off long ago."

"The curse of the Graces," David said with only half his attention on the answer. Was Marguerite really taking notice of his movements?

"Any man dies who proposes marriage without love?" Oliver gave a bark of laughter. "What a tale!"

"I saw it work with her sisters."

"Why is it, then, that no man has loved your Lady Marguerite? She's comely enough to inspire untold flights of passion."

"Who says none has loved her? Such a

man must also be eligible as a husband, which makes the matter more difficult."

Oliver leaned in closer. "Ah, well, but here's the question. If she's protected by this curse, what did she need with rescue from you?"

"Mayhap I was the instrument of it," David said with a direct look at his friend.

"The tool chosen to carry out the deed? Tread carefully, my friend. Repeat such heresy to the wrong person, and you could be accused of believing in black magic."

David's smile was wry as he pushed away from the wall and started toward where Lady Marguerite sat. He spoke over his shoulder. "Who says I don't?"

The ball the ladies had been playing with had leaped out of the cup during Marguerite's turn, and bounced to the floor, rolling toward him. David bent to scoop it up and strolled to where she sat. As he passed the wooden ball to her, he trailed his fingertips over the palm of her hand.

She flinched, her eyes widening at they met his, their centers turning so dark they looked black. A rash of goose bumps feathered over her arm, disappearing under the sleeve of her gown.

David swallowed a curse as his body tightened in response. He could not drag his gaze from the front of her gown where the peaks of her breasts were surely beading under the embroidered silk. He had meant no harm, and yet it seemed as if every eye in the hall turned in their direction. Was it his imagination, or did the rumble of conversation grow quieter, the expression of those who watched become more avid? Was it possible the tale of her abduction at his hands, and retrieval by the king, meant all now waited to see how it might end?

God's blood, but of course they did. How could it be otherwise when so many had borne witness to the beginning? Men might speak with disparagement of women as gossips, but were just as likely to pass on a fine yarn, especially if it had a whiff of scandal in it.

The best he could do at this point was to leave Lady Marguerite alone in public. Bowing, he withdrew, moving off to rejoin Oliver who had thrown himself down on a bench with a number of his other men-at-arms.

He thought Marguerite watched him go. He'd have traded his gold-chased armor to know whether she was glad or sorry for it.

A sudden commotion at the great entrance door provided a welcome distraction. David turned in time to see a thin man with silver hair stride into the hall. That he was a personage of some description was clear from the richness of the cloak he wore and the complement of men-at-arms at his back. A younger man walked beside him, the knife-blade sharpness of his nose and arrogant tilt of his chin proclaiming him to be a near relative, most likely a son. Neither of them was particularly tall, though their upright posture made them appear so. They had been relieved of their swords before being ushered into the presence of the king, but rested their hands upon the empty scabbards with the look of those tonguing spaces where teeth had been pulled.

Men turned to stare. Somewhere a woman gave a nervous titter. Behind and to David's right, a lord spoke in hushed and excited inquiry. "God's blood, is that not . . ."

"Aye, so 'tis," his companion replied with a judicious squint.

"What does he here? One would think he'd be loath to show his face."

"Looking for his lost heiress, I'll be bound." The man chuckled. "That, or redress for her loss. A man to squeeze a penny till it squeals, Lord Halliwell."

"He'll have met his match in our Henry," the first man replied, nudging the other in the ribs.

So this was the man Marguerite was to have wed. David watched him stride through the crowd while a frown settled between his eyes. An aristocrat from his toes to his silver-haired pate, his every move shouted his certainty of his place in the world. He appeared near seventy, an age when only an egotistical idiot would expect to take a bride young enough to be his grand-daughter. To think of him ever having the right to lay his bony and age-spotted hands upon Marguerite made David grind his teeth until his jaws ached.

Even so, he could not blame the man for being incensed at the loss of so fair a prize. It was not often a man could look forward to holding beauty and fortune in the same woman.

Halliwell advanced upon the bench where Marguerite sat. David saw the moment when the crowd parted enough to show the newcomer to her. All color leached from her face, leaving it waxen in its paleness. She swayed a little, but then sat up straight with her hands clasped tightly in her lap.

Her former betrothed drew nearer, stopped before her. Derision crossed his skeletal features. He made her a bow so shallow as to be an insult, and spoke in an undertone while the man beside him looked on. An instant later, Lord Halliwell continued his progress down the room, making for the dais at the far end of the great hall.

David took a hasty step toward Marguerite only to stop with a whispered oath. To go to her now would only make her more conspicuous. There was little he could do to shield her. As she was Henry's ward, that duty and privilege belonged to the king.

Halliwell desired to speak with Henry VII, it seemed, for he approached an equerry with a low-voiced demand. The equerry mounted the dais to whisper in Henry's ear. A negligent gesture of assent, and Halliwell was led forward. His son attempted to follow, but the way was barred to him. Lord Halliwell went to one knee, struggling up again when given leave. The king's face reflected weariness and strained patience as he put the dutiful question that would allow the peer to speak. His eyelids lowered to conceal his gaze as he listened to the harangue that resulted.

Henry was gifted at diplomacy; he had learned to be in the years when he had been dependent upon the goodwill of the rulers of Brittany and France who had given him sanctuary. Edward IV, and his brother Richard III after him, had promised enormous sums if the last Lancastrian heir to the throne should be turned over to them. Had Henry been delivered, his head would have been forfeit in the wink of an eye. Bartering for his life could make a man wily indeed.

It was also true that Henry was a mite stingy. It came, so David had heard, from inheriting a kingdom that was bankrupt from decades of internecine warfare and the depredations of Edward's queen who had enriched her family at crown expense. Whatever Henry might have pledged to Halliwell for his part in this affair, it was unlikely that he would be adding to it.

Where that might leave Lady Marguerite, David could not think. He had Henry's word that she would never again be pressed into marriage, but could he be trusted to keep it? What if Halliwell had decided he wanted her after all? Could Henry refuse agreement, especially if it meant forfeiting Halliwell's support, or even losing him to the Yorkist camp?

At a tug on the skirt of his doublet, David looked down. Astrid was beside him, her piquant features twisted in a furious scowl. She gave a sharp jerk of her head to indicate that he should lean down to hear her. As he bent, she seized his sleeve and dragged him lower to speak into his ear.

"My mistress would have you come to her

with all speed. Lord Halliwell means to have converse with her, and mayhap more. He said just now that he'll be dealing with her after he has spoken to the king. You may wish to know what the old vulture has to say."

There was nothing David wanted more, but he could not consider his desire alone. "Will my presence not make matters worse?"

"How can it?" Astrid spread her short arms. "At least he will not be able to take her away with him if you are by her side."

David straightened again, the better to observe the meeting between the aging peer and the king. "Lady Marguerite fears he may attempt it?"

"You did not see the look on his face," the small woman said with a shudder. "You did not hear him. He said their betrothal stands, and will not be ended until he is done with her."

"Did he now?" David's voice was soft, but resolution rose like a wall of iron in his chest. Astrid's eyes widened and she fell back a step. He forced a smile and extended his hand to her. "Lead on, little one. No one will take your lady from here, this I promise."

It was as well that they were no great

distance away. Henry must have made short work of the impromptu audience, for Lord Halliwell, eyes blazing with suppressed anger, was leaving the dais already. His son moved to intercept him and they stood for an instant in close talk. Both turned then, bearing down upon where Lady Marguerite sat.

David lengthened his stride. He reached her first, and she came to her feet, putting out a hand to him.

"Thank you," she said in quiet fervor. "I would not involve you in this again, but . . ."

"I would have it no other way." Her fingers were like ice and fine tremors shook her. He folded her hand in the warmth of his own as he stood gazing down at her, gauging the depth of her fear. She was upset by the turn of events, he thought, rather than undone by terror. "Take heart. Halliwell can do nothing to harm you here among the king's men."

There was no time for more. The peer and his son were upon them.

Halliwell bared yellow teeth in a fierce grin. "This will be your Golden Knight, I suppose," he said to Lady Marguerite with malice in every drawling syllable, "your gallant rescuer."

Hectic color flared across her cheekbones,

but she remained composed. "May I present Lord Halliwell, David. My lord, this is David, known to all by the title you give him."

"And no other, I believe, nor even a family name of his own." Halliwell looked him up and down in a way David had not endured in years before turning back to Marguerite. "No doubt that explains why you are not wed to him. The question, of course, is what reward he demanded for preventing our marriage."

Her posture became rigid. "No reward was asked or given, I assure you."

"You will pardon me if I choose to doubt it?"

"Nay, she will not," David said with fire in his heart and rasping steel in his voice, "and neither will I. Lady Marguerite speaks naught but the truth."

The narrow face and head of Lord Halliwell turned toward him as swiftly as a striking snake. "And what might the word of a nameless knight be worth?"

David smiled with menace in the slow curl of his lips. "Are you saying I lie, Lord Halliwell?"

Marguerite turned even paler than she had been before. "Sir David was most protective of my virtue, my lord. He slept across the threshold of my . . . my chamber on the night that I was taken. Any of his company will tell you it's so."

David felt his face heat at the reminder. Before he could speak, however, there was a shift of those behind him.

"And a sorry sight it was for his men, and them thinking him such a great hand with the ladies." Oliver stepped forward, moving nearer until he reached David's side. "That would be on top of being a champion known across Europe for his lethal art with sword, lance, bow and every other weapon you may name."

Threat sounded beneath the genial lilt of the Italian's voice. David only hoped the enraged peer had the wit to heed it.

Astrid did without doubt, for she stared up at Oliver with startled approval before giving a decided nod. "Good man."

Lady Marguerite smiled a little, but seemed otherwise unaffected. "Since that night," she went on with simple clarity, "I have naturally been under the protection of the king."

"Who has apparently put you together with your knight at every opportunity, from what I have heard. One wonders if you are meant to be a reward of some sort, after all."

"Idiot," Astrid said.

136

David advanced a slow step. There were times when he didn't mind using his size to intimidate. "You are offensive, sir."

Halliwell jerked back, jostling his son. That gentleman, far from a youth at near fifty, slapped his empty scabbard. His father stopped him with a sharp gesture. "I am surely allowed some degree of choler after being robbed of a bride," he said in grim complaint. "But it doesn't stop there. I was promised Lady Marguerite and her dower lands. I'll settle for no less."

"What you will have is your death," Lady Marguerite said with a lift of her chin. "Recall the curse of the Three Graces."

"Bah! When you are my wife, I will teach you not to prate such nonsense."

"I understood," David said, keeping his voice low so as not to be overheard by others around them, "that the betrothal was a sham and you knew it well. Why pretend otherwise this late in the business?"

"I knew little of the lady, so had not reckoned the worth of the prize taken from me. Knowledge of both has come to me since. I consider I was duped, being brought to give her up for such a pittance."

Astrid tossed her head. "No difficult task, I expect."

Halliwell flicked a glance downward before

looking back to Marguerite. "Shut the mouth of that toad of a female, or I will shut it for her."

"That you won't," Oliver said. He drew a dagger with a leather-wrapped handle from its sheath in the folds of his doublet, letting it be seen only by those in their tight circle. "And I'll thank you not to call our bantam a toad."

Astrid stared up at him, her mouth open though her eyes were bright. For once, she had nothing to say.

"Oliver," David warned, even as Halliwell's son cursed and felt for his eating knife that was slung from his belt.

"Enough!"

That hard command came from the dais. Henry, rising to his feet, stepped to its edge.

Silence came down like a smothering coverlet. Every eye in the room swiveled to watch the king. He surveyed all with a slow sweep of his gray-blue gaze before frowning on the tableau below him.

"My Lord Halliwell," Henry VII said with deliberation, "you and your men must be fatigued from your journey. You may leave us to take your rest."

It was a command phrased as a courtesy. That everyone present realized it was clear from the murmur that swept the great room.

The aging peer bowed with the stiffness of rage. Sharing a glare between Oliver, Marguerite and David, he collected his son with a jerk of his head and began to back from the royal presence.

"And you, Lady Marguerite," Henry continued, "we excuse you, as well."

She flushed, but performed a graceful curtsy of acquiescence. "Thank you, Your Majesty. Astrid and I bid you a fair and good evening."

To let her go alone down the castle's dim corridors lit only by flaring torches was not possible. "If it pleases you, sire," David said, "I will see the lady to her rest."

"And I," Oliver chimed in, with no shame at all.

Something between irritation and amusement flashed in the monarch's face. He flicked his fingers toward them in dismissal. "As you will."

Lady Marguerite put her hand upon the arm David offered and turned to walk beside him. The muscles of his forearm tightened as he felt the chill of her fingers through his sleeve. He placed his other hand over them, offering silent support. As they quitted the room, he could feel the stares stabbing into his back. The only person to speak, however, was Astrid who strutted along beside Oliver with her skirts held up in her tiny hands. "By all the saints," she exclaimed breathlessly, as she took three steps for every one made by the rest, "but 'twould be a fine thing if the curse did get the old devil."

David could not disagree, but he did not depend upon it. A close watch should be kept upon Lord Halliwell. He would see to it.

At her door, Lady Marguerite allowed Astrid to enter the chamber ahead of her. Her smile was tremulous at the edges as she turned to face him. "You have my eternal gratitude for coming to my aid just now. Loath though I am to admit it, something about Lord Halliwell unnerves me."

"You need not fear him," David said in quiet certainty.

"He seems capable of anything to me, anything at all. His damaged pride may well force him to seek redress."

Oliver, just behind them, snorted. "Damaged purse, rather."

David turned his head, giving the Italian a repressive stare. When his squire had shrugged and retreated out of hearing, he turned back. "You will stay out of his way as much as possible?"

"Assuredly," she answered with fervor.

"And send for me if he disturbs you in any way whatsoever?"

Her smile was slow to come, but its warmth rose to shine in her eyes as she spoke. "Aye, so I will."

It was the trust in those few words that undermined his good intentions, that and the way the torchlight farther along the corridor gleamed on the soft planes of her face and the curves of her breasts that peeped above her square, lace-edge bodice. Lifting her fingers from his arm, he brought them to his lips.

Her breath caught, for he heard it. That small sound drove deep inside him, squeezing his heart. Fearful of what she might see in his face, he bowed, then, and released her.

"Sleep well," he said, the words a mere rumble in his chest.

"And you also," she returned.

Her skirts whispered as she stepped away from him, retreating into her chamber. He did not move, however, not until the closing door shut off the last sliver of his view of her.

"So," Oliver said the moment David rejoined him. "What's to do now? Think you Henry will give over to the disappointed bridegroom?"

"He can't do that, not without breaking faith with our agreement. At the moment, I may be more useful to him."

"And when that usefulness is ended?"

"I don't know," David answered in goaded tones. "No one knows. That's the trouble with kings."

Oliver, striding beside him, slanted a look at his set face. "I don't understand why you didn't just take the lady when offered, and her lands with her."

"I know you don't." David's strides increased, as if he would outrun so tempting a suggestion.

"Or why you don't do it now."

"Henry and I made an agreement. That's beyond the more important factor."

"So you made a vow. You were young, things were different. It no longer applies."

David sent his friend a dark look. Admitting the Italian into his confidence about his pledge to Marguerite, on a lonely night when he had thought never again to see England's shores, had doubtless been a mistake. "It applies."

"Because you hold to it, and for no other reason. If you must go by the strict laws of chivalry, then ask to be released from whatever you swore. Surely that's possible."

"You know better."

Oliver cursed and raked his fingers thought his wild, dark curls as if about to tear them from his head. "Only because you are more stubborn than a friar's mule! Meanwhile, it's eating you alive. Mayhap I should put the question to Lady Marguerite. Or to the bantam."

David halted as if he'd hit a stone wall. He swung on Oliver and seized a handful of his doublet on either side of his neck, lifting him to his toes. "You will ask nothing of Lady Marguerite. You will speak only when she addresses you, as if she were a princess royal. You will be the very soul of respect and reverence, or you will answer to me."

"God's blood, David! She's just a woman."

"Nay. There you are wrong." Shoving the Italian from him with rough contempt, he turned and began to walk away.

"*Si,* she is. Yes, and you should thank God for it, you great dolt!" Oliver called after him. "You do her no favor by turning her into some sainted, untouchable angel. That's all very well if you need something to worship, but what of her? What of her wants and needs?"

David strode on without answering. Leaving the castle, he mounted to the outside wall where he stood looking out over the

waving treetops of the forest that surrounded it. Oliver was an earthy bastard, he
told himself as he crossed his arms over his
chest. Let a female of any attraction at all
walk past him, and he was after her in full
cry. His passions ruled him. He had not the
least idea of resistance. He could never
understand the passionless devotion of a
lost youth for a girl so fine and fair. He
would never recognize the adoration a man
could hold for a woman who was the very
reason for everything he had become,
because it had been accomplished to make
himself worthy of her.

Oliver could not comprehend the near-
worship of ten endless years. Aye, even that,
right enough.

So Lady Marguerite was older now, a
woman of near six-and-twenty, old enough
to be considered a spinster? What of it?
Nothing had really changed.

Or had it?

He drew breath hard and deep, let it out
in a groan. Unfolding his arms, he braced
his hands on the parapet before him and let
his head hang forward between his shoulders.

Well enough, a few things were different.
He was not quite as passionless as all that
when he looked at her now, nor was he

unaware of her scent, the sweet torture of her touch, the unconscious seduction of her smiles.

It mattered little. She would never know it.

Ask for release from his vow, Oliver said, as if it were no more than craving forgiveness. That the Italian could suggest it only proved his lack of understanding.

What was he to say? *Your pardon, my lady, but I've changed my mind and would take back the solemn pledge made to you so long ago. Serving your sweet self in the chaste fashion of a knight for his lady as set down in the rules of courtly love has grown cursed inconvenient. I've a mind to take you into my bed for a good, hard tupping before marrying you out of hand. I just need you to release me from my vow so I may set about it.*

David snorted in derision. Marguerite would laugh in his face. If not that, she would give him one of the haughty looks she saved for when she was insulted, and then never speak to him again. Nor would he blame her. To recant his vow would be a deadly insult. It would be as though he had never meant a word of it.

He had meant it with all his soul. He meant it still.

Yes, but what if she should release him of

her own accord, without his urging or even his request. What then?

He lifted his head, staring blindly into the night. His heart tumbled in his chest, and his brain felt like a dead coal blown to sudden hot life in his skull. Yes, what then?

He had almost kissed her, in the midst of their first dance lesson. His mouth had been so close to hers that he inhaled the sweet breath of her, felt her warmth upon his lips like a benediction, knew exactly how she would fit against his body. He had wanted her with such raging, harrowing need that denying it had left him deaf and blind for more minutes than he wanted to count. How long could he bear being around her, touching her without acting on his mad desire?

If he had her consent, could he allow himself to approach her as he would any other woman? Could he taste her, hold her against his aching flesh, shape her gentle curves with his calloused hands? Did he dare?

She was the only person, the only thing in life, he feared. It was not that she was an active danger, but that she alone had the power to annihilate him. She could do it by cutting away that single tender place inside that he kept for no one else.

Oh, aye, but if he was never to tend her womanly desires, then who would? To think of Halliwell or any other man initiating her into the mysteries of it stoked a fury so great his guts twisted with it. Their rough, selfish possession would leave her bruised and torn, dreading all contact with men.

God, no.

She should have a tender wooing, one so slow, caring and skilled that she would open herself to it like some lovely, exotic flower, pleading, finally, to be taken.

Who could do that for her except him?

No one else. No, not like he could, and would if heaven allowed.

For a single instant, he feared that need was no more than an excuse to loose the desire he held so fiercely in check. It was, mayhap, Satan's temptation designed to make him recant his sworn word, to succumb to his cravings instead of thinking of Marguerite's good.

Ah, but if he could have her by her will, then he could marry her. She would be freed from the threat of Halliwell, once and for all. No other man could ever force her to the altar to possess her dowered lands and castles, or even for the sake of her sweet face and form. To guard and protect her always would be his right and privilege.

His honor. Always.

He had to be freed from his vow. She must be brought to see the rightness of it, and so speak the words without prompting or supplication from him. That was the only thing that would serve.

Yes, but could she be persuaded to it? And if so, how was it to be achieved?

7

Marguerite heard the screeching cry before she reached the gateway in the stone wall which led to the drying yard. Her heart jerked in her chest. Picking up her skirts, she broke into a run. It was Astrid's voice that rang in such panic-stricken rage.

Marguerite had been in search of her small serving woman for some time, had looked the castle over before bethinking herself of the yard where linens were hung to dry. She had even looked into the stables on the chance that Astrid had been persuaded to ride out with Oliver. The two of them had begun to tolerate each other in the past few days. They were at loose ends because she and David had been instructed to have their midday meals in private with the king.

Henry occupied these repasts by demonstrating the generosity of a sovereign, illustrating for David the correct method of parceling out to those he favored the food piled upon his dish. Her part was to receive the excess from David's dish as he followed the royal example, to smile and be properly grateful. Marguerite had been more than well fed.

Plunging into the drying yard, she came to an abrupt halt. Oliver had Astrid, holding her facedown over his arm. He was laughing like a madman at her shrieking struggles, while lifting the skirts of her gown and shift.

"Stop! Stop at once!" Marguerite marched down upon the Italian with fury in every step. "How dare you lay hands upon her!"

"Milady!"

Oliver flushed wine-red under his Mediterranean coloring. Eyes wide with alarm, he righted Astrid in haste, shifting her to sit upon his forearm like a half-grown child. She rocked there an instant before throwing her small arms around his neck to secure her perch.

"What are you about? Explain at once!"

"It isn't what it seems, milady, I swear it." The Italian's voice turned desperate as he peered into Astrid's tight little face. "Tell her, for pity's sake, before she has me taken up by the guard."

"He is a very devil," Astrid said between

150

set teeth. "He deserves to be locked away."

Marguerite slowed. For all her small serving woman's indignation, she appeared unhurt. "What passes here? I'll have the truth of it."

" 'Twas like this," Oliver began.

"Don't listen to the honeyed tongue of the man!"

"I was watching poor little Astrid hang linen on the line, and chanced to pick her up to make the task easier . . ."

"I'll poor little Astrid you," the woman in his arms cried, smacking him upside the head. "Put me down. Put me down now!"

"Now, my dumpling," Oliver said, chuckling as he easily caught and held her small hand. Whereupon, she jerked and bucked, trying to free herself while raining insults upon his head.

"Astrid," Marguerite said at her most severe.

A petulant look twisted the serving woman's piquant face, but she ceased fighting. She met Marguerite's eyes no more than an instant before lowering her own.

"I'm waiting." Marguerite folded her arms over her chest.

"Well, I was hanging the linen, right enough, and this great idiot said . . . he said . . ."

"I only said her own braies must be no bigger than a baby's nappies," Oliver explained with a great show of innocence. "It only stands to reason, yes?"

Astrid shot him a fulminating look. "And I said 'twas something he would never know, which . . ."

"Which became an irresistible challenge to see for himself," Marguerite said with a sigh. "Dear Astrid, could you not guess what would happen?"

The serving woman's face turned a darker red. She reached delicate fingers to soothe the red patch on Oliver's cheek where she had struck him. "Well, but how could I think he would care enough to look?"

The silence in the drying yard was suddenly acute. In it could be heard the soft flap of sheets blowing in the light breeze, the rustling of the tree branches that overhung the walls, the calls of men practicing with cudgels in the inner bailey, and the twittering of birds in the eaves of the storage building at one end of the open space.

Oliver broke it with a soft curse. "Astrid, *cara mia,* you are as perfect and pretty as yon house wren. Should that wee thing care that it's not so gawky or big as a goose? Who would not want to see the difference? *Si,* and it's more than your braies I'd be inspecting, if only you would permit it."

Astrid stared at him, her eyes like two blackberries on a polished silver plate. Her lips moved without sound before she managed a croak. "Put me down."

Oliver obeyed, setting her on her feet with as much care as a piece of precious blown glass. Astrid shook out her skirts, straightened her veil that was hardly larger than a handkerchief. Tilting her head back, she stared into Oliver's face in solemn appraisal, as if she would plumb his very soul. Marguerite, watching, felt her heart swell, while tears crowded the back of her throat.

Abruptly, Astrid gave a hoot of laughter, drew back her tiny booted foot and kicked the Italian in the shin. Whirling around, she scurried from the drying yard as fast as she could go.

Oliver yelped, hopping around on one foot, rubbing his injury.

At least, he did so until Astrid was out of sight. He straightened then, and shook his head. Laughter and something much more tender flashed in his dark eyes before he inclined his head. "I am sorry, milady. I meant no harm, I promise. It was only . . ."

"Only a jest. I understand."

His full lips twisted at one corner. "One that got out of hand."

"Yes. And it is not I to whom you owe an apology for it."

"I know." A gusting sigh left him. "And to think I've been giving our David advice on how to handle untouchable females."

Marguerite blinked at him a stunned instant while suspicion stirred in her mind. "You what?"

"Nothing, nothing." The Italian gave her his most ingratiating smile as he bowed and began to back away from her. "Or if you would really know, you might ask him."

Ask David. Yes, of course, she thought as she stood as still as a wooden saint in the center of the drying yard. Except she was not sure she wanted an answer that badly.

It was on the landing, where the stairway leading up from the great hall gave access to the various chambers that opened around its four sides, that Marguerite caught up with Astrid. The petite woman heard her coming and turned back with a quick smile. She fell into step beside her.

"Well," she said in her piping voice, "did you send the lout off with a flea in his ear?"

"You seem to have done a fair job of it yourself," Marguerite answered, as she studied the small face turned up to her.

"Aye, so I did," came the self-satisfied answer.

"And you are quite certain you are all right?" Marguerite searched Astrid's face, fearful she might be more upset than she wanted to appear.

"As ever was." A frown crossed her expressive features. "What said he of me when I left? I know it was something."

"Only that he meant to apologize."

"That should make fine hearing."

"He also gave me something to think about."

"A first for him, I do swear," Astrid said in automatic disparagement. "And this would be?"

Marguerite frowned as she decided how to answer. There seemed no way to come at the thing except to say it. "He hinted David views me as untouchable."

"He actually said that to you?" Astrid stared at her, her brows knit in a frown.

"Certainly not, though it's what he meant."

"Well, but is that not as it should be, given your different stations in life? Aye, and have you not known this age he felt so? Is that not the heart of the vow made to you?"

Marguerite looked away with a sigh. "I suppose."

"But you don't like it."

"I sometimes wish things were different."

"You would have him see you as he does other women, as someone to pleasure and to be pleased by. You would not be looked upon as too singular, not wish to be set above him like some pure Madonna in her niche."

The pain in Astrid's voice said she understood all too well what it was like to be seen as different from other women. Abandoned as a baby, she had been found and taken in by the gypsies. Later, she had joined a group of traveling players that sometimes entertained at noble houses. From the moment she could talk, she was expected to be constantly amusing, a small, feminine buffoon. Though she had earned a place as the Queen's Fool by the time she was twenty, she had learned to expect nothing further of life. Men might be curious about how she was made, but were more likely to laugh at her than to love her. Those at court were the worst, being jaded, cynical and in constant search of novelty. She had been tearfully grateful to be given to Marguerite, had blossomed in the peace of Braesford.

"Yes," Marguerite said, her voice soft.

"Is that not how you feel?" Astrid insisted.

"Would it be so wrong if I did?"

"Nay, milady. It only makes you a female like all others."

"Anyway, it's ridiculous. I'm far from perfect, as David must know. I have a horrid temper, my hair is the color of a field mouse and my hips are shaped like a lyre."

"I notice you didn't deny the purity," Astrid said with an impish smile.

"That's hardly my fault, is it? I would change the state if allowed."

"You could always marry Halliwell."

"I'd rather die a maiden, thank you!"

Astrid lifted a shoulder. "Likely you will, if all goes as Henry and David plan. That's unless you come across a man-at-arms who is handsome, discreet, brave and accommodating."

Marguerite turned upon her in incredulity. "What?"

"Handsome for your pleasure, discreet for your good name, brave so he may risk the consequences and accommodating in that he desires only to please."

"I understand, thank you!"

" 'Tis only an idea, mayhap for when you are chatelaine of your own castle. Though, of course this paragon must not be too worshipful."

"You are a minx to tease with such a prospect." The male image that rose in Marguerite's mind as Astrid described this man-at-arms was David. What did that say of her? Yes, and what chance had she of convincing him she was not as pure in thought as he supposed. Was it at all possible she could persuade him to renounce his knight's vow of chastity toward her?

"What prospect might that be?"

The question came from behind them. The hair on the back of Marguerite's neck prickled in alarm as she recognized that rasping drawl. Whirling with a swing of her skirts, she faced Lord Halliwell. She had thought before that his long and narrow head was like that of an adder. His sudden appearance without sound was the same.

How long had he been behind them? What had he overheard?

"You startled me, sir!" she said in less than gracious welcome.

"Crave pardon, Lady Marguerite. I fear you and your serving woman were engrossed in a conversation of abiding fascination. Shall I depart and leave you to it?"

There was nothing Marguerite would have liked more, though it would be impolite to say so. "Had you a purpose in coming upon us?"

"The same as I gave you before," he said with a tight-lipped smile as he eased nearer. "Being private here, or as close as it comes with so many about, you may now be more inclined to hear it."

The landing was empty. No sound came from the chambers which opened upon it. Astrid was a fine chaperone but hardly of a size to be of aid if needed. It seemed best to hear her former bridegroom without argument, which might escalate into a threat.

"As you please," she said evenly, "though I cannot tarry."

"What I would impart is soon said. Contrary to what you may have been told, I am most anxious for our marriage to go forward. My considerable influence shall be used to see it happens. That is, unless you can give me some reason why Henry allowed your wedding journey to be interrupted by this so-called Golden Knight, some explanation for why he has taken him up as a boon companion?"

Marguerite's mind raced. Halliwell's question was natural enough, on the face of it, but she did not trust the avid look in his eyes. There were those who would pay well to learn what had passed between Henry and David.

Braesford, when the betrothal to Halliwell was first broached, had said the lord was known for switching his allegiance between York to Lancaster at will, depending on who looked to have the firmest grip on the crown. Could being bilked of an heiress cause him to desert Henry's camp, throwing his support to Perkin Warbeck?

"How flattering to be credited with knowing the mind of the king, my lord," she said. "Nevertheless, I can tell you nothing of the matter."

"You surprise me, Lady Marguerite. I was told you and your sisters have Henry's ear due to your extraordinary services to the crown."

She lowered her lashes. "You do us too much honor. If we have been useful at all, it was mere happenstance."

His gaze turned sardonic. "Now, why do I not believe that?"

He meant to suggest extremely personal services provided to Henry. It was the outside of enough. "I could not say, sir. If you will excuse me?" She turned from him, moving toward Astrid who had eased away a few discreet paces.

He lunged to catch her upper arm, spinning her to face him again with his fingers digging into her flesh. "This is not over, Lady Marguerite. You may protest all you please, but I know something is afoot. I will see it stopped, see you returned to me, if it's the last thing I do. And when we are wed and I have you naked in my bed, you will rue the day you dared bandy words with me."

Something cold and hard settled inside Marguerite. "Take care, Lord Halliwell. You may have noticed that I have the protection of the Golden Knight."

"One of Edward's bastards, you mean. He'll forget you soon enough if he's anything like his father. *Inconstant* was the word for our Edward, never satisfied with one woman, reaching under every skirt he saw. Would that he had never died! He was a better king for all his debauchery than pious Henry Tudor."

"You admire debauchery?" she inquired with disdain. "Somehow that doesn't recommend you as a husband." No small part of the anger inside her was for the slur against David. It did not prevent her from noticing that against Henry VII.

"It's just as well you will have no say in it then, isn't it," he answered, openly jeering.

She snatched her arm from his grasp and stepped back from him again. "We shall see, sir."

"So we shall," he called after her in deadly confidence as she and Astrid walked away. "So we shall."

The day crept on. No lesson with David

came to break its monotony, for the king had declared a hiatus. The afternoon was to be enlivened by a competition between the gathered men-at-arms, those who had come with David from France, Halliwell's men, the castle contingent and Henry's own. It was nothing of great moment, no occasion for pomp and pavilions or ladies offering favors. It was merely a series of exercises to keep the soldiery in fighting trim.

At least this was the word Astrid brought from the castle guards.

The news was unsettling. Such competitions were not as mild as they might sound. They were fiercely fought contests with honed weapons that could leave men maimed or dead.

David would naturally be in the thick of it.

Marguerite roamed the castle, moving from one vantage point to the other. None gave a clear view of the area where the competition would take place. It was frustrating beyond words. Added to that, David could not attend upon her to explain how it had come about. She had sent him a message, but Astrid returned with it in hand, saying there was no one in his chamber to receive it. Every male in the castle seemed to be outside the walls, gathered in the open field beyond the gates.

Such mock battles had taken place at her brother-in-law's manse, as well. She recalled with chilling clarity the times she had watched as David drilled with Rand, skipping over the grass, retreating from the great, shining blade wielded against him, or else advancing fearlessly upon it. Her heart had been in her throat in those days.

It was there now. She had a bad feeling about this business.

Dear God, but why did men have this need to throw themselves into such a maelstrom of sweat and effort? What drew them, what fever in the mind moved them to hack and slice at each other as if life meant nothing? How could they look upon the injuries inflicted as if they were piddling scratches, or judge the poor prizes awarded the victors as worth the cost?

The distant yells and deep-voiced shouts followed Marguerite wherever she went. No occupation she found could distract her. She opened the marble-backed book loaned to her by the castle's chatelaine, but soon closed it again. She set stitches in a piece of embroidery she had brought with her, a hood for the baby her sister Cate was expecting in the winter, but had to pick them out again. She sent Astrid for a hot drink flavored with herbs and honey, but left it to cool untouched. She snapped at the petite serving woman for slurping as she drank it herself, and then apologized for the hurt feelings she caused. She felt as if ants were crawling under her skin, felt as though a storm hovered above the castle, growing ever more threatening but refusing to break.

Drums, cheers and a great banging of swords upon shields announced the end of the day's events. Hearing the din, Marguerite dropped down upon a bench in the great hall and leaned her head against the wall behind it.

Over, at last. Sighing, she closed her eyes and whispered a prayer of thanksgiving.

Rousing after a moment, she pushed to her feet. She should seek out Lady Joan and offer her aid. There were bound to be injuries that required tending, and the servants would be run off their feet supplying ale and wine to the thirsty hoard returning to the great hall.

It was as she reached that great open space that she heard the shouting.

"Struck down!"

"Golden Knight . . . stabbed."

"By God's beard . . . cowardly attack!"

There followed a confusion of running footsteps, of calls and yells, of pushing and

164

shoving as men stumbled into the hall bearing a burden. David was in the midst of them, borne on a long shield carried by four of his men. He was pale as death, his eyes closed, his head hanging backward off the shield's edge, bobbing as they walked, and his hair tumbling in golden waves stained with blood. His tremendous strength and force of will were gone, all gone.

Horror washed over Marguerite in an icy wave, shuddering from her head to her heels. Her heart faltered. She ceased to breathe.

One of those who carried the shield skidded upon the rushes that covered the stone floor and recovered with a hard jerk. David groaned, tried to raise his head.

He was not dead. He lived. He lived still.

Released by the knowledge, Marguerite ran forward. Her mind was suddenly calm, clear, focused. Turning to the trestle table left standing after the most recent meal, she swept the tankards and plates from it. They hit the floor around her with a great, metallic clanking and splattering of ale, but she hardly noticed. Her gaze was on David, on the faint rise and fall of his chest, the great, bleeding lump of a bruise that swelled upon his discolored temple, and the blood that wet his shirt, seeping from under his arm.

"Here," she called, "put him here!"

The men swerved toward her, lifting David to the table as she directed. With ungentle hands, they slid him from the shield so he rested on the boards. He made no further sound during the transfer, but lay with his lashes resting on the shadows they cast beneath his eyes and his hands palm up, the fingers lax and open.

He was bleeding, a steady seepage that pooled on the table beneath him. It had to be stopped at once.

"Cloths," Marguerite cried, staring around for Astrid. "Quickly for the love of God!"

What she asked for appeared in an instant, or so it seemed, long, clean strips of old linen. The small serving woman placed a knife in Marguerite's hand at the same time, then reached to take hold of David's shirt in her small fists. Stretching it taut just above his heart, she nodded at her mistress. Marguerite did not hesitate, but began to cut the red-soaked garment from him.

Lady Joan, the chatelaine, pale of face but resolute, appeared at her side. "I have some experience with wounds, my dear. Shall I . . . ?"

"No, I thank you," Marguerite said over her shoulder. "No, he's mine."

The claim held no awkwardness or am-

166

bivalence, nothing except nature's own truth. Nor did anyone contradict her, which was an excellent thing. She could not have been responsible for her temper if they had tried.

The main injury appeared to be a sword or knife thrust. It had entered under his armpit at an awkward angle. If it had gone in straight . . .

It had not. David must have heard something, sensed something, so wrenched away from the blow. He'd changed the direction of the blade so it was deflected by a rib before tearing free. He had lost much blood, regardless, was losing more with every instant that passed.

Oliver stood nearby, his brow furrowed, eyes bleak. He had been one of the men who had carried David into the hall, Marguerite recognized with a distant part of her mind. He hovered now, desperate with worry, ready to be of aid.

"What happened?" she demanded of the squire with a frown while forming a thick pad of cloth and pressing it to the knife slash, holding it in place as she waited for Astrid to make another. "Who did this to him?"

"David left the field," Oliver said with a helpless gesture of one hand. "There was a tent for donning armor, though he wore only chain mail. He walked inside, must have lifted his arms to pull off his hauberk over his head and was blinded by it when he was struck. He twisted away from the blow and hit his head on the tent pole. Or it could have been after, while they fought, I don't know."

"You don't know? Weren't you there?"

"Not at once. It was over by the time I heard the row. The attacker was dead, and David had a dagger in his hand I'd not seen before. Seems he cut the man's throat with his own weapon."

Marguerite closed her eyes as sickness moved over her, but opened them again at once. "Good," she said with tight hardihood, "that's good." She scarcely paused. "Here, hold this pad."

Oliver obeyed. Moments later, they had David's upper body bound with linen strips wound tightly enough to compress the pads she had placed on the wound. Some staining appeared through them, but no more than that. The bleeding had slowed, if not stopped entirely. Still David lay unmoving, unhearing, while the voices of those around him rose and fell with the excitement and outrage of the moment.

That was, until they ceased as if severed

by the headsman's axe.

The cause was the arrival of Henry VII. He cleaved his way through the crowd with force of personality as much as kingly privilege. Men stepped aside, making their bows in a spreading wave before fading back to give him room. He drew close, stopped next to the table and stared down at the quiet figure laid out upon it.

Marguerite made her curtsy in due form and then waited to be addressed. Long moments passed while the king's face remained somber, without expression. When he looked up at last, he met her gaze as if no one else existed in the hall.

"Will he live?" he asked, his gray-blue eyes keen with assessment.

Her nod was as firm as she could make it.

Henry pursed his lips. "Unless the wound turns putrid."

It could not be denied. "Yes, Your Majesty."

"He will have fever."

"It is likely." Indeed it was, as fever was common with such injuries. It could climb dangerously high if the wound was slow to heal.

"Delirium?"

"That may be."

"We must see no greater harm comes

because of it. You will attend to it, Lady Marguerite, attend upon our felled knight."

Any who listened might think he referred to the wound. Marguerite was not deceived, mayhap because she met the full force of the king's gaze. Without doubt, she was to prevent any harm to Henry's plans or his reign from whatever David might say in the delirium of wound fever. She dropped a curtsy of understanding and acquiescence. "As you command, sire."

"Have him taken to his chamber," the king went on with great deliberation. "Order matters there as you please, though with these stipulations. You will not leave his side. No one may enter or leave without your permission. A trusted guard of your selection will be posted outside the chamber at all times. We will tolerate no further injury."

He glanced around with hard eyes, as if to make certain the warning was received. No one spoke. No one coughed, sneezed or swallowed. Even the hound scratching fleas in a corner stopped and looked up.

Marguerite, following the king's gaze, saw that it rested on a pair of noblemen half-hidden behind a square support pillar. Halliwell and his son shifted under Henry's regard, exchanging a darting glance.

Did Henry suspect they were behind the

attack? Nothing was more likely. To strike at a foe when his guard was down was ever the vengeance of a weak man, particularly if he need not sully his own hands with the crime. The only question was if Halliwell was stupid enough to attack a man so high in the king's favor.

Henry looked away with a dismissive flick of his eyelids. He paused to stare down at David again, his features set and eyes shuttered. His lips tightened then he turned from him with an abrupt movement. The king left the great hall, looking neither right nor left while the room bowed in an undulating wave and the mutter of voices rose again behind him.

David's chamber was a mere cell, hardly larger than that of a monk. Against one stone wall was a low and narrow bed that had obviously been knocked together from a few pieces of wood and topped by a straw mattress. Next to it was a rough table holding a bronze basin and an oil pot with a straight spout that served as a lamp. At its foot was a wooden chest for clothes and armor. The deep embrasure of the narrow, shuttered window served as a bench, the only seating in the room.

The wonder, of course, was that David was allotted a private chamber, instead of sleeping cheek-by-jowl with the other men-at-arms in the great hall. The privilege was due to his place in Henry's schemes, no doubt. Marguerite blessed it, whatever the reason. She was in no mood for continued stares and comments.

Oliver had been charged with seeing David carried up the stairs from the great hall. Marguerite went ahead with Astrid to make all ready, to open the shutter to admit light and air, to straighten the single sheet upon his mattress, see that the basin was filled with water and search out cloths for bathing. Once their charge was settled upon the bed, they undressed him with gentle hands, pulling away the sliced and tattered remains of his shirt, stripping off the rough hose he had worn under his knee-length hauberk, leaving only his braies in place.

Marguerite sank down on her knees beside the bed. She took the water-filled basin that Astrid handed her, and dipped a clean cloth into it. With great care, she began to wash away the sweat and blood that streaked David's face. She kept her gaze on what she was doing, trying to ignore the broad width of his chest and the gold-tipped curls that peeped above the bandaging that wrapped it.

Yet she had seen ridges of hard muscle

that had lain over his ribs, also the shield shape of glinting chest hair that made a trail of gold lace over the flat surface of his belly and down to the low edge of his braies. She could feel his body heat through her sleeve and bodice. Her fingertips tingled as she inadvertently brushed them over his skin instead of the cloth. She had known he was tall and strong, but had not realized the extent of it until now, when she was so close, hovering over him, reaching across him to wipe away dried blood. Her heart-beat thudded against her chest wall and she could not quite catch her breath. The curve of her breast, as she leaned over him to swab away a streak of blood on his neck, pressed against the corded muscle of his upper arm. The pressure and heat of that touch made her nipple tighten to stinging hardness.

She sat back on her heels, staring at his inert form in perplexity. What ailed her? He was injured, barely conscious if awake at all, and yet he affected her as if he had reached out to her. How depraved could she be?

More streaks of blood had dried on his upper arm, running under his shoulder to where it joined his back. The skin was puckering around those red tracks, drawing in a manner that looked uncomfortable. If she turned him to the side, she could rid him of it.

Oliver had stepped outside to watch the door. She opened her mouth to call to him, but then changed her mind. With a glance toward Astrid, she said, "Your aid for a moment?"

Astrid put down the old linen cloth she was tearing into more strips. As she saw what Marguerite intended, she reached to push and shove mightily, grunting as they turned David toward the wall, exposing his back. Squeezing out her cloth with one hand, Marguerite wiped at the runnels of red that marred his side. She skimmed her cloth over his shoulder where rust-red had smeared upward to darken the bronze of his skin that had doubtless been gained by sword practice under a Mediterranean sun.

A mark of some kind began to appear from beneath the dried blood. Marguerite tipped her head, wiping around it with care. Bit by bit, it emerged, a curious design that looked as though burned into his skin. The whole thing was no more than three inches square. Small but distinct, it was like nothing she could recall seeing before, being a series of small rings set closely around a smaller inner ring, and with a straight bar dropping down from them. The outlines of the rings were silken smooth, barely raised at all, as if they had been there for years.

It looked very like a brand, she thought in tight concentration. If so, it must have been applied long ago, mayhap when he was a child. Still, she had never seen it before, never in all the years at Braesford Hall. She would have remembered.

She would have, yes, if she had been allowed to see David at such close range and without his shirt. She had never been accorded that indulgence.

No, and neither had she seen him without hose covering the long muscles of his thighs and calves with their glazing of darker gold hair. Not until now. It was true that the knitted pieces worn by most men left little to be imagined, yet it was different when nothing interfered with appreciation for the manifold perfections of the male form. And what a pity it was that the linen braies around his loins had not been left off as well, as they often were by many who wore full hose under short doublets. They offered protection during battle or matches such as the one today, but were still a barrier.

"Milady," Astrid said on an indrawn breath as she peered at the old scar.

Marguerite glanced up, still frowning. "Yes?"

The small serving woman met her gaze an

instant then looked away with a wag of her head. "I almost thought . . . but I don't know."

"What did you think?"

"Foolishness. It has to be. Are . . . are you done?"

Marguerite nodded, sighing as she dropped her cloth back into the basin. Together, they eased David onto his back again. She wondered briefly if he might be better on his stomach, but the mattress sagged too much on its rope supports to make that comfortable. In any case, she should see about washing away the blood from his head wound that was drying in the hair along his temple.

With one hand, she squeezed water from the piece of linen. She turned back, reaching to brush a fall of blond curls back from the dark bruise that crept into his hairline.

Abruptly, David jerked up an arm. Her wrist was snared in a bone-grinding hold. Her breath caught in her throat as she met his eyes. Her heart jolted at the fury and accusation that shone in their metal-hard blue depths.

The cloth she held dropped from her nerveless grip. It landed on his chest with a wet splat.

"Look what you made me do," she exclaimed in tight annoyance at the dampness seeping into his bandaging.

His grasp eased a fraction. Puzzlement invaded his expression, smoothing away accusation, routing anger. "Milady?"

Marguerite snatched her wrist free and picked up the cloth again. She halted in place, her every muscle clenching as relief hit her in a solid wave. David was awake and alive in all his senses. She had been so afraid it would never happen. Just how afraid, she had scarcely realized until this moment, when she was released from it.

"My lady," David said again, the words a mere whisper of sound, "what are you doing?"

"What does it look like?" she asked shortly.

Instead of answering, he glanced around, amazement widening his eyes. "You are in my chamber."

"I am seeing after you at Henry's command. You were stabbed, if you will but remember it." To let him know how despairing she had been, how much she'd feared her task was a death watch, did not seem useful at the moment.

He met her gaze while comprehension welled into his eyes. They darkened, growing bluer, brighter, more alert by the moment.

"You? Alone?" he asked finally.

Her nod was stiff. "And such a change for you it must be, being at someone else's mercy."

"Not such a change," he answered, his gaze probing, "when it's yours."

She smiled, she couldn't help it. "Shall you mind?"

"I can think of worse fates." He moistened his lips as if they were dry.

"So can I," she replied, her smile vanishing with the thought that he could have died instead. She held his eyes, noting the silver gleams, like thousands of tiny knife blades, around his pupils, the shadows that drifted through them, the hint of indecision in their depths. "Is . . . is there anything you need?"

"Ale?" he said with a dry rasp of hope. "I've the devil of a thirst, and my head . . ."

"It hurts, I imagine," she said as he trailed away. She nodded to Astrid who whisked from the chamber at once to bring the drink. Being an intelligent little creature, she would surely bring water, as well.

"Pounds from the top of my skull to the bottom of my feet." He closed his eyes while his jaw muscles clenched then relaxed again. "Also, I see two of you. Two Marguerites, both lovely, yet one more than I can handle just now."

"Two more than you can handle," she corrected, though as much to keep him talking as anything else.

"Do you think so?" He didn't open his eyes, but a corner of his mouth curled.

"I do."

"A fine vow. Remember it when the time comes."

It seemed an odd, disjointed hop from one thought to another. He couldn't be delirious, not yet. Could he? "Which will be never as matters stand, if you will but recall."

"How could I forget?"

She had nothing to say to that, particularly as his words had been flavored with bitterness. What was keeping Astrid? It seemed an age since she had scuttled from the chamber.

"Am I naked?"

The question jerked her attention back to her patient. "Not . . . not entirely," she answered with a quiver in her voice. His eyes were closed, but she refused to allow her gaze to travel down his long length again, as it had many times already. Yes, refused.

One eye opened, but slowly, as if with

great effort. "Too bad."

"David!" He didn't know what he was saying, surely he didn't.

"Who stripped me?"

She swallowed with an audible sound. "Astrid and I," she answered, most cowardly putting the name of her serving woman first.

His eye closed again. He was quiet, as if absorbing the knowledge gained. "I'm sorry I missed that."

Heat rose in a suffocating tide, flooding her body, pooling below her waist. "It was necessary," she assured him in breathless haste. "I would not have you think . . ."

"Too late." A smile twitched his mouth.

"You mean . . ."

"I've thought of it already."

"David . . ."

"Well, I've thought it a hundred times and more, really," he said as if dazed, rambling. "I've pictured you here with me and both of us naked. You've been with me in tents and in palaces, too, and beside a hundred streams and a thousand campfires. I close my eyes and you come to me wearing nothing and with your hair shining, floating. . . ."

She reached out without conscious thought to place her fingertips upon his lips, stopping that flow of disturbing confession. And she shivered as he smiled around them.

"Marguerite?"

"Yes?" Her voice unaccountably husky in her throat. He had not given her the title of lady. She must not be so exalted in the fastnesses of his mind, or mayhap in his dreams.

"Do you have on clothes?"

"Certainly." She snatched her hand away from his mouth, disturbed beyond bearing by the movement of his lips under her sensitive fingertips, the ticklish seep of his warm breath through them.

"Would you . . . ?"

"No," she said before he could finish that quiet request.

"I feared not." He sighed, a long, gusting sound of defeat. He turned his head restlessly, as if maddened by the pain inside it. "Kiss me then."

"Kiss you." The words were a mere whisper.

"Kiss and take away the ache. Kiss and make it well. That much is surely allowed."

8

"Just . . . kiss you," Marguerite repeated.

David could hear the intrigued note in her voice that she tried to hide, one which said she was thinking about it. The very idea made his head throb twice as hard, until it felt as if his brain hit the top of his skull with every beat of his heart. And didn't he deserve the agony?

He was the worst sort of demented fool for teasing her. To resist was impossible, however, as she so obviously thought he was out of his head. Maybe he was, just a little, that he could take the jest so far. He wanted that kiss, by all that was holy, wanted her lips upon his more than he'd wanted anything in years, maybe more than anything in his life.

Still there was more to it. To touch her, to taste her and teach her something of what was between a man and a woman could be a first foray in his campaign to convince her that releasing him from his vow was useful and good. Anything he could do to turn her response into a lover's instead of a friend's should aid the cause. Nothing was quite so helpful in a campaign of seduction as engaging a woman's desires. At least, so he had been told often enough by Oliver and others.

He had never set out to entice where there was no prior inclination, though he had accepted the favors offered when the lady was comely. Truth be told, he was far more apt to succumb to these practiced allures when the woman had some look, however slight, of Lady Marguerite. He was hopeless. Or he had been until this moment when she was so near, so very near.

"My head," he whispered with a wince that was not entirely feigned, " 'twill surely make it better."

Concern and curiosity shadowed her eyes before she lowered her lashes. "Will it?"

"Aye." The single word was a croak.

She shifted with the soft slide of silk and linen. He felt her breast settle gently against his arm and nearly groaned with the sweet, mind-spinning pressure of it. He turned his head in her direction, but could not have spoken again if his life depended on it. Every inch of his skin was rigid with anticipation, while his lips tingled, aching with fiery need.

"Well, if you're sure," she said softly.

The edge of her veil brushed his bare skin beneath his bandaging. It was so much like a caress that he jerked with it. He could catch the sweet, fresh scent that was uniquely her own as she moved nearer, hovering over him from her kneeling position. She touched his face, her fingertips like gentle fire upon the turn of his jaw, quietly rasping over the beard stubble that had sprung up since he scraped them away early that morning. Her breath whispered across his chin.

Her face was so near, her eyes so dark they verged on black. His vision was fractured, showing him two foreheads, two noses, two tender yet firm chins, four soft, soft eyes. He let his eyelids fall as dizziness washed over him.

In that instant, her lips touched his. It was the merest brush; that was all. But then she settled her mouth in place, fitting it to his with perfect fidelity, seam to seam, edge to edge, corner to sweet corner.

The world ceased to exist. He stifled a groan for fear she would move, or in dread that she would not. He didn't breathe, ceased to think, was utterly still as the very tip of her small tongue brushed a hot, wet path over the smooth surface of his lips, tasting him with such innocent hunger that his blood came to a boil in his veins.

He was aware of the tremor that shook her, the sudden clench of her fingers in the hair below the hollow of his neck as he parted his lips so her tongue slipped inside. She started, paused. Still, she did not withdraw as he half expected, lingering instead upon the moist heat of his inner lips as if discovering their texture. He wanted to draw her deeper but forced himself to quiescence.

She touched the glazed edges of his teeth, found the grainy softness of his tongue and played gently along its edge.

Shock moved over him, one more violent than he'd felt at the entry of the dagger into his side. He forgot every kiss he'd ever had from a woman in the delicious flavor of this meeting of mouths and breaths. He wanted to stay as he was for an eternity, allowing her every experiment, giving her access to all that he was or ever intended to be. Mindless with the need of it, he lifted his hand and pushed it under her veil, spreading his fingers wide over the back of her head to hold her forever in place.

God above, but he wanted her, cared for

nothing except having her.

She was his soul's one weakness, and he knew it full well as his blood surged through his veins in hot, brain-pounding waves. She was far more dangerous than any enemy, and he didn't care. She belonged to him and always had, if she could only be brought to know it.

"David . . ."

The sound of his name in that husky plea sent his good intentions reeling. He didn't mean to take advantage of her lips that parted upon that word, but was inside them before he knew. Her sweetness was like drugged wine upon his tongue, heady beyond dreams. He savored her, drank her, discovered her satin secrets while his chest swelled with his indrawn breath of soul-deep content.

The slick velvet of her tongue, the smooth yet sharp edges of her teeth and her warm, wet softness were endless enticements. She clouded his senses, filling his whirling, unhinged brain with nothing except her and the need she stoked inside him. He should stop before he frightened her, stop before the pounding in his head took him away again into blackness or the thunder in his blood burst through the bandaging over the rent in his side. He couldn't do it, lacked the will to release her.

He felt her shudder all the way to his bones. The moan she made of his name, ragged, edged with desperation, was so like the need that raged through him that he finally understood it. With slow, muscle-wrenching reluctance, he forced his hold to loosen, allowed her to lift her mouth from his.

"Thank you," he said, the words such a low rumble in his throat they were more like a growl.

The breath she drew was sharp, as at a sudden awakening. "It . . ." she began. Stopped. Tried again. "It was nothing."

"It was far more than nothing to me." He searched her face as she drew back enough to look down at him again. How black her eyes were, and endlessly deep. He felt as if she was a part of him, and he of her. Clothing and class and space separated them, yes, but it seemed their minds and bodies were one.

"I didn't mean . . ." She glanced down at her hand where her fingers were still entwined in the hair just below the hollow of his throat. Sliding them free in haste, she met his gaze again, her own startled, wary. "It was a small thing, since you asked."

"And if I asked again?"

What she might have answered went unspoken. The chamber door swept open with a mighty creak of hinges. Astrid bustled into the chamber with a beaker of ale sloshing on her tray and one of water beside it.

Though desperately thirsty before, David could have foregone drink forever for another taste of Marguerite's lips. The next best thing was to have her raise his shoulders so he could drink. He could have managed without that aid, or so he thought, but it was far more pleasurable to have Lady Marguerite slide her arm behind him while holding the water to his lips. When he had drunk his fill, she reached for the strong, reviving ale, tipping it down his parched throat, as well.

Afterward, he lay back and watched while she and her little serving woman tidied the room. Idly, he noted the bloodied cloths and metal basin of red-stained water they handed outside to Oliver for disposal. His eyes narrowed as he looked at his lady's hands and wrists, noting a rimming of blood at the edge of her sleeve.

Somewhere in a distant corner of his mind, it seemed he had enjoyed her touch upon him in a soothing caress that provided distraction from pain. It was that which had brought him floating upward from the darkness into light and warmth and her softness beside him. The effort had been immense but worth it. Indeed, it had. With eyes half-closed, he drifted into a waking dream.

The door swung open. Instantly alert, David stared in that direction.

It was only Oliver who stood there, inquiry in his black eyes. His saturnine features relaxed into a mustache-tipping smile, doubtless for the proof that he lived and was awake. His nod of satisfaction was brief yet definite before he looked to Marguerite.

"Your pardon, milady, but I thought you might need the basin returned." He flourished the thing so light from the window struck it in a bronze flash. "I tipped the water down the garderobe and tossed the cloth after it, thinking it might be best if none got a look at them."

"You did well," she said with a glance for Astrid as she came pattering up to take the basin from the Italian. "It will be best if none guess just how serious the wound proved."

"So I thought." Oliver, his face grim, glanced again toward where David lay. "I'd hate for some fool to decide finishing him would be an easy task."

Lady Marguerite's fine brows drew together over her nose. "It's your place to see it doesn't happen. Speaking of which?"

"*Bene,* I'll return to my post. Happen the king will be sending soon to know how fares our Golden Knight. What shall I be telling his seneschal, that no one need disturb you or Sir David in your rest?"

"No one will disturb Lady Marguerite for she will be in her own chamber," David said, annoyed by Oliver's familiarity as well as having them speak as if he wasn't there. "For Henry, you may send word that I am cursed hard to kill. Whoever made this effort will have to try again."

"Don't say that!" Marguerite exclaimed.

"You'll not need me then, I suppose," Oliver said at the same time. "Just as well, as I could use a soft bed and softer . . ."

"Don't," David said in tight warning.

". . . pillow," Oliver ended, and flashed him a crooked grin.

"Don't be absurd." Lady Marguerite darted an exasperated glance between him and the Italian. "You stand guard by the king's order and dare not desert. And though it may pain Sir David to admit it, I'm sure he is grateful for your swift action that saved him from bleeding to death."

"You found me?" David asked, interrupting without compunction. "You brought me here?"

Oliver shrugged, his expression guarded. "In good time, though not before you'd bled like a boar with its throat cut."

"And how is it you failed to undress me?"

"I was posted as guard while the ladies took that duty, so onerous, so thankless, upon themselves."

"Devil's spawn," Astrid muttered, the look she gave him bright with promises of revenge.

The Italian smiled down upon her as if at a fine compliment before he continued, "Truly, I could not persuade them otherwise."

"Not thankless," David said, his mouth lifting at the corner. At least, not for his part. He was thankful indeed.

"Nor could I persuade them to leave your bathing to me."

"Mule's backside," Astrid cried. "As if you ever said a word, being that weak-kneed at the sight of blood."

David listened to the wrangling with half his attention. It had been Lady Marguerite's cool, soft hands he'd felt upon him, just as he'd thought. Even without that vague memory, the rich red color that mantled her face and neck would have told him. He was sorry he had missed the full knowledge of it. With luck, however, he might discover his way toward a repeat performance.

"Astrid is right," Lady Marguerite said to Oliver with some severity. "You, sir, are Satan's own."

"But indispensable, yes? At least while a guard is needed who will not turn enemy when least expected. Well, and to discover if any among the king's men know who attacked Sir David."

It was a point, David knew. He had not recognized his assailant. The man had been a mercenary, one of the many who fought for whoever would pay their wage. It was almost certain the man had come from inside the castle, given the difficulty of joining the ranks of soldiery while the king was in residence. That he had been forced to kill him was a shame. Otherwise he might have been persuaded to name the man who'd paid for this particular job.

With luck, they might yet discover if any had been seen in close talk with the mercenary. The importance of that point could not be ignored, for it was likely the attack was connected with the plan concocted by the king.

Or was it?

"You saw nothing? No one was nearby when you found me?"

Oliver turned to close the door behind

him. Leaning his back against it, he crossed his arms over his chest. "You are thinking of Halliwell?"

"He would not mind seeing me dead." If Halliwell's wrath had not been stirred by the abduction of his betrothed, there was the humbling confrontation in the great hall to stoke it. Men had done worse to soothe offended pride.

Marguerite made a small gesture of protest. When David glanced at her, her expression was distressed, as if she feared herself responsible. Before he could disabuse her of the idea, Oliver spoke again.

"Or his son, as he takes his side with such zeal," Oliver said. "Unfortunately, they were both in the forefront of the crowd during the competition."

"Yes," David said slowly. He recalled seeing the two there in the beginning, though he had lost track of them later.

"Doesn't mean they had no hand in it."

"As you say." Anyone could have hired the mercenary. Nothing would have been easier.

David was suddenly glad that he had coaxed Marguerite into kissing him. The sooner she was protected from whatever Halliwell might do to force a marriage, the better. Who knew how long it would be before Henry decided to put his ruse of a second pretender into effect. These few days, while he recovered from the knife attack, might be all that was allowed.

He had been wrong, he saw, to suggest that she sleep in her own chamber. The more time they spent together, the more opportunities he might find to tempt her. Any number of small encroachments could be made. Such delicate pleasures would surely stir her senses so that releasing him from his vow became the most natural solution in the world.

The troubling thing about his aim was the fevered anticipation it stirred in him. Was it really for her benefit or only an excuse for his unbridled inclinations? Yes, and would he be able to stop with the small touches and gentle caresses he envisioned? He thought he could trust his control, but how was he to be sure when it had never been tested against her?

Marguerite was only marginally aware of the discussion between the two men as she and Astrid finished making the chamber presentable. She was glad Oliver had invaded, even if without permission. That he occupied David's attention gave her time to gather her scattered wits.

How could a simple kiss unsettle her so?

She felt its effects still as a tumbling rush in her veins, an almost painful throbbing in her lips. The center of her belly felt hollow, and an odd weakness in her limbs made her long to lie down, close her eyes and remember.

His mouth had been so very smooth, and warm, so warm. She had not expected it. Somehow, she'd thought it would be rough, prickly with beard and demanding rather than enticing. Her tongue had slipped into his mouth, and he seemed to expect it, even to enjoy it. Strange. She had wanted to extend her discoveries, to probe deeper, searching out every cranny, to taste more of him, and still more.

Was this what seduction was like, this need to draw close to another person, so close that your body and his became one? Could it be this vital urge to mate, a yearning that seemed as natural as the seasons sliding one into the other?

Her purpose in this was not to be enthralled, she told herself with fierce solemnity. The attack today was proof of the danger in David's agreement with Henry. He should not feel he must please the king in order to protect her. No, not at all. A far better safeguard would be to become her husband, as she had thought in the beginning, one who would respect and honor her, yet be immune to the curse that hung over her as the last of the Three Graces.

Such a coil it was, this business of vows and pledges and of honor among men. The trouble it caused was beyond calculation. Yet how much more mean and vicious life would be without it.

Oh, but what could she do to destroy David's hard resolve never to possess her? More kisses, she thought, but surely there was something else? Suppose she were to trail her fingers down his chest, slide them over the flat, hard surface of his belly and down to his long length under his braies. Her palm itched at the thought, while her stomach muscles fluttered in reaction. Would he like that? Would he allow it?

She should have done it while she had the chance, while he lay at her mercy. Even now, Oliver was taking a woven coverlet from the end of the bed and spreading it over him from his chest to his toes. The next time would not be so easy.

The next time. What a wanton she was to anticipate it even now.

"Lady Marguerite? Did you hear?"

She turned so quickly her skirts swirled around her ankles. Meeting the expectant gaze David turned in her direction, she ventured, "You were speaking to me?"

"On the matter of where you will sleep this night . . ." he began.

"I mean to remain here."

His regard did not waver. "Your good name will suffer."

"It is past redemption anyway," she answered with a lift of her chin. "Henry issued his command that I remain with you while you lay in the great hall. If those present suspected there was something between us, after the way you carried me off and the time we've spent closeted together since, it has now been confirmed."

"What can he be thinking?" David asked, grim puzzlement warring with the glimmer of pain in his eyes. "Is he so certain you will remain unwed that he cares nothing for what may be said of you? Or is it something more?"

She met his gaze an instant before looking away again. "I'm not sure what you mean."

"Nor am I, unless . . . but that makes no sense." He paused. "The only certainty is that Henry has a reason."

"Don't trouble about it now," Marguerite said in dismissal. "You should try to sleep."

"If you will order a pallet brought, I will ease down on it while you lie here." He indicated the narrow bed he occupied.

"I shall order two, one for my use and one for Astrid."

"Nay, Lady Marguerite. 'Twill be best if I . . ."

"Can you not call me Marguerite?" she asked with exasperation. "It seems foolish to be so formal while discussing exactly how we will sleep together."

His face darkened, as did the tips of his ears that were exposed where she had brushed back his damp hair after wiping the blood from it. "We will not be sleeping together."

"As near as makes no difference."

"At the king's behest."

Her smile was wry. "I am to guard against whatever you might let fall in delirium, I believe."

"Or anything I might do."

Color invaded her face, for she could feel the burn of it. "Just so."

"God's teeth," he muttered, then closed his eyes with a frown of pain. "You must do what you will then, milady."

She lifted a brow. "Milady?"

"Marguerite," he repeated with the ghost of a smile, though he did not open his eyes.

Taking him at his word, she directed Astrid to the task of finding some manner of sleeping mats for the two of them, and

Oliver to carry them for her.

Oliver gave a grunt that might have meant anything from disgust to approval. "That's all very well," he said, "but what of me?"

"Dullard," Astrid said before Marguerite could answer. "It's your turn to sleep across the doorway."

He sighed, looking as woebegone as a lost child. "*Sì,* but it will be a long night."

"Very well," the serving woman said, "you may have a pallet, too. There, are you satisfied?"

"*Bene,* though it would be better if I had a foot warmer. You are such a short bit you could easily fit across the bottom of my makeshift bed."

"Jackanapes!" Astrid spat at him while setting her hands on her hips. "As if I would sleep with you on any part of it — though you're not so long yourself."

"Long enough," he replied, waggling his brows.

"Bragging dog," she cried. "You may find your own bed, now, for I'll not aid you."

He laughed, and trailed behind her to complete the task assigned.

Marguerite gazed after the Italian with a frown between her eyes. What was he about with his teasing of Astrid? She greatly feared her tiny friend would be hurt by it, and yet

199

so few paid her any attention. It was possible an end should be made before it got out of hand. She would do that, except they both seemed to enjoy it so.

As it happened, no one had time for sleep. David's wound became feverish by nightfall, and grew steadily worse as the hours advanced. Oliver was kept busy carrying water from the spigot in the great hall, one that drained down from a rooftop cistern. He also helped restrain David when he tried to leave his bed and buckle on his sword to go off to fight, and urged him to swallow the bitter brews of herbs and wine that Astrid made from her stores. Marguerite wrung out cloth after cloth, using them to sponge David's skin with endless gentle strokes designed to soothe as well as cool.

She had envisioned trailing her fingers over his body below his bandaging. It had not been like this.

Near dawn the fever lessened somewhat, and her patient fell into a fitful sleep. Oliver returned to his post outside the door. Astrid stretched out on her pallet against the far wall, and was soon asleep in her sound fashion that was near stupor. Marguerite sank down onto her own mat of straw that lay at a right angle to the head of David's bed. Leaning her back against the bed frame near his pillow, she closed her eyes, intending to rest them for a moment or two.

A wafting of cool, fresh air jerked her awake. Henry VII strode into the chamber with his seneschal on his heels and Oliver close behind them. He did not halt until he stood over the low bed where David lay.

"We regret disturbing you, Lady Marguerite," the king said with the briefest of glances in her direction, "though we are pleased to see you are looking after Sir David with such care. No, don't try to rise. We will consider your curtsy as made with the usual grace."

"Your Majesty," she murmured in acknowledgment. Her mind was still fuzzy with sleep, yet she thought there was an undercurrent of satisfaction in the king's voice that had little to do with approval for the way she had carried out his command. A possible reason for it brushed her, but he went on before she could grasp and hold it complete.

"We are told he was fevered during the night."

She agreed, explaining the circumstances.

The king stared down at David, his expression bleak. "We must pray he mends quickly, for much depends upon it."

"Yes, sire."

He was silent a moment. When he spoke again, his tone was brooding. "The Golden Knight. He does, verily, have the look of a Plantagenet."

"So everyone says."

"You would not remember Edward and Richard, I suppose, being so young."

"No, sire."

"Formidable men, they were, in their different ways, running true to the bloodline."

It was a reminder, if any were required, that, though his father had been a Welshman, Edmund Tudor, Henry was a Plantagenet in his mother's line. He and the kings who had ruled immediately before him, the brothers Edward IV and Richard III, were all descended from Edward III. That Henry had come to the throne in this war of cousins was a great oddity of fate, for others had been far closer to the throne by right of birth. Thirty years of bloodletting had cleared his way. And still it had taken an armed invasion, a battle and yet more deaths before he grasped the crown. Was it any wonder he clutched it so fiercely, would do anything to keep it?

Marguerite moistened her lips. "I know little of the Plantagenets, it's true, but David is no uncommon man, either."

"We depend upon it, which is why we are

concerned. There was mention of disturbance to his eyesight?"

The bedclothes behind her stirred, pulling taut behind her shoulders as David levered himself up upon one elbow. "A complaint that is better this morning, Your Majesty."

"We are pleased to hear it," the king said, his gaze searching and less convinced than his words.

"It came from the blow to his head, along with a severe headache," Marguerite informed the king, her voice rigorously even. "Astrid names the malady a concussion."

"Not uncommon, as such things go," David said.

His voice was half as strong as usual, she thought. The king frowned in recognition of that fact, as well. She was just as glad he'd noted it, as she had no wish to point it out.

"So we believe," Henry replied, "still you must not exert yourself or become chilled. Your well-being is too valuable to us to take chances." He turned his gaze upon Marguerite. "You have everything he requires, everything you require, as well?"

"Indeed, sire."

"We would send our personal physician, but came away from Westminster without him as this was to have been a swift hunt with an early return."

She was surprised at Henry's consideration in explaining matters, but could not regret the physician's absence. The man was too fond of his lancet, claiming a good bleeding cured all ills. That seemed the last thing that was needful. "A kind thought, sire, but we will make do with Astrid's skill."

"She belonged to the gypsies, as I recall. Her knowledge of medicaments comes from them?"

"She traveled with them before reaching Your Majesty's court, I believe, but was never of that tribe. Though wellborn, she was put away as an embarrassment to her family."

Henry inclined his head. "Ah, yes, we remember the tale from when she was with our queen. God's ways are inscrutable." He paused. "We will trust in her good offices for now, but may yet send for our physician. Toward that need, you will send word to us if there is any change."

It was a command rather than a request, and doubtless referred to a change for the worse. Marguerite lowered her lashes as she agreed in proper form.

"Excellent." Henry turned from her to meet David's gaze again. "We pray to see you fit and ready for duty again soon."

"Sire." The bedclothes rustled again as

David sketched a truncated bow.

"When your health allows, you will continue with the program of instruction outlined."

"As you will."

"We will look in upon you again to mark your progress."

The king swung around in a flurry of braid-edged wool. Then he was gone, his footsteps and those of his seneschal thudding on the stone floor before fading away down the corridor. Oliver followed the pair, closing the door firmly behind him.

Marguerite closed her eyes and leaned her head back upon the straw mattress. For no good reason that she could think of, tears burned their way into her eyes, rimming her lashes. She sniffed a little, and tried to swallow them down again. Blindly, she sought the well-chewed corner of her veil to blot them.

It was then she felt David's touch on her face, brushing gently over her cheek and under one eye. Collecting the salty wetness on the edge of his finger, he removed it. As she reared back a little, turning her head, she saw him carry it to his lips.

"What are you doing?" she asked in husky surprise.

"Breaking my fast with angel's tears."

A watery laugh gurgled in her throat. "Not very satisfying, I fear."

"Depends on your meaning."

"I suspect you need food." If they were back to him being worshipful she was not sure she liked it.

"I could eat," he said in dry agreement.

It was an excellent sign, one that threatened to make her eyes water again. "Yes," she said, pushing to her feet, swiping away the rest of the stupid tears, "so could I."

The day that followed set the pattern for the rest of the week. David ate, slept and gingerly exercised his torn side. In between, he watched her, touched her with careful familiarity, and seldom allowed her to leave his side. Each afternoon, his fever rose, climbing as the night advanced and only falling again when the midnight hours had passed. Slowly, slowly, he grew stronger and more himself.

Marguerite, mindful of the king's command, began to polish David's speech as he slept less. It was no great task, as he had patterned it after Braesford's long ago. All that was required was to remove some of the army camp roughness and a certain northern inflection. She also drilled him further in the use of titles and the rules of precedence, bowing and curtsying to him as he lay frowning in concentration, giving herself the name of this duke and that earl, of a duchess, a mere lady, or a churchman of higher or lower degree. She noted the way he dealt with wine and meats now, but could find no fault. In fact, he had a certain fastidiousness she thought many English nobles might copy to good effect.

So the days passed. They laughed, they teased, they fed each other. She read to him from *Le Morte d'Arthur* and other such tomes. She changed his bandaging with great care, gave him more red meat as he demanded it and supported him, along with Oliver, as he walked carefully up and down. Yet at no time could Marguerite tell what David was thinking or what he wanted.

It was on a fine morning a week after the attack, when Astrid had gone for bread, beef and ale and asked Oliver to come fetch it back for her, when matters changed. David had refused to remain abed a moment longer. Rising, he'd shaved himself instead of depending upon Oliver's services. He left off his boots, but dressed in hose, shirt and a doublet of plain blue velvet. Over these he strapped his eating knife, yet another gift from Charles VIII of France with its fine hilt of ebony chased with gold.

Now he stood at the narrow window with

the shutter flung open to the morning, his hosed foot on the sill that rose to bench height above the floor and his arm braced upon his knee. His gaze was on some exercise being conducted below, from which shouts and curses and commands rose to where he stood. The day was overcast, with a yellowish hue to its bleak, gray aspect. The pale light threw his features in relief, underlining the hollows in his cheeks and the sallow look of his skin. Despite it, a sheen of vitality lay beneath the surface. It was the mark of strength that no mere knife thrust could ever vanquish, for it was of the spirit instead of muscle and sinew.

"No," she said, "I don't believe you are quite ready to join what's going on below."

He gave her a rueful smile. "Reading my mind again?"

"It's not difficult when you look like a boy forbidden to play."

"I'm no boy." He returned his attention to the window.

No, that was the last thing he was. The boy he had been was gone forever. She grieved for that gentle, fun-loving lad in an odd fashion, though he was safe in her memory.

"I never said you were," she answered as she moved to join him.

"No." He paused. "I suppose you think it comical that I am shut away here."

"Why should I think that?"

The look he gave her had an ironic edge. "You are always shut away, more or less, since a lady can only come and go when permitted."

His understanding of that basic truth made her feel light and warm inside, though she tried for unconcern as she answered. " 'Tis the fate of women. I felt it a beastly trick when I was younger, but seldom think on it now."

"At least you will never require a man's permission again when this is over."

She glanced out the window to where gray clouds gathered above the green of the distant meadow and the blue hills beyond. A meadowlark soared, trilling, into the freedom of the open sky, and she followed its flight while a wry smile twisted her lips. "I had not thought of it in quite that way."

"That is, of course, unless you return to Braesford Hall. You would have the company of your sister Isabel there, but must also come under Braesford's protection, therefore his authority."

"He is a fine man," she said in easy reply, "and not unreasonable. I could say the same thing for Cate's husband, Dunbar. Still, I prefer to live independently."

"I thought as much."

She turned her head to study him where he stood so grimly pensive beside her. "Therefore, your bargain with Henry?"

"He will honor it, I believe. When the time comes, you need only ask that he extend his protection for your remove to one of the properties inherited from your lord father."

He knew well that she and her sisters had inherited considerable wealth from their father who had been killed when Marguerite was but a babe. Her mother had remarried but lived only a few years. Afterward, her second husband and his only heir had both died. As a result, Marguerite and her sisters were heirs to that estate, as well. There was no lack of properties from which to choose.

"It will be a welcome release."

He tipped his head in agreement. "Yet is it a fair exchange, freedom and loneliness in your own manse for family and security with Braesford?"

"Who says I will be lonely or without family?" she asked, the words as light as she could make them.

"You expect to take a husband?" He glanced at her and then away again.

"And hand him the right to claim all I own, to strike a fine figure at court or waste the income on gaming, fine trappings and other women? The thought has no appeal." She sent him a quick look from the corners of her eyes. "Astrid suggested I might take a lover."

"A lover." The words were stiff.

"She thought a man-at-arms, one with no pretension to becoming a husband."

"Don't be fooled," he said in rough disdain. "Any man you take into your bed will begin to think of what else he may gain."

"You think so?" Her voice was layered with frost. "The bedding not being enough to hold him, I suppose."

"Nay, Marguerite. The bedding being certain to set him scheming on how never to lose the privilege."

The quiet timbre of the voice did strange things to her midsection, as did the idea that a man might so enjoy having her. It was an effort to keep her voice even as she replied. "It sounds a dangerous business then. Mayhap that's why you are trying to discourage me."

"Suppose it is?"

"The obvious answer, as I said once before, would be to marry me yourself. Then you need not worry some man will seek greater advantage than I choose to give him."

"Take care," he said, squinting at the distant meadowlark. "There are many who would consider that a proposal."

"But you are not among them."

"You know . . ."

"I know you have already declined to be my husband. But nothing was said of physical love, be it chaste or unchaste."

"Marguerite . . ."

"Henry will like it, I believe, as he insists on putting us together. Mayhap he considers himself a matchmaker, as he did so well by my sisters."

"And mayhap it's merely the gift to the gladiator."

She flushed at the thought of being offered to David as in olden days, a prize before he went to risk death at the will of his king. "Not likely."

"No."

The pain in his eyes acted like a goad, though she could not be sure what caused it. "Forget I mentioned it," she said in dismissal. "I don't know how we strayed onto the subject, anyway."

He turned to face her, tucking his thumbs into his belt as he put his back to the stone edge of the window's frame. "I asked about your future plans."

"I don't see how that concerns you, as you

will do nothing to change them."

"I could, if you like, give you a different view of a husband's purpose."

"What do you mean?" She searched the graven stillness of his features. "You may correct me if I am wrong, but I could have sworn you rode many a long league and risked the wrath of a king to save me from being wed."

"From being wed at Henry's behest, rather, and without your consent," he answered with dogged precision. "You should be married, if you will not be a nun. No protection is so certain for you as a strong husband who can keep all other men at bay."

"And who will protect me from him?"

"That should not be necessary if you choose him for yourself, a husband to your liking rather than a mere lover. Instead of only submitting on your wedding night, you might enjoy his embraces."

"David —" The abrupt, squeezing tightness in her throat would not let her go on.

"You believe otherwise, but I could, if you will permit, show you something of it. I have been long away from Braesford and from you. It would be a rare man, I think, who failed to take advantage of certain opportunities that came his way. I left a boy

213

and have come back a man, and in between . . ."

"I understand," she said shortly.

The gaze he turned upon her was doubtful. "Do you?"

"Oliver was kind enough to enlighten me."

David's scowl was instant and dark. "What said he?"

"Women are drawn to you, and you have had no reason to resist," she replied in unwonted irritation. She didn't want to think of him with other women. It offended some cherished ideal deep within, ached like a bruise struck by accident.

"Well then."

"What of it? We have established that you are not forsworn in . . . in regard to other females."

"The result is more knowledge of what happens between a man and woman than I had when we were at Braesford."

"I'm sure that will be useful to you in future pursuits, but . . ."

"Hear me, Marguerite."

The iron-hard command in his voice was something she had never heard or thought to hear directed at her. She lifted her chin and turned sharply from him then, bent on putting as much space as possible between them.

A soft oath left him. He shot out a hand and grasped her wrist, swinging her back around. In the same move, he circled her waist with his free arm and snatched her against him. Releasing her arm, he slid his hand across her back and upward beneath her veil, thrusting under the fine cloth to tangle his fingers in her thick, loose braid. His hooded gaze scanned her face, her lips that parted to form a blistering order for her release. He met her eyes, his own as gray-blue and forbidding as the looming storm.

"Many are the ways a man may pleasure a woman, Marguerite, ways that have nothing to do with possession. I know most, spent days and long nights enjoying the learning. I've a mind to show them to you, that you are better able to judge whether you will ever desire a husband."

9

Had the blow to his head addled David's brain? Or was this mayhap the result of her small attempt at seduction not so long ago? Had the memory of it lingered, so he sought more of her?

Marguerite had no time to make sense of it. The heat and hardness of him took her breath, clouded all thought. The unbreakable hold of his arms sent a shiver over her. Her heart shuddered in her chest as she watched his gaze fasten upon her mouth, saw him lower his head.

She could not move, not because she lacked the strength but because all will for it fled. Slowly, as if he had all the time in the world, he took her mouth, lapping the finely molded outer ridges with slow strokes of his tongue, tasting the soft surfaces, the indented corners, collecting her flavor as if it was the most precious of nectars. His hand at her waist slid down to press her more firmly to him, and he eased his body against her, nudging her lower abdomen with slow, sure movements.

She inhaled in the shock of sudden hunger, feeling starved for touch and closeness and all the incredible things he promised. Her lips parted without her volition. She matched the opening of his mouth with her own, delicately seeking the meshing of breaths and tongues she had known with him before. He jerked a little, a movement that rippled through him. She murmured deep in her throat, a low sound of need and empathy. The velvet of his doublet was warm, sensuous against her palms. She slid them upward until she could clasp his shoulders, twisting her fingers into the tucks of rich cloth there. She was melting inside, softening to take his hard heat within. Boneless, near mindless, she swayed against him.

He whispered her name, his voice thick, while he kneaded the indentation of her waist as if he would gather all of her into his hands if he could. His clasp moved to her ribs, and higher. He cupped the softness of her breast, weighing its fullness. His thumb, rough with a swordsman's calluses, rasped across the thin wool and linen of her bodice and shift beneath it, again, and yet again. As her nipple hardened to a tight point, he took it between his fingers, rolling it as gently as he might a ripe and tender berry.

A small sound vibrated in her throat. It startled her, and she dragged her mouth free. "What . . . ?" she began in near incoherence.

"Shhh," he said. "It's all right. I wish . . . if you were naked I would . . . and anyway, I . . ."

He was hardly more in command of his senses than she was. The knowledge soothed her. She rested in the support of his arms that seemed to grow ever harder, her eyes closed while he kissed her chin, the hollow of her throat, the turn of her shoulder. When he lowered his head to her breast, she shuddered, needing she knew not what. That was, until she felt the wet heat of his mouth upon her.

Violent need uncurled low in her belly as he carefully closed his teeth upon her beaded nipple under the cloth. Stunned by the sensation, she was unable to move, could only burn as he tugged upon her, breathed in so she was cool and then wet the cloth and took her deep in the fiery heat of his mouth again.

She shivered, clutching at his neck, while in some far recess of her mind a thought struggled to gain ascendancy. He did not mean to take her, but only to show her what went before. What if . . . what if she could slip past his iron will so he took her regardless? Once that happened, his code would force him to marry her. This was her chance, the only one she might be given.

He wanted her, of that there could be no doubt. Proof of it was the swordlike ridge that angled across her belly. She undulated against it with slow care, while lowering one hand to trail down to his chest, seeking his flat nipple under the soft cloth of his doublet. She found it, a tight knot not unlike her own. Carefully, not quite certain of what she was doing, she caught it between her thumb and forefinger and squeezed.

The sound he made was neither groan nor grunt, but something in between. Abruptly, he drew back, caught her arms and set her from him. Perspiration made bright gleams on his brow, and his breathing was fast and hard through his parted lips.

Compunction gripped Marguerite, along with a tremor of distress. "Did I hurt you? Is that why you stopped."

The shake of his head was fast, hard. "No, I . . . You . . ."

"Was I not supposed to touch you?"

"No! This was for you, not me. You can't

do that, not and expect me to . . ."

"What?" she demanded, her voice tight with disappointment and mystification.

"Keep to my vow."

This was a good thing to know, she thought, a very good thing indeed. She reached out to brush her fingertips down his face, all he would allow, while watching carefully to see the effect. The pupils of his eyes darkened, widened. His grip on her arms grew slack.

An oath feathered across his lips while suspicion surfaced in his face. "Marguerite," he began, then stopped as a laugh shook him. "Serves me right."

He swung her toward the bed and pushed her down upon it. For a single terrifying yet glorious moment, she thought he meant to join her there. Instead, he stepped back and shoved his fingers through his hair. His gaze moved over her, resting on her moist and parted lips, on the wet spot on the fabric over the straining peak of her breast, on the quick rise and fall of breathing. Cursing again, he swung from her and stamped from the small chamber.

He had no boots on. She wondered, even as she sank back upon the rustling straw mattress and closed her eyes, how long it would be before he noticed.

■ ■ ■ ■

"David! Wait!

It was Oliver who called after him. David heard him in the dim way he might take note of a buzzing gnat, but did not stop. He could not get away fast enough or far enough from the chamber where he had left Marguerite. If he slowed or stopped, he might go back. If he went back, he might rid her of her veil, loosen the tightness of the braid that held her hair and spread it around her. He might ease every stitch she wore from her and slide his hands over her body until he was stupefied with the pleasure of it. He didn't trust himself to resist seeking the warm, wet center of her then, or sliding into her in hot, hard possession.

God's teeth, but he'd dreamed of it often enough. It would be only a small step more to turn fantasy into reality.

"Hell's bells, man, are your braies on fire? Or have you learned who knifed you and mean to settle the score?"

Oliver, bearing down on him from behind, reached to catch his shoulder. The movement pulled him off balance. David staggered, falling against the near wall. Feeling suddenly like a torn practice dummy with

221

its sand-fill draining away, he turned until his shoulders rested against the stone. Closing his eyes, he breathed in tried gasps.

"Sorry," Oliver said, "didn't intend to be so rough. Are you all right?"

David nodded.

"What happened? Where were you going?"

"Away."

"Away from what? Or shall I guess?"

Opening his eyes a fraction, David stared at his Italian friend. "You couldn't, never in this life."

"No? Only one thing has the power to upset you that I've been able to discover. What did she say to you?"

"Nothing."

It wasn't what she had said at all, but what she had done. A lady, daughter of an earl, should not be so fervent in her responses. She was meant to protest being touched, to avoid having her lips sullied by the unwanted intimacy of a kiss. She was not supposed to set him aflame.

Maybe he had a fire in his braies, after all. Certain parts of him certainly felt hot enough.

"What did she do?" Oliver asked, rubbing over his mustache with thumb and forefinger as he frowned.

David scowled at his friend and squire

while feeling as if the truth must be written on his forehead. The need to protect Marguerite, also to prevent the besmirching of what they had just shared, made his voice brusque. "Nothing. Nothing at all."

"Something must have happened," the Italian said with an inquiring tilt to his head. "What did you do then?"

It wasn't what he'd done so much as the contrast between that and what he'd intended. His plan had been so simple that it seemed foolproof. It was to be a slow campaign to undermine her defenses. He would begin by persuading her to allow another fairly innocent kiss similar to the one he had tricked her into the evening he was injured. He was certain it would take days before he could slip his tongue into her mouth, longer still before he could put a hand upon her elsewhere.

She was not supposed to respond with such hot sweetness that it sent him spinning into need so violent it ripped his control to shreds. He had intended to persuade her to release him from his vow, not become so inflamed that it shattered at the first blow like a faulty sword.

He'd wanted it broken. Above all, he'd wished it unmade. And that was the most ignoble thing of all.

"Well?"

"What?" David gave Oliver a dazed look.

"You did something, didn't you?" Oliver said, narrowing his eyes. "Tell me you didn't . . . Oh, but you did. Didn't you?"

Marguerite had responded to him as if she'd been doing it all her life, David thought in sudden recognition. It stunned him still to think of it. But why? Why? She was meant to be shy and virginal and fearful of the consequences of being intimate with a man. Instead, it was almost as if she wanted to be seduced.

Did she? Was that what she was about?

Or did she intend to seduce him? Was that what he had seen in her face, felt in her touch?

"Do I look such a prize fool?" he demanded as he realized, belatedly, what Oliver was saying. But of course he had been, almost. Almost.

"You look like a man who doesn't know whether he's on his head or his heels. What happened then? Did she ask you to marry her again? She did, and you said yes. That's it. Am I right?"

"Don't be daft. Lady Marguerite is not for the likes of me."

She had suggested before that he marry her, yes, but only to prevent any other from attempting it. Well, and mayhap from reluctance to see him caught up in this political maneuvering of Henry's. Not that he thought her concern was personal. No. She'd have felt the same reluctance to have the injury or death of any man on her conscience.

"Henry didn't think so. He'd have given her to you, had you not been so nobly self-sacrificing."

David felt a great stillness come over him, felt his features set as if in stone. "Who told you that?"

"You did, my friend." Oliver's black gaze took on a look of pity. "You talked out of your head when you were fevered. Did the little one not mention it?"

Out of his head. The very idea left David chilled to the center of his heart. "She didn't, no, if you mean Astrid. Did Lady Marguerite hear?"

"She was asleep, as she had hovered over you for most of three days and nights. Astrid and I watched in her place, as we thought the fever near conquered. We were wrong."

"I am grateful for your care." It was the exact truth that David spoke, though he was even more grateful that it was not Marguerite who had heard his mutterings. Or had she? "Was that the only time?"

"The only one I know about."

He gave a stiff nod. It was as well, for there was no telling what he might have said. Some of his dreams where she appeared made him break into a sweat just remembering them.

"The point is, only misplaced humility prevents you from taking her," Oliver went on, "that and years spent thinking her as far above you as the stars. You should have her and be done, so we may go back to France."

"Only humility and my sworn word." He would not admit he had begun to think the same thing. The Fates had a way of smiting those who dared too much.

"One made when you were green and thought the world a simple place where women were pure, men were brave and honor sacred. What of it?"

"I might have changed, but the vow has not. And the lady deserves better than to be used and discarded as if no more valued than a good dinner with extra sweet wine."

"I did tell you what you might do about that."

"What?" David's scowl was fierce.

"Ask her to release you."

"Impossible. Chivalry will not allow it."

"David, David," Oliver said with a doleful

shake of his head. "You may be the last good man."

"If so, then Marguerite is the last pure lady."

"What odds then," Oliver said with a shrug, "that the two of you will corrupt each other?"

That was his fear, David thought, if he continued with the purpose he intended. Still, how could he not, especially after what had just taken place? He could not bear to think of any other man tasting the pure honey and sunshine that was Marguerite. Somehow, some way, he must find the strength to resist trespassing beyond what was allowed.

He must. It was the only way.

The smile he gave Oliver was sharp-edged. His strength recovered, he pushed away from the wall and turned toward the great hall. "I'd not wager on it, were I you. Shall we go in search of ale?"

"Oh, aye," the Italian said. "But you do know you've no boots on your feet?"

David looked down. His curse was short and vicious. Still, he could not return to his chamber. Not now. Not yet.

"Get them for me. Knock first."

"Don't I always?"

David glared at him. "Just remember it."

Oliver said no more, but his smile as he turned to do as he was bid was wryly diabolical.

Within the hour, the storm that had threatened earlier broke over them. Wind whined around the castle like a demon forbidden entry, snatching slates from the roof and flinging them, clattering, into the inner bailey. It threw rain at the shuttered windows in great handfuls, and sluiced down the walls in sheets.

The dark inside the great hall was like midnight. Lamp flames in their open basins flattened and flared and sent smoke swirling into the upper gloom that was the ceiling. The banners that hung over the high dais swayed as if pushed by unseen hands, and the embroidered horsemen scattered across the tapestry that covered the back wall appeared to gallop with its movement. Those men and women gathered in the gloom raised their voices above the rumble of thunder and drumming hiss of rain, while their faces glowed with ghostly pallor in the lightning flashes that struck through the cracks around the shutter edges.

David, nursing a beaker of watered wine, grew more uneasy with every passing minute. The storm troubled him little, but he did not care for the idea of Marguerite and Astrid remaining alone in the chamber in the upper reaches of the castle. Anything could happen in this semidarkness with the storm's roar to cover the sound.

The king had not gone hunting that morning, and the nobles, courtiers and men-at-arms who traveled with him were at loose ends, not to mention those that had arrived with Halliwell or were attached to the castle. His own men would not ordinarily trespass for fear of reprisal from their leader, but his injury made their conduct less certain. All these bored and randy men were free to roam the place at will, and though most would behave with propriety in the king's presence, there were others who felt themselves privileged, above the rules that applied to lesser men.

There was also at least one who must feel certain he could escape the consequences of whatever he might do. He had paid to have a man killed, after all, and not been caught. At least, he had not been caught yet.

David was just opening his mouth to ask Oliver to fetch Marguerite and Astrid to the great hall when he saw them. They seemed to glow, to walk in mysterious and ethereal magic, though that was only the blue-white throb of lightning behind them and, just possibly, the gleam in Marguerite's eyes.

A rash of goose bumps prickled across his shoulders and down his arms. He felt the hair rise on the back of his neck while his heart tripped in his chest before surging into a faster beat. The need to sweep her up in his arms and carry her far away from all the men who turned to stare at her was an internal fury more powerful than any storm. He wanted to strip her naked, toss off his own clothing and fall into bed with her while the heavens raged and the rain lashed the roof. And if he did, if he had her in his arms, he wouldn't care if God's own paradise blew inside out and the world drowned around them.

"Ah, *sì*," Oliver said, his voice a little thick, "she is fair and fine, all right, your lady."

It was one of heaven's miracles, David thought with strained detachment, that he didn't tear out his squire's tongue. Instead, he turned a stare upon him that was colder than the draft that whipped around their ankles. "Wine," he said in a voice like the honed edge of a sword. "Find a serving wench and have it brought, and fruit as well if any is to be had. Then see if you can recall how to act in the company of a lady."

The last was a mistake, of course. Oliver,

upon his mettle, became exceedingly deferential as Marguerite and Astrid joined them. He was also charming, encroaching and admiring, saying everything a woman might want to hear. He fetched and carried as if to serve was his life's most intense pleasure, all while keeping up a stream of small talk that mixed bits of salacious gossip with a running disparagement of the gowns, veils, girdles and jewelry of the ladies, also the hats, doublets and hose of the gentlemen. He called attention to his own ensemble which included a cloth turban that could be rearranged to form a hood, a striped doublet and parti-colored hose, red on one leg and yellow on the other. That it made David's own gray-blue doublet and darker blue hose seem dull by comparison was his cross to bear.

"Horse's rear," Astrid was heard to murmur to herself after a particularly pointed comment about how difficult it was for a man to care for hair, such as his wild black curls, that must be crushed under a metal coif while on campaign.

David, made all too aware of his own sweat-streaked mane, unwashed since before he was knifed, could only agree.

At least the two females were distracted from the storm.

"Milady, *cara mia*," the Italian was saying while taking Marguerite's hand that lay on the table where they sat, playing with her fingers, "tell us again why you are unwed, if you would be so kind. No, no, not of this Graces curse, for that is of a great stupidity. We would know if you scorn to be a wife, mother of a man's sons. *Si,* and if it comes from some fear in your heart of a man's desires, or if it's only that the men you have met are all imbeciles who cannot see your worth."

The query was too personal by half, this David knew well. He should stop it, could stop it with a single word. Yet he remained silent that he might hear an answer worth knowing.

"You are impertinent, sir," Marguerite told Oliver in cool accents.

"True, but what would you? He who asks nothing receives the same."

"I have no fear."

That much, David could have told his friend. Marguerite feared nothing, nor had she ever.

"You have no trust, either, or so it appears," the Italian returned in idle comment.

Her eyes narrowed. "I trust where it is earned."

"As with our good David." Oliver looked thoughtful. "But who else? Your brothers-in-law, mayhap, Braesford and this Scotsman?"

"Dunbar, my sister Cate's husband. Yes, those two."

"And our good king Henry?"

"Naturally."

Her hesitation before she spoke was so slight only he might have noticed, or so David hoped as he felt tightness invade his chest.

"Naturally," Oliver agreed with great smoothness and a shallow dip of his head. "Such a small number. You will note I don't count myself among them."

He paused to allow her to refute it, but Marguerite did not avail herself of the opportunity. "Why is that, pray?" she asked instead.

"I feel it here." He clutched his doublet over his heart. "Your judgment has been tainted by the small termagant who serves you, I suspect, though what I've done to earn her dislike is more than I can see."

Astrid crossed her arms over her chest and twitched a tiny foot that did not reach the floor. "Other than insult me, abuse me and use me for your amusement?"

"But I don't ignore you," Oliver answered

with great gentleness, "or stare above your head."

Astrid's face turned red and she swung around, putting her back to him.

"As I was saying, such a small number," Oliver went on, turning back to Marguerite. "And none of them available as a husband. If you would be wed, you will have to seek with a wider net."

"Who says I want a husband?"

"Now there is the question, is it not? But women want children, most of them, and matters have been so arranged that a lady has scant choice except to wed the man who may give them to her. Now if you were not of the nobility . . ."

"What? I could have all the children I please, with whomever I please?"

David, watching her face, breathed hard through his nose. Though he honored her right to choose, the idea of it made his hackles rise like those of a rabid dog.

"Well, not that," Oliver hedged.

"I thought not," she took him up at once. "What is the difference, then, between being ward of a king and having a yeoman father who would trade one off for a sheep meadow? Not a great deal, when the bed curtains are closed."

Oliver looked flummoxed by the picture

she painted. David was more attuned to the bitterness in her voice. The truth of what she said was obvious enough, but he had not realized she felt it so keenly.

"She has you there," he said with a twist of humor to his mouth as he watched his squire. He also noted that Marguerite appeared immune to the Italian's smiles, paid no attention to the way he was fondling her hand. Her lack of response was a source of secret amusement, secret pleasure.

That he was inclined to slice off his friend's hand at the wrist was another matter altogether.

Reaching out, he took Marguerite's fingers into his own possession. They were cool and slender, almost fragile as he enclosed them in the warmth of his hands.

"That may be," Oliver said on a sigh, though he recovered in the same instant. "But all the more reason to look around you for the man you want, milady. It is to your advantage to choose first, and then beguile him so completely that he has no idea in his head except to become your husband."

Astrid slewed around on her bench. "And you know exactly how she should go about this beguilement, I suppose."

"Yes," the Italian said simply.

"Jackanapes."

"Ah, my little love," Oliver crooned, "you repeat yourself with these insults. There is hope for me yet."

Astrid turned to her mistress. "Would you listen to him? Would you?"

Marguerite lifted a brow. "You think I should? Or do you feel I shouldn't?"

"Hah! You are curious. I can see it." The small serving woman turned on David's squire, waving with great extravagance. "Very well, let us have your wisdom, O Lord of Seduction."

He leaned toward her, allowing his voice to drop to a whisper as he answered, "For a man, there is no greater lure than a sweetly shaped and unadorned female."

"A naked female, you mean!" Astrid shrilled. "I knew you would say so! I knew it!"

Oliver spread his hands, his face a study in male truth, though his mustache tilted up on one side. "What else?"

God's teeth, but he should have stopped him at the start.

It was too late to think of that now. David's fingers closed around Marguerite's as the image of her, adorned only by the shimmering, golden-brown veil of her hair, bloomed in his mind. The very personification of temptation, she appeared for him alone, stepping delicately through the storm-tinted darkness, lovely beyond comprehension, and gloriously, deliberately naked, smiling with mystery and promise in the darkness of her eyes.

Curse the Italian for being so vividly graphic.

Curse him a thousand times for being right.

10

Naked . . .

If a naked female was what men were least likely to resist, Marguerite thought, then it might be worth trying. Well, and if she could believe David would be so easily swayed by the sight of unclothed female flesh.

Would he push her away and leave her, as he had this morning, if she were in a state of nature? The need to find out was near irresistible.

His control was formidable. Would it survive such a test?

Oliver seemed to think any naked female would do for a man, that yielding flesh and what he might do with it was all that mattered. What of the face, the mind, what a woman was inside? Did these things mean nothing? Was it all about the urge to shove one body part into another until one of them, usually the man from what she could glean, was satisfied? Or was it that coupling roused men to loving affection, as she had also heard? What a strange and cruel arrangement on the Creator's part, that women needed affection before the ultimate intimacy, while men needed the intimacy before they could feel affection.

"It seems to me this naked female would be in a fine way to having a baby and no husband," Astrid said, her piping scorn interrupting Marguerite's thoughts, "for what man will tie himself forever to a female willing to give herself without it?"

"*Sì,*" Oliver said with a devil's gleam in his eyes, "but as it now stands, a man must tie himself to a female without knowing what she looks like naked, or whether he'll enjoy the bedding."

"Oh, aye," the small serving woman agreed at once. "But what you forget is that it's men who would have it this way, as they make the rules."

"The clergy," David said with a trace of laughter in his voice.

"Men who never marry," Oliver agreed, his voice doleful.

Marguerite joined the round of low laughter mixed with rue, but tucked the thought away in the back of her mind in case it might prove useful.

The thunder and lightning rumbled away

toward the north, but the rain continued. Its damp chill permeated everything, making the fire that burned so bright on the great hearth feel like a benediction. Astrid, being closer to the floor where the air currents shifted, complained of being cold. Oliver offered to escort her to the chamber above for her cloak, and the two of them departed on this errand. In their absence, David suggested he and Marguerite stroll around the outer edges of the room to warm their blood. As anything seemed better than sitting in silence, she stood and took the arm he offered.

They were not the only ones who felt the need to promenade. David bowed to first one and then another, as did Marguerite. A few words were exchanged here and there, snippets of news and gossip and comments on the king's absence from the hall. It seemed Henry was shut up with dispatches, which had arrived from London. They had been brought by courier. At sometime in the past days, this messenger had arrived in company with an ambassador of some description. His addition along with outriders and a good dozen mercenaries from across Europe, had filled the hall to capacity.

It was only as Marguerite and David

circled three-quarters of the way about the hall that the crowd thinned, leaving them private enough for speech between them. Marguerite searched her mind for something to say, but found little she and David had not already discussed during his convalescence. Braesford Hall, her sisters, their husbands, her nieces and nephews had all been accounted for and their more embarrassing or exciting stories told. She was left with nothing except niggling concern for her patient. His wound was healed enough that he had dispensed with bandaging, and his headache and distorted vision had departed, but he was not yet back to full strength.

"Would you prefer to return to the chamber?" she asked with a quick glance at his set features. "You have been away from your bed for some time now."

"I seem to be less sore while being about. More, I would not have you return too soon to confinement with me."

He sounded distracted, she thought, as if she was not the only one whose thoughts had been busy elsewhere. "It hardly matters as I have no duties otherwise."

"Surely there are things you would rather do?"

"What? Needlework? The light is much

too dim. Besides, we settled how I feel about the art."

A smile came and went across his face. "So we did." He picked up her left hand and spread her fingers, turning them this way and that.

"What are you doing?"

"Searching for needle pricks," he replied, his lashes shielding his expression. "Ah, there."

The prick was on the end of her middle finger, one received as she stitched the new shirt he wore, made to replace the one lost in the knife attack. He lifted it to his lips, pressing a kiss to the tiny spot before flicking it with his tongue.

Her arm jerked as if she had been stung by an eel. Immediately, he took the end of her finger into the wet heat of his mouth, drawing upon it with gentle suction.

The tender yet grainy surface of his tongue as it moved upon her sensitive fingertip sent fluttering delight along her arm. It spread through her with the intoxication of strong wine, making her feel light-headed. She walked as if by rote, barely aware of where she moved or who was around her. The hall might have been empty except for her and the man whose warm grasp entrapped her.

That was, until a trilling cry came from a

few feet in front of them.

"Sir David! I heard you were in the hall, but had abandoned hope of seeing you this evening!"

The voice, light and rather childish in its breathless delight, belonged to a petite blonde woman. Resplendent in palest aqua-blue to match her eyes, she gleamed with gems set in heavy gold, especially in girdle-draped hips as slender as one of Henry's white hounds. She fluttered forward with her veil of finest silk swirling behind her and her arms outstretched as if she might fly away if not caught and held.

David released Marguerite in time to take the lady's two hands. He spread them wide, though whether to prevent her from clutching at him or to better admire her charms was impossible to say.

"*Comtesse,*" he said, "I am all amazed. I thought you fixed at Charles's court."

The blonde made a moue of distaste. "My dear husband, the *comte,* was persuaded to act as liaison between our Charles and your king Henry. Naturally, I could not allow him to make this journey alone."

"Naturally."

Was that irony in David's tone? Marguerite could not be sure. Glancing beyond the *comtesse,* she saw a round-faced and rather pompous man with thinning brown hair. His rotund shape strained the seams of a short doublet that was liberally decorated with gold lace in the French style. He bowed in distant acknowledgment, but made no effort to join them.

"We arrived in London only to discover your Henry away upon the chase, this so important hunt. As the *comte* and I adore such exercise, *voilá,* we are here. But you, *cher!* I thought you determined never to set foot on English soil again." The Frenchwoman pulled David's hands toward her, pressing them to her breasts that swelled in rosy curves from her tight bodice.

Marguerite, watching the byplay, was struck by sudden aversion to the excitable and bejeweled *comtesse.* How very odd. She was usually more measured in her likes and dislikes.

"Matters change," David answered, disentangling himself as he turned to present the lady. "Lady Marguerite, permit me to make known to you an acquaintance of some years standing, Celestine, the Comtesse de Neve. We met in Paris, she, the *comte* and I, at the court of the young Charles VIII."

Marguerite said everything that was proper, but could not be surprised when the *comtesse* barely acknowledged the introduction. Nor could she prevent herself from wondering if the *comtesse* had been one of the French ladies who had taught David how to make love to a woman in all the diverse ways he had mentioned. The roguish glances she sent him from under her lashes made it appear all too likely.

"*La,* what days of joy we passed together," Celestine said, touching his arm, then wrapping her fingers around it. "My heart smiles at the memories. The dancing and merriment, the fetes, the fury of the tournaments. Do say you recall!"

"Yes, of course."

David was polite enough, but little more than that. Still Marguerite could not help envisioning this merriment at the bright and rich French court. Had David seen the exquisite *comtesse* naked there? Had he?

"And then, *quelle horreur,* the first thing I hear when the *comte* and I arrive at this wild retreat is news of a grievous wound suffered by the Golden Knight. My eyes assure me this was a gross exaggeration, yet you have not been seen until now. Are you quite well again? Will you ride out on the hunt promised for the morrow?"

There was a challenge in the woman's heart-shaped face, Marguerite thought. Toward what end she could not imagine, but she longed to answer her quick, amused questions with a resounding negative.

"I am well, as you see," David answered in grave assurance, "and will naturally join the king in whatever capacity he commands."

"Excellent. I long for this chase with you at my side, for there is little other entertainment in this great stone pile." The *comtesse* turned to Marguerite. "And you, *chère?* Will you be joining us?"

It was the last thing Marguerite wanted, especially as the rain continued to pound on the hall's high roof, sluicing from its eaves into the inner court. If it continued, the hunt would be cold, wet, muddy and miserable.

"Why not?" she inquired with her most genial smile.

"Marguerite, I don't believe . . ." David began.

"I am as fit as you, I feel sure."

How he might have answered that was unknown, for Oliver returned then. His face was grim as he walked up to them, the look in his dark eyes distinctly wary as they rested upon the *comtesse.* The lady, for her part, acknowledged his bow with the brief nod one might bestow on a servant.

"Lady Marguerite," Oliver said, turning

to her, "Astrid asked that I tell you she still feels cold, and means to seek her pallet for the night. She awaits you in Sir David's chamber, but prays you will not cut short your evening to join her there."

The brows of the *comtesse* climbed her low forehead almost to her hairline. Speculation appeared in her pale blue eyes as she stared from Marguerite to David, and then back again. "A thousand pardons if I misunderstood," she said with a brittle smile. "I had not heard of a marriage."

"No," David said before she could go on.

"No," Marguerite said at the same time. "It is a temporary arrangement at the king's order."

"How very intriguing."

"A matter of caring for his wound," Oliver put in, his voice smooth yet freighted with such suggestion he might as well have proclaimed Marguerite to be David's concubine. "You heard of it?"

"We were speaking of it just now," the *comtesse* said with biting precision.

"A vicious thrust, it was," the Italian went on. "It's a thousand wonders he survived. A lesser man would not have done."

"Oliver," David said in warning.

"The truth is the truth." The Italian turned back to the *comtesse*. "How long did you say you have been in residence?"

"Oh, some days now. We arrived not long after this competition began in which you, Sir David, must have been injured. Though I feel sure the contests cannot have been as thrilling as the tournaments of France, I am sorry to have missed the excitement."

Marguerite had little to say to a female who could speak of the mock battle of tournament as mere entertainment. These brutal affairs took place more often on the continent than in England. The thirty years of the War of the Roses had so decimated the noble families of England that people had lost their taste for unnecessary fighting, unnecessary bloodshed.

"I am astounded that I've not seen you about," Oliver said to the *comtesse.*

"Oh, I picked up a fever on the journey from London, so went straight to bed on our arrival." Celestine gave a light laugh. "Picture me shivering and quaking in misery, as much the invalid as Sir David, I promise you. The *comte* quite feared for my life. But the chatelaine, Lady Joan, was a tower of strength, quite literally. Is she not a tall one? And now I am quite well again, as you see."

"You are to be congratulated," Marguerite said shortly. "Now you must excuse me while I see to my serving woman. I fear Astrid has overtaxed her strength, running up and down during these days just past. Or could be the fever you brought with you is now among us."

She half expected David to join her, but he did not. In all fairness, it would be less than polite for him to desert the lady when she had just sought him out. Oliver, it seemed, was back in his position as David's guard, for he stood alert and pugnacious at his side, with not the slightest move to offer himself as escort. Marguerite moved off with only her own thoughts for company.

It was a relief to be away, she told herself. She had no need of either man to walk with her. The way to the chamber was not overly long, just across the hall, up the great stone staircase and along a corridor or two. To be alone and able to let down her guard was a rare luxury. She was also perfectly willing to admit to being bone weary and eager for her own pallet.

She caught a glimpse of Lord Halliwell from the corners of her eyes when she was within striking distance of the stairs. A few more steps and she could disappear up them before he noticed her. She was not certain of outdistancing him, however, and the last thing she wanted was to be caught in some dim stairwell or corridor lit only by a single smoking torch. She kept her steady pace.

"My dear Lady Marguerite," the nobleman called out. "What felicity to see you again after this long absence. Where do you fly in such a hurry? Does your Golden Knight await your coming?"

Innuendo layered his voice, and his eyes were avid as they roamed over her. Marguerite's stomach muscles clenched and she curled her fingers into fists. If Lord Halliwell was unaware that she had left David somewhere behind her, it seemed best not to point out his error.

"My serving woman, rather," she said without inflection as she made to move around him. "She may be ill, and I should go to her."

He reached out to close his fingers around her forearm. "Not yet. I have wished for a chance to speak to you."

"Toward what purpose, sir? I regret that you have been disappointed in the matter of our betrothal, but you must see it's fruitless to pursue it."

"Unless Henry should change his mind."

"That seems unlikely."

"Now why is that? What do you know that I don't?"

She shook her head. Her veil brushed against her cheek, and she reached to hold it back while conquering the urge to clamp her teeth upon a corner in an excess of nerves. "Nothing at all, I do assure you."

"I do swear there's more, and I'll know what it is before I'm finished. You'll not play me for a fool."

She could sympathize with him in some sense. They were both pawns in this game Henry played. Yet she knew Halliwell had agreed to his part in it and been duly compensated. It was unrealistic of him to expect to change the results because he was dissatisfied.

"No one is playing you for anything, my lord."

"I see it differently, especially when a female knows more of affairs of great moment than I've been told. Why was this David of Braesford brought into it? What is the business about? Why could I not take whatever part he's been given?"

It was ludicrous to think of this shrunken, egotistical graybeard with his temper and grown son, playing a golden Plantagenet prince. A smile twitched one corner of her mouth before she could stop it.

"You dare laugh at me?" he exclaimed in fury, his grip digging into her arm like a falcon's talons. "I told you before what will happen to you when you are mine."

"And what will you do to bring that about?" she demanded as anger routed her apprehension. "Will you abandon all honor for the sake of your wounded pride? Will you hire some mercenary to take me unaware, the way you did Sir David? Will you attempt to have me killed if you can't work your will any other way?"

His grip loosened and his sagging features grew slack. "I don't know what you're prattling about."

"I hope for your sake that's true." She twisted from his grasp, taking a hasty step toward the stairs. "David is almost well again. I pity you if he should discover that you lie."

David watched, his breath caught in his throat, as Marguerite threw off the hold Lord Halliwell had upon her arm then left the man standing, mouth agape, as she disappeared up the stairs. Almost, he had gone to her aid. That it had been unnecessary left him awash in a peculiar mix of pride and chagrin: pride that she had stood up to the man, chagrin that she had not required his intervention.

He wanted her to need him. And wasn't

that the height of irony, when what he was doing could well make it certain she never did?

It was a dire chance he was taking, rousing her desire, stoking her curiosity about the marriage bed. What guarantee did he have that she'd ever release him from his vow? What if some other man stepped in and reaped the benefit?

Time was growing short for seduction. Any day now, Henry might wake and give the order to return to London. He could set his plan for a decoy pretender in motion at the same time. Whether Marguerite would ride to Westminster with the king or be sent elsewhere was impossible to know, but they would almost certainly be separated.

To press forward, increasing the intimacy between them, seemed necessary. A fine line lay between enough and too much, however. He did not intend to cross it, but how was he to restrain the ferocious impulses that racked him? She was so incredibly sweet and without artifice, so innocently carnal. He could have her, he knew. All he had to do was abandon honor.

Christ above, but high principles could be a curse!

It was no easy task, breaking free of Celestine, the Comtesse de Neve, and her endless reminiscences of Paris. She had been his lover, or he had been hers. The affair had lasted a week. The *comtesse* had enjoyed coming secretly to him dressed as a servant, had been adept at helping remove his armor. She professed to be stirred profoundly by the scent of horse and sweat upon firm muscles that had been well-oiled by hard effort, and proved it by rubbing her naked body over his until they both smelled the same. She'd enjoyed riding him as much or more than being underneath him. She liked it hard and fast, and rougher than he'd been willing to supply. When she'd moved on to another man, he'd not minded at all.

It was clear she was not averse to taking up where they had left off. He was diplomatic in the extreme, but allowed her to understand that his interest lay with Marguerite. Far from being heartbroken, the *comtesse* shrugged and began a discreet flirtation with a burly man-at-arms.

The rain still pecked against the shutter over his chamber's narrow window when he reached it. All was dark within, especially when he closed the door behind him. He stepped with care and the sour hope that the locations of the pallets being used by Astrid and Marguerite were in the same positions as before. They must have been,

for he had a clear path to his own low bed
with its stumps of wood for legs.

Feeling the frame of it against his shins,
he undressed in a few swift moves and
lowered himself to it. The crackling of its
straw and creak of the rope supports were
loud in the stillness. He winced as he waited
to see if he had awakened anyone, particularly Marguerite whose pallet lay against the
near wall, at a right angle that put her head
just below his own. She didn't stir, however,
and he relaxed by slow degrees.

Minutes passed. David lay listening to
Astrid's soft, snuffling snores and the falling
rain. He was glad that he was not out in the
chill, drenching wetness beyond the shutters. He'd spent many a night in such
discomfort, would likely spend many more.
He could not imagine this feint of Henry's
would be accomplished without many evenings spent riding between widely scattered
meeting places, speaking to gatherings of
yeoman farmers and younger sons, persuading them of the rightness of his claim to the
throne.

His claim. What in the name of heaven
was he doing?

David's skin prickled at the thought, causing the brand on his shoulder to itch.
Reaching up, he soothed it as he had a

thousand times before. It felt smooth yet slightly raised, so he easily followed it with his fingertips, tracing the interlocking circles by rote. Marguerite had asked about it, but he had little to tell her. He could not remember how he had come by it, could not recall a time when it wasn't there. It was simply a part of him in the same way some people had birthmarks. This was not a natural blemish, however, but a brand made by hot iron so long ago it had become a pale scar on the sun-browned surface of his shoulder.

Not that he'd ever seen it, of course. Others had, the women who came to him, the men he fought on the practice field, even Oliver. None had made him so aware of it as Marguerite. He could still feel her fingers smoothing over, or so it seemed, still feel her lips upon it.

He might have dreamed that part of it, of course. Most likely he had.

Flinging to his side, he let his arm drape over the edge of the bed so his fingers grazed the stone floor. Something light and fine touched his hand. He flinched before he realized it must be hair, Marguerite's hair. Usually, she wore it confined in a braid for sleeping. She seemed to have left it loose this night, mayhap because Astrid had been asleep, so unable to plait it properly for her. Its great length would have spread around her as she turned in her sleep.

It was as soft and silken as an angel's wing. The need to slide his fingers deeper into it was more than he could withstand. Faint warmth lingered among the strands. They seemed to have life of their own, as fine, individual hairs clung to his knuckles, his calluses and the rough edges of old injuries. If he wanted to be fanciful, he could imagine they pulled at him, urging him down to the floor, nearer their owner. And he wanted that, needed it, with a power that clamored in his blood, gripped his chest and turned his body to tempered steel.

He longed to stretch out beside Marguerite on her pallet, to pull her close against him, matching curve to curve, breath to breath. He wanted to wake her with the softest of kisses, the most devious of caresses, to incite a thousand sensations that would urge her to turn in shivering surrender. How many times had he possessed her in fervid imagination? How many years had he dropped into sleep with that image burning in his mind?

This was as close as he had ever been, as close as he might ever be.

The warmth in her hair was caused by her

arm that lay beneath its silken cover. He sensed the shape of it and fingered carefully along its length to her wrist. She must be half off her pallet, with her arm flung along the stone floor as if reaching for his bed.

A silent oath feathered his lips as he wondered if she was growing cold, if the rest of her was covered, and what he should do to make her more comfortable. He couldn't just turn over and go to sleep now, not while thinking she might wake up stiff and chilled or even ill.

Astrid was asleep, almost literally dead to the world. He could wake her to see after her mistress, but not without disturbing Marguerite. He didn't want to do that, in part because her nights had been disturbed enough lately, but also because he'd as soon not admit to fondling her in the darkness.

There was only one thing to be done.

Berating himself with battlefield curses in a dozen different languages, David eased from the bed and went to one knee beside Marguerite's pallet. Using only the sensitive tips of his fingers, staring blindly into the blackness above her, he skimmed over the shape of her under a thin summer coverlet, locating the curve of her hip and the bend of her knee. As he had thought, she was lying more on the floor than on her pallet, had somehow rolled over in her sleep so she rested on her stomach.

He eased his hand higher, brushed over her shoulder that was veiled in fine strands of hair. His breath stopped in his chest.

Her shoulder was not covered.

Her shoulder was naked of cover of any kind.

His brain ceased to function for endless seconds. When it began again, it scattered in a dozen directions. Many people slept naked, particularly in summer. They did, of course they did.

Marguerite had not in all the time she had shared his room. She had slept in her clothing, wrapped in her coverlet as if encased in armor.

What did it mean that she was naked now? Could it be an invitation? Should he have returned much earlier and discovered her? Had she been waiting for him in her state of undress?

Did it mean anything at all? Or was she merely weary of being confined in her clothing during the night?

Either way, he could not leave her on the cold, damp floor. She must be chilled, lying there.

Touching her hair, he followed the strands to where they sprang from her head to find her forehead. She was cool, right enough, her skin soft, fine-grained and satin-smooth under the roughness of his palm.

He had best finish what he'd started, before he did something he would regret.

Bending, he slid his hands underneath her, expecting to encounter the edges of her coverlet. It wasn't there. His fingers skimmed beneath her shoulder to find purchase on warm, naked skin. One hand cupped, unerringly, the sweet, round globe of a breast, the other spread over the soft flat surface of her lower abdomen.

Sweat broke out along his backbone, pooling between his shoulder blades. His palms felt on fire. His mouth watered with desperate need to taste the smooth, warm flesh in his grasp. His lower belly clamped down while his braies bulged with his body's sudden tumescence.

God and all his saints aid him.

Clamping his teeth together, he began to lift her, easing her gently back onto her pallet. She stirred, murmuring as she turned toward him. Abruptly, she drew a sharp, gasping breath and stiffened in his hold.

"Don't scream," he whispered as he hovered over her, trying not to think of where his hands were placed. "It's not what you think."

She breathed again, put a hand on his arm for leverage as she righted herself then eased to a sitting position. The shift of position removed her luscious curves from his hands. He groaned at their loss before he could stop himself.

Her fingers tightened upon his arm. "Are you sure it isn't what I think?" she asked, the words as soft as a sigh.

11

She had fallen asleep. How could she have done that?

Marguerite's intention had been to wait for David and sit up as he entered the chamber, artlessly exposing her naked state. Both Astrid and Oliver had said men found that difficult to resist, had they not? Why should he be different?

After a time, the murmur of the rain had made her sleepy. The wick in the small lamp had burned away to nothing, leaving her in darkness. To close her eyes for a moment had seemed harmless.

If she had been awake when he'd first put his hands upon her, she might have feigned sleep and waited to see what he would do next. Having removed herself from his grasp, she would never know. She could have cried. Not only would it have solved her dilemma of how to begin his seduction, but the ripples of pleasure where his hands had been made her think it might have been quite glorious.

She had indicated her willingness to go further. What happened next was up to him. She waited with her heart trembling inside her to discover it.

"You were half on the floor and . . . and I thought you would be chilled," he said, the words a quiet rasp in the darkness. "I only meant to make you more comfortable."

"You touched me."

"It was an accident. I didn't know . . ."

"Didn't know I had thrown off my clothes. I understand." She paused to steady her voice. "It was a mistake, I think, for the night is damp and cool and . . . and the coverlet not enough to warm me."

"You don't know what you are saying," he whispered.

"Do I not? Or is it that you don't want to hear?"

"Oh, I want it, but . . ."

"I've heard much of your prowess with the ladies, but have seen little of it." How she dared say such a thing, she hardly knew. It was as if some more bold spirit had taken possession of her while she slept.

"You've heard — Oliver. I'll wring his neck for him."

"Now, why?"

"He interferes where he should not."

She had thought the same thing a time or two. "Why would he do that?"

"Pure meddlesome spite, because he thinks he knows best, knows my mind better than I do. He thinks he knows what I — God, Marguerite, I'm only a man, and I've so longed . . ."

"For what?" she asked, the words a mere breath of sound.

"To touch you even more." He settled a hand upon her waist in the dark, slid his arm to circle her and draw her up to her knees. Tethered to him by that hard support, she leaned into his strength. "I will not, cannot, take you," he went on against her hair, "but there are sweet pleasures I can show you if you will allow it."

His face was so near she would feel his warm breath against her temple. She turned blindly toward that heat as toward life itself. A great longing pooled inside her. "I could not bear to refuse."

He bent his head and his mouth touched hers, firm and seeking yet incredibly sensual in its smooth surfaces, its tenderness. He brushed against the molded edges of her lips, savoring them with a slow sweep of his tongue's edge as he pulled her closer. Her mouth tingled, swelling with the need for greater pressure, deeper joining. His heat against her cool flesh made her shiver and burrow nearer. The chill tightness she held deep inside began to ease as if she were melting. She relaxed against him with a wordless murmur of need and joy.

He smoothed his palm in circles over her back, easing downward until he captured the turn of her hip. She jerked in surprised pleasure, tilting the softness of her lower body against him. The feeling was so astonishing that she moved against his hard male planes, gathering the fiery, surging sensations it brought in slow discovery. He was so solid and unmovable, his strength forged in fire yet clean and good beyond imagining. The muscles and sinews beneath his skin were a delight, and she swept her hands over them, clasping, smoothing, learning the firm texture and iron hardness of his body. That he held such limitless power in strict obedience to his will while holding her was miraculous. Yet she ached to take it into her, to feel it inside her.

At her soft moan of need, he deepened the meeting of their mouths, plunging inside, brushing the delicate inner surfaces, sliding over her teeth. He sipped the edges of her tongue, drew it into his mouth while lapping the fragile underside.

Greatly daring, she matched his movements, applying suction that brought his
tongue thrusting back into her mouth in
hot demand. Heady pleasure rippled
through her, a tumult of the senses fed by
his hand closing upon her breast, compress-
ing the nipple in rhythmic pulsing.

She was boneless, trembling with a hunger
so deep it was frightening. Her blood
thundered through her veins with primal
force. She thought she was falling, half
fainting, until she realized David was lowering her to her pallet on the floor. He eased
down beside her, his hand spread over her
abdomen as if in possession. He flexed his
fingers, kneading the soft surface while casting lower, ever lower. She tensed, clamping
her thighs together as he slid his hand
between her legs, threaded his fingers into
the fine silk curls to clasp her mound.

"What . . ." she began.

"Shh," he whispered, his lips grazing her
breast, "I won't hurt you."

He wouldn't, and she knew it well. Yet no
one had touched her there in her memory.
The instinct to protect the most vulnerable
center of her being made it difficult to open
to him. It might have taken longer, except
she was distracted as he wet her taut nipple
with his tongue, blew upon it so it knotted

still more, circled it, flicked it with gentle fire.

Heavy urgency filled her. She wanted him closer, wanted him over her, his hard weight against her, upon her. She needed his strength in a way that was beyond understanding.

She reached out to him, trailing her hand along the rough linen of his braies, entranced by the hard ridge that strained against the fabric. The heat of it burned her as she curled her fingers around the long length.

He caught them, transferring her wrist to the hard fingers of his left hand. "No, sweetling. No, this is your lesson."

He wasn't drowning in need and lassitude as she was. He was remote, fixed upon giving her pleasure. And he was doing that with single-minded determination, his long fingers gently probing, separating her fragile folds, easing into her while his thumb circled over a place so sensitive that she hovered between pleasure and pain.

Ah, but he was not entirely unmoved. She could feel the sheen of moisture where his upper body brushed against her, feel the heavy thudding of his heart behind the barrier of his ribs.

He shifted, confining her knees with his

hard thigh as he laid it across them while spreading her thighs wider. She wanted to protest, to break free. That was before he bent his head and took the strutted tip of her breast into his mouth.

All ability to think left her as he laved her with his tongue, suckled her with insistent tugs. She felt the wet slide as he skimmed his tongue down the hillock of her breast to the valley between them. He pressed warm kisses to her stomach, and lower, before nosing into the soft curls at the juncture of her thighs. Shifting, he replaced his caressing thumb with the heat and fervent adhesion of his mouth.

She came apart like precious glass hitting a stone floor, the pieces of her being shattering, scattering under the hardness of his resolve. She swallowed a sob that was half-frantic, gratified joy, half sorrow that she was alone in its glory. Shuddering, she arched toward him, needing to be held to keep her soul from flying out of her body.

He closed his arms around her, rocking her, murmuring into her hair. His hands moved over her, soothing her, pushing away the fire. She felt protected, safe, as if she was where she belonged, had always belonged. Languor seeped into her, pushing her to the edge of sleep.

David was still impossibly strong, impossibly hard against her. That was wrong, she knew, though there was nothing she could do about it. His control was unbreakable, his resistance to temptation supreme. His honor was inviolate.

It was comforting, even gratifying in its way. It was also infuriating. And if she was hurt as well by his ability to resist sharing such completion with her, it was something she refused to admit, even to herself.

David curled his body around Marguerite while he willed his heartbeat to slow and his body to settle down. It wasn't easy, not while the amazing joy of holding her warm and naked body against him simmered in his veins. Her hair tickled him in a thousand places while its scent of sunshine and daisies made his senses reel. Her warm breath against his chest, the feel of her under his hands, satisfied some longing he hadn't known was inside him. He didn't want to move, not now, not ever. For the first time in more than a decade he felt whole, as if he'd been lost and was now found.

How valiant she was to allow him to come to her this way. Her bravery and trust humbled him. The gift of being able to pleasure her was more than he had ever thought to receive. Though he ached to have more, to thrust deep inside her at the peak of need and feel her coalesce around him, to plumb her soft, wet depths until he felt the beat of her heart, he was also content to simply lie and remember and be glad. What would happen on the morrow, next week, next month, he did not know, but at least he'd had tonight.

Astrid made soft snuffling sounds in her dark corner. Still deeply asleep, thank God. The rain had dwindled to a light patter, though it dripped from the roof into the courtyard below. The damp chill of it seeped through the shutter, brushing his fevered skin into a rash of goose bumps. Still, he did not move.

Soon now, he would release Marguerite, easing away, covering her with care. He would return to his own cold and empty bed and try his best to sleep. It was doubtful he would manage it while the taste of her lingered in his mouth, the silken feel of her skin hovered on his hands, spinning over and over in his head. He wasn't sure he wanted to sleep, in truth, not when he could remember instead. He might never sleep again.

He fell into a light doze in his own bed, finally, as morning light began to curl pink fingers around the shutter's edge and a rooster saluted the rain-washed dawn. It lasted barely an hour before Oliver banged his way inside and rousted him out again.

"Up, sir," he growled, thrusting a beaker of ale into his hand. "The king requires your presence in the great hall. You are to have the honor of breaking your fast at the high table."

Oliver's mustache drooped in a dour expression as he made the announcement. David was sure the sentiment was mirrored on his own face. They both knew the king should be taking his ale, beef and bread in his chamber while making ready for the promised hunt. That he was, instead, issuing commands couched as formal invitations did not bode well.

"Lady Marguerite?"

A quick glance had been enough to show her pallet neatly tidied away. She was gone from the chamber, along with Astrid. He should have known. Oliver would not have entered, otherwise.

"Broke her fast in the hall and is now with Lady Joan, awaiting a day in the saddle."

He would like to have seen her before she dressed, awakening to her morning disarray, gloriously naked in the burgeoning light with her hair streaming down her back. He might have snatched a kiss, or even tasted her breast as he cupped it, stroked it, gazed upon its sweet contours instead of learning them in the dark.

There were many things he might have done if men were born equal and life was fair.

"And Astrid?" he asked in gruff courtesy. "She was well when you saw her?"

"As ever was, and like vinegar with it." A sardonic smile crossed his squire's droll features. "The poor little mite was just overtired last night."

"She would 'poor little mite' you, if she heard you."

"Oh, aye." Oliver gave him a narrow look. "And you? Are you well enough to ride out this day?"

David snorted. "I will have to be, won't I?"

"I could make your excuses, say the wound fever is upon you again. The rest could brave the wet and muck while you stay abed with Lady Marguerite to tend you."

The temptation was so strong David felt light-headed with it. Not that he lacked the strength or will to keep up with the king. Still, how sweet it would be to lie abed with Marguerite wrapped up in his coverlet with him while everyone else was away and the rain coming down. For such a day out of time, he could easily forget his duty to his king, forget crowns and plots and honor.

Forget honor, above all else.

David cursed under his breath and rubbed his hands briskly over his face before shoving them through his hair. Pushing up from the bed, he threw on his clothes, pulled on his boots and went to see what Henry wanted of him now.

The king was in a pensive mood, but courteous for all that. Acknowledging David's bow, he waved him to the seat next to his own and piled his trencher with beef from the royal dish. He waited until ale had been poured and the servitor had moved away before he spoke.

"We note that you were in the hall last evening. It is gratifying to us to see you up and about again."

David replied as expected, then waited to see what more would come. Recent days spent hunting had taken some of the strain from the king's face, he thought, but there was trenchant purpose in his gray-blue eyes this morning.

"Lady Marguerite is a capable healer, or so it appears. You are fit to ride?"

That everyone should question his show

of strength was his own fault, David knew. He had deliberately prolonged his convalescence. Part of it was the pleasure of Marguerite's close company, but it was also to protect her. She was safe from Halliwell's attentions while shut away in their chamber, safe also from the snide glances and petty remarks of others. That was beyond the fact that he simply liked lying and watching her as she read to him or stitched a fine seam.

"As you say, sire," he answered.

"You and the lady dealt well together?"

He tipped his head in assent. They had dealt well indeed, particularly the night before, though that was none of the king's affair.

Or was it?

Had Henry somehow divined how matters stood between him and the lady that he asked such a question? For a fleeting instant, David allowed himself to suspect this was the purpose in sending Marguerite to care for him, that Henry meant to see the two of them wed, one way or the other. A part of it could easily be the ruin of Marguerite's good name brought about by the time spent in close quarters with him. Guilt for that undoing could be meant to force him to the altar. Still he could not fathom what purpose of state might be served by it.

That it did, David could not doubt. He liked Henry, approved his rule that combined sternness with forbearance, yet knew him to be something less than open in his dealings. A man did not spend a decade and a half avoiding the trickery and murderous intentions of his royal cousins, Edward IV and Richard III, without learning to be devious in his turn.

"Would you have her ride with us when we depart? Other accommodation can be arranged, but we seek your will before seeing to it."

"Other accommodations?" David kept his gaze on the bread and beef in his hand as he took a bite.

"She might remain here with Lady Joan. Or we will pass a convent or two on the road."

The idea of a nunnery for Marguerite was not new, still everything inside him rose up against it. He chewed with meditative slowness as he thought how to squelch the possibility without committing himself to something barred by his vow.

Henry made an impatient gesture. "Or we might choose another husband for her if you have reconsidered your proposed award for service to the crown."

"No," he said instantly, adding only as an

afterthought, "sire."

"We thought not. Well, then?"

David studied Henry's stern features while facts and inferences assembled in his mind that had nothing to do with Marguerite. "You are ready to go forward as planned to counter the Yorkist threat?"

"The summer is advancing, Warbeck's faction is growing stronger. Reports say his supporters are gathering on the Scots border. If our subterfuge is to be useful, it must be put into place at once. That can't be done here."

"Nor can it be done if I remain in your company, sire. Have you a plan for when and where I am to leave you?"

"An open break will be required. A pretext must be arranged."

David nodded his understanding, though his heart clenched in his chest. A break with Henry would, in essence, be treason against the crown. That crime was punishable by death.

"Afterward, what would you? I mean to say, where am I to go, who should I contact, how am I to proceed?"

"You have no ideas on the subject?"

"Your pardon, sire, but I've given little thought to how a rebellion against you should be mounted."

"You appear to be the only one." Grim humor curled Henry's lips. "As to the logistics of the mock rebellion, we have them to hand."

He turned to gesture to his seneschal who stood behind his chair. The man stepped forward, presenting a leather pouch which he lifted from his belt. Henry accepted it, drew it open to show the rolled sheets of parchment it contained before giving it into David's possession.

"These are . . ." David began.

"Directions to your base of operation, lists of those who will appear to support you, designated places of gathering and so on. Study them well. We will discuss the details as necessary."

David indicated his understanding and acquiescence. A moment later, a useful thought struck him. "If Lady Marguerite rides with me, sire, she may continue to improve my conduct as a future monarch — or at least the pretense of same."

Henry reached up to pull at his bottom lip while thought moved behind his eyes. After a moment, he made a flicking gesture with his fingers. "For our part, you appear regal enough, with fully as much protocol in your grasp as we had when we came to the throne. We had not been brought up to think the crown would be ours, you know, but came to it when those with a better claim perished."

"You are kind to say so." They had perished all right, David thought as he made that polite reply. They had died by sword and axe, the hapless victims of the endless warfare between York and Lancaster. Some claimed this War of the Roses had ended on Bosworth Field, the battle that brought Henry to power. Yet this current insurrection by Warbeck seemed more of the same.

"Nevertheless, it seems you prefer Lady Marguerite to remain at your side. This is your will?"

"It is." David waited, his breath trapped in his gullet.

The king leaned back in his chair, a satisfied smile lighting the solemnity of face. "Excellent. We leave within the hour."

So intent was David on the permission to take Marguerite with him when he went that it was a moment before he could bring his mind to bear on Henry's meaning. "Leave for the hunt?"

"By no means, Sir David," Henry VII answered with a crooked smile. "The time for hunting is over. We are for London and our palace of Westminster."

■ ■ ■ ■

It was nearer two hours before the chaos that followed the king's command settled and the column of horsemen and laden carts could be formed. The lord of the castle and his good lady Joan stood waving from the battlements in misting rain as the cavalcade rode out through the gates. If their farewells seemed a bit hectic, it was no doubt from joy that the king was leaving before their storerooms were stripped completely bare.

David spent the rest of the morning riding up and down the column, settling problems, moving slower carts and wagons to the rear, chivvying stragglers and closing the gaps in the ranks. His own men melded seamlessly with those of the king, he was glad to see, and even surpassed them in discipline and the shine on their armor.

Less impressive by far were the men-at-arms who rode with Lord Halliwell. They made no pretense at formation, much less military precision. Slouching in their saddles as if hungover from the night before, they cursed the mud and wet, their spavined horses and the orders that had dragged them from slumber. They bragged of their conquests among the serving women of the castle and told jokes raw enough to make a Channel sailor blush. Far from pulling them up short, Halliwell and his son joined them in their ribaldry.

David longed to have the disciplining of that company for a single day. Since this was neither his privilege nor his responsibility, he gave them a wide berth. Vigilance was so ingrained, however, that he kept them always under his eye.

In part because of Halliwell's presence on the march, but also for his peace of mind, David maintained a constant watch over Marguerite and Astrid, as well. They rode where he had placed them, in the safe center of the long, ungainly cavalcade. Astrid, wrapped in her cloak with the hood pulled tight around her face, was a picture of misery. Marguerite sat her saddle with straight-backed ease, however, her face framed by the velvet edge of her cloak's hood, her skin dewy from the moist air.

The need to take her upon his saddlebow, to shelter her inside his cloak, against his aching body while kissing away the raindrops that beaded her lashes, was like a knotted fist in his chest. So distracting was the urge that he denied himself the pleasure of riding beside her except for a few minutes here and there. That short time was like a draught of strong wine, both soothing and stimulating.

Not that his attentiveness went unmarked. Grins, snickers and low comments followed him, though hidden the instant he sought out those who dared. Now and then, horsemen crowded Marguerite closer than was seemly. That was until he detailed a guard of his own men to ride ahead of her and behind her.

It was as he had feared. Henry's order that she look after him had robbed her of the respect that was her due. It had been sacrificed to the good of his reign. It was a black mark against him, one that would not be forgotten.

Oliver rode with David for the most part, though he also dropped back to join the ladies now and again. On his return from one such a foray, David gave him a hard stare. His voice was a low growl when he spoke. "If you are so full of energy, you may join the advance riders and report back on what lies ahead of us."

"More muddy road, I'll be bound," Oliver answered with great cheer, "and not much else."

"If it's naught but sheep tracks, I want to know it."

The Italian arched a brow. "*Bene,* but what has you in such a snit? Does your wound pain you?"

"By no means."

"You are overtired then, and wrought at trading your cozy chamber for the saddle."

"No."

"Mayhap it's the presence of a certain *comte* and *comtesse,* and their sudden enjoyment of Lord Halliwell's fine company?"

"Don't play the fool." David had noted the coziness between Halliwell and the French couple, though with little idea of who had instigated it. The aging lord seemed taken with the *comtesse,* but it could easily be that Celestine was bored. If she could not have the blood of the hunt, she would seek it elsewhere. Though if she expected to gain it from him or the *comte,* she would be disappointed. Her husband was far too used to her tricks for jealousy, and David cared not at all who she might take to her bed, or why.

"*Non, bene.* 'Tis the separation from your nursemaid then. I could swear I heard a sweet moan or two last night. Don't tell me, please, that you had nothing to do with it."

The back of David's neck burned under his mailed hood. "What I did or did not do is no affair of yours."

"No, no, but a rainy night and the lady within arm's reach after days of each other's company? Surely you were not so great an idiot as to let such a chance pass you by? In your place, I would have grabbed it, or something, with both hands."

"But you are not in my place," David said with icy menace, "though it seems you would think to be."

"Certainly, being hot-blooded and not backward about such things. The lady intrigues, she remains in the mind far more than those who are merely fair of face. She is made of goodness entire, but intelligent with it. And her passions . . ."

"Are not for you," David said with steel encasing every word.

"But are they for you, my friend? Every man in this draggle-tailed column believes it's so, even the king. You have the repute, so why not the pleasure?"

David gave a short laugh. "Not so long ago, you were warning me against the lady."

"That was before I knew her worth, before I saw her cut your bloody shirt away and stop you from bleeding to death with her bare hands. Allow such fair courage and stout heart to go forever unclaimed, and you play the fool twice over — once for you and once for her."

Hard upon the words, Oliver wheeled his gelding and spurred him into a gallop toward the column's head. David stared after him, his teeth grinding together with such force it made his ears ache.

They rested that night at a priory, a dank and grim religious house where the bread was stale, the wine sour, and the meat limited to a few slivers floating in weak broth. They did not linger past daybreak. The second night came upon them near the newly built manse of some lesser earl, a man who would never have held the title except for the casualties of the recent war. He was embarrassingly pleased to house them, even with but a few hours' notice from the advance riders. While he raided his cellar, his good wife, red-haired, rounded and comely, hounded their cook into a miraculous performance. Between them, they more than made up for the meager fare of the night before.

It had been a clear day at last, but one of hot sun and wind that dried out the mud and turned it to powdery dust underfoot. Men were thirsty, and the wine potent. The faster the libation flowed, the louder grew the company. By the time the cheese and fruit arrived, the noise in the earl's fine hall was a roar.

David, being overtired, could feel the ache from his head wound returning. Marguerite was dropping as well, he thought, while Astrid had simply stretched out on the bench beside her and gone to sleep.

The serving woman's head was in Marguerite's lap. David felt his heart fling itself against the cage of his ribs at the thought of replacing it with his own. Only he would not be sleeping, not with his face and mouth so close to such warm treasure.

The effect of such thoughts was inevitable. Not only did his body harden so fast the stab of it took his breath, but he was suddenly parched for the taste of Marguerite's mouth. With an oath, he rose and stepped over the bench, making for where she sat.

"Your pardon, my lady," he said with a rasp in his voice. "Would you care for a breath of air before you retire for the night?"

A flicker of anticipation appeared in the rich brown depths of her eyes before she lowered her lashes. "I can think of nothing I would like more, but there is this small matter?" She gestured at Astrid.

"Oliver will carry her to wherever you have been assigned to sleep." He glanced around to summon his squire. "Will that serve?"

"Excellently well, though we share a chamber with the young daughters of our host. Their maidservant will show him the way."

Moments later, the thing was arranged. David took Marguerite's arm to help her over the bench then placed her hand on his wrist. Weaving among the tables, he made way through the raucous crowd for the two of them until they passed through the outer door.

The manse was built in the latest fashion, of red brick with a plentiful supply of mullioned windows, fine carving in stone above the door, and minimum effort toward defense. The expanse of a paved and walled court lay before it with a gatehouse to guard the entrance, but there was no true bailey, no portcullis or bridged moat.

Torches flared in their mounts along the outer wall, casting shadows that leaped and danced over the stone ledge that surmounted it. A gray tabby cat, the storehouse mouser, sat on the steps. It rose to follow them, winding around Marguerite's ankles. As they reached the gatehouse, the men-at-arms on duty, the king's own, saluted and allowed them to pass.

Beyond the manse lay a stretch of dirt road, a pale thread in the light of a sickle moon. Black shadows lay upon it, moving gently with the breeze stirring the tree limbs which cast them. David walked in that direction, driven by purpose as imperative as it was wrong. In an effort to disguise his less than worthy intentions, he spoke almost at random. "You will be weary after our long ride today. I would not keep you from your rest for long."

"It matters not at all," she returned.

They walked on a few steps before he found voice again. "You were all right as you rode? No one offered you insult or —"

"No."

He didn't care for that bald answer, nor did he believe it entirely. "I'm sorry that you have been made the butt of wags and gossips. It was never my intention."

"I know."

"I would change it if I could."

"Nothing of it was your fault," she answered with a firm shake of her head. "You would not be in England had I not sent for you. I would not have sent for you if Henry had not arranged my betrothal. We would not be here if Henry had not played us false. Henry would not have chosen his ruse if not for Perkin Warbeck. Warbeck would have no claim if the sons of Edward IV had not disappeared from the Tower. Where does the blame end?"

"Yes, but . . ."

Marguerite stopped, gripping his arm so he paused in midsentence. She half turned to stare back over her shoulder.

"What is it?" he demanded.

"I'm not sure. I thought I heard something."

"The cat, most likely."

"She's here, beside me."

"She?"

"If a male, he's enormously fat," she said with humor in her voice.

"You would notice."

David's comment was light as he probed the darkness along the walled enclosure behind them. He saw nothing to cause alarm, but did not doubt Marguerite's instinct. The sound could have been anything, however, a bird, a servant throwing out scraps, a stray dog hoping to benefit from such largesse, or a man relieving himself after overindulgence in the good wine of their host.

After a moment, he walked on. Marguerite glanced back again, but fell into step beside him.

It was gratifying beyond words to be away from the constant noisy presence of their companions of the road. The air was fresh,

the night wind pleasantly cool. Their footsteps made little sound in the sandy dirt.
The grass they brushed in passing was wet
with dew. The leaves of the oaks that bor-
dered the road had a glassy glitter in the
moonlight, and their shadows covered them
like a dark gray blanket.

Deliberately, David moved deeper into the
darkness until they were even with the trunk
of the great oak. He stopped, then caught
Marguerite around the waist and set her
back to its rough bark.

"David," she whispered.

"I'm sorry for the ploy, but I must . . ."

He kissed her because she drew him like a
wasp to nectar. He kissed her because it had
been an endless two days since he tasted
her lips. He kissed her because Oliver had
goaded him, because he was a fool without
strength of will and because he wanted her
with such blind anguish that he would die if
he did not at least touch her. He kissed her
because sliding his tongue into the moist
heat of her mouth was all he could allow
himself. He kissed her because he must.

And, God, it was sweet enchantment and
everything he'd dreamed. But it was not
enough, would never be enough.

He shivered as she spread her hands over
his doublet, sliding them upward to clasp

them behind his neck. Inhaling in tried control, he eased closer, pressing the heated ridge that tortured him against her while he freed a hand to seek the swell of her breast. The tight, sweet knot of her nipple nudged his palm and he circled over it again and again in mindless fascination. And all the while he plumbed the depths of her mouth, twined around her tongue and showed her in silent mime what he longed to do if only he was allowed.

It was the cat that warned him.

It hissed and leaped in sudden fright, barreling into the calves of his legs. Swifter than thought, he tore away from Marguerite and whirled to shield her. In the same move, he drew his only weapon, his eating knife.

They rushed at him out of the dark, two men with swords glinting in their hands. With no time for finesse, David flipped his knife and threw it with hard and deadly purpose. Before the thud of it striking was heard, he ducked beneath the other man's whistling slash that should have taken off his head. He slammed a booted foot into his knee in the same instant. As the assailant howled in pain, David caught his wrist in a crushing, two-handed grasp and twisted. An instant later, he stood over the body of one attacker, hand fisted on the hilt of the sword he had snatched from his lax fist, breathing hard while he watched the other hobble away into the night with one arm dangling. Watched, also, as another dark figure emerged from the nearby shadows and scurried after the injured attacker.

He could chase the men down and demand answers, but that would leave Marguerite unprotected. Well, and he thought he knew why he had almost been killed, expected them to try again.

Behind him, Marguerite sighed as if letting out a held breath. Moving with the slow steps of a waking nightmare, she came to him. She said nothing, but only slid her arms around him while tremors shook her like an ague. He closed his own around her, squeezing his eyes shut with such force his lashes pricked the skin around them as he tried not to think what might have happened to her if he had died in the assault.

Marguerite put her head against his chest and held him tight.

And he let her.

12

"Murder! Murder!"

The cry went up as the body of the slain man was brought into the hall and laid upon the floor. Gasps, startled grunts and the buzz of conjecture rose to the coffered ceiling overhead. Men gathered around, staring down at the corpse that still had a knife buried to the hilt in the chest, David's eating knife with its handle of ebony chased in gold.

Marguerite drew near the dead man with all the rest. She had returned to the hall with David, though he had left her in the care of the manse's red-haired lady while he gathered men to bring the dead assailant inside. The onlookers parted now, and she saw for the first time the man's lifeless features, gray and blank-eyed with surprise in the flickering lamplight.

She swayed as appalled recognition washed over her.

Halliwell.

The attacker who had tried to kill David was the man she had almost married. He had defied the curse by declaring his intent to force her to the altar. Now the curse had taken him.

The man's son thought otherwise.

"My father has been most foully murdered," he shouted, "and there stands the man who did it. All know his fancy knife!"

He was pointing at David where he stood on the far side of the body. David, who watched them all. His eyes were guarded yet alert and his fair hair gleamed like strands of gold in the flickering lamplight, though he made no effort at defense.

Cold terror skimmed down Marguerite's back.

"No!" she cried, shoving forward. "Lord Halliwell and another man came at us out of the dark. David struck in defense against men armed with swords. But for his great strength and skill at knife throwing, it's he who would lie dead here."

Halliwell's son turned on her. "You defame my father's name. Never would he stoop to so base a deed."

"His death says otherwise," she answered with a lift of her chin.

"So you claim, a wanton unfit for the title

of lady. What did you out in the darkness with this Golden Knight? Answer me that! What magic have you that makes men sniff after you like dogs?"

"Sir!"

"Halliwell!" David's voice crackled with warning.

Halliwell's son plunged on, unheeding. "My father was the same, obsessed beyond reason. You were promised then snatched away, and he meant to have his due, meant to have you at all costs. You must be Satan's own, that you bewitched him so."

Dismay gripped Marguerite at the accusation, clashing with the fury and humiliation inside her. It was a serious charge, the use of black magic to bewitch a man. She could hear the murmurs of condemnation, sense the subtle drawing away of those around her. Among them was the Comtesse Celestine, her eyes avid in her pale face. She leaned to whisper in her husband's ear, though the Comte de Neve winced away with an expression of fastidious distaste.

This danger had always hovered within the curse of the Graces, Marguerite knew, the possibility that she and her sisters would be accused in the deaths attributed to it. So many years had passed, however, near fifteen or more since Isabel first invoked its protection. Marguerite had come to think the worst could never befall.

She had been wrong.

Her gaze went to David. Rage burned like blue flames in his eyes as he shoved his way toward her. The prospect of his support gave her added courage.

"The fault was your lord father's," she said as she turned back to Halliwell's son. "He was unreasoning in his claim upon me."

Hot color flared in the man's narrow face. "You declared before all that my father would die, and here he lies. You are a witch who caused him to be killed. For that, you should burn!"

Cries went up, shouts and yells edged with madness at the prospect of taking a witch. Hands reached out, clamping on Marguerite's arms, clutching at her clothing. She was pinched, struck, pulled this way and that so she stumbled on the hem of her gown.

Suddenly Astrid was beside her. The small serving woman screeched and yelled as she shoved at those who would lay hands on her mistress, beating at them with her small fists.

"Hold!"

The shout came from David. It was followed by the rasp of steel as he snatched a knife from the belt of the nearest man. Behind him was Oliver, his own dagger in his hand.

The hubbub grew louder, ringing with curses and threats. Marguerite felt as if her arms were being pulled from their sockets. A man grasped her backside, pulling her against him, rubbing his hard body over her. Through those crowding around her, she could see Halliwell's men-at-arms gathering at the back of the fallen peer's son who was now Lord Halliwell in his turn.

"Silence! Cease and desist in the name of the king!"

That shouted order, in the ringing accents of Henry's seneschal, stilled the room like a death wind. Men and women spun toward the sound. A soft exclamation rang out. The rustling of clothing and creaking of knee joints filled the quiet as the company jerked into a flurry of bows and curtsies at the rapid approach of their sovereign.

"Release Lady Marguerite," Henry VII said with precision, his voice echoing through the hall.

"But, Your Majesty," the new Lord Halliwell began in protest.

"The lady is our ward, therefore under our protection. Whatever her fate, we shall decide it." Henry waited, his face implacable, until every hand was removed from Marguerite's person and she stood alone. He turned toward David, then, and a path immediately cleared between the two.

"Well, sir. Have aught to say in your defense?"

"It was as Lady Marguerite told, Your Majesty."

"An attack from out of the dark, the result of a quarrel over her betrothal."

"Two men armed with swords came upon us by stealth as we took the air. I slew one and took his sword. The other ran away. A third man who watched followed after him."

"Nay, sire!" Halliwell cried in agitation. " 'Twas the woman. She drew my father there with her wicked ways to cause his death, she and her familiar."

"Familiar?" Henry raised a skeptical brow.

"Her cat. 'Tis well-known Satan keeps company with witches in the guise of a feline. Black it was, and close by her side."

A murmur ran around the room. Those nearest Marguerite made the sign of the cross. She almost did the same as horror skimmed like an icicle down her back. There had been a cat. Indeed, there had been . . .

"You were *there*," she said in abrupt discovery as she turned on Halliwell. "You saw the cat in the dark and thought it black.

You were the third man, else how would you know of it?"

"The cat was gray, and here she is!" Astrid cried in shrill triumph. She reached to pick up the feline that had followed them inside and was winding around her short legs. Grunting, she held the enormously pregnant mouser aloof.

Halliwell's son blanched. "I swear," he began.

"Leave us," Henry said in deadly pronouncement.

"But, sire!"

"Take the body of your father and be gone. Return to the estates that are now yours, and remain until given leave to come to us again. We consider the loss of your father and our favor as just punishment, but may change our mind if forced to hear more wild accusations. Go now, while you may."

Halliwell paled and his lips trembled. He lacked the arrogant confidence of his father, for he said not another word. Bowing, gathering his men with a jerk of his head, he backed away. He did not stop until he was out the door and swallowed up by the dark.

The king swept a hard glance over those who surrounded Marguerite. They moved away, including the *comte* and *comtesse,* making way for David who paced forward to stand at her side in a most public gesture of protection. She felt the strength that radiated from him, felt, too, his relief at the passing of the crisis. She could not share the last, however, for she was far from certain this confrontation was at an end.

Nor was she wrong.

Henry faced David, an intent expression on his long face. The two men exchanged a considering stare while the low hum of comment died away and the great hall was still once more. Tension thrummed in the air, pulling tighter with every breath drawn by the two men.

"We must ask again," the king said in tones of flat rebuke, "if this attack was over no more than the revoke of Lady Marguerite's betrothal."

"I can conceive of no other cause," David answered.

Henry's expression did not change. "None?"

David watched his sovereign for an instant longer before squaring his shoulders. "None, sire."

"Sire," Marguerite began, only to snap her lips shut again. She had almost spoken without leave, almost lodged a protest against something that could not be made public. That the silent communication between David and king had bearing upon it was a prospect that sent a rush of dread like poison along her veins.

The king flashed a look of warning in her direction, though he spoke to David still. "We accept your evaluation. Regardless, Halliwell was a good and loyal subject until this recent event. His death cannot pass without an accounting."

Speculation ran through the crowd. Men pushed closer now, the better to hear. David stood with his head high and eyes blazing with blue fire in his set face. "Should I have allowed myself to be killed, sire?"

"You might have acted with less force, less finality."

There was something going forward, gaining momentum with every word. Marguerite's chest ached with every hard-pressed breath she took. Her eyes burned as she stared from one man to the other.

"So I might, if there had been time," David answered. "Yes, and assurance that the lady with me would not suffer if I failed."

"Enough!" Henry thundered. "You have a witness to your act of defense, so must be absolved of the charge of murder. Nevertheless, we can tolerate no dissension among our followers, nor will we countenance any feud that may come from it. As the son of the man you killed was banished from our sight, so, too, are you, David of Braesford."

"You believe I created this feud."

David faced the king in challenge, feet planted wide. Why would he say such a thing? Henry must know it was not possible, not unless . . .

Marguerite's stomach twisted in dread as presentiment touched her.

Henry's smile was edged with iron. "We believe you love fighting too much, so may have courted the attack against you."

"What, to entice Halliwell to his death? So I might, if I had been certain he paid to have me killed before."

"Our sources say he did, as must yours. Nevertheless, we cannot allow you to usurp our royal right of judgment. More, we have come to think you have too much the look of a Plantagenet about you for our comfort."

David stared at the king while a white line appeared about his mouth. "You would accuse me of treason, sire?"

Dear God in his heaven. This was it, the moment for which all the lessons, all the preparations, had been undertaken. It had come sooner than expected. Yet it made sense to use the excuse of Halliwell's death for its launch.

Cold, Marguerite felt so deadly cold as the recognition settled inside her. With a portion of her mind, she was aware of the *comtesse* somewhere behind her as the Frenchwoman gasped then murmured to her husband in agitation.

"A Plantagenet is always a Yorkist under the skin," Henry stated. "All it requires is the right circumstances to prove it."

"This is a mistake."

"As to that, time will tell. Go! Go now, before we have you clamped in irons for the remainder of this journey, and then lodged in the Tower."

"And Lady Marguerite?"

She quelled inside as every eye in the hall turned upon her once more. Her heart lodged in her throat. So much depended on the answer to the question, so very much.

Henry's stare was grim with condemnation. "It appears she made her choice in these days just past, as well as tonight. Take her. Mayhap you can tame the witch, if such she turns out to be."

David's hot gaze met hers, held it with what seemed dire warning layered with supplication. Slowly, as if he doubted her response, he held out his hand.

She could go or she could stay. Either way, her life would never be the same. Henry had said her choice had been made, but that was not so. The choice was now, here, in this moment.

As if in a dream, Marguerite reached out to place her hand in David's strong, warm clasp. It closed around her fingers with sure strength. He drew her close to his side, within the curve of his free arm. Together, they moved toward the doorway.

"Wait, milady! Wait for me!"

It was Astrid, pushing, sliding, crawling among the legs of those who would bar her way. She was losing her veil, was red-faced and tearful with frustrated anger and something more that looked like grief. Trotting to them in breathless haste, she stopped at Marguerite's side and turned to face the others with her bottom lip thrust out and her hands knotted into tiny fists.

Marguerite reached down to rest her hand on Astrid's shoulder. She suddenly felt less alone, less at bay. As the three of them retreated toward the entrances, she scanned those who watched, searching for one other, for Oliver. Surely he would not let David go without him?

He had vanished. His rakish, rascal's face was nowhere to be seen in the crowd.

Now they were in the doorway. David came to a halt. He turned, his gaze clashing with that of Henry VII there in the dim hall filled with lamplight and night shadows.

"You will regret this decision, sire," he said, his voice ringing in the strained quiet. "I would have served you well all my days. Now that you force this exile upon me, I will claim my birthright."

"Your birthright," Henry said with grim disdain. "It's well-known you are a bastard."

"That I am not. I am Edward V, once a boy king, though the crown was taken from me and I was made a prisoner in the Tower. I am Edward, and you hold what is mine. Neither you nor the pretender who claims to be my brother can keep me from my place. I am Edward, rightful heir to the throne, rightful King of England!"

Astrid gasped, muttering something that was drowned in the babble of consternation that followed. It rose, filling the great vaulted space as men stared wildly around at each other. In it, Marguerite turned her head to stare at the man who held her so close. Her heart beat high in her throat and tears burned the backs of her eyes.

Edward Plantagenet, heir to the throne of England, or David?

He stood tall and golden, gilded with fiery light as if every flickering ray in the vast space was drawn to him. His head was high, his shoulders straight and wide, and pride as natural as breathing shone in the clear blue of his eyes. He seemed invincible, unstoppable, beyond death or fear of it.

He looked every inch a prince with the God-given right to be king.

Terror such as she had never known struck through Marguerite like a lance to the heart. David had declared for the throne as Edward V, and now every hand would be against him. Henry and the Lancastrians who held power from his reign could not let him live. Warbeck must seek his death, as would those who supported the pretender. David would be hunted from one end of England to the other. No place would be safe. Every mercenary within a thousand miles would vie for the price on his head. No man could be counted a friend without reservation.

How was he to survive?

She felt rather than saw him breathe deep. He released her hand but kept her still against him. Lifting his right arm in salute and challenge, he called out to those before him.

"I am Edward, rightful King of England! Who is with me? I am Edward of England! Follow me!"

As if released from some dread spell, the

men of his company, some fifty strong, surged forward. With them came no small number of the king's men. Shouting, laughing, they surrounded David and her beside him, sweeping them out into the night. They clattered in a great mass down the stone steps of the manse, surging into the courtyard.

As they ran, a horseman galloped from the stables hidden in the gloom. He led three horses behind him.

Oliver! It was Oliver.

The Italian reined to a jolting halt and sprang down. Catching Astrid under the armpits, he threw her up on her pony. In the same moment, David helped Marguerite mount, and then swung to his own saddle. Behind them was chaos as his newly declared followers swarmed the stable. Oliver must have warned the stable hands, for more saddled mounts waited.

In a trice, they were mounted and pounding out the gate and down the track, strung out in a ragged line that stretched back far longer than Marguerite would have expected. They were riding into the night. To where she did not know, for how long she could not guess. And she didn't care. She didn't care at all as long as David was beside her.

Something wild and free surged up from somewhere deep inside her, pounding in her heart, burning in her mind. Though tears stung her eyes and streamed back to wet her hair and veil, she refused to think of tomorrow, the next day, or any that came after. She was free, and far beyond the will of any man.

She had made her choice and would abide by it come what may. What would happen when it ended, she could not tell. But she would have now, this moment, and nothing could take it from her.

13

The euphoria did not last.

As mile followed weary mile and darkness turned into the light of day, Marguerite's thoughts returned again and again to what had happened in the great hall. She was positive the confrontation between David and Henry had been staged, albeit upon the spur of the moment, a part of the subterfuge devised to thwart Warbeck's bid for the crown. What else could it be?

Confirmation would have been comforting, but was not forthcoming. It was not a question she could call out to David as they rode, and his preoccupation with military matters prevented her from approaching him during their brief halts to rest. Once or twice, she saw him kindle a flame from his tinderbox, holding it to a set of parchment sheets taken from a pouch at his side. The glimpse she had gotten suggested a map with notations and figures. Correct or not, she thought he appeared satisfied each time he rolled them up again.

Assuming they were embarked on David's role as an alternate pretender, they must have a base of operations, some stronghold to which they could retreat in reasonable safety. If it had a keep and stone walls, then David's company would be able to hold it against all but the most determined attack. Mayhap that was where they were headed now.

It was unlikely that David could have arranged for such a place. That must surely mean that it had been provided by the king. The question, then, was how secure it might be in truth.

The longer Marguerite rode, the more she thought, and the more she thought, the deeper went the roots of her terror. It was lunacy, becoming embroiled in the clashing ambitions of Lancaster and York. David must tread an incredibly fine line in what lay ahead, succeeding enough to prevent the aims of the Yorkist pretender but not so much that he threatened the stability of Henry's reign. He must appear a viable candidate for the throne, a true Plantagenet, but not become so solidly identified as such to the common people that he could not disclaim the title later.

Her misgivings were set aside as Astrid, bouncing along on the back of her pony, reined in beside her on returning from a call of nature. "Milady," she called, her voice high and breathless, "have you seen who rides with us?"

Marguerite, noting the flush of indignation that mantled the petite serving woman's face, felt her nerves tighten. "Who might it be?"

"Yon French count and countess. Can you credit it?"

"God's beard," she muttered under her breath. The Comte and Comtesse de Neve. It was the outside of enough on top of all else.

"What ill wind caused them to cast their lot with our David?" Astrid grumbled. "Does the simmering she-cat yearn that much for him, or is it something else?"

Marguerite turned in her saddle to look back. She could see no sign of the couple, which meant they were far in the rear. Did David know they were there?

But of course he must. He had been riding up and down the column from the beginning.

Astrid nudged her pony closer, speaking in softer tones. "They believe what Sir David said, think you?"

"About what?"

The small serving woman's glance was scathing. "You know."

Of course she knew, as did Astrid, having seen enough of the lessons in past weeks to give it away. To avoid the subject was mere cowardice, as much as she might prefer it. "They must, else they would have remained with Henry. And you, what do you think?"

"I don't like them here, don't like anything about this start." Astrid's scowl was ferocious. "Men who would be king die more often than not, especially when they have no army of size behind them."

"And sometimes when they do," Marguerite said in tight agreement.

"Aye. To have the look of a king is not enough. Mayhap, having the blood would not be, either."

It was too true to be argued. Right without might behind it was useless.

Fresh from watching David's declaration, she could not but wonder at the chance of David being Edward V in all truth. He did have the look and the manner of it. He did indeed.

Could it possibly be that he had somehow lost all memory of being spirited from the Tower and lodged in the nunnery that had been his refuge? Was the tale of his being brought up by nuns mere protective cover?

"It would be a great thing to see David and this Warbeck together," Astrid said with speculation in her voice.

"It would, though it might prove nothing except that both are by-blows of Edward IV."

The miniature serving woman tipped her head like a curious sparrow. "You sound as if that would please you. Have you no wish to see our David a king?"

No, she did not. To think on it was one thing, to accept the possibility quite another. She refused to believe it, for that would make his future even more at risk. So many who claimed that distinction had died violent deaths, so very many.

Beyond that, to be hailed the rightful king would embroil him in royal duties and obligations that would take him forever beyond her reach. He would hold the highest, most noble rank in the land, one far above her own. Only a royal princess would be a suitable wife for him.

She wanted him for herself. She wanted him because she loved him, had loved him since they were lad and lass sitting together in a field of clover, since he had knelt at her feet and given her his pledge as her true knight before marching off to war. She loved him, not for his resemblance to a dead king, but for the iron strength of his soul, for his honor that blazed so bright and for the gentle caring he kept hidden from all except her alone. She loved him because he had come for her against all odds and without thought for himself, because he had the respect and trust of his king, and she knew it merited. She loved him though she didn't know if he was valued as he should be, or if he might be used and discarded.

Dear Holy Mother, but she must stop this madness. Could she trump the request of a king? If she could persuade David to break his vow, even now, would he take her away to France where the Yorkists and Lancastrians could not reach them? How she longed for that, for their halcyon days together of old, without danger and without fear.

She was afraid for him, so afraid. She had to deflect him from this path even if his honor must be forfeit. There had to be a way to win past the control he held on his need, to breech his steely resolve and make him take her. All she had to do was find it. She must, before it was too late.

The day advanced, bright and clear and with no sign of cloud in the sky. Birds sang and swooped in summer delirium, the leaves on the trees whispered above the track they followed, while the sunlight upon them made them appear burnished with oil. Briar roses bloomed in the ditches, along with campanula, dog violets and wild geranium. The rich green of gorse rose above all, with its yellow-gold blooms like globules of purest sunshine.

Gazing upon those blooms as she walked her palfrey to conserve its strength, Marguerite felt a flicker of recognition, a glimmer of something she could not quite catch and hold. The flowers seemed familiar in some strange way. Oh, but naturally, they were, for had she not seen them all her life? Yet something of importance was attached to them, something that niggled at her mind like an itch. Before she could capture it, Astrid called to her, pointing out a wild falcon on the wing, and she let it pass.

It was late afternoon of the next day when they came to the keep. It was Norman, Marguerite thought, built of rough-cut gray stone upon a mounded hill in some time long past. Four-square and massive, it promised few comforts and less grace but was as immovable and enduring as a mountain.

If anyone had sent to say they were coming, it was not evident. The inner bailey was piled high with refuse, the great hall stank

of wet ashes, moldering rushes and can-
kered grease, and the coverlet on the bed in
the solar had not been washed in many a
long day. The few servants who greeted
them were either ancient or slovenly, or
both.

Marguerite looked at Astrid. The woman
pursed her lips, while a militant light rose
in her eyes. She spun around like a small
top to seek out Oliver. Her imperious
gesture brought the squire to them. They all
three rolled up their sleeves.

By the time night came down upon them,
a great fire leaped on the hall's central
hearth, the stone floor had been swept free
of old rushes, dog bones and offal, and the
aromas of roasting meats and baking bread
replaced more sour odors.

"By my faith," David said with relief in
his voice, as he came to Marguerite's side
after seeing to the horses and assigning
places to his followers, "I knew there was a
reason I brought you with me."

She gave him barely a glance as she
supervised a slatternly serving woman who
acted as if she had never used a stone to
scrub a trestle table. "Water has been heated
for bathing. You may make use of it now or
wait until after you have eaten."

"I don't doubt I smell like a boar in rut,

but I'd eat first, if it pleases you."

Polite, he was always so polite. Well, mayhap not always, she thought, remembering certain things he had done while she lay on her pallet in the dark. Though why she should think of such disturbing matters now was a great mystery. Unless, of course, it was his imposing form and the masculine musk of him so close beside her. Well, or because he would soon see that she had designated the solar which lay behind the great hall as his chamber, and meant to share it with him while Astrid slept with the other serving women.

"As you like," she answered, and knew she flushed.

"What I would like," he began, and then stopped as he glanced past her shoulder.

Marguerite turned her head to follow his gaze. The Comte and Comtesse de Neve were settling upon a bench at the table behind her, with the *comtesse* complaining in shrill discontent.

"Pray, why are they here with us?" she asked in low inquiry as she turned back. "The *comtesse* said her husband was in England as liaison between the French king and Henry. Following after you can hardly accomplish his mission."

David's expression took on a sardonic

edge. "Unless the *comte* believes, or hopes, I will take Henry's place."

"A great compliment, to be sure." She and Astrid had come to a similar conclusion, but that did not make it correct.

"Nay, only a sign that Yorkist monarchs have ever dealt more handily with the French. Besides, anything that seems likely to loosen Henry's grasp on the throne may be of benefit to Charles VIII."

"I thought he and Henry were in charity with each other."

"An armed truce based on mutual benefit, one that can change overnight. Charles is an ambitious man with more than his share of daring. Though his attention at present is upon the weaker states of Europe, he would not mind uniting England and France again."

She glanced at David, surprised in spite of herself. It was odd to think of him having the ear of the king of France, also this firm grasp on events beyond England's narrow shores. She must readjust her thinking.

"So he might prefer you upon the throne," she said in an attempt at clarity.

"Or Warbeck. Either will do."

She took up the corner of her veil, biting it while she thought. "The *comte* and *comtesse* will report your progress to their

317

French master then."

"I have little doubt." He reached to take the veil from her fingers and smooth it in place behind her shoulder, trailing his fingers along her neck as he released it.

"And you will allow it?" she asked, her voice not quite steady. Her skin tingled where he had touched, and her knees felt unhinged.

"It would be a great coup to receive aid and endorsement from Charles of France."

"The *comtesse* is . . ."

"What?"

"Pretty, beguiling — attracted to you."

He gazed down at her, his expression considering. "Meaning you believe she is here for my sake alone?"

"Mayhap." As humor rose slowly to brighten his eyes, she went on as if goaded. "I am not jealous. Merely cautious."

"As am I. Shall I send her away?"

"You would do that?"

"Say you wish to see the back of her, and she is gone. The *comtesse* is not necessary. You are."

He meant it, she saw, as she searched the dark blue depths of his eyes until she could no longer sustain their scorching heat. "Let them remain, if they may be useful," she said in a sudden well-being and inclination to generosity.

"As you will."

She smiled a little before she spoke again. "I should tell you, David . . ."

"Later," he said. "There is much to be done before we may find our rest."

Later, indeed, she thought, for she meant to begin her seduction in earnest this night. That was, of course, when they had both attended to their manifold duties, had eaten and scrubbed away the dirt and weariness of the long ride. The thought of it made her quake inside, even as her blood sizzled in her veins.

It was after midnight, however, when David finally joined her in the solar they were to share. Marguerite had bathed long ago, and had the tub with its linen liner refilled. That water had cooled, she was certain, for any warmth from the day that penetrated the stone walls had long since vanished. The coals that had burned in the brazier were no more than dust. The oil in the shallow lamp near the tub must be nearly depleted, for the light flickering on its wick cast jittery shadows over the walls, also over the stone bench beneath the shuttered window and her sewing that she had abandoned there.

David paused in the doorway, his gaze

moving to the bed with its curtains looped back out of the way. It rested on her form beneath the coverlet, she thought, as she watched with her eyes closed to mere slits. He whispered an oath. Moving with care then, he closed the door soundlessly behind him and turned toward the tub.

A stool was drawn up close by. He dropped down upon it to lever off his boots. Rising again, he loosened the doublet he wore and tossed it aside.

How wide his shoulders were, Marguerite thought with a catch in her breathing; he had no need whatever for the padding resorted to by other men. The linen of his shirt stretched over the muscles of his back, defining their shape as he placed a foot on the stool and bent to unfasten the points of his hose. The lean turns of his hips and legs were much more clearly defined without the obscuring skirt of a doublet. The lamp behind him gave them definition beyond anything she had ever seen.

Watching him strip away his shirt in a single smooth movement, and then peel off his hose, made her mouth go dry. She snapped her eyes shut, swallowing convulsively. By the time she opened them again, he was stepping into the tub.

Heavenly Mother, but he was a beautiful

man, far more sublime than the naked saints that writhed in torment in countless church niches. If she had thought to look fully upon his manly parts, however, she must contain her disappointment. His back was to her as he eased down to sit in the tub.

He soaped himself all over, including his hair, and splashed quietly to rinse away the lather. Then he leaned against the tub's wooded side with its linen cover that protected against splinters, stretching his arms along the top rim. Sighing, he settled deeper until only the back of his head and uppermost width of his shoulders could be seen.

The guttering lamp flared up, its light catching the scar that marred the back of his right shoulder. It colored the interlocking circles of it with yellow-gold gleams.

Marguerite drew a sudden, sharp breath. Her eyes widened as she stared at that flame-gilded scar.

She sat up straight in the bed and flung back the coverlet while her heart pumped like a bellows. Sliding from the feather mattress so quickly that her feet thudded on the floor, she started toward David.

"I thought you were asleep," he said, twisting his neck to stare at her. His eyes widened as he saw she had gone naked to her bed

again, without even a shift against the coolness. His face darkened and he looked away
at once, speaking to the water pooled in his
lap. "Is aught amiss?"

"Yes . . . no. I don't know," she said in
something less than coherence. Reaching
the tub, she knelt beside it and touched his
shoulder with gentle fingertips. "Have you
ever seen this mark of yours that lies here? I
mean, have you ever taken a round of
polished steel or hand mirror and looked at
it?"

"Once or twice when I was a lad," he said
with a shrug. "I couldn't see much."

"I daresay not." She smoothed around the
small circles of the design. "So you've never
thought on what it looks like, what it might
be?"

His shoulder twitched under her hand,
the muscles leaping under his skin in reaction. His voice was gruff when he answered. "It seemed some fiend's idea of
marking strays left to the convent, or mayhap a remnant of an odd rite I was too
young to remember."

She leaned to look into his face. "Did it
never occur to you that it might be a
flower?"

"A flower." His voice grated with instinc-
tive manly rejection of such a thought.

"Designed for the purpose of branding."

"Branding? As thieves are marked for their crimes?"

"Not exactly. This would be a gorse flower as rendered in metal, and used, most likely, for identification."

He frowned, though speculation flared in the rich blue of his eyes. "A gorse flower?"

"Exactly. Common broom, the country folk name it as it grows everywhere, or in Latin, *planta genista*. Geoffrey of Anjou, ancestor of Edward III, Henry VI, Edward IV, Richard III and so many others, made a habit of wearing a sprig of it in his hat so he was called by the name. It is now become —"

"The symbol and namesake of the Plantagenets," he finished for her with the rasp of anger in his throat. "No, Marguerite."

"Is it really so impossible? You have their look, David. Even Henry said it, who should know better than any."

"No matter what I claimed back there before them all, I am not Edward V. I have never been that poor lad, despite what you or any other might wish to make of me."

"Are you sure?"

"I was never born in a castle, never shut up in the Tower," he answered with a hard shake of his head. "I remember the convent from my earliest days, recall too well the nuns, the short rations, the birch as punishment and the constant clanging of the bells for prayer."

"But what of this scar? Who would do such a thing to a child? Surely it must have been something more than a whim, must be a sign of —"

"Of what, Marguerite? And for whom? And why?"

"I don't know, but . . ."

" 'Tis only an old mark mayhap from injury or falling into a fire or against hot metal as a toddler. That it has the look of anything else is happenstance."

She didn't believe it. He could not see the scar as she could, had never seen it in close detail.

Such a mark had not been acquired by chance. No, not at all. It had been deliberately pressed into his skin so it was clear in every line. So shiny and pale was it against the sun-burnished musculature of his shoulder that he must have been a mere babe when it was done.

The horror of it brought tears that burned the back of her nose and clustered along the edges of her lashes. How he must have cried with the pain, poor deserted child without mother or father to protect him.

Dipping her head, she pressed her lips to that small flower design.

Her mouth tingled against the incredible heat of his skin, setting off a palsied quake of need that struck deep inside her. David jerked, and a prickling of goose bumps ran across his shoulders that she felt under her lips. Blindly she skimmed her palms over them, as if to soothe them away.

"Marguerite . . ."

"Yes?"

"You . . . you shouldn't."

"Should I not?" Her voice was low and a little breathless. "Come to bed, and take your rest. Come to bed, and show me what else I should not do."

14

"If I go anywhere near that bed with you," David said in a threat-laced growl, "the last thing I will take is rest."

"Oh." It was all she could say, for the promise of giddy, unbridled pleasure beneath the words took her breath.

"I can't lie next to you while you are clothed in nothing but your hair with its shades of honey and cured hay, ale and new chestnuts, and not touch you. But if I touch you . . ."

"Yes?" she said when he ground to a halt.

"I will be even less able to sleep."

"You intend that I sleep alone here?" she murmured while sliding her hand over the turn of his unblemished shoulder again, mindlessly tracing the muscles that lay in hard ridges across it.

"I'll stretch out on the floor. That should be penance enough to distract me."

"It's cold. And gritty."

"Good."

He surged to his feet in a cascade of water and sliding suds. Marguerite's fingertips trailed down his body. They burned as she deliberately let them rake over the muscles of his back to the tight curve of his backside.

His breath left him in a sibilant whisper. Abruptly, he whipped around and caught her arm, drawing her up so fast that she fell against him. Her face pressed against the flat, wet surface of his abdomen for an instant, while the iron-hard length of him nestled between her breasts. She gasped, choking at the feel of that wet, slick slide of hard flesh. He swore again and pulled her higher, thrusting an arm behind her hips before swinging her up against his chest. A few dripping strides, and he tossed her onto the mattress of the bed. He followed her down, half crawling, half falling over her.

Glad triumph surged up inside her. This time they would not be interrupted nor would he stop. She would know the caresses he was capable of giving a woman, the bliss he had squandered on the ladies of France. She lay quite still with her hair spread around her, her breathing fast and shallow, her heartbeats jarring her breasts.

He shifted to one elbow, though a long leg anchored her at the knees. Slowly, he let his gaze drift from her hair to the rounded hillocks of her breasts, and lower to where her abdomen quivered. Without haste, he took her wrist and raised it above her head to clasp it in his other hand. He caught the other, and imprisoned it with the first.

She had no protection from him. She was at his mercy and uncertain if he meant to be kind. Though she had invited this, wanted it, knew it to be necessary, fear stirred inside her. She watched him, her eyelids twitching a little as he leaned closer.

His irises were azure-blue, yet almost obliterated by the widening black circles of his pupils. She could see herself reflected in their surfaces, edged in the red-gold of lamplight. She looked wanton and unafraid, with little sign of the turmoil inside her.

He touched her hair, removing a silky strand that half covered her mouth, sliding his fingers down it until it became part of a skein that lay like gold mesh over one breast. His gaze lowered to that screen and the tight nipple beneath it. He bent his head farther, until his warm breath whispered over the sensitive flesh. Until she arched her back, offering it to him.

He took the gift, closing his mouth over the berried tightness of the tip, using her hair as friction as he rubbed his tongue over it, around it in endless incitement. He wanted her response, it seemed, waited for it with patience and guile. He spanned the indentation of her waist with his long and hard swordsman's fingers, lifting her, turning her closer against him.

Every sense in her body rushed to where he laved and suckled her. She felt as if she was being drawn like a bow, tighter and tighter, yet controlled by his strength, his incredible virility. Still, his grasp was careful, his full power in abeyance. He would do nothing she did not wish. That was a false impression, however, for he had the skill and patience to persuade her to anything.

The force of that male power surrounded her, pressed upon her inexorably. She was infinitely aware of it in the glide of his muscles against her, the taut surface of his belly, the turgid length of him that lay along her thigh. His control was absolute, but he could release it at will, could use it to take from her whatever he wanted, any way he wanted it.

It was enthralling, yet frightening, too. She made a soft sound in the back of her throat while her stomach muscles rippled in a tremor that shook her to her toes. He hesitated, lifted his head to meet her gaze again.

"What would you, my lady?" he asked in strained demand. "Is there nothing you would ask of me?"

She had no idea what he meant, could not think for the sensual haze that held her. "All," she said, the most she could find to reply.

"All?" He lowered his head as if he would take her lips, but drew back again.

She watched him through quivering lashes. "I want you . . . would have as much of you as you would ask of me."

"I can ask nothing," he said on a harsh laugh, "while you . . ."

Was he thinking of kingdoms or titles or other monetary things? "I will ask nothing, not ever."

The answer did not seem to please him. He grasp tightened as he unleashed his strength.

He brought his mouth down upon hers, sweeping in to plunder its depths, taking her every breath. He stole her thoughts, her responses so she was caught in the maelstrom of his desire. She took him, drank him with soft murmurs while her very being rose in flood, flowing warm and heavy with the riptide of her longing, breaking against the rock of his will and pounding higher, ever higher.

His hands clenched upon her, kneading her thighs and spreading them while he shifted his leg to push it between her knees. He sought the moist heat of her, cupped and held and rotated the heel of his hand upon her. He separated the tender, exquisitely sensitive folds, slid a finger into her, and another, while he deepened the incursion and withdrew, went deeper.

It burned with a sharp sting as he touched her maidenhead, and she moaned in protest. He soothed her but did not take his hand away. Instead, he stroked less deep, centering his attention upon the single, exquisitely sensitive point at the apex of her thighs. Waves of sensation raced in upon her, growing ever wilder.

She wanted to touch him, to close her hands upon him and draw him close, but he prevented it. She wanted to protest, but lacked the words, could not catch her breath for the sensual tension that gripped her. She yearned for more of his heat, more of his strength, all of his power, yet felt curiously alone and bereft in her need.

The storm inside broke in a sudden torrent. Her cry was one of loss that he swallowed, inhaling the sound. She convulsed against him, needing to feel his skin against hers in any way she could, aching for his weight, for his hard flesh inside her. Yet even as her being contracted in rhythmic pulses that flooded her with heat and beatitude, she felt the tears gather.

His will was unbroken.

She had failed.

She could not save him, could not even save herself.

Her breathing slowed. Chill crept over her. She tugged on her arms, and he let her go. He was a weight upon her, burning still. She eased away from him and turned to her side, pulling up the coverlet as she huddled in upon herself.

He reached out to pull strands of her hair from under her shoulder and smooth them down her back to her hips. She didn't move, gave no sign that she felt it. She heard him sigh as he turned to his back. Not long afterward, the lamp burned away the last of the oil and flickered out. Later, perhaps an hour, maybe two, David's breathing slowed and he slept.

Marguerite lay staring into the darkness. Finally, as dawn began to finger the window shutter's edges, she closed her eyes.

"You will have to marry me," David said.

He made the announcement as soon as Astrid left the chamber again after putting the tray she carried across her mistress's lap. He'd followed the small serving woman for no other purpose. He'd broken his fast already, showing himself in the great hall for the benefit of the men who were now his cadre, the core of his campaign. Now he had this task to complete before he rode out for the day.

Marguerite had drawn a short cape around her shoulders against the early-morning coolness. He would have preferred that she wore only her hair as a covering, but had no right, as yet, to insist. He soon would, however, even if he exercised no other.

His mind flowed to the night before, giving him a vivid picture of how she looked as he touched her, the way she had come apart in his arms, burying her face in his neck. Her lips had been rose-red and swollen from his kisses, and her breasts the same. Though he had not taken her, she had still been his for those brief moments.

It was almost enough. Almost.

"What are you saying?" she asked with wariness in her brandy-gold eyes. "I thought marriage between us was impossible."

"A true union is. This would be a legal

tie, for your protection. I am not Henry, able to ward off any encroachment with a royal command and the claim of wardship. Any man might offer you insult, or worse, while I am absent on this business for the king. I would prevent that."

"Being married to you will be of little use if I am still left alone." She picked up the beaker before her and sipped the wine, ignoring the bread.

"It will give me the right to pursue and kill anyone who harms you."

Her lips tightened at the corners. "A strong deterrent, I suppose."

"And the crucial point."

"But it would not be a real marriage." Her voice was tight with something that sounded oddly like despair.

"It will be an exchange of vows before the church doors. You need not fear any falseness."

She put the beaker back on the tray. "What, then, makes it less than true?"

That was the rub, the thing he had little wish to bring out into the open. Once it was put into words, he would be unable to change his mind. "You know well. Nothing about the past has changed."

Desolation rose in her eyes as she watched him. The ends of her fingers turned white as she clasped them in her lap. She moistened her lips, pressed them together before she spoke. "And I am to understand that nothing *will* change. You offer marriage so I will be less a burden to your conscience as you go on as agreed with Henry."

"So you may be safe while I am about it, rather," he answered, concern for her distress adding sharpness to his voice.

"It isn't to remove the condition you imposed upon the king? His pledge to allow me to remain unwed?"

That meant something to her, he thought, but could not work out what it might be for the angry ache inside him at her rejection. "You have been named a wanton through no fault of your own, and a witch, as well," he said with a scowl. "The notoriety puts you at risk from any man who may come upon you. Would you chance insult, and worse, rather than accept the security of becoming my wife?"

"I prefer a live husband to a dead one!" she returned with fire in her eyes. She sat forward, so the sheet that covered her loosened, revealing the creamy curves of her breast. "If you marry me, then Henry will have your service for nothing. You wipe out your reason for undertaking the role of pretender. There will be no point in continuing with it."

"Except that I gave my word," he said in quiet contradiction. "Except that I will have you as my wife."

"For what use it may be to you as I am to be untouched, still."

The look he gave her was edged with hot and stringent remembrance. "Not quite untouched."

Wild rose color flared across her cheekbones. It also mantled her neck and shoulders like a pennon announcing the approach of desire. Fiery remembrance lay in the soft depths of her eyes, along with embarrassment that it hurt him to see. Above this, however, was accusation.

"But something less than a wife in true consummation," she said evenly.

He'd not known she knew the meaning of the word. Heat burned the tops of his ears as he wondered how much else she knew. God, but she was so soft and warm and malleable, so easily aroused. He loved how she responded to his kisses and the marauding search of his hands. Her breasts were pale and lovely, softly rounded, delectably rose-tipped. They were sweet as honey in his mouth, and so tender it was all he could do not to strip away the coverlet that hid them and feast upon them again, this moment.

There would be time enough for that, and more, later. Once they were wed, he would teach her to feel only joy at her response to him, or at anything they might do together. He would let her know exactly what he wanted of her and how much he wanted it. When she had spoken the words he needed to hear, he would be free to show her a thousand treasures, and to take from her all she had to give. Meanwhile, he required her acquiescence without argument or further delay.

"I am deadly serious, Marguerite. This is too urgent to be left undone."

"Is it, indeed?"

"You wanted it once, you offered it to me. Why dillydally now?"

"You refuse to give me children." She pulled the sheet higher as she spoke, tucking it more securely under her arms.

Frustration moved over him as he watched that protective gesture. Yet he could hardly tell her he expected her to become so used to his gaze, his touch, his possession that she would abandon all modesty. Nor could he say she could have all the children she pleased if she would but release him from his vow. It smacked of bribery at best and extortion at worst, and had no vestige of principle in it.

Jaws clamped tight, he looked away for an instant before he spoke. "It was ever to be that way between us."

"At your decision. I don't remember being asked."

He gave a hard shake of his head. "You would have been denied motherhood as a nun."

"I abandoned all idea of the nunnery ages ago. My ambition now is quite otherwise."

"And that would be?" he demanded in tried patience. His men awaited him in the bailey below. He had miles to ride and appointments to keep.

"Nothing of great moment, only love and a family, a home and hearth to call my own."

He had never had those things beyond the few shining months at Braesford, had long given up hope of them. "We don't always get what we want."

"No," she answered, looking away in her turn.

"I will give you whatever is in my power," he said with as much sincerity as he could manage. "I know it isn't what you might have chosen, but you will have little to regret."

"You don't understand," she whispered.

That was beyond true, but he had no time to go into it. "At least give thought to what I have said. We will speak of it again when I return."

She swung her head to look back at him again. "Where do you go?"

"To a gathering of barons who may join me, or at least pretend to change their allegiance that others may do the same."

"Pretend?"

"At Henry's instigation, to lend credence to my supposed claim as Edward V."

"That seems a dangerous game," she said, her voice a thread of sound. "How do you know they won't capture and kill you to be rid of the Yorkist threat you represent?"

He lifted a shoulder. "I don't. My dependence is on the word of Henry VII."

She did not look any happier. "He seems to be wasting no time in carrying the thing forward."

"As you say."

"Who rides with you?"

"My men-at-arms. Oliver. The Comte de Neve."

"Not the *comtesse?*"

"It is no venture for females."

"Well enough. You will take care, nonetheless?"

He stared at her a moment while bemusement shifted through him. His mind was so beset that he spoke before he thought. "Are you — can you be — jealous, after all?"

"Don't be daft," she answered with a glance as sharp as the rebuff.

She was, no matter how she denied it. This lady he had revered for long years as an angelic being was all too human. More, she was jealous of him who had never been worthy of it before, never thought he would be. "No," he said softly.

"I'm only fearful of what may happen."

"Yes." His voice turned harsh as he absorbed that evidence of her concern.

And because of it, he had to swoop down upon her and take her lips in a kiss so fast she could not protest. With the taste of it upon his mouth, he left her then. He left her before he could decide that Henry's crown would be well lost in exchange for a day spent in bed with Marguerite.

The meeting of barons was a strained affair with plentiful displays of arrogance, suspicion and bombast. It would have proceeded with more dispatch and less recrimination if Henry could have been present, but was concluded with some degree of satisfaction anyway. By the time David returned to the Norman keep, he was bone weary, disgusted at the task imposed upon him, and his temper as frayed as the moth-eaten banners that swayed above the hall's dais.

It did nothing for his state of mind to discover that Marguerite was not in the solar they shared. Not that he expected to find her there as naked as when he had left, but it had been a persistent fantasy. She was not in the hall, the kitchens, the storerooms or the stable. She had not left through the gate on horseback, though the guards could not say she had not slipped past them afoot. No one had seen her in at least an hour, possibly longer, and none could say where she had last been occupied.

Climbing to the battlements to scan the wooded area around the keep was a last resort. David took the steps two at a time with fear as his companion. He could think of far too many things that might have happened to her, each worse than the last. He should have made certain the guards knew she was not to leave the keep under any circumstances, should have set men to guard her as he had during the journey hither, should have taken her with him, should have told her how he would mourn if she came to harm. He should have told her he loved her, and made her believe it this time.

By the time he reached the top of the steps, his heart was clamoring in his chest, his stomach twisted in a knot and his brain curdling in the acid of his regret. He was desperate to look down from the height he'd reached, yet dreaded what he might find. He slowed, stood for a moment at the top, holding the healed slash in his side that still hurt after a day of exertion, trying to catch his breath.

He heard her first, the lilt of her voice like a melody on the light wind that blew around the battlements. It came to him from the far side of where he stood, beyond the bulk of the main rooftop. Relief shuddered down his spine and circled his chest to squeeze it tight. He took a fast step in that direction, then paused as he caught another voice in answer to whatever Marguerite had said.

Celestine, the Comtesse de Neve. That languorous yet breathy voice was unmistakable. She was here on the battlements with Marguerite.

Celestine had ignored Marguerite's existence in days past, except for glances tinged with petty resentment. Marguerite had returned the favor. What, then, could have brought them together?

For all her flighty manner, Celestine doted on intrigue. The few short days he had been involved with her in Paris had been marked by her delight in the hide-and-seek of cuckolding her husband. She had been ecstatic over repaying him for his numerous affairs, and in the same coin. The lady had also been more than familiar with Charles VIII, and was an enthusiastic advocate for whatever might benefit her royal lover. The *comte* might have the diplomatic title from the French king, but it was the *comtesse* who was most often closeted with him.

These things could have nothing whatever to do with the discussion between Celestine and Marguerite. Then again they might have every bearing. Either way, David could not let the opportunity to discover what the *comtesse* was about pass him by.

With silent footsteps, he eased along the rooftop, following the windblown sound of feminine voices. They stood at the battlements at the rear of the castle, he thought, overlooking the densest section of the surrounding woodland. As the words they tossed back and forth grew clearer, he stopped and put his back to the wall he followed, leaning against the sun-warmed stone.

"A onetime Master of Revels to your Henry? But no, *ma chère.* How can you think I would know this Leon de Amboise?"

"He always seemed something more than a mere musician or director of entertainments," Marguerite said in idle tones. "My sisters and I felt sure he was in service to Charles VIII. This was years ago, of course."

"C'est vrai?" The Frenchwoman's indifference could not have been plainer. "I never heard his name."

"He was most handsome, which made me think he might have come to your notice."

David remembered Leon as well, though he'd not thought him particularly handsome. Leon's sister had been a mistress to Henry before his marriage, had borne a child, little Madeleine, who was taken as their own by Isabel and Braesford when the child's mother had been killed. Leon had disappeared not long afterward.

If Leon was an agent for the French king, it was never proven. Nor had David seen anything of the man on his adventures across the continent. Still, Marguerite might well suppose that Celestine could know him if both were in the pay of France.

Celestine gave a tinkling laugh. "Another golden one like David?"

"Dark, rather, but accomplished."

"In bed, yes? Ah, but I refuse to believe he could compete!"

It was a moment before Marguerite spoke,

and her voice had a compressed sound. "You are saying . . ."

"But yes, a most prodigious lover, our David, truly insatiable, I give you my word. Large, also! Large in all ways, you comprehend! Well, you have seen the *comte*'s lack of stature, so understand my awe, yes?"

David felt sweat trickle between his shoulder blades. Sainted Mother. The woman's artless lack of restraint brought back forgotten memories. As uninhibited and demanding as a cat in heat, the *comtesse* had instructed him in myriad ways to please a woman. So busy was he in wondering if Marguerite would like them that he almost missed her reply.

"I can imagine."

Could she indeed. The top of his head felt sun-blasted as he thought of it.

"Such natural talent he had, such sure hands," the *comtesse* went on. "Never have I known a man with greater veneration for a woman's body. He did not simply grab and push himself inside like most, certain that the woman must of course be satisfied if they hammer fast, fast on their way to pleasure. Idiots! No, no, he took half his joy in tending the enjoyment of his partner." She sighed. "I have found no other so caring, so selfless."

"He . . . he completed the act?" Marguerite asked, though distaste was strong
beneath the curiosity in her voice.

"But of course he did, *ma chère!* Have I
not said he was prodigious! Such strength,
such endurance, such absolute control held
until the ultimate moment! It makes my
soul quake to think of it even now."

"I . . . I'm sure."

"Forgive me," Celestine said with an arch
pretense of compunction. "You will be ready
to scratch my eyes out, yes? I did not mean
to dwell on these delights. You must not be
jealous."

"Jealous? Why should everyone . . . I
mean, why should you think that."

She sounded bored, David thought, not at
all as she had sounded just that morning.
What in the name of heaven was going on?

"Shall I admit I would like you to be?"
Celestine asked. "I was quite crushed to see
him with you. He left me, you know, walked
away as if I meant nothing, as if none of the
skill as a lover I imparted to him meant
anything at all."

"David left you?"

Heat burned the back of his neck at he
listened. The urge to break up the discussion nearly propelled him into the middle
of it. What held him back was dread that it

was too late already.

"He tired of me and moved on," Celestine said, "the only man ever to so insult me."

"I can see it would have been a trial to come upon him again here with Henry."

Was that sympathy for the Frenchwoman in Marguerite's voice? David frowned as he considered it.

"Indeed. A woman has her pride."

"Though surely you had been in the habit of seeing him in France? He was a favorite with Charles, after all."

Celestine's laugh was sharp. "I made sure our paths seldom crossed."

"But you joined him, joined us, when we left Henry. Why put yourself to the pain of it? Unless you have hope?"

"Of rekindling his interest? I am not so foolish. I've seen the way he looks at you."

"I'm sure you are mistaken."

For an instant, Marguerite's voice sounded diffident, as if she wished to be convinced. It was a task David would have relished had things been different.

"Not about such a thing, *chère.* I am told he abducted you as you rode to be married, carried you off upon his saddlebow. This is so?"

"It happened that way, yes."

"*Quelle horreur!* How terrifying it must

have been to be at his mercy. Yes, and how devastating to know the deed meant your ruin. One doesn't soon recover from such a tragedy."

"Tragedy?"

Celestine's laugh was brittle. "Was it not so bad, then, being in his power? I confess I would not have fought his seduction so very hard myself. But then Henry ordered you to tend him after his injury in the attack. Not only were you subject to his will before, but all were shown clearly that your good name meant nothing to him or to your king."

A choking sensation caught David in his throat as he waited for Marguerite's answer. That he saw a glimmering of what might be going forward helped it not at all.

"These things happen," Marguerite returned in even tones. "As the king's ward, I must do as I am bid."

Blackness descended over him. He had thought Marguerite willing, had been sure her care, her smiles and companionship while he was injured meant she returned what he felt. He had been certain that she welcomed his kisses, was enthralled by what he had shown her of desire. Could it all have been from mere acceptance of her fate, or worse, the pretense of it?

"You would like to escape him, yes? Or see to it he can hold you no longer?"

Marguerite was silent.

"It can be arranged, I believe," Celestine went on in her light voice, so at odds with what she was saying. "That is, if you were to persuade him to ride out in a small party, were to lead him in a certain direction that might be suggested to you?"

David's heartbeat faded into near stillness. He cared nothing for the plotting of the *comtesse,* could not even be surprised she and the *comte* might seek to prevent his interference in Warbeck's bid for the throne. Loyalties were hopelessly tangled in this business of kings and crowns, and gold could sway anyone from one side to the other. No, it was Marguerite's reaction that mattered.

Surely she must realize this morning ride so casually mentioned could end in ambush. She had to see there could be no escape for her, as Celestine viewed it, unless he was taken prisoner or killed.

She must know that all she need do to be free of him was tell him to his face that she wished it?

David held his breath, the better to hear what she would answer.

Long moments passed while he longed to

be able to see her face, to know what she was thinking and feeling. Finally, she spoke.

"David has weighty matters on his mind. I misdoubt he will set them aside for a pleasure outing."

"I feel sure," Celestine said, her voice heavy with suggestion, "that you may convince him of the benefit."

"Supposing I could . . ."

"Yes, *chère?*"

"What direction had you in mind?"

David closed his eyes, swallowing hard as he let his head fall back against the stone wall behind him. Marguerite had agreed, was even now listening as Celestine told her what she must do and when. He could not believe it. Everything he knew of her, everything he had ever known, said she would never stoop to such a thing. He'd have expected her to spit fire at the mere idea, not only for his sake but because it assumed she was without heart or principles.

Why was she doing it? Why?

Had she changed so much in the years since they were together at Braesford? Or had the change come about since his return? Was this about her need to escape the prospect of being married to him rather than a betrayal?

Excuses, he was making excuses for her.

She wouldn't go through with it. She couldn't. He would stake his life on it.

It was his life that would be at stake, indeed, because he would follow wherever she led. He would go for this ride with her. Yes, he would follow where she led and see what came of it.

It was not necessary by any means. He could call a halt, here and now, or else force her tonight to tell him what was planned. The last appealed mightily. He would take white-hot enjoyment from questioning her while she lay naked in his bed.

God, no, he couldn't do that. He must first allow her to prove herself disloyal. Then he would call a halt to the threat, stop it short of riding into an ambuscade.

Or would he? If it meant so much to her to be free of him?

Easing away from the wall, retreating from the soft and deadly murmur of female voices, he left the battlements. In the great hall, he called for wine. Morose and short of temper, he fended off all efforts to join him while he attempted to drink the memory of those voices under the table.

15

"You should tell him," Astrid said, as she stood on top of the chamber's stool, braiding Marguerite's hair with quick competence. "It's too dangerous, otherwise."

"How can I? He and Celestine were lovers. He will never believe she would plot against him. He will say I am accusing her falsely out of jealousy."

"And you are not?" Astrid jumped down from the stool to reach the brown ribbon that lay across the bed, using it to confine the long plait for riding.

"You know better."

"If the *comtesse* made much of his prowess . . ."

"She wished me to be jealous, but that's a different thing altogether," Marguerite said with finality.

Astrid gave her a long look, but made no reply.

"I shall tell him, of course, when it's

necessary," Marguerite said in answer to the disapproval in Astrid's face.

"But you'll not give him time to prepare against it."

She gave a small shake of her head while doubt burned a hole in her stomach. "He would make none if he didn't believe me."

"He could be killed, milady."

"I know that!" she snapped. "I would not have agreed to this confounded ride, otherwise. He must be put on his guard against the *comtesse*. She must not be allowed to seek out others willing to betray him."

"Best pray he doesn't discover what you have done. He has shown only his gentle side to you, but that doesn't mean he has no other."

An anxious tremor skimmed over Marguerite's nerves. It was true that David had never turned his wrath upon her, but she had seen strong men turned to shivering, sniveling wrecks by it. It wasn't something she wanted to face.

He had not been his usual self on his return the evening before. He had seemed hard, forbidding, with frost rimming the blue of his eyes as he stared at her. There had been no smiles, no kisses or further mention of the marriage he had proposed. His late-evening meal had been eaten with

Oliver. He had agreed to ride with her this morning, but had not come to bed last night.

Where had he slept? She suspected it was in the great hall with his men, but would not ask. If it was elsewhere, with someone else, she didn't want to know it.

Mayhap she had made too many difficulties about taking him as her husband, especially after proposing it herself not so long ago. He had not been pleased at her hesitation, she knew. Yet what wonder that she had misgivings, when he said one day they could never marry and demanded it the next, declared he must love her only in chaste fashion then proceeded to make a wanton of her?

As he could not slake his desire upon her, mayhap he had found a female permitted to him. One lay near at hand and no doubt available, for all her ire at his escape from her bed. The *comtesse* might even abandon her threat against him for the sake of being in his arms again. It seemed personal vengeance moved her as much as any political advantage.

No. She would not think of that. She would not.

David waited for her in the inner bailey when she swept down the steps with Astrid trotting along at her side. He was not alone, but had Oliver for a companion. To see the Italian mounted and ready to ride was a distinct relief. Whoever awaited them might think twice with his addition to their party.

She was hardly seated upon her palfrey, and Astrid upon her pony, when the *comte* and *comtesse* joined them. The *comte* was irascible and half-asleep, but Celestine more than made up for it. With a forest-green riding gown, and matching hat draped by a fine purple plume perched upon her blond curls, the Frenchwoman was so colorful she made Marguerite feel drab in her serviceable brown wool. The lady greeted everyone with bright cheer, chattering with merriment about the fine morning, her mount, her serving woman's failure to wake her in good time and the excellence of the wine brought with her morning bread. She was still talking when they clattered out the gate and into the dew-damp morning.

At the *comte*'s suggestion, they turned from the road onto a dim pathway, little more than an animal track, that meandered through the woodland, which crowded the back of the keep. That gentleman took the lead and Oliver fell in beside him. He was followed closely by David with Celestine, while Astrid and Marguerite came last. How their places were decided, Marguerite could not have said, but she didn't care for the odd pairing. Short of pushing forward to dislodge the *comtesse,* there was no way she could have a private word with David.

She could not think trouble would come this early in the jaunt. Any attack was likely to be launched a good distance from the keep. They would stop at some point to rest the horses and refresh themselves with the wine, cheese and bread attached to Astrid's saddle. She would find a way to warn David then.

Oliver, she noticed after a moment, carried a pair of longbows behind his saddle, as well as a plentiful supply of arrows. She was gratified beyond words to see them, yet could not help wondering at it.

"Do we hunt while we are out?" she called to those ahead of her. "Should I be alert for game?"

"Meat for the larder is always an excellent thing," David answered her over his shoulder, "as is staying alert."

Were his words significant? She could not say, yet her skin twitched as if a spider crawled under her clothing. "Why, we might even stumble upon a Yorkist party," she returned with ironic optimism. "Think what a diversion that would be."

"*Mon Dieu,* never say so!" Celestine exclaimed with a theatrical shudder and quick frown over her shoulder at Marguerite.

"No telling where they might be riding," Astrid said in stout support.

"I was certain Warbeck tarried in Scotland," the Frenchwoman said, reaching out to put a gloved hand on David's arm. "Pray tell me there has been no word otherwise!"

"None," David answered.

The curtness of his tone pleased Marguerite. At least he was not short with her alone.

David's mouth was set in a grim line, she saw on closer inspection, and his eyes were more than a little bloodshot. Yet he sat his saddle with ease, appearing stalwart, strong and outrageously handsome with the early-morning light striking silver from the buttons on his blue-green doublet. His gaze was keen, and he appeared to miss no detail of what they were passing or what lay ahead of them.

The tightness in Marguerite's chest eased a fraction, though she kept her own vigilance.

They flushed a deer a few minutes after the sun cleared the treetops. Oliver, being in the lead, gave chase. They heard him crashing through the trees and underbrush, heard his faint shout of triumph as he brought down the animal. The place was marked so servants could retrieve the venison later. As they were halted already, refreshment was brought out. They sat about under a great, spreading oak, drinking wine poured from a skin into metal beakers and nibbling on chunks of cheese and bread.

Marguerite tossed her crust toward a trio of jays and pushed to her feet. Carrying her small beaker of wine, she strolled with a fine pretense of idleness toward where David squatted with his back to the oak's thick trunk. "Shall we go back now?" she asked as she approached.

"Go back? But we have hardly begun," Celestine said in frowning protest.

"We would not want Oliver's kill to spoil." Marguerite sent a small smile toward the Italian. "Besides, I don't believe Astrid is feeling quite well, though she would never complain." She waited with a suspended feeling in her chest for David's decision.

He rose to his full height, slowly looming above her. He searched her face, his eyes darkly blue and far too penetrating. "You are pale, Lady Marguerite. Are you certain it's not you who is unwell?"

They were back to formal address and politeness. Something had clearly changed between them.

"Not in the way you mean. But . . . but you will remember, mayhap, that I sometimes have a feel for ill tidings?"

"Don't be silly!" The look Celestine gave Marguerite was sharp with suspicion and fury. "What passes with you?"

David paid no attention to the *comtesse,* never removed his gaze from Marguerite's face. It seemed the breath he took was deeper than usual. "You have such a thing now?"

"I believe so. Truly."

The *comte* got to his feet. His florid face shone with perspiration in spite of the mid-morning coolness, and his fleshy mouth had a contemptuous twist. "Return now? *C'est ridicule.* We come so small a distance it is hardly worth leaving one's bed."

"I believe I may have eaten bad beef," Astrid said, resting a tiny hand to her stomach.

Oliver contributed nothing, but only squatted where he was, looking grimly amused as he smoothed his mustache.

"We can always ride another day," David said after a long moment.

"Yes," Marguerite breathed in heartfelt relief. "Another day."

"But no!" The *comtesse* stamped a booted

foot. "I insist we go on."

David still held Marguerite's gaze as he answered. "You and the *comte* may continue, if it pleases you. Lady Marguerite and I will make our way back with Astrid."

"Bene," Oliver drawled. "I will go also."

There was more in the same vein, but finally the Comtesse Celestine threw up her hands. "Very well, then! It is a pity of the greatest, but we shall all turn back."

They mounted and returned to the forest trace, this time with David and Marguerite in the lead. They were followed by the *comte* and *comtesse,* with Astrid and Oliver bringing up the rear.

Gladness was a tripping refrain inside Marguerite. With every mile traveled, she shed a portion of her fear. It was all she could do not to kick her palfrey into a gallop, tearing back down the woodland track toward the safety of the keep. She stood on the single stirrup of her sidesaddle, searching ahead for the sight of its stone walls rising above the trees. Yes, and for David's pennon, with its stylized green crown on a pale blue ground, fluttering in the breeze above it.

She glanced at him as he rode in grim watchfulness beside her. Her smile was tentative, but she could not stop it, did not try. Long ago, the two of them had ridden at breakneck speed through meadow and field, across streams and through woodlands where the fallen leaves of a hundred years and more had muffled the hooves of their mounts. How reckless they had been, and how full of the joy of being alive. It was a good memory.

David turned his head to meet her eyes, his own guarded yet inquiring.

"Race you to the keep," she said, the challenge ringing like a low chime in her voice.

His laugh was short, but his smile, when it came, held the warmth of old. "Done," he said, and leaned forward, spurring his mount.

His stallion leaped into a gallop. Marguerite, unprepared for such quick acceptance, was an instant behind him.

The arrow whistled as it streaked through the air where David had been. Its barbed head pierced Marguerite's cloak. It skimmed her chest, and bit into her arm.

She reeled, thrown off balance by the snagging blow. Pain took her breath. Shock and the stunning unreality of the fletched shaft bobbing through the rent in her clothing stopped her anguished cry in her throat.

Another shaft flew over her head and struck the tree beside her with a solid thwack. More sped about her, before her and behind her, slicing through leaves and branches and things softer and less solid. A man screamed, or it might have been a horse; Marguerite could not tell as her palfrey reared in terror, dancing on its hind legs.

A shout rang out in hard command. David had turned, was coming back, pounding closer. She wanted to warn him away. The words would not come. Somewhere behind her, Oliver's bow twanged and he gave the same triumphant yell as when he brought down the deer.

A dark shape flashed before her. She flinched, tried to rein away, but her arm had no strength. She dropped her reins, reeling in the saddle.

Abruptly, a band of steel wrapped her waist. She was lifted free of her saddle. What breath she still had left her in a moan as she hit a wall of solid muscle. Searing agony streaked from her arm up to her shoulder and into her head.

Even in the midst of it, she knew David's scent. His heat and strength surrounded her, though she saw nothing except the red mist behind her eyelids. Darkness closed in upon her as his stallion jolted into a run. The hooves around her of other horses were muffled thunder, but it was impossible to tell if they carried friend or foe.

She caught at David, twisting her good hand into the thick wool of his doublet. She held on as if she would never let go.

David cursed in vicious phrases from a half-dozen languages as he bent low over Marguerite, protecting her with his body. He wore mail beneath his doublet, while she had none. He had escaped the arrow with his name on it, but she had not.

He'd thought himself the only person in danger, but he'd been wrong. He knew not how many men were hidden among the trees, who had sent them or what they would do now. And he couldn't think, couldn't plan or retaliate until Marguerite was safe.

He suspected the arrow was in her shoulder or arm, but couldn't be sure and had no time to look. It could be in her chest, draining her life's blood around it. He could feel that warm wetness against his side, and nothing had ever struck such despair into his soul.

Oliver was behind him. The Italian had the reins of Astrid's pony looped around his arm while he drew bow from the saddle at some target behind them. The Comte de

Neve had been hit, for David had seen him fall. He had no idea what had become of the *comtesse* and cared not a whit.

She or her noble husband, or the two of them together, had designed this ambuscade. If Celestine had seen fit to join the attackers, what odds? Had she fallen, it meant even less. He need not accuse her or the *comte* then, or explain how he had come to know they were behind the attack. No, and neither would he be forced to mention Marguerite's part in it.

She had tried to warn him. Was it a change of heart, that warning, or something more, some plan or purpose he could not define? Whatever it might be, she had paid for it. He only prayed the price was not more than he could bear.

The keep loomed ahead. He swept through the gate well ahead of Astrid and Oliver. Dragging his white stallion to a halt with such wrenching force the great beast went back on its haunches, he swung down. He reached for Marguerite, pulling her carefully into his arms, and then stumbled up the wide front steps with her. He did not pause in the great hall, made no answer to the men who swarmed around, shouting and exclaiming in concerned fury. With his blood pumping madly through his veins, he made for the solar with giant strides, not slowing, not stopping until he had laid her upon the mattress of the bed.

She was so pale, so still for endless moments. Slowly, she lifted her lashes. She gazed up at him with pain and sorrow in the soft, dark brown of her eyes. He could not hold that gaze for fear of what else he might see, or what she might discover in his.

The arrow that thrust up above her body, tenting the brown wool of her cloak around it, was an obscenity. He stripped off his gloves, unsheathed his knife and made a fast slash through the cloth, cutting from the arrow's hole to the center edge. Unfastening the heavy garment at the throat, he spread it open.

The arrow's shaft was lodged in her arm with the barb protruding from the underside. Blood welled around it, soaking into her sleeve, darkening the waist of her gown. David closed his eyes for a bare instant, swallowing on sickness such as he had not felt on seeing any of a hundred battle wounds.

Astrid was beside him, pushing at his thigh as if to make him move, speaking, instructing, questioning. David paid no heed. He lifted his eyes to Marguerite's again. "It has to come out," he said, his voice carefully, rigorously even. "Now. At once. Will you allow me?"

She searched his face, probed the depths of his eyes while looking from one to the other. What she saw there must have satisfied her, for trust welled into her face and she gave a slow nod.

He would have kissed her if the arrow had not been in the way. Instead, he touched the soft skin of her cheek, wiping away a single tear that tracked across the fine, pale skin. Mouth set in a grim line, he sliced away the sleeve of her gown. Moving quickly, before she could understand quite what he meant to do, he caught the arrow's shaft in his two hands and broke it off above the flesh of her arm. He heard her stifled moan, but would not let it deter him. With his long fingers wrapped around her elbow, he lifted it then grasped the arrow's head. Clenching his teeth, closing his eyes, he pulled what was left of the shaft out from the back side.

She gave a sigh and her eyes fell shut. For an instant, David thought she had fainted. He was not surprised, for he had seen hardened soldiers pass out from far less.

An instant later, a wobbly smile curved her lips. "Thank you," she whispered.

No accolade had ever meant so much.

A fiery ache hovered behind his nose, crowding his eyes until they burned, while regret lay like a stone inside him. He stepped back as if stunned, with the piece of arrow gripped in his fist and Marguerite's blood staining his hands.

"Move," Astrid said, shoving at him with both childlike hands. "Out of my way, dolt, unless you want her to bleed to death."

"Astrid, love," Oliver, who had come quietly into the solar behind them, muttered in protest.

"Silence, fool. If you would make yourself useful, go and ask for water that has been well boiled with a goodly handful of salt."

While Oliver was gone, Astrid folded thick pads of linen and held them firmly to the wounds on either side of her arm to slow the bleeding. Afterward, the punctures were bathed with the salt water until she was certain no fragments of cloth or other matter were left embedded between them. When the arm was bound in clean linen, the small serving woman pressed a soothing herbal drink upon Marguerite. She stood for long moments, holding her mistress's hand and smoothing tendrils of hair back from her face. When Marguerite finally slept, she sat down on the three-legged stool to wait.

David had a dozen things he should be doing. He sent Oliver to see to them, instead. Moving to the window where the shutters hung open, he stood looking out with his legs spread and his arms crossed over his chest.

After a moment, he spoke over his shoulder in soft inquiry. "What do you think?"

"She will be all right if the wounds don't fester."

"If." He was not overly optimistic. He'd seen too many minor injuries become septic, mere scratches received at tournaments and in battles. They killed more seasoned soldiers than any weapon ever forged.

Astrid gave him a jaundiced look. "We tended you, she and I between us, and you healed in good time."

A tight smile came and went across his lips. "So you did."

"You need not stay," Astrid said, knitting her short fingers together and folding her hands in her lap. "I will be here."

"I can't go."

"As it pleases you, sir."

A short silence fell in which could be heard the rumble of voices from below, along with birdsong and the lazy hum of bees. The breeze through the window was warm and scented with green growing things. He wondered if it was too cool for Marguerite, but she slept on as if she didn't feel it. Or he thought she slept. She was so still that he turned and walked back to the bed, staring down.

Yes. Her chest rose and fell. Still.

"She isn't going to die," Astrid said with compassion in her light voice.

"She almost did. The arrow came close, so close. An arrow meant . . ."

"For you? Praise be to God that you were also spared. And Oliver."

A spasm of pain gripped his chest so fast and hard he could barely breathe. He strode back to the window and settled with one hip on the stone embrasure that made a shallow bench in front of it.

"You would rather it was you who was hit, I expect," Astrid said in sharp tones. "But she'd not have it that way."

"Why in the name of heaven did she have to go? What made her agree? She knew something was planned. She tried to warn me, you heard her. Wasn't that what she intended?"

"Aye, it was. As to the why of it, she didn't think you would believe evildoings of the *comtesse,* but had to see it for yourself. If

369

you didn't see it, then that lady and her husband might try again when there was no one to warn you."

David was not accustomed to concern for his well-being. So tough was he in body and mind that it never occurred to him that Marguerite might be afraid for him. It was difficult to realize, too, that she might have felt he would not listen to her, or believe what she told him. The idea made his chest ache.

Celestine had come to him not long after he'd been taken up by Charles of France. As with so many ladies of the court, she had been drawn to his prowess on the field, his strength and honors. It had not taken him long to understand that she cared nothing for him beyond these things. She had been demanding and condescending in bed, with less modesty than the meanest street trollop. The affair, if it could be called that, was instructive, but too cold-blooded to hold him for long. She had screamed and thrown things when he left her.

That she had been all smiles when she appeared at Henry's court had been a surprise. He might have known she had her reasons.

So Celestine had dropped her poison in Marguerite's ear, but far from being taken in by it, Marguerite had used it to cause the

Frenchwoman's undoing. Brave, bright Marguerite, who did not understand — might never understand — how much he was hers and how much he wanted her to belong to him.

God's teeth, but what was he doing? How had he become involved with Henry and his schemes? Why should he continue, if it could mean losing the one thing he had ever wanted, the one person who had ever meant anything to him?

Yet what could he do now? He was in the middle of the quarrel between York and Lancaster, and there was no way out except absolution from Henry.

Absolution or death.

16

"Has there been no word from the *comtesse?*"

Marguerite put that question to David on the third morning after the incident in the forest. It had been troubling her for some time, but Astrid did not know the answer and she was asleep when David was there, or else he slept on the floor beside her bed when she chanced to awake, and she would not disturb him.

"There was no sign of her in the woods where the attack took place," he answered, his voice even and a little distant. "Blood was found where the *comte* fell, but that was all. The two of them seem to have escaped with the men who set upon us. Well, or were taken away by them. Either way, they are gone."

"You don't sound greatly concerned," she ventured.

"No. The *comte* and *comtesse* almost got

you killed. Their fate doesn't interest me."

The pair could have gone to Henry, who was surely in London by now, or else taken ship for France to report events to Charles VIII. Fear of retribution would surely keep them well away from David now, a thought that brought infinite relief.

She watched him where he sat at the window. He looked perfectly at home, as she had seen him there often as she drifted between sleep and awakening. The morning light slanted across his features, making them appear strained, almost gaunt. It shone in his hair and caught in the sincere blue of his eyes as he turned his gaze upon her.

She could only sustain that intense scrutiny for brief seconds. Lowering her lashes, she watched her fingers as she pleated the sheet that lay across her. "Astrid said she told you . . . that you understand what I was about."

He tipped his head. "Think no more of it. I only regret it ended as it did."

"What was the point of it all? Was it for the French king? Did Charles learn somehow of your purpose and fear he had let the true heir to England's throne slip through his fingers?"

"What? You think the *comtesse* was to lure

me back to France or, failing that, truss me up and carry me?"

"Something of the sort, I suppose."

"Nay, my lady. The men in the wood loosed their arrows with the intent to kill. What use might I be as a pawn in Charles's game against England if delivered to him as dead meat?"

"Don't!" she said sharply.

"Forgive me, but facts are facts."

"Unfortunately," she muttered without looking at him, "I would almost rather you were a guest of the French king, even if under lock and key, than pretending to be Edward V."

He turned a scowl upon her. "Is that what you thought, that it wouldn't matter if I were taken as it would be better than this business of Henry's? I should tell you, then, that it would not have served at all. Like Henry before me when he was a guest of Louis XI, my best use as a hostage might well have been to hand me over to the English crown in exchange for certain concessions."

"Charles would have done that?"

"Without a second thought."

"But you were his friend!" Her chest hurt as she saw his calm, almost fatalistic acceptance of that deceit. He was so alone, so very alone.

"Yes, but far less dear to him than the glory of his crown. He would love to be the king who made England and France one again. The how of it would mean nothing and less than nothing."

To veer away from that hurtful subject seemed a kindness. "In spite of which, we don't know the *comtesse* was acting for Charles."

He drew up his legs, placing his feet on the embrasure seat and then bracing his folded arms on his knees. The gaze he sent her was both interested and doubtful. "Who then?"

Lacking a veil to mangle, as was her habit, she lifted the corner of the sheet and nibbled upon it. "She is a proud woman. For herself, then, for revenge?"

"A vain woman," he corrected. "But if her intent was retribution for past rejection, why wait so long? The contact between us was years ago."

That he could answer so readily was proof he had considered it. If it troubled him, nothing of it could be heard in his voice. "She may have fallen in with the aims of others because of it."

"Yorkists, you think? Or some arrangement with Halliwell's heir? If so, I would imagine it was gold that swayed her. To maintain a position at the French court is no cheap undertaking."

Marguerite thought he underestimated the woman's jealous attachment, and her anger that stemmed from it. She did not say so, however. "Mayhap it was Henry. Suppose he has decided you could actually be the Plantagenet heir?"

"So he'd also have reason to see the end of me? I do see the trend of your thoughts," he said with a glimmer of irony in his eyes.

"It would explain why he was suddenly determined to arrange a betrothal for me after all these years," she said, tearing at the linen corner, speaking almost at random and with little belief in what she said. "He could not reach you so long as you remained in France. He sent messages, I believe you said, asking that you return to England, messages you disregarded. He might have been clever enough to realize I would send a plea for your aid if threatened with marriage."

"And that I would answer it as surely as winter follows autumn," he said, turning to gaze out the window with a thoughtful expression on his face. "But no. Henry would never have chanced making me an alternate pretender in such a case. More, it's well-known that Charles VIII supports Warbeck's pretensions, and I suspect the *comte* felt my demise would best serve the French crown. As it is to Celestine's advantage to support her husband, she involved herself in the intrigue — or may even have suggested it. Certain it is that she knew the best method for waylaying me would be to entice you into it."

"So it would seem." She paused, finished on a whisper. "I'm sorry, desperately sorry."

"Don't." He turned his head to stare across at her. "You were used, and that's an end to it."

Her lips turned down at the corners. "I allowed myself to be used."

"Out of concern and fear and a thousand other things that no longer matter."

"You are too kind."

"Should I shout and curse and threaten chastisement? That would be stupid, as I knew what was to happen and did nothing to stop it."

Sickness shifted inside her. "You knew? But how could you?"

"I heard you and Celestine speaking of it, up on the battlements."

"But then . . ." She stopped, tried again. "Why did you ride out with us?"

"I could not believe that you meant

harm." He lifted a shoulder. "If you did, it didn't much matter what came after."

"You trusted me." She could not think about the rest of what he'd said, with its suggestion that it didn't matter whether he lived or died if she meant to betray him.

He uncoiled from the seat and came toward her. Going to his knees beside the bed, he took her hand, being careful not to jostle her bandaged arm. "I trusted you, yes, as you have always trusted me. One thing you and I have never done, my sweet Marguerite, is hurt each other."

It wasn't true, she thought as she shielded her eyes with her lashes, at least, not entirely. He had hurt her by proposing a marriage that offered nothing except his protection and his name. He had hurt her every time he withdrew from her arms, leaving her craving something more from him in the way of closeness, craving the completion he would not give her, would not take from her. These things were unintentional, however, so could not be allowed to matter. He even thought they were for her benefit.

"Marguerite?"

"No, we haven't hurt each other. Not on purpose." She met his gaze an instant before looking down again.

"Nonetheless, you took the arrow that was

meant for me. For that pain, I beg forgiveness."

"It was my own fault."

He rubbed his thumb across the top of her hand, the movement soothing yet oddly entrancing, deliciously exciting. "I should never have agreed to a race, and wouldn't have except it seemed an excuse for making for the keep that much faster."

Her smile was wry. "My thought, as well."

His long fingers settled on her pulse beneath her wrist, pressing gently. She thought briefly of them touching her elsewhere, and with the same sure care. The drawing sensation in the lower part of her body made her shift a little on the mattress.

"I also regret dragging you into this business," he went on, his voice a deep rumble in his chest. "It appears you would have been safer with Henry, and yet I thought . . ."

"Yes? You thought?" she inquired as he stopped.

He met her gaze, his own starkly blue. "I feared you might become a target of reprisal for my actions, or be taken as hostage for them."

"Hostage."

"My hands would have been tied if you fell into Yorkist control. And if the demand was to exchange my life for yours?" He lifted a shoulder in a gesture of resignation.

"You would have done that?" she asked, though the words were like knives in her throat. "Exchanged your life for mine?"

He bent his head to brush his lips across her knuckles without answering directly. "I thought I'd be better able to protect you if you were by my side. I was wrong."

"Or not. Who can say what might have happened if I had remained with Henry."

"You would be safe at Westminster this day, instead of lying here in pain."

"It doesn't hurt so much."

"You lie," he said without heat.

She reached with her free hand to touch his face where golden beard stubble lurked under the skin. A soft wing of sandy-gold hair fell forward at his temple and she smoothed it back, tucking it behind his ear. To touch him in this way satisfied some deep need inside her while making her feel warm and fluid inside. His brow was broad, classic in its proportions. His brows and lashes were darker than his hair yet bleached to gold at the tips. Deep in his eyes were facets of blue that were both darker and lighter than could be seen at a distance.

He was so gentle with her, and yet she had seen the hard, unyielding side he showed to others. His strength had nothing to do with shouting and bluster, but came from inside, from bedrock confidence. He was a warrior, one hard and dangerous to cross. And yet, he did have the bearing of a prince, of a man who should be king.

He had the fair looks, the demeanor and also the branded mark of the Plantagenets. What if he were one indeed, a true son of Edward IV, and not some by-blow from a brief affair? What if he truly was one of those young boys who had disappeared? Such a terrible miscarriage of justice if Henry used him to keep his hold on a throne that should be David's by right.

If the pretender Warbeck claimed to be Richard, the second son of Edward IV, then David would have to be Edward, proclaimed as Edward V on the death of his father when he was little more than a boy. It could be no other way.

The idea of it haunted her, had lingered at the back of her mind from the moment David stood so proud and strong and proclaimed himself a Plantagenet to Henry's face. She longed to know if he was more correct than he realized. Someone, some-where, must know the truth. There had to be a way to discover it.

If so it transpired, Henry would have to

be told as a matter of loyalty. After everything he had done for her and her two sisters, she could not leave him in ignorance.

What might he do if convinced beyond a doubt that David was the true heir to the throne? It was impossible to say with any degree of certainty. The least he would do, surely, would be to recall David from his role as a divider of the Yorkist force.

That recall was necessary. David would never abandon the course he was set upon, otherwise. He had given his word to King Henry and would not depart from it, something she should have known from the start.

If David was dismissed by the king, however, he could accept that turn of events with good grace and no damage to his honor. He could go about his affairs as before, either returning to France or remaining here in England. They could be done with this business of princes and kings forever.

First, however, was the matter of discovering his birth.

It would have to begin with the convent where David had been reared. Surely the order of nuns domiciled there kept records for the children left in their care? If not that, then the Mother Superior might remember the circumstances. It could not hurt to ask.

She had sent messages flying across Europe to bring David to her. It should be easier to do something similar in England. She need not leave the keep or make a noise about it. All she had to do was pen the messages and wait with what patience she could manage to receive answers.

She would start tomorrow. And would it not be strange if she proved that David was the least false of all the pretenders to the throne of England, more truly a king than the man who held it?

Marguerite was up to something, David knew it. Brooding speculation was in her eyes and determination in the set of her chin. It had always been one of her charms that what she thought and felt registered on her expressive face.

He only wished he knew exactly what she had in mind so he could prevent it. He could not endure another such incident as the ambuscade.

The devil in it was that he could not remain to discover it. Now that she was mending, he had to return to the arrangements made by Henry. Meetings of vital importance had been postponed, meetings with those who would pretend to support him and provide funds, men and armor to make his cause appear strong and viable. These appointments must be kept if he was to maintain the momentum he had gained.

He had gathered some few supporters on his own, young men ready for change, those grown tired of the endless machinations of the old regimes, the constant shifts of power that robbed noble and merchant, rich and poor alike of their peaceful futures. None could prosper while all looked over their shoulders for the next invasion, the next overthrow of Lancastrians by Yorkists or Yorkists by Lancastrians. The common people were so sick of war that they were ready to cheer any man who could promise an end to armies marching across their fields and common lands, taking whatever they produced and raping their wives and daughters.

He was ready for an end to it himself, David thought, and he had been a child when it began. How much more ready must Henry be for peace?

If he survived this Yorkist revolt, if Henry prevailed and kept his word to allow Marguerite to remain unwed, then he would escort her to one of the properties left to her by her father. There, if she would but allow it, he would become her husband in name only. Failing that, he would be her

seneschal and captain of her guard. He
would watch over her for the rest of her
days. And if by chance she should decide of
her own will to take another man as husband, then he would leave her, returning to
France. He would leave her because he
could not bear to watch her with another
man, could not endure seeing her bear
another man's children.

He would go back to the tournaments and
wars where he had won his fame. What happened afterward would not matter at all.

"When do you go?"

Marguerite's question ran so closely with
his thoughts that it was an instant before he
realized she was asking when he would leave
the keep again. He glanced at her, wondering why she wanted to know even as he
noted, with tightness in his chest, the
shadows caused by pain and worry that lay
under her eyes.

"In the morning," he answered.

"So soon? Can you not wait a few more
days?"

"I should have been away already. They
say Warbeck is making ready to march, in
part from fear of losing his followers." The
gentle touch of her fingers upon him made
the blood boil through his vein, afflicting
him with greater hardness than the roomful

of naked dancing girls he had once seen in Italy. The pleasure of it was so great it must surely be sinful.

"Losing them to you, you mean."

"So I'm told."

Her smile was a mere tug at one corner of her lips. "It must be gratifying that they are willing to risk it."

"It might be, if it wasn't so useless." He caught her fingers that she was threading through his hair, making his scalp prickle down the back of his neck and all the way to his spine. With her hand captured in his, he went on. "I would remain if not certain your fever is gone and your wounds beginning to heal."

"I know you would," she murmured. "And when do you return?"

He twitched a shoulder. "Who can say? It depends on how many men come to my standard and what news they bring of others who may join me."

"They will be disappointed, all those men, when you resign your claim to the throne. I hope Henry won't be too hard on them for breaking away to follow you."

He smiled a little because it was so like her to think of the fate of others when this was over. "He will have enough to worry about, dealing with those who ride with

Warbeck."

"Let us hope so," she said on a grimace for the inevitable bloodshed that must accompany a victory.

Female softness was the perfect antidote for thoughts of death. The need to gather her into his arms, to press her against him from neck to his knees, clawed at him. He yearned to bury himself in her, felt with certainty beyond all reason that her touch would take away the grimness of what he was about, just as his might make her well and unscarred by her ordeal. To lie beside her in that narrow bed, naked skin to naked skin, seemed an earthly paradise that he would give his soul to know.

Such sweet damnation. All he had to do for it was to forsake the vow he had made.

That was all.

"Speaking of riding," he said, the words strangled in his throat as he released her and got to his feet, "I had best go and see that all is in readiness."

"Yes, I suppose so." Her gaze was dark brown and deep as she stared up at him, searching his face. "You won't forget to come and say goodbye?"

"No. No, I won't do that."

It was the last thing he would do, in fact. His leave-takings were his most perfect excuse for holding her, kissing her. For that, he would never fail to seek her out. No, not even if it killed him.

Treading down the stairs and into the great hall, David searched the gathered men for Oliver. He saw him playing at dice with a handful of others. A small jerk of his head brought his squire to him.

"You've a frown on you like an abbess with only one nun to order about," Oliver said as he strolled within hearing distance. "Is something amiss?"

"The very thing I would ask you. Has Astrid said anything of what might be troubling Marguerite?"

"Other than a double-punctured arm and nearly getting you killed? Naught at all."

"She came nowhere near getting me killed. That was my own stupidity."

Oliver held up his hands. "You said it, not I."

David ignored that sally. "Astrid's mentioned nothing of what her mistress might intend when she is well again?"

"Shall I ask her? Is that what you want?"

"If you can do it without making too much of it," he said in agreement. "And without delay, either, as I'd know the answer before morning."

"Before we leave," Oliver clarified.

David nodded, but then put out a hand to touch his arm as he turned away. "Wait. I think . . ."

Oliver paused in midstep, one brow arched in interrogation.

"You will remain here in the morning. Whatever you do, don't let Marguerite beyond the gate without you, don't let her out of your sight, don't let anyone near her."

Oliver's eyes narrowed. "You think she is in danger, or is it . . ."

"I don't know. But I cannot do what I must if I have to worry she is being insulted for my sake or that something may happen to her, with her, while I'm away."

"No. I see that."

"Explain it to her. Make her understand that she is to remain near the keep."

"Be easy. I'll look after her."

David looked at him through narrowed eyelids. "From a distance."

Oliver chuckled, the skin around his eyes crinkling with his amusement. "Oh, that was understood."

"Good," David said under his breath, though worry clung like a burr caught on the back of his mind. "Good."

17

Marguerite wrote the first of the messages on the day after David left. It was not the easiest of tasks. To hold the parchment steady required pressure from her left hand that caused her upper arm to throb. She could only manage a few lines before she was forced to stop. Resuming again in the afternoon, she finally completed it. The effort actually seemed to ease some of the soreness from the injury, which was encouraging. She might soon regain use of the arm.

Sanding the missive and pouring the fine grains back into their box, she looked toward Oliver who sat in the window embrasure, picking a tune from a lute. Calling him to her where she sat at the narrow table she had ordered brought into the solar for her correspondence, she explained what she wanted done.

"My most abject apologies, milady," he said gravely as he stared down at the lute in his hands as if he'd never seen it before, "but I am to abide near you. Sir David's orders."

She was taken aback. "But why?" As another thought struck her, she frowned. "You aren't a prisoner?"

"Not yet, milady, but I could be if I fail him."

"Fail him in what?" she asked in dawning suspicion.

"Looking after you, milady. I am charged with your safety, warned not to let you out of my sight."

"So it is I who am the prisoner."

"Nay, milady, nay!" he said in alarm. "Nothing was said of preventing you from going, though you can't be allowed to go alone."

"You are my guard."

"In part, as I have been since you were taken on the road. Nothing has really changed."

She turned over that information in her mind. It seemed straightforward enough. "Let us see if I have this correctly. If I were to go to London, to Westminster, you would be obliged to go with me."

Oliver looked pained. "Milady . . ."

"Answer, jackanapes," Astrid said, looking up from where she sat mending the torn corner of Marguerite's linen veil in the light from the window.

"But it isn't safe!" The beleaguered look he cast toward the small serving woman made it difficult to say whether he spoke to her or to Marguerite.

"Not safe to answer?"

"Not safe to go," he said with exasperation as he turned back again. "I am to keep you safe at all costs."

"I am shut up in a keep with a goodly number of men-at-arms around me, am I not?"

"Half the number David brought with him," he agreed with a decided nod.

"How much more safe could I be?"

"It matters not. I must stay with you."

"Because David said so, I see." She drummed her fingers on the tabletop. "Very well. I need a trustworthy man to deliver this message. Yes, and two additional men-at-arms to ride with him in case of trouble. You will see to it?"

"Three? It requires three men to do the task I was to undertake alone." His outrage was comical, mainly because it was tempered with such obvious relief.

"Are you not flattered?" Oliver could have been trusted with the task, Marguerite thought. For the others, it was to be hoped each of the three would keep the others mindful of the swift completion of their assignment.

"Exceedingly." He drew a breath that swelled his chest. "And I believe I know just which ones to send, milady."

"I was sure you would. Mind you, they are to wait for a reply and ride straight back here with it."

"*Bene,* so it will be done."

"See that it is, or next time I'll send Astrid."

The Italian sent a sly glance toward where her serving woman watched them, her sewing in her lap. "Could you not send her now, with or without extra men-at-arms?"

Marguerite laughed, she couldn't help it. "She can't be spared. I require her help to dress with this stiff arm." She lifted it in a brief gesture. "Besides, you know you would miss her as you would your morning ale if she was not here."

"One grows used to doing without," he said stoutly, his gaze going to the window seat once more.

"Scoundrel," Astrid said without heat as she tied a knot and then bit off the thread with a click of sharp teeth. "You know you love me."

"No such thing!" Oliver protested.

"Ha! You do, you love me. You want my body. You want to see how I am made under my skirts."

He turned to Marguerite with beseeching eyes. "Milady, only listen to her."

"You did start it, you know," she said without compunction. Pushing back her stool, she got to her feet and went away, leaving them to it.

The reply she sought took the best part of two weeks to be returned, and then was negative. The Mother Superior of the convent near Westminster, from which David had been apprenticed to a tanner of skins before his rescue at Braesford's hands, regretted that she could not be helpful. She had no personal knowledge of a blond-haired, blue-eyed baby born at the nunnery more than a score years before then branded on the shoulder, though she did agree the incident should have been memorable. However, she had held her post a mere five years, taking it after the former abbess died of the sweating sickness. In pursuit of the information sought, she had spoken to several elderly nuns who were in residence at that early period. They well remembered a young man named David who had carried a brand such as Lady Marguerite described, but said he came to them as a boy rather than a baby. By some peculiar oversight, no record could be found of his arrival, leaving the Mother Superior unable to say precisely when he came to St. Theresa's. The woman regretted she was unable to be of greater aid.

Marguerite was disappointed but not discouraged. She had suspected this would be no easy task. At her desk once more, she wrote four new missives and sent them forth to the convents within a reasonable day's travel of the London nunnery.

Another two weeks and some few days dragged past before the trio of messengers, men from Bruges, who had been with David and Oliver for years, returned at last. They were dusty, sweaty, exhausted and riding different horses from those they had set out upon. Marguerite barely allowed their spokesman time to down a glass of ale before sending for him.

"Have you an answer for me?" she demanded the instant he appeared.

"Aye, milady, four of them." He fumbled at the pouch that hung from his belt, but brought out only one rather grubby sheet with a wax seal crumbling at its folded edge.

"What is this?" Marguerite said as she accepted the message from his hand. Oliver, standing at her side, stepped forward as the messenger gave her a dogged look.

"The crones at the first three convents gave us to understand they have better things to do than keep track of every nameless babe left on their doorsteps. The fourth said the same. As we were on the point of leaving there, an old nun with a cast in one eye ran after us. She said word was flying from one convent to another of someone asking for information about a certain baby born many years ago."

Marguerite had not anticipated this development. She should have, of course. Anything as unusual as pointed questions about a former foundling was bound to stir up curiosity. Though the life passed behind convent walls was quiet and restricted, there was near constant communication between the different domiciles of an order.

She only hoped the interest she had caused remained within the narrow religious community. She did not like to think of what might happen if it was spread abroad.

"Had this woman anything to tell you?" she inquired.

Dust flew from the messenger's hair as he shook his head. "Said nothing more than that, only shoved the letter at me and ran off as if the devil's imps were on her heels."

Marguerite's fingers were less than steady

as she broke the seal and unfolded what appeared to be a piece of wrinkled parchment torn from a religious manuscript. The writing upon it was in some vegetable ink so pale it was nearly invisible. That was until she stepped to the window and held the sheet to the light.

The words were badly formed and the spelling inventive, but the sense of it was clear enough. An elderly nun, one Sister Beatrice, who had befriended the writer when she was but a novice, told a strange tale of a baby which might be the one sought. Sister Beatrice might speak more freely now, as the matter had long weighed upon her conscience. Anyone who would hear her must come without delay, for the good sister was full of years and soon to leave this world.

Marguerite dismissed the messenger with ample reward for him and the men who had ridden with him. When he was gone, she stood tapping the parchment against her thumb. There was little to consider, however, when all was said and done. She must go. Her arm was almost healed after near a month of rest. It sometimes ached at night, but she thought she could handle the reins. The keep could spare a contingent of men-at-arms to accompany her.

Oliver would go with her, of course, and Astrid, as neither would countenance being left behind. They could be away by daylight on the morrow.

David would not like it.

No, but David wasn't here. If he had been, if he were not about the king's business, then the journey would not be necessary.

"Oliver," she said, turning to the Italian with purpose in her eyes.

"Nay, milady. I know you long to speak with this nun of the message, but it can't be done."

"Not to her, but to another who may know more." She related the contents of the missive in a few succinct phrases.

" 'Tis too dangerous to go, milady. Half the countryside is up in arms over this business of the pretender, and you've no notion who you may meet on the roads. It's as much as my life is worth if I allow you to venture beyond the keep's walls. David will kill me, I promise you."

"Allow?" she asked, at her most aristocratic.

"Your pardon, milady, but . . ."

"You cannot stop me. I am my own woman, now, with no father, brother, husband or any other man over me." How good it felt to speak those words aloud. It was as if a great weight had been lifted from her, the weight of a lifetime of expectation, prohibition and bowing to the dictates of others. No matter what happened after this, she would never again resign herself to any man's will.

"But, Lady Marguerite, only consider my position," Oliver moaned.

Astrid came to stand beside Marguerite. She looked up into her face, her eyes bright with understanding. With a glance for Oliver, she spoke up in her piping voice. "Lady Marguerite may feel for your position, you addlepated dunce, but has a purpose more important. She would be about business of her own that has naught to do with the affairs of men."

"The king will not be pleased."

"We aren't that pleased with him, if it comes to that," Astrid countered with a toss of her head. "What has he done except use us for his own ends? Bustle about now and make ready, or my mistress and I will go without you."

Oliver cajoled, threatened and pulled his curly hair, but it was for naught. The end was never in doubt.

They left at daybreak on their grueling journey. Set at the pace kept by men-at-arms, it was no royal amble through the countryside, but a race that took them in fast stages from the Yorkist area in northwest England to the south and east of London. Their way was paved by plentiful coin and myriad curses. Fresh horses, cold food and rough beds upon fireside settles were their lot. By the end of the third day, Marguerite was forced to support her arm in a sling. Still every hoof beat that struck the ground over the next two sent a lance of pain from her fingertips to her spine. She was almost ready to admit the endeavor was beyond her strength when they came finally to the convent that held Sister Beatrice.

It was a sleepy enclave where sheep grazed, cattle lowed and the walls, built for defense against Norsemen in centuries past, enclosed a huddle of buildings of no particular comfort or beauty. They consisted of a Norman church rising four-square and solid at one end, a quadrangle of long dormitories edged by a cloister that enclosed an herb garden, and a collection of outbuildings that had been added over the centuries for purely practical purposes. Its location at the edge of a marsh provided reeds for thatching the humped roofs, and a thousand other plants to keep the body alive and in working order.

The Mother Superior was a most practical lady. On hearing that they wished to speak to a certain elderly nun, she arranged it with dispatch and little curiosity. This may have been the result of Marguerite's announcement that they were upon the king's business, but could just as easily have been because the woman was too busy to care about deathbed reminiscences.

Marguerite, with Oliver and Astrid close behind her, was shown into a four-square cell. It was more airy than most, but boasted few comforts beyond a prie-dieu in the corner and a window that overlooked the garden where herbs in flower murmured with bees. Sun-warmed, sweet and pungent, their scents drifted into the room where the elderly woman they sought lay dying. That this was her fate seemed certain from the inescapable odors of old age and disease, which lingered beneath the herbal freshness.

The woman on the bed ran her rosary through gnarled fingers as if in constant prayer. She had a sweet face with thin, fragile skin that was unlined except for grooves of pain on either side of her mouth. Her eyes, sunk deep in their sockets, were clouded with age. Flustered and fearful at first, she grew calmer as she learned the purpose of their visit.

"All praise to our dear Lord that you have

come," she said in a voice so soft it was barely a whisper. "The pain in my side grows wearisome, and will soon take me away. Now you are come, I may seek my rest, knowing justice may be done."

"Justice?" Marguerite inquired, stepping closer to the bed while Oliver and Astrid moved forward on either side of her.

"I've waited long, so long I had given up hope. So many deaths, so many, and for nothing. I have prayed without ceasing . . ."

"Justice for what?" Fear that the woman was wandering in her head, that she could tell them nothing because she knew not what she was saying, was like a live coal inside Marguerite's chest.

"For whom, you mean to say. For poor Lady Eleanor, who did not deserve such use, such betrayal. Father Joseph said the sin of fornication was upon her, that this is why she was brought to bed of a child here. I made so bold as to ask how that could be, when she had her marriage lines that said the union enjoyed the blessing of the church. Yes, and when the man who brought her to childbed was a king such as no woman dared refuse."

"A king? You mean . . ."

"Edward IV, he was, though he's dead now, has been these many years. Oh, aye, and the sweet Lady Eleanor, as well. They sent her away afterward, you know. I heard it was to the convent at Norwich. Aye, and heard, too, she died there of the shame and heartbreak." The elderly nun's unseeing gaze wandered to the window while her pale, bloodless fingers still turned the black beads, like some kind of flower seeds, in her hands. The soft clicking was like music in the somnolent quiet. "I sometimes wonder if she was not helped to her death."

"Because of the marriage, you mean." Marguerite took a slow, deep breath, aware of Oliver and Astrid exchanging a grim look behind her back.

"And the marriage lines, yes. Poor lamb, to be enticed into indiscretion with her betrothed, a man all saw as her husband, only to be put aside when Edward lusted after the Woodville woman. Secret, it was, his marriage to that witch, because he feared Lady Eleanor would cry out against it. As if she would have, ever. She'd too much pride, you know, even if her family had not received royal favor to see to it she was put away."

Astrid, at Marguerite's side, looked up at her with wide eyes. She doubtless remembered when much of this was brought out as Richard III became king. He had used the tale to have parliament declare Edward's children by Elizabeth Woodville illegitimate, a first step in taking over his brother's throne. It was not long afterward that his two young nephews, Edward's sons, were noticed playing outside their Tower chamber a last time, and then were seen no more.

It seemed apiece with everything else that Lady Eleanor Butler had conveniently died while shut up in her convent. But it had little bearing on why Marguerite had come.

"What about the baby?" she asked, raising her voice a little to bring the nun's thoughts back from the past. "Was it a boy? And if so, what became of him?"

"A boy child, yes, and so beautiful with soft gorse-yellow curls and blue eyes. I was there when he was born. I helped him into the world, helped him take his first breath, though I misdoubt it was a good deed."

A frown knotted Marguerite's forehead. "Why would you say that?"

"What? Oh, his father was there to see him born, you know. He named him Edward after himself. Then he took him away and had his mark put upon him. How the dear little mite cried, such agony it was to me to hear it. Aye, and why should he not cry when he was greeted with pain the moment he arrived in the world? And because it was his own father who ordered that great ugly burn, ordered it for his own glory."

Oliver whispered an oath. Astrid clapped her hands to her mouth as if to stifle a cry or contain sickness.

Marguerite's heart ached at the tale, as it had twisted with anguish for the brand burned into David's skin. At the same time, she was gripped by febrile excitement. A mark, a burn ordered by a Plantagenet king. She had been right to follow the trail left by it. She had been right to come here.

"Edward did that?" she asked, her tongue almost too stiff to form the words. "But why? Why?"

The rosary beads moved faster, a sign of the elderly woman's disturbance of mind. "The baby was a son, you see. Edward had married the Woodville woman by then, but she had not conceived. He thought to mark the babe so he might know him again if he had no other sons. Arrogant, selfish man, to use a child so. He was well paid that his sons born of Elizabeth Woodville did not long survive him."

"You mean . . . You are thinking of the princes in the Tower?"

"Are they not in the thoughts of all who have lived through these terrible times? Pity those young boys, their lives cut short for so base a reason." Tears rose, glimmering in the nun's fine old eyes, pooling in her eye sockets. "What do children care for crowns? They should have been permitted to laugh and play without care. But no, that they had been born made them pawns, and so they died from the ambition of another king."

"And the branded babe, what became of him?" Marguerite held her breath as she waited for the answer. So much depended upon it, so very much.

A fretful look came into the ancient face. She turned her head back and forth upon her thin pillow. "Ah, the poor wee thing. He was sent away after a few years, though I know not where. Some place close by the king, 'twas said, where he might be brought forth at need."

The convent where Braesford had discovered David was a mere stone's throw from the back gate of Westminster Palace. That was close indeed, most conveniently close.

Even as Marguerite realized it, Astrid caught her sleeve and gave it a tug. She drew her down and whispered a suggestion in her ear.

Marguerite gave a single nod and straightened again, clasping her fingers tightly together at her waist. "Mayhap you tended the burn you mentioned as it healed? You saw where it was and how it appeared, the size and shape of it?"

Sister Beatrice turned even more fretful. " 'Twas the size of my palm, and large on that tiny shoulder, monstrous raw on his sweet skin. The look of it? Some heretic's symbol, a few circles with a straight mark under them, such as a child might draw for a tree and its trunk. I could hardly bear to look upon such a mark of the devil. Besides, only holding and walking the babe made him stop crying."

"Dio," Oliver breathed. "Ah, *Dio."*

Marguerite could only echo the sentiment. What the nun had just described was the brand on David's shoulder. Though it might have been large once, David had grown so it was now much smaller by comparison. It was still the same, however, still exactly the same.

It also meant he was not Edward V whom everyone said had died in the Tower. He had never been that vanished boy king.

No, he was better. If Edward IV's sons by Elizabeth Woodville were illegitimate, as claimed by his brother Richard III, then the marriage to Lady Eleanor Talbot Butler was legal and binding. The child of that marriage was his only legitimate offspring. David was, then, the true and rightful heir to

407

the throne of England.

Marguerite cleared her throat of a sudden tightness. "I am glad, so very glad Edward's son had someone to hold him when he cried."

Tears glazed the milky eyes of the old nun. "Such a sweet mite, so sweet," she said, stumbling over the words while her fingers worked feverishly at her beads. "I've wondered often what became of him, if he lived and where he is now. He would be a man grown, and should have been a king. My conscience smites me often that I did nothing when his father died. I should have, I know I should."

"If Richard III had learned of the boy, he might have eliminated him as he did the others," Marguerite said in soothing reason.

The elderly woman turned her head back and forth on the pillow. "So I tell myself, but would he? Did he take the throne from ambition to wear a crown or because he thought it right? Too late to know, too late. I let that dear child be shunted away and forgotten. Edward IV died, and his sons afterward, and that was that. The little one was robbed of his birthright because I would not speak."

"If you had tried, you might easily have been silenced."

"Aye, and so I let fear make me a coward. Now I will die in spite of it. We should not live our lives in fear of death, for there are things far worse."

What was there to say to that? All Marguerite could offer for comfort was the truth. "Mayhap it makes no difference," she said, reaching out to still the fingers turning the rosary beads, giving them a gentle squeeze. "It's possible he would rather not be a king."

The woman's lips twisted a little as she managed a watery smile. "What manner of man would turn away from it? Who would not accept a crown if all he had to do was reach out his hand? No, no, I failed. The babe was a fine, braw boy, but may have been too weak to hold it. Still, he should have had his chance. Yes, he should." She let her eyes close as if suddenly too weary to hold them open. "I have confessed my sin and done penance for it. It lies heavy in my heart still, but I am ready to go to my maker. The rest, I must leave it to you."

Standing there, Marguerite was suddenly aware of the terrible responsibility that went with what she had just learned. People had died for such knowledge, had been killed in battle, been executed or quietly smothered in the night. If the truth had become known after Edward died, then David might easily have been among the victims, just as she had said.

He could become one still.

What would he do if presented with what she had learned here? Would he shrug it off and continue as he was, keeping to the letter of the agreement he had forged with Henry? Or would he use the forces that were even now gathering around him to strike at the man holding the crown that was his by right?

Most men would choose the latter course. And who could blame them when a kingdom with its power and riches was at stake?

Henry Tudor had won his crown in battle at Bosworth Field. He had risked everything for it, including his life, and would not give it up without a fight. To him, as a Lancastrian king, Edward IV had been a usurper who had stolen the crown from his uncle, Henry VI. Who Edward's son might or might not be mattered little, as he had no real right to be king in Henry's view. Such had been the reasoning behind the vicious battles of the War of the Roses, and so it remained.

What would Henry do, then, if suddenly presented with David as the rightful Plantagenet king? Would he dissolve the agreement between them, call David away from his role as a false pretender and allow him to leave the country? Or would he simply have him killed and so end the threat at the source?

What had she done? Dear God, what had she done?

Henry was not the only one who must make a life-or-death decision. She must somehow make up her mind what she was going to do now.

Should she tell David what she had discovered and leave what he would do with it to him? Or should she forget she had ever made this journey and keep the knowledge of his birth from him forever?

Should she remain loyal to Henry VII who had done so much for her and her sisters, placing the facts before him that he might act upon them as he saw fit? Or should she transfer her loyalty to David while knowing she must lose him, that if he became king he would be consumed by royal obligations, among them the need for a dynastic marriage to some foreign princess?

What choices, each more terrible than the last.

It was then, there in that nun's small cell, that Marguerite knew she loved David beyond all reason. She knew because the dearest wish of her heart was to let this bit-

ter cup pass her by while she made no decision at all. She longed to have everything as
it was before, that she might have the joy of
being near him in whatever manner honor
allowed. If his being a king meant she could
never again taste his kiss, feel his arms
around her, watch him smile, then she
wanted him to be just a man.

"Milady? Lady Marguerite?"

A shudder moved over her as she roused
from her inspection of the bleak gray land-
scape of her heart. Turning toward Oliver,
she raised her brow in inquiry.

"The old woman sleeps. What would you
now?"

"Let us go back," she said, "back to the
keep."

"And when we get there?"

"Imbecile," Astrid said with tears in her
voice. "How can she know the answer to
that? Or knowing, how can she say it?"

How indeed, Marguerite asked herself.
But she had the whole long ride back to
make up her mind.

18

Marguerite was not at the keep. She had not been there for many days.

David, receiving the news from the captain who had been left in charge of the keep's guard, felt the blood in his veins turn to winter's black ice.

Lady Marguerite had ridden out with a complement of men-at-arms not quite two weeks ago. No one knew her destination. None could say when she would return.

None knew if she intended to return.

David stood in the great hall with his white-faced and stoic guard captain in front of him. He removed his gauntlets with slow care and dropped them on the table beside him as he fought to restrain his temper. Unclenching his teeth, he asked the question that concerned him most.

"Who rode out with her?"

"Her little serving woman and your squire, with a complement of six men-at-arms."

"Only six."

"Aye, sir."

The captain, his gaze wary, shut his lips on anything more he might have added. It was just as well, as David might otherwise have decided to take his head off. That Oliver was with Marguerite should have allowed him to breathe again, but his Italian squire had a soft spot for the lady, as well as for her small henchwoman. He could be depended upon to trade his life for hers if need be, but he would also be a willing slave in whatever mad undertaking Marguerite required.

"No other?" David demanded. "No one was sent from the king to fetch her? No one arrived from Braesford?"

"No one, Sir David."

"She received no noble visitor?" He scowled in sudden dread. "Lord Halliwell's son was not here?"

"No, sir."

David cursed under his breath, flinging away from the man. Striding away a few steps, he stopped, whipped around and came back again. "What went forward in my absence?"

"Sir?"

"What did my lady — Lady Marguerite — do in the days before she left here? Did she turn ill again? Did she embroider, walk into the countryside, ride? What?"

"She mostly penned letters, sir, and sent them far and wide."

A tingle of foreboding prickled over his scalp. "Had she answers to these messages?"

"Aye, sir, one or two."

When prompted, the captain expanded upon that news, saying who had been her messenger, also what the man had said in the great hall about where he had been and who he had seen. David's heartbeat slowed as he began to see what Marguerite might be about, but his anger burned hotter.

He had been away too long. Knowing he might be, he'd tried to guard against this pass. It had not sufficed.

His instructions for Lady Marguerite, left with Oliver, were that she was to remain near the keep, if not inside it. She had ignored that order. In willful disobedience of his provisions for her safety, she had put herself in danger.

What in the name of heaven possessed her to ride out? She had not been in any shape for it when he left. Had her wound healed in his absence, or was it still raw so it might turn putrid from the dirt of travel? What if she lost her arm? What if she died?

God in heaven.

Anything could happen to her upon the road, especially with the bands of men moving here and there, some for York, some for Lancaster, and some for no one and nothing except their personal gain, personal pleasure. It could have happened already with him none the wiser. She could be lying somewhere beaten and raped. She could be dead and the crows feasting upon her lovely brown eyes.

David's gut twisted. He slung his head from side to side to rid his brain of the images he could not bear. The need to see her, touch her, hold her was an ache of such desperate, raking necessity that it threatened his sanity.

"Pass the order to mount up," he said, his voice rasping in his throat.

"Sir?"

Incredulity was in the captain's voice. His men had been riding for days, had done little else for weeks as they gathered followers to the erstwhile cause of Edward V, or rather to Henry's. They were tired, hungry, gritty with the dirt of the road and rank with the smells of sweat, horse, campfire smoke, bad ale, bad food and boots and mail worn too long without airing. Every mother's son of them wanted nothing more than a bath, a hot meal and somewhere to sleep from sundown to sunrise.

David wanted the same, with the addition of Marguerite beside him.

None of it mattered.

"You heard me." He scooped up his gauntlets, began to pull them on again. "We go!"

It was less than two hours away from the keep that the dust cloud was spied.

Topping a hill that gave a spreading view of fen and dale, they saw it floating, drifting above the winding roadway. Beneath it bobbed the moving shapes of horsemen riding hard, while behind pounded a troop twice their number, giving chase. The second mass of horsemen flashed with armor and bristled with lances.

David halted with his men behind him. He narrowed his eyes, trying to make out the figures that fled ahead of their pursuers. They leaned too low over the necks of their mounts for certain identification, but he thought one, at least, perched upon a side-saddle.

Beside him, a man reached out to touch his arm while staring at the head of the column. "Your pennon, sir."

His pennon?

David rode under it of course, that blue banner with its stylized circle representing a crown of leaves. He and his men carried it, but no other.

No other except, just possibly . . .

David shouted an order, though what it was he could not have said. He spurred into a gallop, thundering down off the hill while asking for every ounce of power his destrier yet possessed. His men drummed after him, shouting, cursing as they threw themselves into the race.

His heart battered against the wall of his chest. His skin felt on fire beneath his mail. He could hear the harsh whistle of his every breath, feel them searing his throat. The wind of his passage made his eyes water until he could barely see. And though he knew he was closing the gap between that small group ahead and his own, it seemed that the world slowed, that trees and rocky outcroppings and bracken-strewn slopes moved past at the speed of an old man hobbling.

Every leaf, every rock and wildflower was startling clear. Every hazard was seen and avoided with ease and no help from his mind. His concentration was upon the lady, his lady, Lady Marguerite who was riding toward him with her veil streaming behind her and grim purpose in her face. His lady who rode under his banner.

Another snapped order, and his column opened down the center. The men swerved wide in a double line, one half pounding along the right while the other held to the left. The oncoming troop of nine riders, two women among them, did not slacken. They plowed forward, their faces red, their mouth set in grim lines while their mounts strained, wide-eyed and splattering lather. They drew nearer, gaining, gaining, gaining.

They flashed through the middle of David's troop with elbows flying and hooves flinging up grit. David had a glimpse of Marguerite's pale face with the wings of her veil flapping behind her, Oliver's dust-mustachioed grin, Astrid's face screwed up with terrified rage. Then they were past.

His men closed the lane behind them. Marguerite's troop galloped on without slowing, certainly without stopping, making for the keep as if the devil himself was after them.

He would be, and soon, David swore. He would personally be on their heels.

"Halt!" he called, throwing up a hand.

His men grunted, swearing as they drew rein and clattered to a jarring stop behind him. David swung his destrier broadside to the road and drew his sword. Easing his weight in the saddle, he sat in grim anticipation. A goodly exchange of hacking, slicing combat would suit his mood exactly. He needed it, wanted it, prayed for it.

It was not to be.

The horsemen ahead slowed to a prancing walk. A distant order rang out. The column wheeled in formation and rode back the way they had come.

The need to chase after them was a roaring fire in David's chest. He burned to know who led them, who had ordered them out and what they wanted with Lady Marguerite. He needed, still, to be rid of the rage that throbbed in his head, needed to vent it on an enemy who could fight back blow for blow.

He couldn't ride after them. The company was as large as his own. If he should be defeated, should be killed or taken, they might yet ride down and capture Marguerite. The risk was too great.

David's mouth set in a straight line. He wheeled his destrier and made for the keep with his men straggling along behind him.

Marguerite was waiting for him in the great hall. He saluted her courage, but derided her common sense. Far better if she had retired to the solar, thrown off her clothing and awaited him naked in his bed. It might have at least given a different direction to his rage. To see her travel-weary and begrimed, with half a dozen men-at-arms at her back like an armed guard, only added to its burn.

"My lady," he said as he strode toward her, sweeping off cloak and helm as he walked and sending them flying into the arms of a servant. "How kind of you to rejoin us. Of course, you almost brought half of Warbeck's army with you, but what of it? A fast clash of arms before supper would have whetted our appetites right well."

Her lips had curved in a smile of joyous welcome, but it faded at the harshness of his voice. Her chin came up. Shock and resentment chased the warmth from her eyes. "Warbeck's army? Was that who they were?"

For an instant, David regretted her distress, also the loss of her smile. It couldn't be helped. She needed to understand what was at stake.

"You didn't tarry to be introduced? Wise, I would imagine, for I misdoubt you would have liked their manner of greeting. Too rough, by half, for a lady, though only to be expected *if you will not do as you are bid*."

Her chin came up and gold fire flashed in the brown depths of her eyes. "Bid by whom, sir? I am not yours to command. But never mind that. I wanted to express my gratitude for your timely arrival, and my gladness that you were not required to fight your way free after our rescue."

"Gratitude would not have been necessary if you had remained where you belong," he declared in grating condemnation. "This isn't a May game, Lady Marguerite. This is bloody war, with no quarter asked or given. The men trying to ride you down weren't about to kiss your fingertips. They would as soon tumble you in a ditch as look at you, and leave you lying there bleeding and broken. If you haven't the wit to know it, then you need someone to command you."

Astrid, frowning at him from where she stood half-obscured by the drape of her mistress's cloak, stepped forward. "You forget yourself, Sir David. Milady is weary, for she has ridden far on your behalf . . ."

Oliver gasped, and stepped forward, pulling the serving woman against his thigh. "Astrid, my sweet little love, have done. Can you not see you'll make matters worse, that he's beside himself with all the horrors that could have happened to her?"

His friend and squire's words were for him as well, David knew, but he was past heed-ing. They only made him turn upon the Italian.

"How could you let her go?" he demanded in growling ire. "Or if you could not stop her headstrong flight, could you not have sent word of what she was doing and where she was going so I could do it?"

Oliver laughed without mirth. "You could have tried."

"Oliver said everything you could wish in warning," Marguerite declared, cutting across their exchange. "Not that it was necessary, being that I am no idiot. Some things are simply more important."

"Are they now?" David said, his voice dropping to a softer note. "And what would they be?"

She gave him stare for stare, as proud as any princess and twice as chilly as she looked down her nose at him. "I will discuss it with you when you are in a more reasonable frame of mind," she said with honed steel in her voice. "For now, I bid you good night."

She was turning away. She had dismissed him and meant to leave him standing there like the near-servant he had always been in her brother-in-law's house. She refused to see that he was past that, could not acknowledge how far he had come since the days

423

when they had frolicked together. Faster than thought, he reached out and seized her arm, swinging her back to him.

A cry of anguish left her and she swayed toward him, all boneless grace and failing strength. The shock of what he had done, the instant recognition that his hard, calloused fingers gripped her injured arm, robbed him of agility. He let her go as if he had touched an open flame. Before he could move to catch her, she was at his feet in a travesty of a curtsy, kneeling in the spreading pool of her cloak and skirts.

"God, Marguerite, no," he whispered.

Astrid screamed and began to beat on his hip with her small fists. David barely felt it. Nor did he feel the glares, the angry stares directed at him in the sudden silence. In some still, dark fastness of his mind, shame lashed at him, but he could no more heed it than any of the rest.

Bending with desperate strength, he slid an arm behind Marguerite's back and one under her knees and lifted her against him. Her head fell forward to rest against his chest, and he pressed his beard-rough cheek against her forehead for a fleeting moment. Turning then, he went swiftly to the steps that led to the solar.

Somewhere behind him, a man muttered

in a salacious aside. Another guffawed. David spun around, snapped an order to the captain of his guard that wiped the snide smiles from a score of faces.

The silence took on a different timbre, one freighted with the dread that underpins respect among men. In it, he turned again and climbed the stone steps with hard and steady purpose. Nor did he stop until he was in the solar with the door closed behind him.

He paused, then wavered in the middle of the cramped room. There was really only one thing to do, one place to put her down.

He didn't want to do it. She felt so right in his arms, so soft against him, yet with innate strength that showed she was his match in all the ways that mattered. She was his match, had been in those days when she emerged from childhood, was even more so now. She was his friend, the mate to his soul, and he might have lost her.

Desire clashed inside him with storm fury. It hardened his body until every muscle cramped like forged steel and the gripping in his loins took his breath. He wanted her with every last particle of his being, every frantic thud of his miserable heart.

"Put me down," she said.

Her voice was even, but he could feel the

tremors that shook her. It was a moment before it came to him that they were not from frustrated desire, fear or weakness, but from rage as great as his own had been.

He hesitated only a moment before moving to the bed. He placed her upon it with care then stepped back. Fatalism and stubbornness layered his voice when he spoke. "I didn't mean to hurt you."

"But you did." She sat up, scooted backward on the mattress until her shoulders were against the headboard. "You also humiliated me, speaking to me as if I lacked a brain and the sense to use it. Do you honestly think I have no understanding of what could have happened on the road? Can you not conceive that just as you have a purpose that takes you away from here, I might have had one that was worth the journey?"

The quiet pitch of her voice was unsettling. He would have preferred that she scream at him, call him names, throw things. At the same time, he caught a shading of disdain in her voice that made his eyes narrow. "And what might that have been?"

"I discovered the whereabouts of a woman who was present when you were born, a woman who knew your mother. Yes, and your father."

The hair on the back of his neck stood up, stinging with premonition. In an effort to stave off a revelation he might not like, he said the first thing that came to mind. "That was the purpose of the messages you sent."

"What else? Did you think I was plotting treason? Or mayhap your thought was that I wrote to request a seamstress and silk merchant that I might replenish my wardrobe like some court flirt? God's blood, David, do you not know me at all?"

To hear the oath on her lips might have amused him at another time. He was in no mood for that now.

"How was I to know what you were about when you failed to tell me? Did it never occur to you, while you were sending men here and there over half of England, to direct a message to me?"

Anger glittered in her eyes. "What, and have you send orders that my requests were not to be obeyed? That I was not to leave here? Not likely! I don't require the guidance of a man for my actions. No, nor his permission."

"Have you no consideration for the fact that I am responsible for your safety? That Henry would expect an explanation if you were killed while under my protection?"

"Your protection? What protection is this, since you were not here and I had no idea when you would return? You could have been dead for all I knew, killed on the road, captured and executed, tortured, maimed, left to starve in some hole of a dungeon."

David blinked as he recognized the truth of what she said, also that she might have feared for him exactly as he had feared for her. Still, he could not leave it alone. "You didn't have to go hieing off to wherever it was you found this woman, if that's where you have been. You could have waited until I returned."

"But would you have made the journey? Or would you have set it aside until Warbeck's rebellion is over? It seemed important to know what this nun had to say. And it was important, David. It was."

"How is this? I told you before and I tell you again, I am not Edward V. No matter what I said when leaving Henry, I have no legal trace of royal bloodline."

"Oh, but you do," she answered in soft yet clear conviction. "Yes, you do."

He stared at her while the stinging at the back of his neck moved to the brand on his shoulder where it throbbed in time with his heartbeat. Inside him rose an intolerable ache to have it be true, to be born a legiti-mate Plantagenet rather than a discarded by-blow, accidental result of a moment of kingly lust. It had nothing to do with crowns or thrones, but was about acceptance, about knowing where he belonged.

"Impossible," he answered, all his tight throat would allow.

"No, it isn't."

She told him then. She described the nun-nery, the cell, the old woman and her rambling tale. She left out nothing of the horror of the brand on a helpless babe, or of how he had been shuffled off, hidden away and finally lost.

"You don't . . ." he began, then stopped, tried again. "How could something, some-one as vital as a son and heir be overlooked? How could it be allowed to happen?"

"You weren't overlooked," she said, her face earnest as she slid off the bed and came toward him. "Rather, your birth was ig-nored. Your mother's legal betrothal and consummation of the marriage were simply set aside because Edward, being young and fickle, decided he wanted Elizabeth Wood-ville and she would not succumb to him without marriage. He was ever a man easily controlled by his desires. But you were kept close at the convent near Westminster in case his illegal queen failed him. His first three children by her were girls, if you remember. He hid you away in case no sons ever appeared, hidden yet marked to be certain who you were. Oh, but then he had Edward and Richard by the Woodville woman, and so . . ."

"And so I was discarded," David said in hollow certainty.

"Lady Eleanor, your mother, had died by then. Convenient, was it not? And the nun who had tended her when you were born was shut away at her country convent, left to fade from memory as so many women have been within such walls. Only they forgot that women talk among themselves even in nunneries, that they keep each other and their stories alive in memory."

"No," David said in stubborn refusal of belief. "It has to be a mistake, some fancy told by an old woman wandering in her mind. My mother was, must have been, just another of Edward's women, one sent to a convent to hide her shame."

Marguerite caught his cuirass, shaking him. "What of the brand then? Why would Edward do something like that to a bastard child? It makes no sense, not unless he wanted to know you, know a child called Edward for his father, when the time came."

"You don't know he did, being there's naught but an old woman's word for it. The mark might be from an accident, as I said before, and nothing to do with Edward IV at all."

"You have the look of him, David," she said, meeting his gaze with determination, as if willing him to believe her.

He wanted to do that. Oh, yes. Never had he wanted anything more. But that small act of credence, innocent as it sounded, opened up such dire possibilities and dread decisions that his head spun with them.

The question that plagued him most was whether anyone else knew this story, and if they accepted it as true. Was it, for instance, at the bottom of the attacks against him? And if so, who was behind them? Was it the leader of the Yorkist rebellion, Perkin Warbeck? Or could it be Henry, after all?

"Before God, my lady," he said in a bellicose whisper, "I wish you had left well enough alone."

Her smile was strained around the edges. "Do you really think things would be different?"

An excellent question. It would be helpful if he knew the answer.

"David, David," she said, shaking him again, "you are the king. You must accept it.

You must, and then decide what you will do next."

"Henry is the king, Marguerite. He won his crown by right of arms at Bosworth Field."

"He is a usurper."

"Is he, when this bloody crown has been fought over for decades, tossed back and forth so many times that no man alive can tell who has the truest right to wear it? Even if I am who you say, what good is it? Nothing can be done when there is no proof."

The look she gave him was wondering. "But there is proof. Did I not say? I brought it back with me."

"Impossible," he declared, his voice hoarse, though it was as much a protest against fate as it was a denial.

She paid him no heed, but stepped back and unfastened her cloak. Throwing it aside, she loosened a velvet drawstring bag from the girdle at her waist. She drew it open and took from it a rolled parchment tied with ribbon and affixed with seals. With this resting on the palms of her hands, she held it out to him.

"These are the marriage lines of Lady Eleanor Talbot Butler who gave birth to a child branded at birth with the mark of the Plantagenets," she said softly. "These pages are your mother's legal contract of betrothal, and therefore of marriage, with Edward IV of England."

19

Marguerite watched with care as David hesitated then reached to take the parchment she offered. He unrolled it, scanned the Latin phrases with swift comprehension. She saw the instant when belief finally came to him, saw his eyes widen while dark color rose in his face and receded again. Though she looked closely for triumph, for pride or greedy anticipation, these things did not appear. Swinging away with the marriage contract clenched in one fist, he moved to the window and stood staring out.

"What did you intend doing with this proof?" he asked without turning.

"Beyond handing it to you? What would you have me do?" She waited, her heart tumbling in her chest, for his answer.

Breath left him in a wry laugh. "Destroy it, if I would consult my wish alone."

She saw his point. If his life was in danger before, it would be ten times worse if he were revealed as the rightful king. "And if I don't?"

"It seems clear it should be placed in Henry's hands."

"Henry's," she said in faltering comprehension.

He inclined his head. "It makes Warbeck's claim to the throne as nothing, since it proves Richard III was right, and Elizabeth Woodville was Edward's concubine rather than his queen."

He meant, of course, that Warbeck, claiming to be Edward's second son, Richard, had no legal claim whatever to the throne. "But will Henry use it, since it makes his own queen illegitimate, as well?"

"Under ordinary circumstances, no. But if it means saving his crown . . ."

"Yes, I see," she said, keeping her voice even with an effort. "But . . . but that isn't the real reason, is it?"

"Not entirely."

She stared at his profile from which all emotion had been banished, leaving his expression remote, cold, not quite focused. "It's a matter of honor. That's it?"

"I can't leave him in ignorance of something so vital to his welfare."

"What of your welfare?" she demanded, clenching her fists at her sides. "What if

Henry is so incensed, or so threatened by your rise to royalty, that he has you dragged out and beheaded at once?"

"It's a chance that must be taken," he answered, his face grim. "I will ride in the morning to deliver the evidence into his hands."

"We will ride, if it must be done."

He shook his head. "This is something I need to do alone."

She recognized the finality in his voice. He would not be moved from what he thought was right, even if it meant his death. He would not allow her to go with him because he didn't want her to see him die.

She had thought she would be forced to choose between her love for David and her loyalty to Henry. She should have known better. David had made the choice for her. All she had to do was accept the inevitable as she had with so much else in her life.

And why not? It was, as David had said, the right thing to do. That it was also the easiest did not make it less true. She would have that consolation if worse came to worst and David was seized for the king's justice.

"No!"

That defiance came to her tongue unbidden. She followed it up at once, moving to David's side to place her hand on his arm.

"Send the marriage contract to Henry if you must. When it is on its way, let us ride for France. If you would not be king, then this coming battle between Henry's forces and those of Warbeck have nothing to do with you. Let them kill each other over a piece of metal set with a few jewels. Only let them do it when we are far away."

He eased his stance, turned slowly to face her. "You would go with me?"

"Yes, if you would have me."

A corner of his mouth lifted. "Oh, I would have you, if it would serve. But you know it will not. You would miss your sisters, miss Braesford and the Scotsman Cate married and all your nephews and nieces that have been born and are to come. You would miss England's narrow little shores that hold so much of heart and home."

"You . . . you are saying that because you missed them while away on the continent." An ache pierced her chest at the idea of it.

"Oh, aye, and I left not half so much behind as you would be leaving. Still, it was all I'd ever known."

"We . . . we could make our own family."

His smile took on a rueful edge. "We could. Charles of France gave me lands, you know, with a fair castle of stone as pale as cream, and sundry villages to go with them.

We could make a home there, rear our children, grow fat and lazy and old together in the fullness of our years. We could, but for one small thing."

"Charles could well seize you for use as a pawn, might trade you to Henry for sundry concessions."

"There is that possibility, though it is not the whole."

What else could it be? She searched her mind, found the inevitable answer. "Your vow."

He inclined his head. "My vow, made when I thought you far above me as the stars, and just as out of my reach. When I was young and innocent and full of high ideals."

"And when you feared you might die in battle for the sake of Henry VII."

"That, as well."

"But you didn't die," she said, her voice tight in her throat. "You left me instead, just as you intend to leave me now."

"Not by choice."

"It comes to the same thing."

He stared down at her, and she could see the longing that darkened his eyes. His gaze moved over her face, rested on her lips. She felt them tingle, swelling, and felt, too, the tightening of her nipples under the binding she had used for comfort while riding. His heat reached out to her, surrounding her with the scent of horse and hot man. Her eyelids felt heavy, so heavy. She could not look away from the beautiful molding of his mouth, the smooth surfaces of his lips, the small pulse that throbbed in the bottom one.

He wanted her and she wanted him, and what odds that she might yet seduce him from the strict path of duty that he had chosen, might find some place in the wide world where they could be safe, could be together?

It was her only hope.

She stepped closer, caught his cuirass again and urged him toward her. He came in a swift move that brought his hard body up against her, pressed her against the stone of the window embrasure. She could feel the hard muscles of his thighs, the hot metal of his cuirass against her breasts, the corded strength of his arms that held her. He reached up to sweep her veil from her head, to spear his fingers under her thick braid where it had loosened. Then he lowered his head and took her mouth.

This was no tentative meeting of the lips but his full possession. He swooped in with his tongue in hot domination, commanding the ultimate surrender. She gave it to him, twining her tongue with his, moaning a little with the slick friction, the advance and retreat like a maddeningly intimate test of wills. She wanted to entice him, to incite his greater possession, yet could not hold the intention in mind as her excitement flared.

His arms locked ever tighter around her. Awareness receded as her senses whirled. She melted against him, sliding her arms upward to clasp his neck, threading her fingers into his hair and clutching it to bring his mouth even harder against hers. She wanted more of his sweetness, his heat, his tongue, more of him deeper inside her. She ached with emptiness and ratcheting need. She was desperate for the feel of his bare skin, the heft of his weight upon her.

His hands molded her hips, lifting her closer against him. She could feel the hot length of him against her belly, the way he shifted against her in yearning. Desire and despair flavored his kiss as he suckled her bottom lip, set his teeth gently upon it. Heat mounted to her head in a red mist. Blindly, she followed where he led, offering everything, taking everything.

Stone was at her back and metal pressed against her. She could breathe only in panting gasps. A small sound of distress escaped in her throat.

He inhaled, his every muscle hardening to steel in revolt against his will. An instant later, he pushed away from her.

Air rushed into her lungs in a gasp so deep she turned dizzy with it. Before she could recover, he caught her up, carried her to the bed and dropped her upon it. He stepped back then, twisting to unbuckle his cuirass and fling it from him so it clanged against a bedpost. As he stripped off the mail he wore underneath, and the shirt under that, his gaze returned to her. His eyes burned as they roved over her, as if searing every detail into his memory, the softness of her breasts, the scoop of her waist and flare of her hips, every curve and hollow. He tore the points of his hose from his shirt, stripped off boots and hose until he was rampantly, magnificently naked.

She watched him, noting with avid attention the masculine grace of his every move, the width of his chest and the muscles that glided under the skin, the stalwart strength of his thighs, the glint of light on the curls that spread over his chest and tapered downward to the rigid length of him. She should look away, pretend to modesty, but she wanted to see him, to remember every inch of his skin, his power and beauty, if this was the only time she would have him.

He came toward her in a soundless and powerful glide, bounding up to land beside her on the jouncing mattress. Before she could move, he rolled her toward him, his fingers busy at the back of her gown. She allowed him access while spreading her hands over his chest, absorbing his heat and scent of metal and male energy.

He wanted her, she knew. How much of her did he want? How much would he take if she offered everything she had to give? Was his control as strong as his body, his will equal to his desire? And what could she do to tip the scales?

He drew her gown off her shoulder and down, easing the sleeves from her arms. Her girdle was next, slithering away over the edge of the bed. He exclaimed in impatience at the binding that flattened her breasts, but unwound it with care, saluting the curves as they appeared, licking at the red marks left by the cloth, tasting a nipple as it peeped between the layers of wrapping. He cupped the mounds when they were free, molding them in his hands. And when he bent his head to take a hard and beaded tip into the heated suction of his mouth, it was so sensitized that she shuddered, keening in the back of her throat.

The sound seemed to rake him like a spur.

He jerked, shuddered, even as he suckled. With a hard, competent hand, he shoved at her gown while being careful of her injured arm. He pushed the fabric down over her hips, dragging it from under her and slinging it away. Her braies that had prevented saddle sores were stripped off next. When they were gone he splayed his hand over the flat surface of her abdomen and then slid it down, down until his long, hard fingers delved into her soft folds, spreading them while his thumb stroked over the tender bud at their apex.

Marguerite shifted, opening her legs at his nudge. It felt so erotic, so freeing, especially as he slipped a finger inside her. She spread her thighs wide, and wider still. She wanted him deeper, needed more of him.

He gave it to her, a second finger thrusting with care, with concentrated intent and masterful precision. Fire ran from her breasts to where he probed and back again. Her breathing grew shallow, ceased altogether as her very being burst in silent brilliance that sent tiny shooting stars across the backs of her eyelids. She turned, arching against him with her eyes squeezed shut while internal muscles pulsed in frantic rhythm.

"Please," she whispered against his shoulder. "Please come into me. Please love me. . . ."

He stroked her back, her hips, ran his palm up her spine and pushed his fingers into her hair. She could feel the throb of his heart, hear his ragged breathing. "Do you know what you're saying, sweet Marguerite?" he asked in hoarse demand. "Are you releasing me from my vow?"

"Yes, yes," she gasped, while amazement for what he had asked flitted through her mind.

It was banished as he surged up, pressing her to her back again as he covered her. He supported himself above her, hovering with a hand sinking into the mattress on either side of her face. "It is your will and not mine?"

His arms were trembling with the effort of his control, the muscles like stone. His thighs were firm between her legs, though not as hard as the iron rod that prodded her. She pressed her palms to his chest, reveling in the silken crispness of his chest hair against them, before she skimmed them down his abdomen and lower, until she held his power and pulsing heat between her two hands.

"Mine, yes," she answered in near incoherence, and could not have said whether she was answering his question or claiming possession. "Now, David. Now!"

"As you will, my lady," he said in echo of the words he'd spoken so often long ago. "And when you will."

She met his eyes then, saw them ablaze with bright azure triumph and something more that stopped her heart for an instant before sending it into a harder beat. Holding his gaze, she eased upward a little and positioned the tip of his male member against her wet, moist center. Greatly daring, she lifted her hips to take him in, parting her folds for easier access with one hand as he rocked against her. Releasing him, she grasped his waist and drew him down.

His groan sounded strangled as he eased deeper, retreated, and went deeper still. She shivered with the exquisite joy of it, the fulfillment. He stretched her, sent pleasure spiraling through her in a thousand small lightning strikes of sensation. She spread her legs wider, pulled him deeper, pressed against him with small shifts of her hips.

A deep burning promised pain. She stifled a low moan, but would not stop. She pressed up against him again, and again, but could not breach that last fastness protected by her maidenhead.

"Forgive me, sweetling," he murmured.

With a powerful thrust and twist of his hips, he plunged deep. He was perfectly still, holding her pinioned to the bed.

She cried out, but found beatitude before the cry ended. With a sob, she wrapped her arms around him and held him close while tears leaked from under her lashes. She was stretched to the fullest extent, encompassing, holding as she relaxed by degrees, adjusting to the length and thickness of him as if made for him alone. David was hers for this moment, if for no other.

"Are you all right?" he whispered against her hair.

"Perfect."

He kissed her temple, her eyes, licked the salt of her tears, brushed her nose with his lips. He took her mouth then, and slowly, with an inexorable bunching of muscles, lifted away from her and slid back again. And again. And yet again.

It was a slow ravishment of the senses, a deep plundering, as if he meant to leave no small corner of her body unplumbed. He glided, lifting her with him, tilting her hips to take more of him, all of him. It was an endless beguilement as he swirled with deliberate friction upon her swollen entrance before plunging in again.

She was enthralled by the smooth flexing

and stretching of his muscles, the perspiration veiling his skin, his heat, his effortless strength and infinite control. She filled her hands with him, grasped his hips, slipped them over his back, clutched his shoulders as she moved with him, against him, with him again. Her very being expanded. Ripples of goose bumps moved over her as years of strain and frustration fell away from her.

Still he moved, relentless in his power, implacable in his will. His eyes were fiercely tender, his jaws clenched as he held himself in unwavering restraint. He focused every ounce of his attention upon her, tending her responses while unheeding of his own, urging her toward some supreme moment.

It surged through her like on onrushing storm, a thunderous cataclysm of the blood. It broke deep inside, sweeping her up in elemental fury that had David at its center. She coalesced around him in mindless wonder, drawing him into her very core, caressing him in violent internal waves. She took him as he had taken her, surrendered even as she triumphed. And in that moment, she felt his full power as he drove into her a final time, sounding her as if he meant to make them one.

And he did, he did, while the blood

pounded through their veins, their heart-beats matched and melded and their breaths mingled. He took her mouth, whispering her name into it, holding the future at bay, protecting her from all the tomorrows, making this evening, this moment, enough to last a lifetime.

David lay watching Marguerite sleep, propped on one elbow beside her. The gray light that heralded dawn lay beyond the open window. A breeze drifted inside that was ripe with the scents of wood smoke and horse dung and green growing things. He should be up and away, but could not bring himself to move.

He didn't want to leave her, not now, not ever.

By Our Lady, but she was valiant and caring, also passionately intelligent, intelligently passionate. None of it was obvious or studied or designed to attract, and yet it swept him toward her like a hurricane. He had known more beautiful women but none that intrigued him so. None that he could love forevermore.

He had been as gentle as he could with her, but feared he had tried her sorely. He could not seem to get his fill of her. They had bathed together, eaten together, then he had taken her a second time, a third, a fourth. In the small hours of the morning he had been so lost in her, so fearful he would never hold her again, that his control had slipped. He winced now, remembering how demanding he had been, how consumed with need. He had been rougher than he intended, rougher than she deserved, rougher than she might be able to forgive.

God, beheading was too good for him.

Yet he would do it again. This night just past could be all he would ever have of this sweetest Grace of Graydon, this generous lady to whom he had pledged his life so many years ago. He had once thought it would be sufficient if he could persuade her to release him from his vow, that he could then arrange matters to suit his most fervent desire.

He had been wrong. The news brought by Marguerite set aside all his plans, destroyed his long-held dream.

Henry might well want his head, and who could blame him? The king had thought to nullify the chances for success of one pretender by creating another that was patently false. He had not known he was inviting a worse threat into his realm. That he would strike to remove it was only to be expected. Henry was a pragmatic man who never underestimated his enemies.

Marguerite had crowned him with clover once, when they were young and the world was green and new. Mayhap she was something of a witch, after all, that she had felt it appropriate back then. Now she had crowned him again, in effect, by seeking out and returning with proof of his birth. She had, but he would readily exchange that proof for the chance to go back and live this night again.

He had no wish to be king, David thought. Such had never been his ambition, and nothing had changed in that regard. It was enough to know that he was no bastard, but had been conceived in what his mother had known to be lawful wedlock.

Edward, he had been christened Edward, after all. How typical of his royal father, to name both his firstborn sons, though from different mothers, for his own arrogant self.

Edward IV had kept him close as a babe, and as long afterward as he had a chance of being useful. He had abandoned him when other sons arrived. What connection, David thought, did he have, or wish to have, to that user of women, King Edward IV, heroic in war but incapable of anything beyond raging lust that would brook no refusal? He wanted nothing to do with his Yorkist crown, Yorkist ambition for an immortal royal line.

He could not expect Henry to believe that. It would take a supremely confident king to act on such a belief, even if he could accept it.

The greatest danger, so far as David could see, was the chance Henry might consider Marguerite's actions a betrayal. That the attempt to rescue her from an unwanted marriage could end with her being imprisoned or banished to a convent was unthinkable. It could not be allowed to happen.

He must leave her behind as he rode to confront Henry, then, must go now while she slept. That was bad enough, but he must also leave her without saying farewell. He could not kiss her for fear she would wake, could not have one last taste of her, no final possession.

It was a high price to pay for honor.

And yet, he was glad that she slept on, exhausted by long hours of riding over the past few days and also the love they had shared. He was not sure he could have retained his much vaunted honor if he had been forced to say goodbye.

Easing from the bed, he dressed quickly in the dark. He woke Oliver and gave the order designed to have his company saddled and ready by the time he had bathed once more and dressed in raiment fit for an audience with a king. By the time dawn rendered the eastern sky in shades of rose and gold, they were upon the road.

What lay ahead, David could not tell. All he knew was that Marguerite lay warm and safe behind him.

20

Marguerite woke with a start, hovering on the edge of a perilous nightmare. She stared at the ceiling of coffered wood, her heart throbbing against her ribs. The dream faded without leaving her the sense of it, yet she felt something was wrong.

In a single moment, she understood what it was. She was alone in the bed. The mattress surface beside her was cool. David had gone.

She sat up in a rush, staring around the room. His clothing and armor were missing, and his boots. Beyond the window, the warm and golden light told its tale. The morning was advanced, two hours past dawn at least. Sounds from below were muted, infrequent, a sign that the largest part of David's company were either not stirring or had departed, as well.

David was gone, and so was the marriage contract that had been laid aside the night before. He had gone to confront the king, and he had left her behind.

"Astrid!" Marguerite cried in anger and a terrible desolation that nearly stole her voice. Whipping back the coverlet, she leaped from the bed and began to gather up her scattered clothing. "Astrid, where are you?"

"Here, milady!" The small serving woman swung open the door, closing it hastily behind her at the sight of her mistress's state of undress. "What is it? Are you ill? In pain?"

"When did Sir David leave? Did you see him go? Why didn't you wake me?"

Astrid bent and picked up Marguerite's girdle, placing it across the foot of the bed. "He was away early, milady," she said without meeting her gaze, "or so they said in the kitchen. Most of his company went with him, those not needed on guard here. I was not awake at the time."

Marguerite stepped to the three-legged stool and dropped down upon it with her gown crushed in her fists and sudden tears rimming her eyes. "He went without me, Astrid. Why? Why did he leave me behind?"

Astrid sighed as she came to stand beside her. She put an arm around her shoulders in a tight hug. "Oliver is gone, as well."

"Yes, of course he is," she said bitterly.

David would take his friend, but not her, the one person, next to him, who was most intimately concerned with what was going forth.

She had thought that making love would change things between them, that he might be willing to abandon England and this dangerous business of kings and crowns. Oh, she knew he had said he must go to Henry, but she had hoped to persuade him otherwise.

Their closeness made no difference, or so it seemed. What had been an upheaval of the senses reaching to the bottom of her soul had affected him not at all. He had gone about the manly pursuit of his honor without a thought for how she might feel or what might become of her if he was killed.

Dearest heaven, but she had gloried in his touch, his possession. He had used her with such tenderness, such caring when he could surely have been far rougher. He could have ridden her, driving into her untried body without remorse. The power and need for it was there in his savagely held control. Almost, almost, she wished he had unleashed his full strength, taking her as he might a woman who had known love often instead of an untried virgin. He had come close the last time he woke her, she knew, close enough that she had felt the potential for pain beneath the exquisite pleasure. Yet he had stopped short of it.

She did not know if she could have sustained it. It hurt her beyond bearing that she might never find out.

It was possible that she would never see him again, never know his kiss, his touch, the joy of lying with him, sleeping with his body curved protectively around hers. He could ride to this audience with the king at Westminster and simply disappear. It had happened before. A king did not require reason, need adhere to no rules. A word, a gesture and it was done.

David was such a king, or would have been if the world was a just place and all men honorable. Mayhap he was riding now to eliminate Henry and take his rightful place on the throne? Men had done more dangerous things while driven by the greed for power.

What if he had not taken her with him because he had tried her and found her wanting? He had satisfied his lust and was done with her?

What if he had decided that he deserved no less than a princess as his consort? She had suspected he might, had she not?

Yes, or it could be he knew it was what

was due the crown, what parliament and the people would require of their sovereign. The two of them had signed no marriage contract, and he was his father's son.

He was the son of Edward IV, who had allowed his true wife to bear their son in secret, had branded him as his own then abandoned lady and child for the sake of Elizabeth Woodville's beautiful smiles and calculated surrender.

Anguish squeezed the breath from Marguerite's chest. Suppose she had conceived during the night just past. Would David allow her to give birth in a convent? Would he brand the child of their union in case his dynastic lady produced no heir to the throne?

Marguerite clasped her arms around her upper body, rocking back and forth with the pain of the possible, the agony of not knowing what David intended, or what would become of them both.

Astrid held her closer, resting her cheek against Marguerite's hair. With no idea of what was in the mind of her mistress, she went on. " 'Tis because they think it men's work that yon fools went without us. They believe they grant us a favor by leaving us behind to stitch and see that food is prepared, and wait with what patience we may to hear what will befall them."

"They don't know Henry, not really," Marguerite said, her voice thick with tears. "They will make a muddle of it."

"Very likely, but what would you?" Astrid leaned forward to peer into her face. "They have such a head start. It's hardly worthwhile to go after them. Besides that . . ."

"Yes?"

"You know what I would say, milady. You know, if you will only think on it without fear, why Sir David left while you slept."

Did she? Did she really?

She knew what she wanted to think, but that was not the same thing. Or was it? Could it be that David had thought only to protect her? Had he taken this terrible decision upon himself so she need never bear responsibility for it?

If that was really the reason, what did it say of her that she could sit here and permit it?

It might be too late to prevent what would happen. David could be dead before she arrived, executed while she was on the road. The dream that had awakened her might have been a warning of it.

Might, might, might. Anything might have happened. She did not know for sure, nor would she discover it by sitting moaning upon a stool.

Whatever her fate, she would not learn it here.

"Astrid?"

"Aye, milady."

"We are for Westminster and an audience with the king. Tell them to make ready."

" 'Tis done, milady. I attended to it the instant I heard that Sir David had gone without you."

A smile flickered across Marguerite's mouth. "You are a pearl among women, though I have a feeling this was done because you would chase after Oliver."

"Oh, yes, yon great braggart is all I desire," Astrid declared with a toss of her head, but she grinned to herself as she said it.

Westminster was crowded, noisy and fetid from too many people squatting within too small an area. The royal palace with its walls and towers, gates and spires, churches, cloisters and jam-packed hall, dominated all. Every person that passed by Marguerite's cavalcade carried something for the court, pulled it on a sled, rolled it in a barrow or drove it in a cart. That did not, of course, count the sheep and pigs and cows that were herded on their own four feet.

All gave way for the pennon of the Golden

Knight that waved above the torches they carried as evening drew close around them. Some cursed the necessity, some shouted invective, but many whispered with awe about the second and true pretender. It was instructive.

After the austerity of the old Norman keep that had been David's stronghold, by the grace of the king, the palace seemed sumptuous, rich beyond imagining with its silk hangings, paneled walls and floors of polished marble. The chamber to which Marguerite was shown was small and drear, but even it was larger than the solar at the keep.

She had sent ahead to apprise Henry of her coming, and to beg a private word at his mercy. When she passed through the gates, the news was taken to Henry. By the time she had bathed, slacked her thirst and donned the most impressive of the gowns from her wedding trousseau, of scarlet silk edged with braid and with brocaded sleeves, an escort appeared to take her to the king's apartments.

She could have done with more time to rest. She was weary beyond words and still sore in body and spirit from her night with David. She had not dreamed a bed could be so strenuous a place, or that muscles and depths she had never used could ache so from being tried. It seemed, she thought with heat in her face, that more internal massage of a particular kind might ease it. That she would ever prove the right of it seemed most unlikely.

It was as she and her escort of two men-at-arms swept along a vast corridor lit by fat candles on floor stands that she saw David. He came toward her, resplendent in a cloud-gray velvet doublet edged with gold braid, and so regally handsome that her heart faltered along with her footsteps. He wore hose of a lighter gray and a black cloak flung back from his wide shoulders so the lining of russet silk made a frame around him. Behind him walked his own escort of the king's men, though Henry had sent four to deliver him. They were, she saw in some concern, not mere guards but members of his council.

It was only then that she realized the corridors they traveled were deserted. They were wending through the back reaches of the palace, well away from where the rest of the court enjoyed their evening entertainment. David's visit was naturally being treated as clandestine, kept secret for the benefit of the state and his pose as an alternate pretender, but then so was hers. Whether that boded good or ill for either of them was something else again.

David paused as he saw her. His face turned grim. With a brief glance at the men treading on his heels, he came on again.

"Lady Marguerite," he said in a voice that cut like the slash of a sword, "what brings you hither? I thought I left you otherwise engaged."

"So you did, but such pleasant duty can only occupy for a time." She kept her voice even, being all too well aware that their six silent and stern escorts had a dozen ears between them. She moved as she spoke, and David fell into step beside her. The two escorts blended as one, following as they turned in step down a bisecting corridor.

David gave her a hard stare. "What are you saying? Why are you here?"

Did he think she meant to betray him to Henry? The pain in that question took her breath for an instant. "Why, the same as you, Sir David," she answered when she could speak again. "What else?"

"If you are here to see Henry . . ."

"The only reason I would travel so far or set foot in this benighted palace in summer." Her smile was brittle. "Besides, we have a history, my family and the king. I've little doubt he will hear me out while I make a tale of my need."

"And what will you ask, my lady, in exchange for whatever information you have for him?"

"Only what will bring my happiness. I have no need for more."

"Freedom? Escape from yet another unwanted husband?"

"At the very least."

He leaned closer, speaking rapidly as they were nearing the king's apartments. "If you are doing this out of anger that I left you behind —"

"You give yourself too much credit, sir," she said with her coolest smile. "Why should I have expected you to take me with you? I am nothing to you, after all."

He paled there with the light of a hundred candles limning his features in orange and gold. The shift in his throat as he swallowed was fast and uneven. His eyes darkened and his mouth set in a hard line. He straightened his shoulders so they appeared impossibly broad, capable of holding up any weight.

"So be it," he said, and nodded to the leader of his escort that he was ready to face the king.

David barely recognized this elegant lady in her scarlet silk, her scarlet veil of near transparency and necklace of rare pearls. Or rather he did, but was reluctant to accept it. This was Lady Marguerite Milton, daughter of a lord, one of the greatest heiresses in the kingdom, the lady he had revered for years as being above him. It seemed impossible that he had held her in his arms, had taken her cry of pleasure into his mouth before burying himself in her soft depths. She had little resemblance to the passionate siren who had come to him the evening before and pulled him into her kiss while shivering with desire.

He had thought he knew the Marguerite he had left behind, would have wagered his life on what she would and would not do. This great lady he knew not at all. And it made no difference whatever that his birth was now proven as greater than hers. It was too new, too beyond belief, this change in his rank. In his blighted and doubtful heart, he was once again the orphan lad unworthy to touch the hem of her gown, certainly unworthy to touch the lady.

The entrance to the king's apartments opened before them. They trod their way through empty antechambers, past guards standing at blank-faced attention. They waited in a dim chamber that smelled of old candle wax, dust and nervous perspiration, saying little. The king's seneschal announced them. He and Marguerite were ushered into the presence of Henry VII.

The audience chamber was long and narrow, marked by a row of tall, arched windows filled with thick glass divided by mullions. Linen-fold panels formed the walls, with paintings in jewel colors adding interest to the open spaces between them, as well as adorning the ceiling. A dais rose beneath the windows, set so the faces of those who came before it would be well illuminated while the king's remained in shadow. That stratagem was of little use at the moment, as the sky was night-dark beyond the windows, and rain streaked the small glass panes.

"We admit to surprise to see you here," Henry VII said, his gaze upon David when he had raised him from his bow and Marguerite from her curtsy. "We thought you occupied in the north upon our service."

"So I was, Your Majesty," David answered in firm assurance. "Only something has come to light that —"

Henry lifted a hand to stay the flow of words. "All goes well with our endeavor?"

"Better than expected, sire."

"We have also taken note of recent interest in the Golden Knight. You have done well."

"I am gratified that you think so," David answered, "though you may be less pleased when you hear what I have learned."

Henry leaned an elbow on the arm of the chair that served him as a throne in this informal audience chamber and cupped his chin in his hand. His gray-blue eyes were shrewd under level brows. On this day, he wore a circlet of gold that came down on his forehead, holding back the shoulder-length waves of his gray-dusted sandy hair. His clothing was simple, being merely an embroidered wool doublet, dark hose and boots that came to his knees.

"And what might that be?" he asked after a moment.

David, his face grim and heart crowding his throat, removed the bag of oiled silk kept close under his cloak. From it he took the marriage lines which officially united Edward IV of England and Lady Eleanor Talbot Butler. With an openhanded gesture, he presented them.

The seneschal stepped forward and took the parchment, conveying it into the king's hands. Silence descended as Henry, a frown growing between his brows, perused the document.

"This is extraordinary," he said when he

looked up at last. "How came you by the pages?"

Marguerite stirred beside him. With a bow, David indicated that the tale was hers to relate. She did so with admirable brevity, but in full disclosure of all that confirmed the document in its origin.

Henry sat back in his chair. "You realize that this makes our queen consort illegitimate?"

"Indeed, sire," Marguerite answered. "I'm sorry for it, but thought it important you have this proof."

Henry made a sound of agreement. "And this babe, this son you say was born to Lady Eleanor and branded by Edward as his own? The child's claim to the throne must supersede that of other Yorkist claimants, including our Elizabeth's brothers. What know you of it?"

David drew a deep breath and squared his shoulders. "Forgive me, sire, but I am that child."

Henry's eyes narrowed. "You?"

"Brought up in a convent where orphans were taken in, and bearing a brand that is the mark of the Plantagenets."

"We would see this brand."

Hard on the words, Henry made a brusque gesture. The seneschal walked to the door of the antechamber and returned with the escort that had waited outside. They marched forward, surrounding David. A moment later, he was thrust to his knees with his cloak and doublet stripped away, and shirt torn open to expose the brand.

"Sire!" Marguerite exclaimed with shock strong in her voice. "Sir David came to you with this news. He could have continued to gather his force under your aegis, instead. He could have played you false until strong enough to become a foe."

If she meant to help, it was the wrong way to go about it, David thought in tight despair. The last thing he needed was for Henry to think of him as a potential enemy.

"And we are to accept the existence of this mark on faith, Lady Marguerite?" the king demanded. "We are not to inspect it to see if it be new or old, real or a fake, a true brand or something built upon a random scar?"

"Why would he lie?" she demanded in her turn. "He might have kept it hidden until crowned, if that had been his wish. He was already recognized as a pretender, the returned Edward."

The king did not answer, but dismissed the men of his escort with a gesture. David breathed somewhat easier once they left the chamber. At least he had not been taken to the Tower forthwith. He shrugged his clothing back into place, but remained on one knee. It seemed best to assume nothing, at least for the moment.

"He was recognized at my instigation and with my aid," the king answered Marguerite at last. "You will understand if we suspect we have been duped."

"Never, sire," David answered with all the hard conviction at his command.

"In what way?" Marguerite inquired, standing tall and proud as she faced Henry, though her clasped hands trembled visibly. "You sent for him yourself in the beginning. When he would not come, you arranged a stratagem you thought could not fail. You were correct in it, for when faced with a betrothal I could not abide, I sent for him and he appeared. Afterward, you, and you alone, put forth the suggestion that David become a pretender. He could be forgiven for thinking himself the dupe, enticed here that you might destroy him."

"Marguerite," David breathed.

"You go too far, Lady Marguerite," Henry said in hard warning. "We are not so devoid of reason as to propose insurrection against us from a true heir."

"Nor is David imbecile enough to set

himself against you. He agreed to your subterfuge for no reason except your sworn word that I need never wed. And if he has succeeded beyond your expectation or your need, it is through no fault of his own but mayhap because the people noted something of royalty in his face and manner. Where in all this is there room for betrayal or malice? Where is anything, except the honor that is his watchword?"

That plea sounded as if she was for him, after all. David heard her out with amazed hope flaring behind his breastbone, staring at her while searching for the truth of it. Her face was pale and her eyes shadowed with desperation, however, and she would not look at him.

Henry shifted in his chair, clasping its arm a moment before beginning to tap his fingertips upon it. "We are to allow him to continue building a force against us that may become greater than Warbeck's?"

"He would not . . ."

"Nay, sire," David said, overriding Marguerite's protest. "You may destroy the evidence of my birthright at your will. I have no desire whatever to wear your crown. You earned the worry and woe of it on Bosworth Field. Even should I be proved Edward's son ten times over, I would not take that from you."

Henry snorted. "Easily said, but men have been talked into royal ambition before by those who would use them for their own ends."

"But none with such strength of will or little yen for a crown," Marguerite insisted.

"Nay, sire," David repeated most earnestly. "You may destroy the evidence of my birthright at your will. I was never brought up to think myself fit for a castle, much less a kingdom. High honors were never expected, nor the high duties that go with them. What I have was earned by my own hand, with main strength and the favor of heaven. I am my own man, and would never trade that to become the master of all England who is, in truth, the minion of all."

"Fine words and fair," Henry returned with a twist of his lips, "but how should we wager everything on them, not only our throne, but our queen, our heirs and our future? If we are wrong, these things must be forfeit, for you can no more allow us to live than I can permit you that boon now."

It was a death sentence, for all its measured reason. David heard it over the drumming of his heart as his fear grew that he would not go alone to the axe or gallows.

"But, sire," Marguerite said with the rasp

471

of anxiety in her voice as she moved forward a quick step. "To take David's life now can only lend credence to the tale of his birth given out before. He has gained fame near to legend under his pennon of the Golden Knight. The people could turn from your cause should it become known that you executed him out of hand. Warbeck is still out there, you will recall, and unlike David, he does covet your crown."

David could feel the sting of the wool carpet under his hose-covered knee, smell the odor of hot lamp oil, dust and a hint of sandalwood from Henry's clothing. It was better to concentrate on these things than on the decision Henry would hand down in the next brief moments. The tapping sound of the king's fingers on the arm of his thronelike chair was loud in the quiet. Abruptly, it stopped.

"Who else knows this tale, Lady Marguerite?" he asked in meditative tones. "Other than you and Sir David?"

It was a trap, one that yawned wide and deep. David felt cold strike to the marrow of his bones as he saw it. "Marguerite," he began.

"The elderly nun in her convent, also those who were with me when she told it," she answered, her voice rigorously even.

"Who else, I cannot say, not knowing how many others might have listened to her ramblings."

David breathed again. If only he and Marguerite had known of his birthright, they could both have been ordered to the Tower at once. She had sidestepped that pitfall. He would not be forced to see her arrested with him on that account.

"More than that," Marguerite went on, her face clear yet intense, "you were wise enough to destroy the *Titulus Regius* by which parliament, under Richard, declared Edward's children from Elizabeth Woodville to be born out of wedlock. The queen's favor with the people as Edward's eldest daughter forms the bedrock for your reign. As you suggested just now, raking up the matter of her legitimacy again is unlikely to be useful."

Henry's face turned stone-hard. "Our queen is well loved, but our reign does not require support derived from her or from her father."

"No, no, I only meant that . . ."

"We know what you meant," Henry said in forbidding decisiveness.

Quiet settled upon them again. They were deadlocked, poised on the cusp of two threats. And in that moment, David suddenly knew what he had to do. He knew it, even if he could not be sure of what Marguerite wanted or how she would respond if what he was about to say was accepted. He cleared his throat, speaking with every ounce of persuasion at his command.

"The story of my birth has been kept hidden these many years. No reason exists for it to be brought to light. My purpose as a false pretender has been served, for Warbeck's forces are weaker now. The report from his camp is that he will invade in a matter of days before his supporters may rally to me. I will disband my forces and renounce all claim to the throne, as planned from the beginning. Afterward, I will name myself as an imposter, no son of Edward IV's at all, and be content to remain so all my days."

Henry was no fool. "A generous offer, Sir David. And in return?"

Here was the crux of the matter, the chance of a bargain Henry might accept more readily than an abdication for mere honor, with nothing gained for it. "Though I've no use for your crown, there is one thing for which it will be well lost, one and one only I would have in recompense."

David heard Marguerite's soft gasp, felt the look she turned upon him. He glanced up to meet her eyes for endless moments, seeing the fear in their dark brown depths, the doubt and the pain.

"And that is?" Henry inquired in dry mockery.

He inhaled to the deepest depth of his lungs, and in sudden certainty that what he was doing was right. When he answered, his voice was strong and sure. "The hand of your ward, Lady Marguerite Milton, as my lady and my wife."

21

Astonishment beat up into Marguerite's brain along with wild exhilaration. David thought to gain a concession from Henry that might nullify suspicion while proving his sincerity. He meant to give up all claim to the throne in exchange for her hand.

Was it possible the night spent together had meant something to him after all? Had her fear that he had abandoned her been for nothing? Or was this merely another example of his care for her welfare, a sign that he actually had no desire to be king, just as he had said.

The answer was unknowable. She hoped, all the same.

"We thought," the king said in deliberate irony, "that you were forbidden to marry. We distinctly remember being told you swore away this joy when offered the lady before."

"My oath was for Lady Marguerite and

no other, sire. It was an act of youthful idealism, though binding for all that."

"A knight's vow of platonic love, I apprehend."

"Just so, sire, one I would have abided by, no matter the cost."

"Idealistic indeed."

"Or foolish." David's lips curved into a wry smile, for Marguerite saw it as he met Henry's gaze squarely and without evasion.

Henry removed his hand from his chin. "And now?"

"And now I am no longer bound. The lady released me of her own will."

She had done that, Marguerite saw in dawning recognition. David had made certain of it with his question that she had repeated in her extremity, while he hovered with his heat and hardness at her entrance and she was so awash in pounding desire she barely knew her name. It had been imperative to give him her assurance at the time, though she was not certain what to make of it now.

"Is this true, Lady Marguerite?"

Henry was looking at her, waiting for her answer. She tipped her head in assent, while the blood throbbed so hard in her veins she felt light-headed with it.

"And this matter of a marriage to Sir David is agreeable to you?"

She met the king's stern gaze, hardly able to believe she was being consulted. A tremor of panic moved over her at the official nature of that query. Once made, her consent could not be rescinded. Yet this was David to whom she would be given in wedlock if this terrible quandary could be resolved.

"It is, sire," she answered in strained composure.

Henry turned back to David. "Should we sanction your proposal, what security have we that you will not regret it later? What warranty can you give us that you will never seek to overturn this bargain?"

"My word, sire," David said.

It should have been enough, but was it? Could it ever be, when so much was at stake?

"Also the pledge of my heart, sire," Marguerite said with a lift of her chin. "My sisters and I first came to your notice for the sake of a babe held hostage, your small daughter, Madeleine. I am here now because of this other little one that was born and abandoned at Edward's order. It seems fitting that a similar young life should stand surety for the promise you have heard. Allow me, then, to offer the firstborn child of my marriage to Sir David to be fostered in your household as pledge against our loyalty and service to you and your heirs after you."

"Marguerite . . ." David whispered.

She met his gaze, her own clear, though edged with tears. "There is no danger for this child of ours, for you will never go back on your word. I know this well."

"No, but it will rend your heart to let our babe go. And mine."

"Yes." She found a smile, but it trembled around the edges. "But to lose its father before it can be born is more than I can bear."

Silence gathered from the corners of the long room, hovering around them. A candle flame sputtered and shadows leaped. A faint draft stirred Marguerite's skirts around her ankles.

Henry made an abrupt, staying gesture. "A fitting sacrifice, Lady Marguerite, though one too painful to accept."

"But, sire . . ."

"We shall hold it in abeyance for now, but leave the promise open against the need of a perilous future."

Henry was a kind man but wary of trust. He would not take her child, but reserved the option to demand it at any whiff of betrayal. It was as good a bargain as she could achieve, and better than she had expected. Marguerite curtsied with all humility. "Thank you, sire."

He turned to David with narrowed eyes. "Where will this child be born? Have you thought on it?"

"If you ask where we will go from this place, then it shall be as you command," he answered with gravel in his voice. "I have property of some worth in France. Failing that, Lady Marguerite has holdings from her father that may provide a suitable retreat."

Henry's brooding gaze rested upon him for long seconds. Then he made a judicious gesture. "Our thought is that it will be sufficient, and mayhap safer, should you retire to the north of England. I have an estate no great distance from those grants made to the husbands of Lady Marguerite's two sisters. If you should be willing to exchange these French holdings of yours for it —"

"Done, sire."

Marguerite gave David a quick, warning glance. He had not seen this estate of Henry's. The king, being a canny man, was unlikely to be offering an even exchange.

David, catching her eyes, lifted one shoulder in token of his resignation. He was right; she saw it in that same instant. They had scant choice. This was all still supposition. The king had not yet made a final decision, but was still speaking.

"We would have it understood that travel beyond these northern lands and environs shall be forbidden without our permission. Any appearance at court must be by strict invitation."

David inclined his head in acknowledgment. "And my men-at-arms?"

Henry tipped up his strong chin. "They must be disbanded as suggested but for those, like your squire, who may stay by your side from friendship or personal allegiance."

Marguerite, listening intently to the unspoken words as well as the commands, felt the slow rise of hope. Henry seemed intent on keeping David confined in such a way that he could never again be a threat, yet within England's borders so he might remain under his eye. Stringent these rules might be, but were better by far than a sentence of death.

"Then my usefulness as an alternate pretender is ended here," David said.

Henry's smile was wintry. "Beyond a doubt. The ruse will be exposed as our stratagem, and that will be the sum of it."

David's features turned grim and a muscle

flexed in his jaw. "And when Warbeck invades?"

Silence descended while Henry settled back in his chair. The only sounds were the drumming of his finger on his chair arm once more, and the whisper of insects against the windows above them.

The king's lips flattened and he folded his fingers into a fist. Then he relaxed them again as he breathed a long sigh. "Once on the battlefield at Stoke, Sir David, you saved my life at the risk of your own, saved my pennon, as well. I am not unmindful of that heroism nor of what I owe you because of it."

"It was my duty, sire."

" 'Twas more than that," Henry corrected. "Rather, it was a demonstration of supreme loyalty, one that turned the tide of battle for a Lancastrian victory. We are not a superstitious man, yet have long felt you arrived as a sign of God's blessing upon our reign that day. We summoned you here this summer, arranged for your arrival by cunning, from the conviction that you should be here to support us in this Warbeck affair."

"You truly did not know the story of my birth then, had no idea who I was?"

Henry gave a laugh that was remarkably like a snort. "Think you we would scheme to bring such a viper into our nest? Unlike the eagle that feeds such to its young, we are not so arrogant or certain of our might. We do pride ourselves, however, on recognizing the worth in your blood and breeding."

It was a reminder, if any were required, that David, as Edward's son, was a cousin to Henry, though several times removed. And who could say that blood had not called to blood in the midst of battle at Stoke-on-Trent? Stranger things had happened.

Henry glanced above David's head while the lines in his face deepened as if what he saw weighed upon his soul. "Let us say, too, that I am weary unto death of the senseless bloodletting, and feel it would be the basest of ingratitude should I fail to take your past service into account. Because of these things, and because the abdication you have proposed is so rare in the history of the crown I wear, I cannot do less than match you in honor. Rise, Sir David, and know I will be proud to have you at my side should I be forced once more to defend my crown."

A flush mantled David's face, Marguerite saw, as he came to his feet with easy, muscular strength. "You mean, sire . . . ?"

"We will send for you at need, this I swear.

For now, you may leave us. Go from here with the lady who has spoken so ably in your defense, promised so much in your name, Lady Marguerite whose hand you risked your life to gain. Go with my permission to wed and my blessing." A wintry smile tugged at his lips. "It seems we have played matchmaker right well for a third time with the Graces of Graydon, assuring that none are now accursed, if so they ever were. But though you are both dear to our sight, we trust you will understand our fervent wish that it is long months before we need set eyes upon you again."

"Farewell, sire," David said with a profound bow that only briefly hid his burgeoning smile.

Marguerite curtsied and began to back away. "Fare thee well, indeed," she said, her voice not quite even. "May you reign long and well, and your children after you."

There was warmth in Henry VII's face, benediction in his gesture of grace. "We thank you, Lady Marguerite. Remember us, and our queen, to your sisters."

A few steps more and the door of the audience chamber opened and closed behind them. Their escort rejoined them in the antechamber and moved with them to the corridor that led back to the living quarters. There, they were left alone.

David took Marguerite's hand and placed it on his arm. Together, they walked toward the room that had been allotted to her. Their footsteps echoed around them for several yards on the marble-floored passage. Silence had been only prudent with the escort at their heels, but now that they were released, Marguerite could think of little to say. Or rather, there was much she would express, but no words deep enough.

David turned his head to study her set face, glanced ahead at the empty corridor and then back again. When he spoke, his voice was rough. "You are angry?"

Was she? Mayhap she should be, as she had not been consulted in the matter of her wedding. Yet that was not what was paramount inside her. "I am relieved." She held his gaze. "And you?"

"What about me?"

"Are you angry at how things have turned out?"

"Angry that I am alive? Hardly."

"I meant the loss of your birthright."

"To know the name of my father and my heritage to bear is all I ever wanted, more than I expected. It is enough, even if no one else will ever learn of it. As for the crown, it isn't mine and never was, sweetling, no matter how legal the marriage between my parents. Edward wrested it from his uncle, Henry VI, and then murdered him to keep it. Now Henry VII has it back. So be it."

She watched him closely. "You are sure? Henry has your mother's marriage lines now. He will surely burn them, as he burned the *Titulus Regius* that declared his queen a bastard."

"I am positive of it."

"With the only proof of your birth in his hands, there was no need to tell him, surely, that it was only Astrid and Oliver who heard the old nun's confession so can bear witness."

"We may send to give him that surety and heart's ease later, when we are settled on the lands Henry promised. But don't try to distract me. I was asking how you felt about being wed."

She pursed her lips while her heart vibrated wildly against the cage of her ribs. "If the purpose is to give me the protection of your name, now that you've had what you wanted of me, I'm not sure I care for it."

He halted, swung to face her. "You can't believe that."

"Why should I not, as I've been told no different. All has been arranged without consulting me in the slightest. I am to be taken north without my leave —"

"Surely you will be happy there where you can visit back and forth with your sisters, take Christmas and Easter with them and have them close in time of need."

"Yes, of course, and with Astrid and Oliver near us with the small ones they will surely have between them. But that isn't the point."

"What is then?" he demanded in exasperation.

"The odd truth that I have no more been wooed or persuaded now than I was before being handed over to Halliwell."

"There was no time, no other way. I needed a bargain to offer Henry so he would believe —"

She was awash in fury now, as she had not been before. "And I happened to be handy?"

"God, no, Marguerite!" He caught her hands, pressing them to his chest, spreading her fingers over his pounding heart. "I offered him something for which I had no use in exchange for the one thing I could not do without. I gave up a crown for a wife, and am well satisfied with the exchange."

"Well, cry hosanna for you. But what am I to gain from it?"

"Nothing of great worth, only my heart, my love, my life, though you have had them these ten years and more. Did you think I didn't want you, that I would not claim you before last night? God, but I hated that infernal vow, cursed my stupidity a thousand times over for making it. You cannot know the cost of it. To touch you would have been my damnation, for I would have been forced to sample and taste and savor until my brain boiled in my skull and desire tied my entrails in knots. I would have taken you and bid good riddance to salvation and my every hope of heaven."

She searched the burning blue of his eyes with their shading of desperation. "But I set out to seduce you, and you would not allow it. You . . . you touched me until I was mad with need, taught me the diverse ways of passion but would take nothing from me."

"And a double-edged sword it was, my lady, for I could not hurt you without slicing myself into leading strings."

"You wanted me all along?"

"Have I not been saying so? My need for you was so fierce that I set myself to seduce you in all but deed, to force from you the words I needed to hear, had to hear before I could make you mine."

"That I release you from your vow."

"Just that, no more."

She shook away the excuse with a twist of her head, her voice thick as she replied, "You could have asked. The release would have been freely given. Freely."

"To ask would have been to negate the vow, to make it worthless in the sight of God. The release had to come from you, as a sign of your favor, your need. Even . . . even your love."

"It was. Oh, it was," she whispered.

He caught her against him, whirled her down the corridor for a few dizzying turns. "Say it," he demanded when he came to a halt. "Say you love me."

"Yes," she said her eyes burning with tears for his exultant happiness, the bright hope and the love that was in his face. "I do love you, have loved you since we were a lad and lass sitting in the clover. Do you remember?"

"I remember," he said, his voice so gruff it was hard to understand him. Releasing her, he reached for the bag that still hung from his waist. From it he took a square of silk wrapped around another of parchment. His hand shaking a little, he unwrapped it, took from it a circlet that formed a crown of dry and crumbling clover.

"Oh, David," she said with love aching in

her voice. A crown of clover. The crown she had made him so long ago. It was, she saw with sudden, poignant clarity, the very base of his pennon of pale blue marked with a leafy crown, the symbol of who and what he was, and all he had become by his own merit. "You kept it all this time."

"It is the only crown I have ever valued, all I ever wanted or needed." Handling it with the care he might give a precious relic, he took her hand and placed it upon the palm. "Crown me once more, consort of my heart, my secret queen. Be my wife."

"As you will, Your Majesty." She placed the clover circlet gently upon his bent head then offered him her mouth, her heart, her life. "As you will."

AUTHOR'S NOTE

The eternal question used when plotting a story is "What if . . . ?" David's birthright as the eldest son of Edward IV and rightful king of England was constructed in this time-honored tradition.

History records that Edward IV was already married by legally binding contract to a young widow, Lady Eleanor Talbot Butler, at the time of his secret marriage to Elizabeth Woodville, the woman who became his queen. A priest identified as Robert Stillington, Bishop of Bath and Wells, swore he also performed the rite of marriage between Edward and Eleanor. On Edward's death in 1483, his brother Richard used this information to declare the marriage to Elizabeth Woodville invalid and the children from it illegitimate. His subsequent seizing of the crown as Richard III was based on this legal maneuver.

Henry VII invaded England and defeated

Richard III at the Battle of Bosworth in 1485. To strengthen his grasp and unite the warring factions of York and Lancaster, Henry then married Elizabeth of York, eldest daughter of Edward IV and Elizabeth Woodville. The finding of illegitimacy for the children of Edward IV was revoked on his order and the papers pertaining to it destroyed. This move returned his queen to legitimate status.

Edward IV was a notorious womanizer known to have fathered a number of illegitimate children, among them one or two who have traceable modern descendants. It's claimed that he proposed to Lady Eleanor because she refused to have sex with him without marriage. It seems reasonable to assume that Edward, having met her terms, received his reward. There is no evidence to show that Lady Eleanor ever had a child, but she did enter a convent near the time that Edward's marriage to Elizabeth Woodville was made public, and died there some four years later, in 1468. No birth date is given for her, but as women were considered ready for marriage at fifteen, and she was left a widow after ten years with her first husband, she could well have been only thirty years old, or less, at her death.

If Lady Eleanor was indeed the legal wife of Edward IV, and if she chanced to retreat to a convent in order to give birth to a son, that child would have been the rightful heir to England's throne. From this intriguing "What if . . . ?" *Seduced by Grace,* and its hero, was born.

The Perkin Warbeck insurrection was a lengthy affair, beginning in 1491 and ending in 1497 with Warbeck's defeat by the forces of Henry VII. A number of modern scholars and novelists like to point to the backing of this would-be prince by James IV of Scotland, Charles VIII of France and the duchess of Burgundy as proof that the royal houses of Europe recognized and accepted him as the fifth duke of York, or Richard, second son of Edward IV. They contend that he was removed from the Tower for safety by his uncle, Richard III, and surfaced again at his propitious time. This has never been proven. Moreover, the politics of the time were rife with alliances that had more to do with territorial concessions and ancient feuds than royal birthrights. And in fact, Warbeck penned a full confession after his capture. In it, he admits to being an imposter and gives his surname and humble origins.

Henry's treatment of the defeated Warbeck was humane compared to the retribution handed out for treason by his predecessors. He took Perkin Warbeck and his wife into his household, making them members of his court in a form of house arrest. It was only two years later, after an escape by Warbeck and another attempt at rebellion hatched with the earl of Warwick, that this pretender to the throne was finally hanged.

In 1501, Sir James Tyrell confessed to arranging the murders of the princes in the Tower — though no confirmation exists as he was executed for treason before evidence could be introduced at trial. With this public acknowledgment of the demise of Edward IV's sons, the danger of insurrection from those backing another pretender to the throne declined. It did not end, however, until the Yorkist line was nearly extinguished during the reign of the next Tudor king, Henry VIII.

Jennifer Blake
March 24, 2011